ENIGMA'S CODA

ENIGMA'S CODA

Mike King

Stochastic Press

mike@jnani.org

Version 1.0 © 2016

This book is also available in Kindle format.

ISBN-13: 978-0995648005

ISBN-10: 099564800X

London: Stochastic Press

one

ØØØØØØ Looking out of his office window a familiar view
_____ presented itself looking north. It included the roofs
and facades of various classically-styled buildings
including the Royal Geographical Society; it included something of the
curve of Kensington Gore; but mostly it terminated in the trees a little
further on which border South Carriage Drive. To see further than that
one needs greater elevation, he thought wryly. The vista reminded him
of the funeral procession of Princess Diana and of a day which was
perhaps the first herald of the whole sorry mess. Back then he was just
twenty-seven and had been appointed with a modest office affording a
much truncated view, three stories lower. He smiled as he recalled the
reaction of his younger self to the events of the whole week and to the
funeral in particular; this to him had been an excessive and rather un-
English display of emotion that he, frankly, had disapproved of. But his
curiosity had led him to leave work that day and walk through the
detritus of mass grief – the flowers lapping in waves up to the gates of
Kensington Palace were admittedly moving – and head by some instinct
towards Buckingham Palace. Was it a million mourners? Who knows,
but the rows upon rows of Portaloos spelled out a kind of reassuring
competence. This feeling had grown in him: that whatever irrational
excess the day had been the culmination of, it had all worked rather
smoothly. He had glimpsed moments of the state funeral on televisions
in the staff lounge: the cortege, the two dignified boys, Elton John's
Candle in the Wind and so on – it was at the very least well orchestrated.
As he approached Buckingham Palace workers were beginning to collect
up the litter of the day; again it seemed like simple competence. And the
institutions of state: the Palace, the Houses of Parliament, the Abbey;
even the BBC and its grave but reassuring news reporters – all this had

made him feel somewhat reconciled to the national hysteria otherwise rather alien to him.

Not normally given to any extensive walking, he had rested on benches at various junctures in this rather unusual outing. After enjoying the evening sun at Buckingham Palace he crossed into St James' Park where the ducks and geese he observed when leaning over the little bridge were busily unconcerned with funerals and the workings of authority; it was the same for the pelicans – though one might class them as officers of state considering their source of livelihood. Coming into Parliament Square he passed things he had not previously noticed, such as the Institution of Mechanical Engineers, the statue of Abraham Lincoln and the Middlesex Guildhall. He was predictably out of breath and so sat down on the little stone wall with Lincoln behind him, taking in the view of Parliament's buildings. He looked around the full panorama which also included Westminster Abbey, which he knew, St Margaret's Church which he did not; neither the rear of a statue of Benjamin Disraeli. What he did know was that there could hardly be another spot in Britain so absolutely caked with history and the institutions of national governance. His father may have been a nominally anti-Establishment figure, it had struck him, but in reality he had grown up with a sense of ease regarding institutional Britain: after all, here he was with a professorship at Imperial College, not a name to conjure up radicalism, not at least, of the political sort. Few people would have heard of Magnus, an Imperial project that in his own field was considered rather wild. He had in fact been the youngest professor ever appointed there. As a minor mathematical prodigy – he always modestly qualified it that way – his ascent had been steep yet apparently effortless: a degree while at Merton College and the Mathematical Institute, a Masters and doctorate and then postdoctoral studies at the Programming Research Group – all these at Oxford – which had naturally led to his chair in the mathematics of artificial intelligence at Imperial. None of the gate-keepers on this trajectory had doubted his ability but somehow their task of selection had been eased, or even made pleasurable, by the quality generally noted in him: his affability.

Something drew him back to the view from his window; he found that he must have got up from his desk a while ago, lost in thought. Yes, at the time of Lady Diana's funeral he had not long laboured in the footsteps of the great Igor Aleksander and Emil Piatigorsky, with the recent blessings of Oxford dons such as Sir Roger Penrose, Andrew Hodges and David Deutsch. And now! He would go up and break the news to Emil. It was a colossal triumph but he had got past the bitterness; he would not crow.

ØØØØØ1   Something made him linger at the window however, thinking back to that day twelve years ago. After asthma had struck him at eighteen he was naturally reluctant to walk much, so he had sat for some time on that low wall in Parliament Square, ruminating on the strange week leading up to the funeral and the national outpouring of grief. It was all faintly ridiculous. He had tested himself: how would he have reacted to the sudden death – God forbid – of his wife Ros, then his girlfriend? Yes, he could feel the hypothetical grief. This public demonstration was unsettling however, not like the funeral he could imagine for Ros, transposed in his imagination into the Cotswold churchyard of Chipping Norton where his grandmother's service had been held with such simple gravity. It had the proper privacy demanded by such occasions. Diana's funeral on the other hand was not just so very public, but also so full of 'personalities' offering their irritating assessments. It had been, according to the consensus, a very New Labour moment, a national turn to a more caring, more emotional outlook. He had found it hard to laud this development, yet in the end the modern Blair government had seemed acceptable to him, political differences set aside for the day in the concerted efficient workings of contemporary institutions. Perhaps the affair did – if you looked at it aright – have some proper Britishness about it.

He had raised himself from his seat, taking one last look at the Abbey where Elton John's song had earlier reverberated around the marble and stonework, and headed towards the Embankment. He was in a fine mood on a warm September evening, not being capable of holding an irritation about anything for long, and in this spirit had passed by the construction site that was the joint Westminster Tube and Portcullis House project.

That reminiscence brought him back to the present again, and he turned to look southward down Exhibition Road: this was a huge improvement, a real modernisation. His eyes followed the receding perspective of the new lighting masts and the somehow satisfyingly clean lines and texture of the kerbless street and pavement, in contrast to which Portcullis House was a missed opportunity, he thought – it was the past projected into the future, not radically modern. That day he had walked along the Embankment, not yet adorned with the Millennium projects that he did approve of: the Eye, the 'Wobbly Bridge', and the

Charing Cross footbridges. The river on the other hand was timeless, and a natural accompaniment to all the organs of state that had functioned so well in support of the funeral. Perhaps he had been – if he were honest – a little swept up in the emotion of the day.

In any case there was no doubt that all his difficulties had begun then, or were at the very least presaged by the funeral and his unusually extended walk. He had spotted some benches in Victoria Gardens as he headed towards Embankment Tube and tucked into the little park. Sitting down to catch his breath again, he became aware of a sculpture opposite him, one of a series commemorating the heroes and anonymous fallen of various wars. Something made him get to his feet, despite still panting a little, in order to take a closer look at the stone inscription at the monument's base, which told him that it was the 'Fleet Air Arm Memorial', to him an old-fashioned thing expressing pointless sentiment for the lost in war. He looked up at the figure, mounted at head height on a plinth, and made of cast iron, he had supposed, a substance redolent of antiquated industries. It was actually a brand new sculpture, just installed, portraying an airman with wings held above him as shields.

'Fleet Air Arm.' What was that? Thinking about it he guessed that they were airmen of the Royal Navy. Poor sods, he had thought, most of them probably drowned, but there was enough grief for the departed already on that day and further extending empathy to people even more remote than a TV princess was beyond him. She had been undeniably captivating; dead airmen were not.

But he did not walk on. He continued to stare up at the sculpture – somehow the detail of it had fascinated him, despite his remove from its context and purpose: the rather androgynous face of the generic pilot was largely encased in its thin, presumably leather, helmet; the oxygen mask detached on one side and hanging down; the expression vaguely horrified. He had thought perhaps it is made of bronze, not iron. Leather, iron, bronze. These were all antiquated materials, all symbols of the past, of wars fought with brutal weapons made of crude material substance.

ØØØØ1Ø   After a long while lost in thought as he stood there by
————————   the memorial he had realised how tired he was, stirred
                    himself and went for the Underground. It was typical of his optimism that, where his colleagues liked to complain about the Tube, he estimated that his average wait for a train was only two minutes, a figure they had scoffed at. He was not to be budged on this

however, having made an empirical investigation of the matter. On that day, not only was his wait for a train a mere ten seconds, but a seat was immediately available despite all the talk of public transport overload. His mood was buoyant – as it mostly was – but tinged with a curiously reflective aspect.

That night, he was sure about this, he had dreamt for the first time of a descent into water with friends. He had woken, finding it odd how vivid the impressions had been, and, in going over the details a number of times, had therefore committed the entire scene to his waking memory. It was a dive towards water in some kind of seaplane, accompanied by shouts of: 'We're going in too fast!' and 'The sea's too rough!' The dream had been laden with poignancy as though it was a recollection of something significant for him, and of people who were important to him. Though not prone to the sort of psychologising his wife was fond of, he had established for himself quite empirically that dreams could contain vivid and coherent presentations of people and places you knew, and equally people and places you did not. In the following three years before he married his beloved Ros the dream recurred now and again, but he had given little further thought to it, as the subject matter of these dreams belonged to an unloved domain for him: history.

Paying attention again to the view from his fifth-floor office at Imperial he realised how that had all been so long ago. He and Ros had moved into their home in Fulham around that time, a chance find that had suited them both: it was a modernist offering originally built by the architect Timothy Rendle for himself in an otherwise leafy Victorian neighbourhood not far from Chelsea Harbour, where they would keep their Thames cruiser. The exterior was a little dull perhaps, though impeccably clean-lined, but he and Ros had carefully updated the interior, something of a joint project that brought them together despite their very different professions. The early years of marriage were exhilarating, with both careers going so well: brief holidays abroad or sailing up the Thames to Oxford for the day – both found it hard to tear themselves away from their work for any extended period – and the expansive open plan dwelling a delight to which they invited colleagues from the world of academia and marketing, including Professor Richard May, and of course, Emil Piatigorsky. Ros had set up the marketing company Pierce & Fine with a colleague; she was the Pierce half. At home their dinner parties put Imperial innovators together with potential backers, though Ros would tease her husband in front of guests for being so 'blue-sky'.

'I am determined to be useless,' he would say under the fond gaze of Piatigorsky, and the more wary smile of his head of department. Ros had been a modern literature student at St Margaret's Hall, turning up at teatime one day in his family home in Parktown through a connection with his mother. Ros had instantly set about criticising his appearance and otherwise teasing him, all of which he had batted away with good humour. He loved maths and had no aptitude for English literature, he told her; why, he couldn't even spell the language. Where his almost-blond hair dangled rather uncontrollably over his forehead and blue eyes, she was physically trim and precise. Where he was languid and seemingly haphazard in his mathematical research, she was highly organised and purposeful. And ambitious. They would have a very modern marriage, she later asserted, to which he laughingly agreed. The Oxford years had been marvellous and very much shared with another couple they had met there as students, the Chatterjees, not to mention a friend of Ros's called Patricia Elleworthy, something of a strident feminist.

ØØØØ11   His odd dreams about crashing in water recurred now and again, but then something intensified them and brought an even stranger scene to his dream life, not that he cared to call it such in those days. A conference in 2001 had taken him for a week to Princeton where he had delivered a paper on his new work. It had been well received, and was the first hint for him that his direction – then tentative but clearly divergent from that of Piatigorsky – could be the right one. He might appear like a swan gliding on the surface of still water, as he liked to tell Ros, but he had damn powerful paddling legs, and here was the proof of it: he had been keynote speaker with an impressive fee and all expenses paid. It had proved a useful bit of networking – the human dimension of his profession – which was something Ros could understand and he was perfectly at home with. He was in fact no less ambitious than his wife, it merely showed in a different way. For example, unlike his father's corduroyed approach to academic dress, he was happy for Ros to kit him out in an understated but expensive style that he carried well and which set him a little apart from his university colleagues. And they had a truly enormous mortgage on the house, a loan outstanding on the boat, and generally sophisticated tastes, his rather conservative, hers always on the lookout for the new.

At the end of the week he had taken a late night connection to Kennedy airport for the leg back to London. He had managed with half a night's sleep in one of the airport hotels and found himself on an early plane the following morning, looking out awkwardly through the little elliptical window towards New York, its towers clearly visible though nearly ten miles away.

It was a day – it turned out – that the world would never forget: the eleventh of September. If Princess Diana's funeral had been a small but not insignificant emotional shock to his system, as his doctor later insisted, then 9/11 was to be a huge one.

two

∅∅∅1∅∅   William had sat in a window seat on the London-
———————   bound jet at Kennedy airport, facing west, and
               conscious that there was some delay. Then he had
glimpsed small plumes of smoke in the distance, connected he thought,
with skyscrapers just visible to him. Although he vigorously approved of
glass and steel high-rise blocks in principle, in practice his interest in
architectural or cultural landmarks was insufficient for him to have then
known the names of those towers, or the larger vocabulary of WTC1,
WTC2, WTC7 and so on that was to be drummed into him – and the
rest of the world – in the following days.

     So, there were plumes in the distance apparently rising from two
adjacent skyscrapers located pretty much on the horizon as he saw it, in
a place he knew as New York, but not further detailed in his mind as
Manhattan. Not long afterwards the pilot announced a further delay; he
would inform them as soon as he knew more. But passengers got the
news slowly by mobile phone: he could hear fragments of horrified
conversation, and then they were evacuated and he was forced back to
the hotel, after interminable queuing, in a place that he had also not
previously put a name to but rapidly discovered was called Long Island.
Every receptionist and hotel porter was keen to tell him of events in a
hushed voice, and as soon as he was in his room alone he turned on the
TV. To start with nothing made sense to him as news flashes updated
and contradicted each other, but by late afternoon footage of the
appalling destruction of the towers was broadcast; more and more of
them; more scenes of pedestrians running from the collapse and
covered in dust as the huge clouds billowed out and punched their way
through the man-made canyons of hi-rise office blocks. He kept trying
to call Ros, and finally got through to her: she had only just heard the
news and was worried sick for him, having a vague idea that he would

be in New York around then. He had to reassure her over and over again that he was all right, and that he was ten miles away from the disaster. No, there would be no flights, as far as he could work out, until the authorities were absolutely sure it would be safe. Yes, he was sure there would be very thorough searches before any planes took off again. Strip-searches even! Ha! Yes, I love you too. Love you. Love you.

Beyond eating in the lounge, staring with others at the repeated footage and hearing escalating casualty estimates, he could only return to his room, watch more footage, sleep, and then make his way on foot to the terminal to find yet again that all flights remained cancelled. On the morning after the second night of this ordeal – made bearable only by continuous phone conversations with Ros – he ran out of his asthma medication: he had only taken enough for the week, and so was forced to find a local doctor who could prescribe him more.

He had been shocked to find how much he relied on the medication: in the hour or so that it took to track down a doctor, deal with the paperwork as a foreign national, be seen, and collect the medication from a pharmacy, his wheezing had led to something close to a panic attack. The stressful images crowding in on him of so many deaths in close proximity – less than ten miles away – and the bodies being recovered, and his being alone in his room all rather placed demands on his instinctive bonhomie, and there was no doubt that by the time he had finally got home to Fulham – met at Heathrow by a frantic Ros – he had undergone a considerable shock; later his doctor would insist that it went beyond the ordinary pressures of coping with the unexpected, and that the experience really had triggered a post-traumatic stress disorder. However apparently robust a personality, the four days and nights of delay, on one's own in a hotel filled with the stranded, and bombarded with scenes of nearby horror, can be sufficient to set off a train of self-doubt, at the very least.

He had then started living with a second recurring dream, which was coherent though even more mystifying than the one about descent into water. The immigration control personnel at Kennedy airport – who he had encountered coming into the country in real life – were now mutated in his dream into armed and threatening presences repeating a strange question to him. It took a well-known form, but was bizarrely mutated to reference a key figure from his own profession, and was uttered with cold menace:

Are you now, or have you ever been, Alan Turing?

After the first occurrence he had woken up with a grin on his face, despite its unsettling nature. You had to see the funny side of it. But as it recurred from time to time he was more impressed by its hostility, and the dream began to annoy him: it was related in some way perhaps to the shock of 9/11, but what on earth was the connection with Turing?

If people asked about the fact that he had been pretty much a witness to the tragedy he would nod and say yes of course it had affected him, but would then add: 'Do you know, the odd thing was that when we were evacuated from that grounded plane along with hundreds of others I had no idea that it was Sir Paul McCartney they got off first. Only heard about it later.' He could generally turn an awkward moment into something a little lighter-hearted, and had a truly endearing grin, which is what spread across his face as he stood there looking down Exhibition Road. It was time to go up and see Professor Emil Piatigorsky: he has two things to show him.

ØØØ101 Walking back to his desk from the window he collected an envelope and a journal offprint and then left the office; as he walked down the corridor his grin fleetingly emerged again as he saw the panel on the wall commemorating the Turing exhibition at the Science Museum. His name was on it, as was that of the collaborating institute, Birkbeck College, and also the word that caused him the most amusement – he could afford that now – 'interdisciplinarity'. Spurning the lift he bounded up the single flight to the most coveted office in the Department of Computing, that of Professor Piatigorsky – actually, that was not such a good idea, as he was panting and had to wait a moment in the corridor to get his breath back. He was in better shape now than for years, but not that much. Well, the moment had come, he decided: he knocked, and after a barked 'come in', he entered with a soft 'Hello Emil.'

His long term line manager turned and said 'Ah, hello Willy', though as he had never lost his Russian-German accent it came out 'Villy'. William walked over to the window. It had that effect on people: it drew you to it because you could see north right over the neighbouring buildings, past the dome of the Albert Hall to the complete panorama of Hyde Park. It was a far better view than from his own office, and the envy of all their colleagues.

'So what is new in the Chinese Room?' This was the nickname that Emil had given William's office – wherever it happened to be located –

because of a well-known thought experiment concerning artificial intelligence.

'Symbols come in; symbols go out,' said William casually, looking over his shoulder from the window. Emil merely grunted at this tired piece of banter, clearly absorbed in some mathematical scribbling with pencil on paper, so William contented himself with the view again. It held a new significance because of the papers he held in his hand, but he did not yet offer them to Emil. The head of department would have prepared Emil for what was to come, though it felt somehow correct that it should not interrupt a train of mathematical thought.

His first interview with Piatigorsky came to mind, way back when he was a post-doc. As today there had been a gruff but kindly welcome, though followed by a startling move: the acknowledged genius in computational mathematics and natural heir to the legacy of Igor Aleksander had walked over to the open window, stepped up on a chair obviously left there for the purpose ... and climbed out! No visitor, unfamiliar with his habits or the layout of the building, could do anything but start because of the six story drop assumed on the other side. There was no such thing, of course, but a small rooftop with an old weather-beaten armchair. It was how Piatigorsky could pursue his smoking habit.

'There is no smoking *in* the building,' he would say. 'It was decreed thus. *Verboten*. But there has been no decree forbidding smoking *on* the building.'

The interview was therefore conducted with William standing on one side of the open window and Emil seated on the other in a haze of smoke, with Hyde Park in the distance. Looking at the view William was reminded again of how the Albert Hall symbolised everything he disliked about the older buildings surrounding the college, including Imperial's original entrance encrusted with wreaths, cherubs, cornices and porticos. It was not that he would have made the effort to choose the family home or research modern architects or leaf through glossy books on modernism and its schools: Ros did all that. But still, he resolutely stood for the future not the past.

ØØØ11Ø William rehearsed his long-standing antipathy: Albertopolis! The Albert Hall, the Royal College of Music, the Royal College of Art, the Royal College of Mines, etc, etc. His own Imperial College. Stuffy buildings for a stuffy past and archaic disciplines, all kept watch over by Albert himself from his twiddly gilded memorial. Only the Royal College of Art had a modern feeling in its gallery, not that he cared for modern art that much either; he had just enjoyed some private views there with his wife and her professional set. Sometimes she hired a room there, other times at the Tate Modern, when the marketing people – with their white wine and canapés – were too numerous to be crammed into their home. William and Ros liked to share in each other's professional lives this way; she would come to Imperial now and again while he willingly attended functions in the more up-market world his wife inhabited; and, far from looking out of place, William was in fact an asset to her: an academic who did not look or behave as one, but rather as a man genially comfortable in the business world. Now, he reflected, Imperial would have a hospitality suite to rival those others.

Since the sudden onset of his asthma condition in his eighteenth year William had been forced to give up rowing and other athletic activities that he had enjoyed and shown some talent for, but punting, which required mostly skill and a little strength, was an activity he could still pursue as long as it did not turn into a race. It was through this that he wooed Ros in their Oxford days, and it was their mutual love of being on water later led to their cruiser in Chelsea Harbour. Skill with a long pole and picnic hamper – and a habit of never talking about his mathematics – had done the trick. She had dazzled him with her knowledge of contemporary English literature, the energetic recounting of which she had no inhibitions about. William's reticence about mathematics had been inherited from his father, who made a point of never discussing his discipline or college gossip at home. 'Enthusiasm,' he would say to William's bemusement, 'has simply not been, well, very *English* since Lord Shaftesbury declared it a menace to the good order of society.'

Enthusiasm. That's what he had reacted against on the day of Diana's funeral, William reflected, still waiting for Emil to finish his train of mathematical thought.

Having adopted his father's reluctance to speak about work, William had become instead a good listener, and it was only much later that he felt something of a philistine compared to his wife. For Ros the creative impulse was the most admirable in humankind, and in particular the creative entrepreneurial impulse, though most inventors and businessmen had no real idea of what they had come up with; it was people like her with the broader imagination and keen feel for the culture of artefacts that could see, properly see, the potential of them. And then sell them to the world. A better mousetrap never left the enthusiast's shed she would declare; that old saying was rot. He in turn would say that computer science was changing the world more totally than any of the previous revolutions, either political or technological. Actually he couldn't really have put flesh to his argument as Ros could to hers, but this was ground she never challenged.

ØØØ111   Christ! He had survived an absolute catastrophe. In his hands were the two documents that marked his complete rehabilitation, the return to who he was meant to be. None of it, as it turned out, had been his fault. Not entirely that is. There was no doubt some blot on his conscience but, like a mildly aching tooth, he could live with it. Had to. It was the scar – the pain of which could flare up in the emotional equivalent of bad weather – that corrected him perhaps. In all events it is sobering to have one's childhood certainties undermined.

His growing up in the Parktown enclave of conservative North Oxford had been typical of donnish families in the area. His father, Edward, was kindly enough if a bit remote, but it was his mother, Belinda, who was the greater influence. She liked to tease her husband about his politics.

'Your father,' she would tell William, 'is not a champagne socialist. He is clear about that, because he doesn't drink the stuff. Or drive fast cars, or tup fast women as Shakespeare would say, all of which, apparently goes with champagne. So I like to call him a "shareholding socialist" but he says that I can't just make up terms like that. They have, apparently no circulation. I protested that if I were to use it often enough perhaps it would catch on. But he says you can't introduce terms by fiat.'

William's father – more usually known as 'Pop' – would grunt in annoyance from his armchair.

'And I tell him,' his mother would say conspiratorially as she leant closer to the teenage William, 'what has a little Italian car got to do with it?'

In turn Edward would huff that his wife's claims to be a 'One Nation Tory' should really be recast as a 'Non-Two-Nation Tory' on account of the subtitle of Disraeli's novel. This was a veiled criticism of her Conservative family background and their pretence to have more compassion for the working poor than he did, given that he had actually read *Capital*. He did agree however that it was quite correct, after the Thatcher years, to call such conservatives 'wets'. Just because Thatcher had popularised the term didn't make it one arising by fiat … and so they were back to little Italian cars. In turn this would annoy Belinda, or at least she would pretend as much. William's growing up knew banter and sport, though Edward was no match for his wife in banter – even if he was in erudition – but he did love to talk about cricket, the Boat Race, and that trusty fall back, the weather.

William's elder brother Paul was more like Pop perhaps, and a stern critic of William. He had no precocious talent at anything, but had made a solid career in law, and could be just as critical of his mother as of his younger brother. After the conversation about champagne socialism he had turned to his father.

'"Tup" is a rude word, isn't it Pop?'

'Yes,' grunted Edward.

'Well, please get Mother to stop saying it.'

'Can't, old boy. It's Shakespeare.'

'Surely, just because it's Shakespeare doesn't mean Mother should say it.'

'If we lived in Shakespeare's time I would agree with you. But we have strictly equal opportunities now. Hence the following construct is equally permissible to both genders: "The Moor tupped the bright-eyed Desdemona by moonlight."' This last was added in a vaguely thespian style.

There was a pause.

'Father,' said Paul sternly.

'Yes?'

'I'm shocked.'

'Why?'

'Your use of the qualifier "bright-eyed" suggests enthusiasm.'

'And?'

'I thought you were against enthusiasm. Lord Shaftesbury and all that.'

'Dear Paul. Lord Shaftesbury quite properly expressed dismay at enthusiasm for *ideas*. It's just not British to be enthusiastic about ideas, particularly religious ones, in public. Private displays of enthusiasm are quite a different matter.'

'I see,' said Paul slowly.

Belinda stifled a laugh as she stared at her eldest son, raising her eyebrows in a challenge for him to take it further. He just shook his head and looked away.

Emil had played an unwelcome role in all the turmoil of the recent years, but it was all water under the bridge now, and William knew that he was not himself completely excused by the seemingly random nature of the events that had crowded in on them. Taking in the view as Emil scribbled away, William had a number of further thoughts. First, that the view would soon be his. Second, and related to the first, that he had a bombshell to drop on the poor professor, whatever their head of department might have said to ease its passage. And third, that Adriana was the start of the real trouble. In 1997 his professorship was perhaps the maiden voyage of what promised to be an ever more prestigious life on the waves of fame and social success. The disturbing dreams after the funeral of Princess Diana were merely ice-cubes lost on the frolicking swell. In 2001 – after the shock of 9/11 – the more bizarre visitations of the night were like loaf-sized lumps of ice, yet quickly melting in the tropic waters of progress and contentment. But in 2006 a woman called Adriana Russett was to be the iceberg that would hole him, the previous icy harbingers having no more suggested catastrophe to him than a head cold suggest the hangman's noose.

three

Ø Ø 1 Ø Ø Ø   Ros had been shaken by 9/11, as much as he had. It is
———————— one thing to watch the tragedy unfold on TV, and
another to realise that your husband had actually seen
the planes hit the towers, however indistinctly. She also knew a least two
of those who had died in the disaster, as her marketing connections
extended into the world of finance: her friends had been employees of
British firms with offices at the World Trade Center. It was illogical, but
William could just as easily have been one of them. After meeting him at
Heathrow she had fussed over William quite obsessively, and no doubt
the idea of having a baby took hold of her mind about then. She had a
Japanese friend called Yukiko who had given no thought to childrearing
until the Kobe earthquake struck, she told William, but the shock of all
that death, including that of her aged cat, had made Yukiko seek a
husband soon afterwards. Before 9/11 it had been something for the
indefinite future; now Ros began to plan a definite schedule. She had
friends that William, despite his liberal upbringing, privately thought to
be rather too stridently feminist. They rather mocked Ros for this
emotional response, but she silenced them with her candour – Britain
post-Diana and post-9/11 had become a place more used to open
expressions of feeling; a place anyway where the 'great moderation' of
economic boom favoured women like Ros, and so created the
impression that many if not all the goals of equality had been won. She
was going to have a baby and William had been all for it.

Still it was over four years later, having scaled down her role in her
company a little, before she gave birth to a baby son. The household
was suitably transformed, though possibly with the dawning realisation
in the couple's mind that total modernism does not completely
acknowledge the world of baby clothes, toys, nappies, and a live-in
nanny from Iceland. This particular young woman had come for

interview at their house and seemed to naturally fall in with its modernist tenor: even her accent seemed to suggest clean modern lines. The heavily pregnant Ros loved it that the surname of this economics student was Birgisdóttir, meaning the daughter of someone called Birgis. That's what we need! Ros had been tickled by the linguistic constructions so suggested, like Robertsdaughter, Smithsdaughter etc, indicating a matrilineal line. This conversation had established a friendly feeling with the young woman, and immediately after her departure William and Ros had agreed to hire her. Ros continued to enthuse on the theme of 'dóttir', pronouncing the foreign syllables so as to give them some exotic significance.

'Strangedaughter?' William had queried, not entirely convinced that the system could be adopted in Britain.

'Probably,' answered Ros. 'Knowing us.'

Little Tommy was born in January – a son, not a daughter, and plain 'Strange' rather than 'Strangeson' – an event that naturally changed much in the outlook of both Ros and William, though neither made particularly significant concessions to parenthood. William took a few week's paternity leave, working at home with occasional visits to Imperial, while Ros continued to conduct some of her business, again from home. It was a little later, once William was back full-time at Imperial, that his life began to face a seriously destabilising influence. He wasn't the same after 9/11, Ros would remark in tenderness and concern for him. William had these recurring dreams about a crash in water and the Kennedy airport scene, which Ros interpreted for him: it was anxiety, she would say, stroking his hair. You did say how that video of a man jumping out of the burning tower had shocked you more than anything, so crashing into water is just another way your subconscious is dealing with falling to one's death. And the whole Turing thing is anxiety about your career. You are like Icarus, she said, flying too close to the sun. You're a maths genius. But you are not going to crash, and your career is stellar and your best work is yet to come – that last thought was a conviction gleaned from an aside by William's head of department, Richard May. They were confident enough in each other's ambition, and drawn closer now with the arrival of their son. William, it is true, was not a great one for the 'subconscious', but Ros's repetition of this idea was comforting when he felt a little down.

None of this really signified any great change in his life however, instead it was a conference trip in May of that year that became the turning point, though William was a reluctant to go with a son so young. The conference was in Geneva this time, held in honour of Igor

Aleksander, and it would have been unthinkable not to attend; effectively this was to be the last public celebration of the work of Emil's intellectual godfather, and therefore also in the academic lineage leading to William. Ros insisted on coming with the baby to Stansted airport, their live-in au pair Maria Birgisdóttir in tow, and so a loving wife, a burbling babe, and an Icelandic nanny waved him off: the first separation from the household at 54 Britannia Road since Tommy was born.

ØØ1ØØ1   The Grand Hotel Kempinski provides its guests with a
———————   fine view of the fountain on Lake Geneva, but only from certain rooms. Not William's. He came down to the hotel breakfast lounge, other conference delegates sitting clearly marked with their name-badges in an area set aside for them. He missed Ros and little Tommy, and wasn't interested in fountains, and didn't even approve as he usually would that the Kempinski was a modernist structure – a 'concrete bunker' as some would have it. He was tired from the flight and concerned that his asthma was playing up. Of more concern still had been the negotiation with the continental breakfast selection; that stuff was what? Garlic sausage? He did prefer America as a conference destination, he realised, where they at least spoke English and garlic was not the default ingredient in everything – you never knew where it would turn up next. That it could lurk in a sausage – Toulouse – or in a cheese – Boursin – he was well aware of, but on the Continent you were just as likely to be ambushed by garlic lurking amongst innocent things like potatoes.

He had not immediately recognised the other delegates seated singly and in small groups over breakfast and was anyway more in the mood to sit by himself and go over his lecture material. He was not the keynote speaker – that was Emil's privilege this time – but was still looking forward to getting some response to his recent developments. Hence it took him a little while to realise that a tall, rather shy-looking young woman wearing the conference badge had been hovering by him. She stood there rather wandily, clutching her conference pack in one hand and a coffee cup in the other.

'May I join you?' she asked, having now caught his attention. 'I couldn't help noticing that you are from Imperial. I guess you are with Piatigorsky?'

'Sure and yes,' he managed. 'I'm William Strange.'

'I'm Adriana Russett, and I read one of your papers a while back.'

'Only one?' commented William mournfully, but with the beginnings of his characteristic grin. Adriana settled in, and then rose to collect further breakfast necessities – he couldn't help noticing that she was rather beautiful.

On her return she said: 'I'm doing a PhD in the history of computing, looking at Ada Lovelace and Alan Turing as the origins of Artificial Intelligence.'

ØØ1Ø1Ø William looked at her for a moment, considering this. 'Hmm', he said, 'In my view, Alan Turing to Artificial Intelligence is rather like a Stone Age man to an Enzo Ferrari. Sure, he invented the wheel, but that's all.'

Adriana sat bolt upright, which gave her the edge on him, height wise. Her face coloured. 'That's outrageous!' she said, and thought furiously for a moment. 'Look, Bill, surely it's nothing like that. It's more that Turing invented the sports car, perhaps an old MG like the one I drive, and er, Ferrari developed it on.'

She paused as he merely smiled at her. 'Oh. Is it alright to call you Bill?'

'Sure,' he said amiably. It was just typical student-lecturer banter as you might expect on the first day of a conference, indeed he was waking up a bit and beginning to enjoy the further ramblings between them. When he got up to say that he was replenishing his coffee she suggested that they take their drinks onto the veranda which she pointed out to him; he had not noticed it, a large dining area overlooking the lake, and he had to admit on taking in the view that perhaps Switzerland had its merits. Their panorama included the famous fountain, the city itself, and the mountains that encircled them, all quite attractive in the clear morning sun. More awake now, he did finally register the modern furniture and the taut stainless cables that served as railings and the modernist ambience of the whole thing. Okay, he told himself as he settled with the young woman at a table near the edge – the waterfront trees just below them making a discrete canopy over the road and yet affording them a perfect panorama – this is better, and perhaps asthma won't be a nuisance in this fine mountain air. Above all what he felt on that first morning was gratitude that his moping over separation from Ros and Tommy – and Maria for that matter, whose breezy efficiency he had come to enjoy as part of the household – had been displaced by something bright and entertaining.

ØØ1Ø11

By the time he had retired to his room that night – again most pleasing in its unfussy decor he had decided – he couldn't fend off the nagging feeling that something more had happened at breakfast and during other moments in the day when the tall figure of Adriana came into view, smiling at his presence, and joining him for more banter over Turing and Stone Age man. She simply wouldn't let him off with his dismissal of Turing's seminal work.

'Sure, "seminal",' he had countered, 'that's the right word. I think it means seed. But a full grown plant, I don't know what, a, a, cauliflower, for example ...' Adriana burst out laughing at this. 'No,' he said frowning with mock seriousness, 'a *mature* cauliflower is structurally equivalent to any other plant or tree or whatnot in its maturity ...' He knew he was going round in circles, but persisted doggedly, his blondish hair a little damp from the early summer heat. 'So, any mature plant – and I don't see why we shouldn't consider a cauliflower over any more attractive species – involves a development that it fantastically removed from the seed.' He was extemporising rather wildly now but getting to his point: 'It's an utterly different thing to be served, um, cauliflower *cheese* for lunch, rather than cauliflower *seeds*.'

This got another laugh. Yes, he had to admit to himself, that was rather good. 'What I am saying,' he continued, 'is that Turing's contribution was perhaps a brilliant insight in its day, but that the original insight has been piled upon by countless other contributors. This means that for those actually working in the field it is long buried. We have no call to make reference to it.'

'Are you saying that the very notion of the Turing machine doesn't affect your thinking at every moment in your mathematical research?'

William paused and then said: 'No, not really. Any more than Ferrari would need to think every moment about the wheel.'

Adriana could not think of anything to say to this so she explained that she was a history graduate who had happened to have also pursued some mathematics modules through university. History gave her the feeling that the beginnings of things were very important, but she could not of course argue with him on his own territory. She was sure he was wrong however, to which he nodded graciously. How could this woman possibly offend him? He concluded that she was pretty bright and well, very pretty. She could argue the historical case for Turing rather well, having made her first line of study that equally antiquated pioneer, Ada Lovelace, daughter of Byron. Lovelace, though admittedly female and therefore conventionally beyond criticism – having also had a programming language named after her – was, to William, made even more irrelevant through her association with Romantic poetry. Adriana's thinking was obviously unscientific, like his wife's, a determined defender of the humanities and the social sciences. But, out of politeness, he had to concede in the end that Alan Turing had been a giant of his time, and that his, William's, discipline would not have existed without Turing.

Adriana in turn was intrigued that William's father was a medieval historian at Wadham College, Oxford, but hadn't heard of him because her academic studies had been in the redbrick universities and were focussed on the last two hundred years. She did have an eye for her surroundings and their little incongruities however. On the second day at breakfast, meeting out on the veranda at one of the little tables with the fantastic view, she complained with fresh-faced delight about how conventional the Swiss were. Electric trains, cuckoo-clocks, pristine everything, she observed. Not a scrap of graffiti anywhere in Geneva, Bill! He just grinned; it wasn't something he thought about one way or the other.

She leant towards him, captivating in her unmannered way: 'The most radical thing I saw all yesterday was a teenager in Goth style, though of course it was all off-the-shelf and expensively coordinated. He had purple hair and was riding a *moped*. Wild!' She imitated this by slipping her feet out of her sandals, bringing them up to rest on the edge of the chair, her knees now up to her chest, while leaning forward clutching imaginary handlebars. 'Zeeee ... ding ding ding ding ding,' she imitated the sound of the moped's two-stroke engine. 'Zeeee ... ding ding ding ding ding.' She twisted the imaginary throttle for him.

He burst out laughing, shaking his head. This long-limbed female in summer dress with the bare feet imitating mopeds against the backdrop of Swiss mountains was, well ... was, well, what? As he later rested in his hotel room he didn't want to put a name to it. He rolled over on his bed and dialled London, and the images of Britannia Road dispelled any 'well whats', as he conversed with Ros, listened to Tommy's gurglings or wailings, and wished Maria well.

'What do you think of the hotel?' he had later asked Adriana, after she had cheerfully complained about Geneva again, this time that there was no litter anywhere.

'Oh, very comfortable,' she replied. 'It's way above my normal budget.' She sniggered a little. 'It's all courtesy of the British Academy in my case, you know. And down to the latest academic interest in interdisciplinarity.'

'No, I mean the hotel itself, you know, the architecture.'

'Oh. Hideous. I bet they tore down some absolutely beautiful Victorian block with proper "eyebrows" over each window.'

He stared at her. 'Eyebrows?'

'Yes. Eyebrows. Cornices. It's what the Austrian emperor complained of as missing when he spotted the first modernist block opposite his city residence in Vienna. Ornament. You know, Adolf Loos and all that.'

He didn't know, reflecting that this was Ros's department and he was out of his depth again. Shouldn't have started it.

Daytimes were a delight, but his nights were a little fraught. Apart from missing Ros by his side, and the nagging feeling that he was enjoying Adriana's company too much, he woke up each morning with vivid recollections of his two dreams, all mixed up. The seaplane was now crashing into Lake Geneva, while the shouts 'We're going in too fast,' and 'the sea's too rough' were more urgent, and, more disturbingly, clearly enunciated in wartime English. As usual they belonged to men he held dear, while the Turing dream was transposed into the Swiss airport. Ros's old reassurances didn't help much here. And within, what, four days, he was becoming disturbingly comfortable with this new life, so that he had to make an effort to remember his house in Fulham at 54 Britannia Road; he had to make an effort to remember its bedrooms and balconies; to remember, God forbid, even his wife and child. The Grand Hotel Kempinski, the conference hall and breakout rooms, the walks by the lake, and above all Adriana, all seemed to construct a terrifyingly complete new life, rounded off it seemed with these dreams. Actually, it was not that this life was complete so much as it tantalisingly hinted at another even more complete and significant life of people and places at a double remove from Fulham. Ridiculous! He would shake his head, ring up Ros, and quickly reclaim the parts of himself that seemed to be receding.

The stay went fast in the end. On the last day the delegates were invited for a banquet and dance on a refitted paddle steamer on the lake. As they walked over the gangway to the gently rocking vessel Adriana's usual gaiety subsided and she become inexplicably sombre. He glanced at her and, finding her all the more beautiful in that mood with her high cheekbones, small rounded lips and grey eyes, had felt strangely protective towards her. In the slow numbers they danced surprisingly close. Physically close. No doubt Piatigorsky had noticed, William realised much later.

On that last evening, after he had spoken to Ros, he felt the unusual urge to flip through the TV channels for some adult material and pleasure himself. It was true, after all, that Ros had gone off sex after a difficult birth, and he had adjusted to it with forbearance. In fact he dared not think how long it was since they had proper sex together. But now he was all fired up. Four and a half days had let Adriana leach into his soul: there was no doubting that her waist-clinging summer dresses and sandaled feet and funny anecdotes had entered him unfathomably. That, he had thought on the plane home, was understandable. He was lucky to have escaped from the Kempinski now, back to his real self and real life, and suffering only a vague pang of guilt. A man has needs. You could never escape the wisdom of Freud, as his wife would say, so it was natural to look at Adriana and let his mind wander; it wasn't the same thing as a roving eye, was it? A man has an imagination and he had imagined Adriana naked and he was sure that he wouldn't if he had been allowed his conjugals. You couldn't really say that he was at fault. But he hadn't been able to fathom why each night brought progressively more intense repetitions of those two strange dreams, or why he had to fight so hard to retain the memory of who he had been, including the sweep of his life as a mathematician at Imperial College, or his recently becoming the father of a baby boy. Sitting on the plane absently looking down at the coast of Belgium formed from tiny white brush-strokes that had pencilled in the waves, impressionist-style, he did feel a little put out by it all.

He and Ros liked to joke about an imagined French word: *discombobulé*.

'Tu es un peu discombobulé?' he would ask Ros in an atrocious French accent when she looked a bit frustrated over her marketing portfolios.

'Un peu, chéri, un peu,' she would reply, more convincingly.

Well, right now he felt a bit *discombobulé*. A jarring note, a disagreeable sense of unforeseen difficulties ahead, weighed him down a little.

four

ØØ11ØØ   'So, you brought me the paper you published?' Emil's
————————   voice cut across William's reminiscences.
         'Yes.' William had waited a long, long time for this
moment; had first imagined it when gripped with unforgivably vengeful
thoughts towards his colleague; had rehearsed it recently in more sober
and equitable frame; and now felt more like the sad bearer of harsh
news than its author. He walked over from the window and handed the
paper to Emil, who grimaced at it.

'Yes, yes,' said William, 'I know, it's the wrong journal. It's the
Judean People's Front instead of the People's Front of Judea.'

'Willy, I have no idea what you are talking about,' said Piatigorsky,
doubly annoyed.

'Well it means, I guess, that you didn't read it.'

'No, of course not,' said Emil, looking slightly worried now he had
absorbed the abstract. He made excuses for himself: 'I should have, of
course. I keep telling myself to read outside my field. But I take it to
mean well out of my field. Maybe I miss what's near.' It was an odd
admission: the abstract alone had clearly rattled him.

The senior professor sat down and began to concentrate on the
paper, and in these moods Emil struck William as resembling Lenin or
Trotsky perhaps, where the narrow glasses and piebald goatee all added
to the long-familiar but undeniably Soviet sonorities in his unbudgeable
accent. As Piatigorsky's focus intensified and naturally withdrew from
his surroundings, William's thoughts returned to the flight home from
Geneva. He wandered back to the window. It was an appropriate
moment to allow this involuntary but relevant recapitulation to take its
course, yielding perhaps some last additional insight into this dreadful
period in his life.

What first came to mind regarding the aftermath of Geneva had been Adriana's request for him to be an external advisor for her project, made even then, on the Lake. Birkbeck encouraged interdisciplinary and multi-institutional input, she had said. Her intention had been to ask Professor Piatigorsky, but she could see now that William would be better.

'Maths I can do, history I can do, but my Department agreed that for Artificial Intelligence I needed someone from your place. And you would make me work that much harder to get at Turing's precise historical contribution.'

As far as he could recall, he had made a pretty thorough job of telling her why he could not help her out, and that Emil, really, was the perfect fit. 'Professor Piatigorsky, you will find, is a Renaissance man, unlike me,' he had told her self-deprecatingly. 'You can ask my wife who has a degree in literature: I'm a complete philistine.' He had gaily continued to Adriana under the Swiss early-summer sky: 'You see, Pop – my father that is – rather inoculated me against history of any kind. I just don't have the sort of mind that would want to spend time considering the 1930s or whenever Turing was making his seminal developments.' He had clearly and firmly turned down her request, but he could see now that there had been no real resolve behind his words.

William had returned to a cold grey English May in Fulham and the spell of the mountain lake slowly receded in his mind. He had been overjoyed to see Ros and Tommy and his good humour extended once again to Maria who, it had to be said, kept the household running most efficiently. It was also true that she seemed to have egged Ros on with rather exotic menus, just when he was looking forward to proper food again, but he felt a great relief to be home and able to forget Geneva. And perhaps he could get used to sushi, at least it didn't seem to have any garlic in it.

Professor May had been impressed with William's talk at the conference and judged that Imperial had scored something of a triumph in the interdisciplinary area of artificial intelligence applications in the humanities. It had been a hat trick of Aleksander, Piatigorsky, and Strange. May wanted to see William a month later: Geneva had landed Imperial with a possible new consultancy, code name 'Eliza II'. It was an expert system that would replace call centres.

'It's part of the repatriation or reverse outsourcing strategies currently in their infancy in developed economies ...' May droned on.

William was all bright cheery enthusiasm as usual, nodded at the idea of an improved office space, and only later recalled that he would have to share it with a postdoctoral student under his supervision. All he knew was that he should behave when it came to a planned meeting with the research team of the company, scheduled later in the year. And that Geneva had been a Good Thing.

ØØ11Ø1 In bed that first night back from the Kempinski Ros and William were in a loving mood, and got as far as kissing which aroused him terribly, but then she backed off.

'Darling, I'm just not ready yet. I'm terribly sorry. I have to be honest, I am all healed up down there, at least I think I am, but I've been a bit low, or something. And I do have mastitis and breastfeeding is still hard. I'm not in the mood. But you'll see it will turn round before long. It's pretty common in the postnatal group I'm in. My friends say it will just go away and we'll be back to normal in no time. As long as there's no pressure.'

'Sure, sure,' William had said, though he was a bit dubious of the postnatal group as it included the same feminists who had earlier expressed scepticism over Ros's conversion to motherhood. Patricia Elleworthy had led this scepticism to such an extent, and so tartly, that he reminded Ros of something in bed one night when conversation had strayed to their Oxford friend: 'Do you remember darling, I found a name for Patricia not long after you introduced her: "Vinegar Central"?'

'Oh, shut up William,' Ros had giggled. 'That's most unkind. Without strong-minded females like her we women would still be in the kitchen.'

He was of course supportive of feminism; his mother had instilled it into her boys from a young age, and William had always found a simple sense of justice in it. And surely it wasn't completely against the spirit of feminism if a man happened to have noticed a woman's underwear and the image of it had impressed itself on his brain? Freud must always be allowed for, whatever the political correctness otherwise quite properly adhered to. Ros was clear on that. Anyhow, despite all Patricia's earlier theorising, she announced one day that she too was going to have a baby – with her lesbian partner. 'A sister for your little girl,' she had solemnly told the Stranges well ahead of both deliveries. William raised his eyebrows at this, but had not shared with them his quick statistical estimate: that there only was about a thirty-six percentage chance of their combined baby production turning out like that.

In the morning after his return he found himself with a raging erection in the shower and masturbated. What worried him was that it was the image of Adriana that spurred him on – he hadn't been able to prevent a glance at her underwear as she had pulled her legs up that morning on the lake to imitate the Goth on a moped. God forgive him, he was only human.

At work he now found himself having to read lengthy irrelevant documents related to the Eliza II project, at least they were irrelevant to his own research, which was increasingly diverging from the path set out by Aleksander and Piatigorsky. Indeed, though his talk in Geneva had gone down well with Professor May – especially after the consultancy offer – it had rather cooled his relations with Emil.

All in all Geneva did fade from his mind and his dreams became less frequent, though he found himself struggling to fend off some melancholy moments: perhaps Ros's slight postnatal depression was rubbing off on him. The lack of sex for this long period was odd, and as a thirty-six year old male in reasonable health it did grate on him. It was true that any significant cardiovascular activity had long been out of bounds for William, but he liked to think he was a decent enough lover if you were not expecting long athletic sessions: Ros had always reassured him in the past on this subject. In truth both were highly focussed on their careers again as Ros took back much of the key management of her firm, aided by her loyal PA, Jonathan Gries. An evening discussion of their family finances also provided another spur: the addition of Maria to the household added a significant expenditure to their budget, previously stretched as it was by the house, its extensive refurbishment, and the boat at Chelsea.

It was also young Tommy that provided William with the focus beyond his work and which in many ways motivated him to strive harder still. Like most first-time fathers he had been unable to imagine in advance how much a child would change him. Okay, so sex was rather puzzlingly off the agenda, but he saw that too in a different light: the outcome of love-making was far more mysterious and satisfying than he could have imagined. Maria took the burden off the boy's parents when it came to sleepless nights and full nappies, and so his delight in having his son on his knee was pretty much unalloyed.

When he received an email from Adriana asking again if he would consider being an external advisor to her doctoral thesis, he was not much affected by dashing off a reply – with all due courtesy of course – in the negative. William was not even that bothered when Adriana put up a fight, arguing as she was so capable of regarding the benefits to both parties of the proposed arrangement. Her emails were charming and persuasive, and he did have a rather rosy picture in his mind of the days on Lake Geneva, so he didn't turn her down when she suggested they meet in Carluccio's Restaurant near South Kensington Tube. Why not? She was pleasant company, and his resolve was complete. He had ten years on her and as much again in terms of his precocious career development, so it would not be hard to play the senior academic in his scholarly field and put an end to it.

∅∅1110   It did not work. The whole idea of interdisciplinarity, she had explained, was at the heart of Turing's breakthrough, didn't he think so? In truth he couldn't help realising that his pure science background looked philistine next to her humanities reach: she could bring in Plato – whose philosophy he had never read – and Eddington – whose popular science books he had never read – and also the whole context of the birth of modern computing in the collective effort of wartime code breaking, of which he had no idea and no interest in whatsoever. He felt like someone who had never read anything in fact, and what the hell was the Bloomsbury Group? Up to now such a lack of broader cultural mastery had never bothered him, his affable good humour quite adequate to the task of deflecting such claims on his time or self-image. But Adriana's animation, the mercurial flow from maths to history and back again, was captivating.

Still his bottom line was no: Professor Piatigorsky was her man, he of the keen love of interdisciplinarity, why didn't she approach him? But a sinking feeling right through their conversation made him feel increasingly powerless. She was, and there were no other words for it, incredibly beautiful.

Some part of his mind was conscious now that his confident assumption of adequate defences against her might be mistaken. He had quietly observed to himself that various opportunities in the house to respond to Maria's very real appeal had been left unavailed of: it was almost a little joke between them. The young woman knew her sexual power; he acknowledged it as a gentleman should; they left it at that. So why should Adriana be different? Objectively, and in an unanimated state, she was hardly more fetching than the au pair. And, fun as it was, the massive power of his mathematical ambition surely made it impossible for all this chatter about Turing's life and society and the humanities to dent it. However something beyond his grasp was drawing him out of his rigid orbit. Something quite tangential was setting an unknown course for him, steering him into danger. He inwardly steeled himself: if this was a car crash in the making then his inability to turn the wheel in evasive action, and the dread that this paralysis arose in him, was, it had to be said, accompanied by another emotion.

He was exhilarated.

It was simply marvellous to sit in a window seat at Carluccio's with a forgotten baguette on his plate and a fast-cooling cappuccino opposite the woman from the Grand Kempinski. Adriana was wearing jeans this time in the cooler air of London and a light angora sweater, all of which hugged the lines of her body. Her rapid-fire and enthusiastic defence of Turing's significance was a world away from the few sentences he had ever prised out of his father about medieval history, from a man quite set against public enthusiasms of any sort. He gradually felt the unwelcome inevitability of it: that he was going to be her advisor after all. He blinked at this realisation, though he kept deflecting her as best he could.

He finally agreed because something else was dimly pressing on his thoughts. Not just excitement, or for that matter the very real frisson of sexual promise, or guilt that he could even contemplate such possibilities: it was the matter of his dreams. This was not part of some elaborate justification for the whole disaster that he had constructed after the event: he distinctly recalled that, as Adriana's arguments mounted up, his thought processes had not of course completely shunned her overwhelming attractiveness, or overlooked a wild sense of excitement, hard suppressed. But behind that there was a sombre curiosity, perhaps even a self-preserving desire, to follow up the connection between this woman and the strange dreams that her presence had amplified in frequency and impact while in Geneva. They may have subsided since then, but, he realised, he felt incomplete while they remained unexplained and unresolved. The equation had tipped. Not further knowing her was a worse prospect than the horrible damage an affair might wreak on his marriage. He loved his wife, he loved his son, he loved the household. Yet its measured course was fathomable, familiar – it was a world bounded by the slow charming evolution of family life, such as he had known in his own growing up. Wrecking that would be terrible. This other thing had however some nameless sombre potential: not knowing that thing would be – strangely – even worse.

He agreed that supervision would start the following week.

ØØ1111

After the meeting with Adriana his dreams had returned: there *was* a link. They were suddenly more insistent and detailed. He was sure now that the voices crying 'We're going in too fast,' and 'the sea's too rough' – voices of men he had never met but now knew well – were talking about some kind of seaplane making an unscheduled landing on water which might be Lake Geneva. And the scene at Kennedy airport – it wasn't Geneva International, he was sure of that now – went like this: he walked up to the booth in which an armed immigration official sat expressionless and somehow menacing. The man took his British passport and opened it as gingerly as if it were laced with ricin. After a long silence in which the officer breathed heavily, he closed the passport with a hissed exhalation and asked:

'Purpose of visit, Professor Strange?'

'Conference,' William blurted out in his dream.

Pause.

'Con-ven-tion', articulated the official slowly as he wrote it down. The manner was hostile, no doubt about it. Then, after another silence the man looked up and around and beckoned armed police to approach William.

'Professor Strange.' It was a statement, an accusation. The official then brought his head forward, staring with boundless icy aggression at William, and slowly enunciated the line:

Are you now, or have you ever been, Alan Turing?

To start with this dream was more comical than threatening. What a strange thing the mind is! He could see an obvious connection with Adriana here, because of Turing, but not with the other dream. While contact with her definitely seemed to trigger repeated experiences of these dreams – which he strangely craved for – he struggled of course with his decision over seeing her. It was mathematically a waste of time, just when he felt all kinds of pressures to apply himself more ferociously to his research, and the guilt over his attraction to her multiplied: what was he thinking of? He loved his wife and baby son. He made enormous efforts to blot out Adriana's physical attractiveness; he also had the feeling that she was doing the same; that of course made it all the harder.

'Just my imagination,' he would tell himself. 'She knows I'm married with a child. She must have a boyfriend – umpteen far fitter and younger men to flirt with. I'm just imagining that she's drawn to me. You know. In *that* kind of way.'

But some five weeks after supervision began it was a warm summer evening in his office – he was working late and was squeezing in a tutorial before going home – and Adriana's light flowing dress that covered her body next to his somehow sank him. Heated debate led to a kiss. A real kiss. Both were startled by it; both were breathing heavily. Both hastily made conversation about practical arrangements over the next tutorial and agreed her writing schedule all over again. As she rose to leave, flushed, her hand absently brushed over his crotch as if some hoary instinct made her test whether his primal response to her was adequate.

It was.

five

Ø1ØØØØ William's sense of guilt over that kiss became the
———————— dominant emotion in his life, accentuated every
moment he had with Ros, and particularly with
Tommy. It fuelled intense bouts of determination to avoid any
repetition, but there was still no physical intimacy between William and
his wife, and he knew it was just a rationalisation of his own guilt over
Adriana, but he wondered: is Ros also having an affair? Could it possibly
be with that mincing Jonathan Gries, her PA? Come to think of it Gries
had always quietly provided those cultural references that he, William,
failed to volunteer when conversation demanded it – had this upstart
been mocking him all along? Had Ros turned to him because William
had failed her here? And how is he to deal with the fact that Adriana has
a long-term boyfriend whom she loves? This was the unwelcome
though entirely predictable discovery made on another day with Adriana
where all resolve had evaporated in an instant.

'It's a difficult situation we're in,' Adriana said after they had kissed
and fondled in his office, this now a regular part of the meeting for
supervision, 'but one can love more than one person at a time you
know.'

Her comment had finally prompted him to ask outright about a
boyfriend, but all she would say was that his name was Francis and that
she could not leave him at that stage. William was not sure how to take
this, so remained silent.

'We can't solve any of this by thought,' she added brightly – which
struck him as odd – but she was right, he later realised; none of the
thinking he pursued on the subject appeared to resolve anything, so he
confined his rationality to where it did some good: to his mathematics.
After their first kiss and the memory of her hand brushing so lightly, or
even accidentally, across his fly, William had in fact made a series of

resolutions, all of which came to nothing. He would transfer Adriana to Emil. The thought of that was so painful however that he abandoned it immediately – it was the pain of livid jealousy. No, he would simply have it out with her: he could not risk the hurt to his son Tommy if this led to a divorce. Or, they could meet at Birkbeck in the postgraduate lounge in full view of other students, or at Imperial in the staff lounge. But he never did say anything, because the thought of her alone with him in his little office drove him mad with desire. He was absolutely besotted, he admitted to himself in the mirror. Christ! He must be a special sort of chap after all to have this young woman so keen to kiss him. It was only a kiss after all. Okay, his hands had wandered far up her skirt. But it wasn't as if they had slept together. Round and round churned his irrationality.

It was in the middle of such a train of thought that the office phone rang one day: a call from Jane Wozniak, Professor May's secretary – would he have a minute to pop up to May's office? Christ! Has his affair got out? Don't be stupid. Just act calm. It isn't an affair. He has not slept with her. But William arrived in May's office to find two businessmen keen to shake his hand, research directors of SharpSoft, the company behind the Eliza II project. He had been recommended to them by their top research scientist, they assured him, and May was finalising the contractual arrangements. It meant a substantial additional income for William, and the rather mean-spirited sense of satisfaction that his line of research had not just led to this but also rather left Piatigorsky out in the cold.

It was some positive news he could share with Ros, and he took the opportunity to raise the idea with her of moving into larger premises. Britannia Road had been fine for the two of them, but dinner parties were increasingly difficult, and Ros was getting back into schmoozing mode. It was true of course that they still had a rather large mortgage, and that Pierce & Fine itself was experiencing a dip in profitability with its own recent move into more prestigious offices. But the very idea of choosing a new home for the four of them and having the pleasure of dealing with architects and interior decorators gave them new energy, and their estimated future earning potential far outweighed any old-fashioned caution. At least it did for Ros, and William was only too glad to have some project that they could share in, one which would mask his anxieties over where things were going with Adriana.

Ø1ØØØ1   William had been buoyed both by the new consultancy
_____   and the prospect of a larger home. After Geneva's

conference with its interdisciplinary basis he also found himself with a wider range of invitations to speak. There was no doubt that his talk in Switzerland had been not just competent, but stimulating, perhaps even entertaining: Adriana had been the spur then, of course, though his reason for accepting an invitation to give a keynote address at Stirling University had a contrasting motive. It would give him a few days away from both Ros and Adriana and perhaps a chance to think in a constructive way about his difficult situation.

So, immersed in his professional milieu on a Scottish hillside, his anxieties dropped away a little and for the first time since starting tutorials with Adriana he had a couple of nights without either of his dreams. He took stock. Despite kisses and other intimacies with Adriana, he had not had sex with her. He could escape this with some honour. But how? He slowly resigned himself to what had been unthinkable up to now: he *must* transfer her to Piatigorsky. William had additional workloads with the Eliza II project and an increasing list of invitations as keynote speaker so Professor May would not be in the least suspicious over the move, and Emil would be delighted. He would have to do it over Adriana's head and simply confront her with it once the arrangements had been made. If his strange dreams had a meaning they would make it known without Adriana's presence, and if not, sod them. Even as he thought this to himself he had to admit that here was the tug on his resolve. Sex with Adriana – or for that matter sex with any woman – was something he needed badly. But not badly enough to endanger his marriage, to lose his baby son. This other thing, well, perhaps he could seek counselling over it. For that matter perhaps he and Ros should seek marriage guidance over the no-sex thing. Anything. He had to *act* when he got back, however out of character all these options might seem.

After this marathon of a soul-search alone in his VIP suite one evening he slept soundly and felt better than he had for a long time. He had even been relaxed enough to join the conference outing on the last day, taking the delegates by coach to Glasgow for dinner and a visit to Hill House, the home of the renowned architect Rennie Mackintosh. As he toured the rather unremarkable and uninteresting structure William found himself making a mental effort to remember some aspects of the artist's life to recount to Adriana. He had to grin wryly to himself as he realised that he was doing this to impress her. Then he suddenly remembered his resolution, and changed it in his mind: he was doing this for Ros. They needed more things in common.

On the way back in the coach some American postgrads started singing Old MacDonald's Farm in funny variations, with someone finally shouting 'humming version!' He was in such a good mood by then that he joined in, again something out of character for him. But the humming version was not quite finished when his mobile phone vibrated in his jacket pocket and he broke off in the middle of a hummed 'ee ay ee ay oh' to answer it, being sure it was Ros. When he flipped the lid open he was shocked to see that it was Adriana's number – he had a fleeting thought to ignore it, but found himself pressing the receive button. He spoke briefly with her, snapped the lid shut and sat there, his equilibrium shattered. He was both so elated and so gripped by anxiety that he resorted heavily to his inhaler, which was hard to do discretely on a packed coach.

Would he like to pop over to Lake Windermere on his return trip for a little break and a tutorial? That had been Adriana's question. She was on holiday there for a few days in advance of her father joining her, and it was a lovely hotel, and they had vacant rooms; could he stay a night or two? William had not been able to make a direct refusal, merely saying he would call her back after looking into the possibility of re-arranging appointments. But he knew full well that he had no appointments on the first two days of the coming week, and that what he had to resolve was merely what excuse he would make to Ros. He felt sick. The image of a car hurtling towards a barrier returned to him: he was powerless to put on the brakes or turn the wheel. Instead his mind raced, working out possibilities: he had a vague idea that Lancaster University was on the route home and he could tell Ros that he had received an invitation from it to run an impromptu workshop there. Ros was well aware of his recently heightened professional profile and would buy it. He stared blankly at the Scottish moorland from the window of the coach, now feeling far removed from the student jollity, which had moved onto Swing Low Sweet Chariot. 'Americans,' he muttered to himself.

The next day found him on a series of train connections to Windermere. Roughly speaking he was heading towards Lancaster, and so his call to Ros from the train had some plausibility – this subterfuge being part of the first serious lie he had told her. He stared out of the window, not conscious at all of the beautiful landscape, but only of a sense of powerlessness.

Adrianna picked him up from the Windermere train station in an old MG. At first they were rather awkward with each other.

'I didn't realise you had a sports car,' is all he commented as she led him to it in the car park.

'I told you,' she said. 'In Geneva. Compared it to a Ferrari, like Turing to contemporary AI.'

'Oh yes.'

It was a short drive, on a fine summer's day, she confident at the wheel, and he glancing at her profile, her initial reserve giving way to gaiety and grace and chatter. The lake stretched out on her right, and so she was framed alternately by houses, trees and water. She pulled into the drive of the Belsfield Hotel, wheels crunching on gravel. William was suddenly gripped by a vertiginous déjà vu – he gripped the handle of the car door and looked away from her, not wanting to betray his confusion.

'Are you okay?' she said, as he shook his head, blinking.

'Sure,' he replied a little slowly, 'Must have been the whisky tasting session at Stirling. They have a dozen malts in a two mile radius, and the tasting seems to be a standard end-of-conference event.' This was true. He shook his head again, as if clearing it. 'Oh,' he added casually, 'we also had an outing to the Rennie Mackintosh Hill House.'

Ø1ØØ1Ø After William had checked into his room he came down to join Adriana. They had a few snacks for lunch in the lounge overlooking the lake, still awkward with each other, and commenting on how different it was to Geneva – this was an old-fashioned grand hotel, built in Victorian times, impeccably restored to the gilded opulence of that age, and located in several acres of ground with a view north of Lake Windermere. So much more enjoyable than that concrete bunker in the litter- and graffiti-free land of the millisecond-accurate cuckoo clock, suggested Adriana. I liked the Grand whatever-it-was called, returned William, conceding however that at least there was proper English landscape here and weather. And proper English food. Ah, countered Adriana, we are real opposites: I can't get enough of that continental cuisine. William looked out over the lake and reminded himself: he had a right to a little holiday, why not, and it was part of his professional duties to supervise, or at least advise, as in this case, doctoral students. Conferences had junkets, this was just an extension of that principle. Crap, said his conscience, for that is what he was clearly labelling the sober voice in his head that kept reminding him of the outrageous foolishness of this venture. Neither of them had even touched the other yet.

They settled in a bay window with coffees. Adriana pulled out the latest draft chapter in her thesis, but for him to comment on it he had to shuffle a little closer; after a while she closed the gap a little more. He couldn't bear it. He could feel the warmth of her thigh through her thin dress and his summer slacks – a spare Paul Smith sourced by Ros from the Vogue collection to go with his classic Church's Oxfords, the memory of their origins causing a pang for him. He suddenly got up to go to the gentlemen's and looked at himself in the mirror as he washed his hands. The fittings must have been recent, that much he could work out from having perused bathroom catalogues with Ros: they were ultramodern for some reason, where one might have expected Victorian replicas. It soothed him. He lingered over his reflection – in truth he was still a little giddy from the jolt he had received on arriving at the hotel. Déjà vu – what was that exactly? It was not really a bad feeling; it was, ironically, one that you might actually want to repeat. It had the strange promise of meaning in it, but meaning tantalisingly withheld – and that was the whole essence of this liaison with Adriana, the only justification he could cling to when exposed to the withering critique of his own conscience. He looked hard at himself, realising that one cannot quite capture one's own image in a mirror. What he did see clearly enough was a complete lack of determination. His heart was actually thumping; it had been the entire time he had sat next to Adriana on the padded bench by the table in the bay window, with a view over their shoulders of the lake in the hazy July sunshine. He would return to the second half of the chapter, they would lean over the document, their shoulders, their hips would touch, and he would be lost.

He had seated himself on the bench leaving a good gap between his thighs and Adriana's, unsure of how to continue with their tutorial. Something prompted him to ask: 'Déjà vu is French isn't it?' She looked up from her chapter. He persisted: 'Aren't there whole novels written about it?'

Adriana smiled, and then frowned thoughtfully. 'Actually that's a good question. There's Proust of course, but that isn't exactly déjà vu.'

William looked at her blankly, which made her smile broaden into a grin. 'Of course some have tried to explain it with the theory of eternal recurrence,' she continued. 'The ancient Greeks believed in it, and both Nietzsche and Ouspensky revived the idea, though in rather different ways.' The grin didn't leave her face: she was winding him up, and his exaggerated grimace was her reward. 'Nietzsche thought that you should live your life with absolutely no regrets, so the prospect of repeating it an infinite number of times would be a joyful one,' she said with big eyes, looking straight into his, half mocking. He raised his eyebrows, and looked from side to side in a worried fashion. She leant towards him, and softly suggested, as she slid a little curtain of his hair to the left on his comically furrowed brow: 'How about a walk by the lake, and we can get back to the chapter later on?'

Their stroll by the water's edge saw the restoration, in William's mind at least, of the chaste mood established earlier. His heart had stopped pounding – nothing like literary topics for that, he thought – and it now seemed to him that a friendly lakeside amble with a woman effectively his colleague was quite in order. He had worked hard for the Stirling conference, improved the status of Imperial College and himself in the field, and was entitled to a little holiday. A coach trip to a heritage site with a crowd of Americans was hardly much of a break. This was more like it. He had avoided physical contact with Adriana just now by an adroit turn of question; it was easy enough to steer her to literature, the humanities, philosophy or any ardour-cooling darn thing. He would get through this and get home after some walks in England's best countryside and, hopefully, after some of its best food.

Suddenly Adriana stopped and turned to him, taking his hand and drawing him close. He was overwhelmed in an instant. Despite the call of birds and the sounds of marine engines on the lake and a little traffic in the distance, it actually seemed that a profound silence now permeated the bubble they found themselves in. He kissed her with restraint but soon lost it in the urgency of her response; his heart began to pound again and he was conscious of laboured breathing. After a long while she whispered to him: 'Bill, I have missed you so.' He ran his hands down the smooth fabric of her dress at her back as he drew her waist tight to his; they remained pressed together for some time. He then nodded, took half a step away from her, clasped her hand and they walked on a little, slow, in a rhythm with each other and with the lapping waves on the shoreline and the little bleached roots they stepped over. He was dizzy and could not think a coherent sentence, let alone speak it. As they turned into a small creek a redshank flew up in alarm, its call sending its mate into flight; they made a wide circle above black-headed gulls bobbing amiably and unperturbed on the water. A cormorant took that moment to dive for its supper. These were all seagulls to William – had he even noticed them – but to a metaphor-constructing ornithologist the redshank might have been his conscience, the black-headed gull the grinning face of fate and the cormorant the bewildered seeker of truth in the depths of his unconscious.

They returned to their tutorial, this time next to each other in another comfortable spot, their thighs and shoulders touching easily and in oddly good form to look at the intricacies of Turing's early deliberations on thinking machines. It was just a kiss, he kept thinking. A kiss is just a kiss – the tune went round his head. The physical memory of their groins pressed together said something different, but he refused to acknowledge the contradiction. Instead he was sharp with Adriana.

'It's no use speculating on what Turing may or may not have thought. You can only use the written evidence, and must avoid all interpolation based on any of your own preoccupations. You have to work with that short early piece of writing, what was it called? His "Nature of Spirit". It's not my job to read it, that's for the historian in you. But you have to remember that he was a mathematician first and foremost and that the Turing Machine is a hypothetical device that manipulates mathematical symbols, nothing more.'

Adriana nodded, eager, busily correcting her paragraphs with a red biro. It was her turn to steal glances at her companion, a well-known prodigy in mathematics, a man with a beguiling tumble of blondish hair and blue eyes of passion and depth. He had the ease and confidence of a man of the world, or so it appeared to her.

For himself he had the ease and confidence of a man knowingly driving a car at full speed into a concrete barrier. Once the decision has formed one can afford the appearance of calm, indeed it is no effort to maintain it. Conscience had done its pitiful best, and now remained a silent observer as the vanquished antagonist. But while she made notes his thoughts kept returning to that question, the one from the dream, a question that no longer seemed funny, but grating. It was clear: her very presence triggered the wretched recollection:

Are you now, or have you ever been, Alan Turing?

He pushed the ridiculous thing away from his mind and looked at Adriana, focussed on her papers. She was absolutely beautiful, and he was past the point of no return. That was obvious now. He had no choice in this unfolding, and so he would yield with grace at least, and give himself to her wholly, yield to the serendipity of their commingling in this specially marked-out place. It *is* marked out, he had thought, another strange conviction that welled up in him. Time did not really progress for them, though it paced out certain inevitabilities. They finished the chapter on a constructive note, found themselves ready for an evening meal, ate it harmoniously to the satisfaction of their rather different tastes, and drank a progression of glasses of wine, the provenance of which they could comment on with equal approval. The sun set in a deep reddening haze behind mountains over the opposite shore – it was a soundless, timeless progression in which all things were ordained and prescribed. No thought could break this flow, though conversation tumbled between them, laughing at memories of his cauliflower and her moped on Lake Geneva, or debating his hopeless attempts to avoid his academic fate at Carluccio's. He agreed pleasantly: his had been lousy arguments against Turing's legacy. Cauliflowers were not serious vegetables – equally, mopeds were not serious means of transport. While one set of hands were clasped, the other alternately or sometimes together raised glasses to their lips. Thus were they joined in the growing stillness between them, and thus it was inevitable that they should go up as if to their separate bedrooms, linger at her door while she found the key, and after the smallest pretence that he was off then, tumble into her room, both of them flushed, and each to the other utterly beautiful. William lightly kicked her door closed as he grasped Adriana's waist, and she pulled him onto her bed.

Ø1ØØ11   The following morning William was locked in his own en-suite bathroom, where he had said he needed to go to retrieve his sponge bag. He paid no attention to the admirably modern fittings this time, which was a loss to his project for the new family home. Perhaps part of him did acknowledge the translucent perfection of the one-third hemispherical glass hand-wash basin with its polished interior and ground exterior, set on a dark marble base via a satisfyingly clean-lined cylindrical stainless fitting, but really it was his overwhelming sense of anxiety that had sent him there to suck heavily on his inhaler. Again he looked at himself in the mirror. He had taken a step beyond his marriage that was terrifying, but the guilt was not the major thing he had to acknowledge: it was a sense of heaviness. Not a good heaviness at all, not the heaviness of après-sex. His dreams in the night, mingled with the exhilaration of Adriana's presence next to him, made for a newness that was at once liberating and dreadful. That dread was nothing to do with his sense of guilt however, it was not the dread of his wife discovering this infidelity – how would she anyway? It was a dread he could not name at all.

Anyhow, it was too late for guilt, and perhaps his wife was having an affair as well. This thought stopped him in his tracks. He never did like that PA of hers, too toadying. Come on. It had been six months since the birth of Tommy and they had not had sex, and it had been who knows how many months leading up to the birth. That can't be normal. Perhaps this business of an open marriage will work. Perhaps simply not talking about it will work. What binds him and Ros is Tommy, nothing will come in the way of that. What binds him and Adriana is their shared intellectual journey. He stared at himself in the mirror: this train of rationalisation was not that convincing, but it would have to get him through the day. He shrugged and then showered. Some things can't be thought through; Adriana was right on that. Physically he glowed, and he would cling to that even if mentally he felt unbalanced.

He and Adriana had breakfast, and at his suggestion would go out on the lake at midday – he had negotiated the hire of a dinghy with an outboard motor and suitably equipped with neat little life jackets. Thus attired he stood in the stern, started the engine with a flourish and steered it expertly out of the small marina. At his request, the hotel had made up a classic picnic hamper. Adriana reclined opposite him, looking up at a confident, humorous Oxbridge male, a lover and friend, a man ten years older than herself, a man meeting some deep need in her that she could name no more clearly than he could.

It was blissful on the lake. William switched off the engine after progressing up the water for some time, and again the silence seemed to burst upon them. The waves slapped against the side and he joined Adriana in the prow of the dinghy: they kissed long and hard. The sun beat down on them. For now they would forget their larger circumstances as William got out pristine white napkins, glasses, a bottle of champagne and began to explore the various delights of the hamper, spreading things out for Adriana.

'No need for a great jetting Swiss fountain,' she murmured, her eyes full of both simplicity and mischief, 'when I have a lover like you.'

Much later he started the engine again and turned the boat around. Without warning, as his eyes scanned the nearby shoreline and what appeared to be a resort with little jetties and holiday makers, he was gripped by an utter panic. The familiar dream scene of a seaplane crashing into water came to him, but it was overlaid with the strange sensation that he was now rowing their little boat and that the person in the prow was someone quite different to Adriana. The sun seemed blotted out, it was cold. He gasped at the tiller, his knees buckling for a moment, and then righted himself. Adriana was turned around, looking forward out of the boat at the same scene and did not notice his discomfort. He would need all his reserves of humour and bonhomie to cover over this horrible disjunction that had suddenly riven him. Somehow, he made it through the rest of the day.

'What on earth is happening to me?' he whispered to the mirror in her ensuite bathroom as they changed that evening. 'Is this some kind of breakdown?' How could one transition from contented lover on the lake – albeit with a conscience nagging like toothache – with confident command of boat and hamper and pleasantly stimulated by a good champagne – in small quantities of course, one had a craft and passenger in one's charge – to a head-case in less than an instant? In the fraction of a second it took to scan an absolutely innocent stretch of unfamiliar shoreline? Or, on the other hand, was it in some inscrutable and horrible way actually familiar? Isn't that what déjà vu means?

They went to a restaurant in the town of Windermere for the evening. By this time his mood had recovered somewhat as they teased each other over the menu with its mix of traditional English fare and the 'invasion', as William put it, of foreign dishes. Out of gentlemanly feeling he had initially refused her suggestion that he could drink but she should not as she was driving, but after a little gentle persuasion he capitulated; he had needed it, and was grateful for the light-headedness the wine produced. He was having a fantastic time with Adriana but in the lulls in the conversation or when either of them left the table for the bathroom conflicting emotions would surface. How on earth had he gone from that confident master of the punt in which he had proposed to Ros, certain of the fixed course of future marriage, career and children due to his station in life, to that seemingly confident master of an outboard motor from which he stared at his lightly-clad mistress in the bow of a dinghy, beautiful under a Lake District sun, and now fearful for the outcome? And in which he had experienced such a horrible brainstorm? What words could describe it anyway? He had heard of the term 'brown study', but that implied a genteel absent-mindedness in an armchair in the library. He had heard of the term 'psychotic episode.' That made him wince inwardly. Or 'breakdown'. The terms multiplied, all of them alarming and previously only applicable to other people.

It was still light as they returned in Adriana's MG. She drove competently along the shore-hugging little road.

'You must like driving,' he remarked, realising that she would have had to endure hours on the motorway from London, and wanting to talk about any trivial thing.

'I hated the whole idea to start with,' she replied. 'I took my test at eighteen, but scorned the motor car just like Sylvia Plath – my mother's influence, you know. But then, like Plath, I realised that what I disliked was other people driving cars.' She laughed at herself. 'When Daddy was going to get rid of his old MG he persuaded me to take it on a holiday in the West Country, just in case it turned out that I would like it after all. And I did. I found it quite liberating.'

'Well, that makes three things so far,' said William thoughtfully. 'Three things where we have opposite tastes: food, buildings and cars.'

'I'm sure there's more,' she said gaily, but William found himself oddly steeling himself for the moment when they would arrive at the hotel. He was mindful of both moments of disjunction – today on the lake and the previous day at the hotel – and was glad that Adriana could not see the expression on his face in the fading light. She slowed down, indicated right, and waited for some cyclists before crossing the oncoming carriageway. She brought the little sports car gently to rest on the gravel drive of the old hotel.

six

Ø1Ø1ØØ The tyres of the old MG crunched loudly on the driveway gravel of the Belsfield Hotel as the car came to a sudden halt. The low light on the lake made all things luminous; there was a warm breeze. He was in a thoughtful mood. After switching off the engine they turned and kissed each other.

'We've had a wonderful day,' he commented as he drew himself out of the driving seat and strode lopsidedly around the front of the car to open the door for her. She swung her stockinged legs out from the cracked leather upholstery of the sports saloon, an MG TA Midget which had seen better days. She looks smashing with the new rank insignia on her cuffs, he thought, as he had so often in the weeks since her promotion to Assistant Section Officer. The Women's Auxiliary Air Force uniform did nothing to hide her shapely curves, and, in his opinion, she stood out from the whole cohort at the officers' training school housed at the requisitioned Belsfield, but in reality it was he who turned heads as they entered the extensive lounge. As a WW1 veteran with a limp he could not exactly strut up to the bar to order drinks for them: his progress was too halting to be that of the stereotyped male officer of the British armed forces, but his pirate eyes and vigorous manner were none the less thirstily gazed upon in a man-starved world.

'Deirdre, darling, are you having the usual?' he boomed out.

'The usual, Peter,' she called as she walked over to the bay window. Yes, he thought, he, ordinary old Peter Darby, had netted quite a catch in that Deirdre Haviland, daughter of a high-up in the Admiralty. She had plenty of rivals, though they were friendly enough and welcomed the couple as they settled into the bay window with a view of the lake, he with a pint of best and her with a G&T. He *was* in a thoughtful mood. After they were left alone by Deirdre's friends she commented on it, concerned for him.

'You know,' he turned to her, 'I have never told anyone this, but my worst fear is of drowning. Not on the lake of course. Not when you are there with me. But on the high seas. That's why I do the work I do. For some reason it's been on my mind today.'

'But you spend more time at sea than you should, or are allowed to in fact, darling. Why do you do it then?'

'Because of all our sailors lost on the convoys. Did you know that every German U-boat in the Atlantic has tipped around two hundred of our boys into the drink? On average that is. Can you imagine what it's like? What a horrible way to die? I don't want to kill Germans at all, or have them drown in their submarines. But each sub we destroy saves two hundred of our sailors. That's what drives me.'

Deirdre looked at him for a moment and gripped his hand. After a while she said: 'Peter darling, I hate to mention it, but can we turn to my studies?' He half-grimaced, half-grinned.

Ø1Ø1Ø1   Deirdre fished out a brown folder from her leather satchel and spread a few papers in front of them.

'I want to understand more about the operational oversight of the Sunderlands,' she said, coaxingly.

'Humph,' he complained, 'do all our evenings have to turn into tutorials?'

'Peter, darling, you know I have more officer exams coming up. It would be fantastic if I could serve in the Atlantic air support with the Sunderlands, don't you think? After all I can't stay here after graduation. So far we have only covered a bit of history regarding Squadrons 204, 210 and the Royal Australians who you met on the Medway.'

'Yes of course, dear, you are right. I just fancy getting a bit blotto tonight.'

'Later, Peter, later. Plenty of time for that. And anyway you shouldn't be driving back to White Cross Bay if you're blotto.'

'Okay, okay. Where were we with all this?'

'I wanted to understand the operation of RAF Marham. If I could get transferred to Marham, I would be in contact with you on a regular basis.'

'Your father knows all that, if you wanted to ask him.'

'I can't ask him, darling. *You* know that.'

And so they went on for a while, she asking questions and making notes on his answers. The uniformed women of the WAAF came and went, the lucky few with a sweetheart on one arm, the rest content to socialise with their own sex. The big lounge with its shabby reminders of past opulence was open to all, but beyond it and the lobby there was strictly no access for the men. The optics behind the bar were mostly empty and dusty, waiting for better days and more plentiful spirits. A dull ale or a stout for the men, and gin with a dubious tonic for the women, was pretty much it, but on the scuffed and worn oak bar next to the only two pumps in operation was a very modern Bakelite telephone. Its shiny black surface was moulded into a most up-to-date sculptural form, and its handset deliberately shaped to divorce the whole thing from its lineage. The war effort needed everywhere the very best in communications, and, curiously, also needed to spell out the stubborn fact that technology was everywhere changing tradition. It rang.

'Peter!' called the barmaid across the large room. 'Peter Darby?'

'Sorry darling,' Peter said as he got up awkwardly and went to the bar. He took the call with a serious face, nodded, and then put down the receiver. 'Boat coming in. Bit shot up,' he confided to Deirdre when he got back. They continued for another hour with her studies, amidst the low hubbub of voices. Blackout blinds came down on the windows and the lights came on.

Ø1Ø11Ø   'Swot,' came a pleasant voice from over them.

'Hello Barbara,' said Deirdre.

'Get your flying boatman to buy me a drink will you?'

'Of course,' said Peter, rising to his feet more vigorously this time, and shuffling Deirdre's papers into a pile: enough with studying. Barbara sat down next to Deirdre and followed Peter with her eyes.

'You, Deirdre Haviland, are going to get me into the Shorts factory, or there will be a serious falling out.'

Deirdre laughed. 'You, Barbara Stevens, won't find any more Peters down there, you know.'

'Thank God for that. One Peter is enough for womankind. I want a limber young thing with sawdust between the ears, who doesn't know his tensile strength from a train station.'

Deirdre grinned. Her friend's father had been an engineer, which might explain why Barbara's vocabulary made ready reference to mechanical things, but where she got her strange expressions from nobody could tell. Barbara cocked her head, eyebrows up, accusingly, waiting for a response.

'Oh, okay, I'll get you in somehow,' said Deirdre.

'There's my girl.'

'But engineering isn't dull you know, it's full of ...'

'Yes it is,' cut in Barbara. 'I should know.'

At that moment they were joined by an RAF officer with a thin moustache.

'Buy you girls a drink?' he announced.

'We are fine thank you Alasdair,' said Barbara, 'Young Peter Darby is tending to our needs.'

A barely-disguised irritation passed over the officer's face. 'That Peter Darby is going to get caught out one of these fine days. And he's not so young any more.' He glanced to the bar at Peter. 'Everybody knows that his sidekick at the factory is Clarence Marshall, a real rough type who's done time, I'm sure of it.'

'Rough diamond,' agreed Barbara sweetly, looking at him with big eyes. 'I hear he did twenty years for collecting faggots on your estate. Made him a little bitter, I suppose.'

Alasdair grimaced at this. He didn't waste any more breath on Barbara, but turned to Deirdre: 'There's a Coastal Command officers' dance at Barrow-in-Furness in two week's time. Would you like to accompany me?'

'No thanks, Alasdair.' The officer stiffened at Deirdre's curt response. He stood scowling for a moment but was drawn away by two WAAF women who appeared to know him.

'Alasdair can't bear it that you are Peter's girl,' said Barbara.

'Nor can my father,' said Deirdre with a sigh. 'But I tell you this,' she said defiantly, turning to Barbara. 'He's worth ten of that Farnham-Smythe.'

Peter made his way back with the usual G&T for Barbara, having observed the retreating officer without comment. The lounge of the Belsfield was increasingly packed. 'Thank you, young man,' said Barbara, prompting a quizzical raising of his eyebrows as he settled into his chair. He was however now following the progress of a stout man with spectacles ploughing his way towards them.

'Ecky,' said Peter softly as the man reached them.

'Aye, evening, ladies. Evening Mr Darby.' He leant closer to Peter and asked if he could have a word. Barbara blinked at him, his pronounced Scottish accent making it a little hard for her to follow what he was saying. She too leant towards Peter and his friend in order to engage them.

'Engineering, Mr Turnbull,' she said firmly, breaking into their conversation. 'It's a discipline used equally to design flying boats and ladies' bras.'

'Aye, Sergeant Stevens.' He looked at her for a moment over his spectacle rims and then turned back to Peter.

'Would you say that engineering is a boring topic for conversation in a hotel lounge bar, Mr Turnbull?' she asked.

'I would nae know, Sergeant Stevens,' he responded, quite unruffled, 'I have nae been bored in my entire life.'

'Which, I dare say, is why you are not a ladies' man,' responded Barbara thoughtfully.

Ecky turned back to contemplate her. 'Am I nae a ladies' man, Sergeant Stevens?' he asked slowly.

'I would nae know,' she mocked him, to which he did not respond. She added: 'But you *are* the only man permitted upstairs at the Belsfield.'

Ecky turned back to Peter with a faint sigh, his head cocked questioningly.

'I'll come by your office around eight,' said Peter.

'Around eight, Mr Darby,' repeated Ecky and turned to leave.

They watched him row back in the direction of the bar. A piano started up a few notes of 'It's a Long Way to Tipperary' upon which the group surrounding the pianist burst into song. Alasdair belted it forth with gusto but as he turned and caught the trio of Peter, Deirdre and Barbara looking at him across the lounge his smile turned to a scowl.

'That's the wrong way to tickle Mary …' sang Deirdre quietly with a smile.

'Too right, my girl,' said Barbara.

Ø1Ø111 Deirdre then turned to Peter with a mischievous grin on her face. For the benefit of Barbara she said: 'So, what's on when you get back to the factory? Are you going to work on that issue of the tensile strength of the forward wing member strut flange, er, collet, er ...' she laughingly groped for a suitable word: 'bracket?'

Peter's brow furrowed at this nonsense, spoken so sweetly, and making such a bewitching contrast with the formality of the WAAF uniform.

'The *forward* wing member strut flange collet bracket?' queried Barbara with precise and rapid enunciation; her eyebrows arched, leaning all serious towards Peter. She could be counted on to rise to such prompting. He sat stony faced, ignoring Barbara, but conscious that here was the root of his attraction to Deirdre: one moment, and in certain moods, she could look quite spinsterish in that outfit, but then she could puncture it the next with such quaint and funny ramblings. The two women burst out laughing. He frowned exaggeratedly.

'If you must know there is a Sunderland in with major repairs. I am indeed trying out some new ideas on forward weaponry. It's so hush-hush that I've had to tell the local newspaper to only print ten thousand copies in German. But if your have three or four hours to spare, I can go into the details for you. There is a whole new range of angle-pivot cleats I am testing on the, er, forward flange, strut, bracket, erm ...'

'Aargh,' cried Barbara, getting up and ruffling Peter's hair. She knocked back her drink in two gulps and then looked down at him. 'I actually think you *are* German. You always fall for it, taking us so seriously. But engineering talk reminds me how much I have been looking forward to doing my laundry. It's so much more exciting you understand. See you next time, old sailor.'

'Enough of the "old",' spluttered Peter, actually annoyed by now and forgetting that she had called him 'young' earlier on.

Barbara took this as a prompt for further banter. 'Thursday night is silk undies night. I am faced with hours of rubbing those darling little soap flakes into gusset after gusset. And you know how slimy the little flakes get as they dissolve in the warm suds. You can't imagine how tired my fingers get from all that rubbing! Or how hard it is to restore the pristine purity of the ruby-red silken fabric!'

Peter glared at her in irritation as she flounced off, waggling her behind. He shook his head and muttered: 'Pristine purity ...'

Turning briefly, Barbara repeated loudly from across the lounge, to the bemusement of onlookers: 'Rub, rub, rub! Rub, rub, rub!' Others were singing 'To the sweetest girl I know,' over the general din of conversation. Peter screwed up his face. Deirdre was highly amused and took his hand, murmuring: 'Don't take any notice, darling. They're all jealous you know.'

They looked at each other for a while, and then she asked: 'So what is on at the factory, apart from repairs?'

'I do have a new boat with some modifications in progress,' Peter replied. 'And I am working on the weapons. Not the forward weapons though, which is all I can say. I am serious about secrecy you know. Just as you are.'

Ø11ØØØ   William was absorbed in his reverie while absently taking in the view over Hyde Park, his eyes resting on familiar landmarks here and there including the gilded Prince Albert. He was startled into the present by a grunt from Emil. The learned senior professor leapt to his feet and crossed the room to take a dirty old cloth and furiously rub out a long sequence of equations on his whiteboard, completely ignoring the guest in his office. Grabbing a marker pen Emil then peered at William's paper and scribbled down some symbols on the smeared off-white surface. He stood back and added further marks, and then peered at the paper again. After a while William stopped following Emil's line of thought on the board; he was quietly confident that he had long ago covered all the possible objections that Emil was now raising. He found again to his great relief that he was not bitter any more. Emil is finished, he acknowledged to himself, but took no pleasure in it: it is a simple fact.

He turned back to other thoughts. Things had gone badly wrong after Windermere: it had been a terrible mistake to start an affair with a student just because his wife wasn't ready for sex after childbirth. But anyway that wasn't quite right. It wasn't just a sex thing with Adriana. On the other hand it definitely wasn't a no-sex thing either – he had been round this a thousand times in his head, moralising it from all possible angles and finding no real hiding place from his conscience. He wasn't the man he had thought he was, that was clear.

At the time he had felt that despite the trap he had created for himself, the situation wasn't entirely dreadful. Leaving aside the frighteningly wonderful times spent with Adriana, there was the other strange upside to this turmoil, a promise of revelation. His rational side had immediately recoiled from that word – 'revelation' – but the broader feeling remained, that whatever this confusion was about, it felt like some clarity would eventually emerge from it. Meanwhile the most terrifying problem for him in that period was that his research was stalling.

He had returned home from Windermere with the glow of Adriana's loving on him. He realised that he looked a little sunburnt from the days on and by the lake and had a story ready about walking with colleagues in the hills behind Stirling University. That hazy mountain sun can be deceptively bright! He had taken the Underground from St Pancras station to Fulham Broadway with his suitcase and walked the short distance home to number fifty four, its familiar brick and glass facade picked out with thin black-painted steel. It just didn't feel that familiar. The rumble of the little wheels of his suitcase had seemed oddly annoying, and at each kerb it was something of a jolt to get the thing to mount it. At one point his suit carrier slipped off the extended handle of the suitcase and fell on the pavement; it was a fiddly job to secure it again and it all added to his nervousness. He was definitely *discombobulé*. He opened the gate with the big block numerals, bronze on black, let himself in, and shouted 'Hi darling!'

He was alarmed to realise that the emotion he felt above all others was fear. But how could Ros know anything of his affair? Nothing to worry about. He hung up his light summer jacket and the suit carrier, dumped the annoying suitcase by the rack, and walked up the stairs to the main living space. A Bjork tune was playing loudly – not that he could have identified the artist – so he had to announce himself a second time to the little trio that constituted his domestic ensemble: Ros, Tommy and Maria. Ros had a magazine in her hands, Maria had Tommy on her lap, and the coffee table was strewn with estate agents' brochures and books on architecture and modern furniture. Ros rose up and gave him a hug and a kiss. The music still played loudly. Many confused thoughts ran round his head, including that Maria looked a little flushed and that when she handed Tommy to him he thought she should keep away from the baby if she had the 'flu. Or perhaps she had got it from Tommy, in which case he was being quite unfair on her. All this was overlaid by thoughts of guilt and how quite one kisses one's wife after sex with another woman. But, as 'All is Love' was turned off, Ros was enthusiastically telling him how Maria had an unexpected knowledge of contemporary furniture, and they had been daydreaming about the new residence.

'Just daydreaming, Will. You have to be fully involved in all the decisions. And how was your trip?' Ros spoke rapidly.

He mumbled various things about how artificial intelligence was permeating new disciplines, and how the Scottish air and whisky had given him something of a glow. Ros thought he looked a bit pale, actually, but then that was the fluorescent strips perhaps: they had never been that flattering. They would get a lighting consultant in on the new home. Somehow he negotiated all these initial exchanges, a kiss in bed, and drifted off to sleep with his wife next to him. Part of him was simply appalled at what he had done. It was in some ways not that different after the first passionate kiss with Adriana; surely that had been the central transgression. But sex, actual sex? He had crossed some boundary that was not just a moral one, but – and his fear returned suddenly, bitingly – a legal one. Lawyers. Did not colleagues, in going through their terrible divorces, bring in lawyers, who it seemed ensured that the fathers saw nothing, or next to nothing of their children? The loss of Ros was a horrible prospect but he deserved it, if that is how it was going to be. The loss of Tommy? That was unthinkable.

Nothing of this materialised however, so over the following days he settled back into his old routine, though not without the feeling that there was now something tangibly unstable about it. He made as good a show as he could at home and at work, and even with Adriana, but the fact was that he was down. His mood was laid low in some indeterminate fashion though definitely connected with those moments of déjà vu at the lake. He frowned to himself. Where had the uncomplicated William of old gone? And how had he gone so quickly?

Several months later he had made another excuse to Ros about a lecture at Lancaster and made a second trip, alone, to Windermere. He had to do it, even if it was precious time away from his work and involved lying to Ros again; he had to do it because he needed to push forward into the dark morass in his mind that centred on the lake, Adriana and Turing. It was September now, and turning unexpectedly cold. The Belsfield Hotel felt bleak to him; he was hoping that it would hold some clue to his increasingly depressed mood, but all it did in the end was to make him miss Adriana horribly, as each location in the hotel reminded him of those incredible few days with her. It was another place that he really wanted to see however: the holiday camp he had spotted when on the lake with Adriana and which had churned his stomach so. How could an innocent bit of holiday shoreline in the Lake District do that to a person? He had looked the place up: it had been the site of a military flying boat factory in the war – apparently Short Brothers, which had made the Sunderland flying boat in Rochester, had been targeted by

German bombers and so it had moved its operations to Windermere in 1940 – this surely must be the site associated with that bizarre dream of crashing into the sea. Or was it perhaps a flying boat crashing into Lake Windermere? He had stood holding the handle of the outboard motor, gripped with that terrible déjà vu, a carefree Adriana dangling her hand in the water and looking south down the lake to Bowness, and had viscerally felt for a moment that he was rowing a dinghy. Not a dinghy actually. Had that strange hallucination been perhaps an escape in a life-raft?

Worse than any of these speculations had been this question: why on earth was he so overwhelmed by them as to force a clandestine two-day break from his work and family life?

The holiday park, also looking rather forlorn and end-of-season, told him little. His taxi waited for him as he went into the camp facility, the 'White Cross Bay restaurant & family lounge bar' as it said in the brochure. Its walls were covered with old photos of Sunderland flying boats and the crew and workers of the site, but nothing of the original factory or slipways remained. He made some polite conversation with the receptionist there about bringing his family next year, interspersed with questions about the wartime use of the place, but nothing triggered any insight. At the receptionist's invitation he had walked around the camp, pausing at the water's edge where a cold wind driving down the lake had raised sufficient wavelets for them to lap insistently at the little jetties and on the gravel shoreline. It was not at all soothing – something was lurking here that he could not get at. He returned home even more depressed, a mood that he hid from both Ros and Adriana, but which continued to prevent any serious research. Whatever other fears he had, this was the worst: what if he failed to make that mathematical breakthrough he was convinced lay just around the corner? He knew well enough the ferocious intensity of application needed to turn the various clues and half-formed insights so far gathered into a substantial ground-breaker. He felt the pressure both of his own mathematical genius and of the more mundane need for success: a better salary. The house project as Ros and Maria were conceiving of it was on a truly substantial scale. He needed to make it happen. He needed the excitement of it to keep Ros and Maria happy.

Ø11ØØ1   William and Adriana had resumed tutorials after Windermere but there was no obvious place where they could make love again. They kissed and fondled and drove each other to a pitch of desire, but that was it – Adriana would not hear of a hotel room or anything like that. She went home to her boyfriend and William to his wife – it was symmetrical enough, he supposed, but he was in agonies of jealousy over Adriana's boyfriend Francis, made worse by his own sense of justice. How could he complain, how could he expect anything different?

William now really suspected Ros of having an affair while she was running her business from home and he was at work, but could not tackle her with his suspicions. If she was having an affair, then wasn't it a good thing? Perhaps Ros was guiltily hiding from him what he was hiding from her: she had plenty of opportunity at work and in her business trips around the country, now resumed on a small scale as the baby was less dependent. Or was he feeling a little shut out because it seemed that Ros mostly discussed plans about the new home with Maria, not him? He felt again his lack of education in the arts: he had mentioned Rennie Mackintosh to Ros, but, as with Adriana, couldn't follow through in the slightest.

In October William had agreed with Ros that it would be good to attend a function at Imperial, something they could do together. Richard May was enthusing over various new consultancies, including the Eliza II project, and put on a party for corporate sponsors of such projects; he was always angling for Ros's involvement and was keen to see her back in action after her pregnancy. Ros and William hadn't been anywhere together as a couple in ages, but William hadn't counted on Adriana being invited as the Birkbeck contact for a proposed inter-college project she had mentioned to him, and so it had been an awkward evening, even though Adriana seemed long-practiced in putting on a remote and professional air. William spent a little time with his head of department, who then buttonholed Ros and asked her opinion about hospitality suites: was Imperial really in the game with its current facilities? Ros had delicately hinted perhaps not, but why not join her at an event on the sixth floor of the Tate Modern, it had quite spectacular views and was becoming the location of choice for the discerning event manager. Better than the Royal College of Art.

Piatigorsky suddenly turned up and joined Ros and Professor May. He was his usual self, charming in his exotic East European way, one that rather ignored the more British deference given to husbands. William had long been used to what seemed like his rather obvious flirting, just as Emil's wife Hilde was entirely unfazed by it. She was asking Ros where the baby was, and, on learning that Tommy was with an au pair, Hilde proceeded to lecture Ros that it was exploitation when a wealthy woman paid a poor woman for babysitting. Feminism in East

Germany insisted on equality for all women, Hilde told her, unlike feminism in the West which just wanted women – some women at that – to have careers like men and make money out of social divisions.

'In my student holidays,' Hilde told her, 'I worked with women road gangs in rural areas south of Berlin, and when I looked for work as a lecturer here in London I made sure it was a polytechnic, not a university. Pah, now they are all the same.'

As William watched Ros with the Piatigorskys he had a sudden horrible thought. Was Emil tupping his wife? He kept a fixed grin on his face as Emil scolded Hilde over her prejudice about universities and reassured Ros that some limited wage differentials were not ruled out by Marxist theory, all perfectly innocent perhaps. But his mind was racing. He had no idea about Emil's movements during the week. Of course he always assumed that the senior professor was in his office, but how often did William visit him there? Certainly since Geneva there had been less casual dropping by, but Ros's strange behaviour went back much earlier than that; he felt only confusion and drifted off. Adriana caught his eye and against his better judgement he made his way to her, lifting a glass of wine off one proffered tray and a canapé off another, rather wishing that there was a more obvious person with whom he could engage in conversation. They spoke together rather awkwardly.

'Quail's eggs,' he mumbled. 'No garlic. Good.'

Adriana responded by listing the contents so far of the other edible offerings, pointing out the distinctly Continental tinge to many of them. Actually that annoyed him, so he said sarcastically that he was waiting for them to develop a canapé based on roast beef and Yorkshire pudding; he was in an edgy mood. Adriana was half way through suggesting why not bacon and eggs when they were interrupted.

'Hello Miss Russett,' boomed Emil's voice suddenly – he must have followed William over. 'William, you never introduced us. I can't forgive you.'

William went through the motions of a cheery introduction while eyeing Piatigorsky closely, as if this would reveal the truth about him and Ros. They could easily have had lunch-time liaisons for years, he thought. Meet in an Italian café close to Britannia Road, and then slide between the marital sheets.

Snap out of it! William berated himself, the rictus of his fixed smile actually beginning to hurt. This is ridiculous. But now Emil was in animated conversation over Turing, explaining to a fascinated Adriana how the seminal genius of computational mathematics had set a wrong course for the development of the field. The older man had actually manoeuvred himself between William and Ros and was charming the pants off her. William felt his jealousy rise. He also felt ridiculous to himself. What a lost opportunity! If only he had stuck to his resolve while at Stirling, declined Adriana's invitation to Windermere, and had quietly transferred her to Piatigorsky. He mused bitterly on this for a while, but then shrugged his shoulders. It was no use regretting events: he was a man used to buoyancy, not gloom.

Through his confused emotions about the suave émigré there surfaced another more satisfying thought: it was Adriana's manner to engage with intellectuals with such vivacity, but it was William she chose at Geneva and all of the initial suggestions that she take Piatigorsky as advisor had been firmly resisted. William wandered off again, this time in search of the Stilton and blackberry canapés and another large glass of wine. Ros would have observed nothing more than his brief conversation with a student and a handing over to the Professor for small talk.

Later on William was unavoidably talking with Adriana again, while watching Emil on a return visit to Ros's side, engaging her animatedly. At one point Emil seemed to be indicating to Ros in the direction of William and Adriana, making William uncomfortable. Damn it, he was nervous about everything, suspicious of everybody, and he needed yet another glass of wine. He felt deeply uncomfortable with himself: how was he going to do any good mathematics when his easy conventional life had now gained such aggravating undercurrents? Damned unwelcome complications.

Ros was rather cool with him on the way home, and said nothing as they prepared for bed. He had definitely drunk too much and so fell asleep barely conscious that the space between them under the sheets had grown larger. At breakfast Ros seemed to be studying him in silence. He had shaved with a splitting headache, not in the mood for conversation, and headed straight out, but when he got home that night Ros announced frostily that they needed to talk.

'Emil tells me that you have a new research student.'

'Ah, yes,' William responded.

'You didn't mention it,' Ros said, looking him straight in the eye.

'I didn't think to,' said William with an effort at carelessness.

'Emil says you met her in Geneva. And that you literally pinched her from under his nose.'

William just shook his head.

'I saw her at the Imperial do, talking with you,' insisted Ros. 'She is very attractive. Called Adriana, I gather.'

'And?' William was genuinely annoyed.

'Emil says you have regular tutorials with her and she would have been at the Stirling conference with you. That's all rather a lot of opportunities for a man whose wife has recently been pregnant and is still recovering from a difficult birth.'

This was all too fast for William. This was both about things he was desperate to talk about and things he was desperate not to talk about. It was also quite outrageous for his wife to speak with him like this. But his real annoyance was with Emil. He would play it calm however.

'Ros, darling, Emil is just jealous. *Academically* jealous that is,' William hastily corrected himself, and realised that it probably made things worse as he saw Ros's eyebrows go up. He was going to finish however. 'Listen. I did meet Adriana in Geneva, and Emil is quite right in one respect that he should have supervised her. But Adriana was clear that his approach to Turing – you know the mathematician – the one she is doing her research on – was all wrong. It's purely an academic choice. But his nose was put out of joint and so he made up that silly story of her going to Stirling with me.'

Ros was taken aback. 'She wasn't in Stirling with you?'

'No darling. I have the delegate list if you want to look through it. You can see all the PhDs attending, they are always in a list of their own. It's just an unwarranted extrapolation by Emil, who is bloody annoying when he starts meddling in people's affairs. Bull in a china shop.'

'Mmm,' said Ros, now more uncertain. She paused. 'It's still odd that you didn't mention her to me. You always said that the college would be so much better without students. You hate having students.'

'Oh, that's just me sounding off darling. The realities of academic life are that you have to have students. I only did it because May is on our backs.'

'I thought you were his new darling.'

'That doesn't mean we escape his quotas.'

'Mmm.'

Ros took a deep breath, as if to raise another point. William cut across her. 'I could ask you the same kind of questions, you know,' he began. She looked at him with a growing frown. 'You spend your time in the company of who knows what men,' he continued. 'What if I started making similar accusations? Where would our marriage go then?'

'Like who?' she demanded, apparently thunderstruck.

'Like Jonathan Gries. Like Emil himself.'

Ros could not contain herself.

'You are absolutely out of your mind!' she practically yelled at him.

He was taken aback. 'It's no more ridiculous than what you are accusing me of.'

'Oh yes it is. This Adriana Appletree, or whatever her name is, is stunning. I saw you next to her, chatting away. So did Emil. But me have an affair with Emil? Are you crazy? He has thirty years on me! And Jonathan!' Her eyes were wide open with disbelief. William was getting nervous again: he had the disadvantage of knowing his own lies but not being at all sure of hers. Ros was shaking her head and looking around the room. 'I can't believe what you have just come out with!' she shouted at him. 'You think I could have an affair with a man like Emil? Or a man like Jonathan? What do you take me for!'

William summoned his own anger and hurt pride.

'Now, you listen to me. You, my beloved wife, have refused me sex for what, eight, nine months! We are modern people, we are supposed to talk about such things, but you just fobbed me off. Okay, I understand that you had mastitis for a while, but you've long given up breastfeeding. Okay, you had to get on top of your business again, so young Jonathan ponces in and out of our house like he owns it! And you think I am an idiot for thinking you are having an affair! I tell you, you are having a something! I don't know what! And I'm shut out from you!'

They glared at each other.

William continued: 'Nothing has happened between me and this woman, Emil is just being spiteful, letting his imagination run riot, I guess he can't imagine not sleeping with her if she was his student. But goddamn it a man has needs! Do you want to drive me into the arms of someone like that?'

Ros stared at him. Suddenly she was livid with rage. 'How dare you! How absolutely dare you! That's pure blackmail! You are demanding your conjugal rights – so-called – or you are going to have sex with some student? Are they all like that then? Simply allocated to this or that supervisor for their gratification?'

He yelled at her: 'Adriana means nothing to me! But I'm an ordinary man with ordinary needs and our much-vaunted modern honest marriage gives me no space to explain my needs to you. Don't you understand? How could you imagine that I was okay with all of this? This … sexual desert!'

She stared at him. 'That,' she said coldly, 'is blackmail. You are demanding sex from me or you will turn to some willing – allegedly, and I can't understand how a student would want to compromise their education in this way with a dull married man like you ...' she groped for her meaning and then found it with grim satisfaction: '... slut!'

He did not have time to untangle all the exact implications of her last confused outburst because she suddenly got up, ran to their bedroom and slammed the door. Just as suddenly she opened the door, shouted 'Separate bedrooms!' at him, and slammed it again.

He propelled himself from the sofa and ran to the closed door.

'What?' he shouted at it. 'Separate bedrooms because of a suspicion? An *absolutely unfounded* suspicion?'

Ros opened the door without warning.

'Because you just tried to blackmail me for sex!' she shouted and slammed the door so hard that Tommy woke up and started wailing from his nearby bedroom. William could just hear Ros say loudly from within the room: 'Patricia warned me about you, but I didn't listen! I was a fool!' Maria ran past William, glaring at him, and entered Tommy's room to comfort the boy.

William stared at the closed door for a while and then walked back and slumped on the sofa. 'Dull?' He was a dull married man? Was his wife bored with him? It hurt him terribly, yet he had to admit after a little reflection that he had got off lightly. His actual act of infidelity lay undiscovered, though he felt the sour taste of compromise linger in him over all the lies he had shouted at her. Then he gritted his teeth in sudden anger. How could Emil interfere like this, on a hunch? He was certain that Emil could not have seen him and Adriana together, not in any compromising situation. Okay, he and Adriana had danced a little intimately on Lake Geneva, but Piatigorsky had often been seen doing the same. With all comers actually.

He has been utterly stupid on Windermere, of course. It was playing with fire. He should just take all this as a terrible warning of what he faced if he continued with Adriana and was found out. Ros was just angry, that's why she called him dull. It was the feminist thing. Sex was not a right. He was the husband, the male, but he should wait for the invitation, otherwise it would be marital rape. He had heard all this in the discussions between Ros, Yukiko, Patricia and other feminist friends where he had been presented as the modern male, the equality husband, and to which he had freely assented. Oh, how he wanted to wind the clock back and restore things to how they had been: any number of feminist dinner guests was worth peace in the marital bed. Well, he would end it with Adriana, ride out Ros's anger and hope to return to her bed before long. *Our* bed, for Christ's sake. Perhaps it was all just postnatal depression.

He was puzzled by it though. He hadn't really slept with Adriana out of mere sexual deprivation. He was unshakeably confident that he wasn't that kind of man. This was something different. Or do all married men say that to themselves when they have an affair? And another useless lie stuck in his mind: that Adriana meant nothing to him. Adriana meant everything to him, though here was the real problem: he could not even begin to define this exact 'everything'. At the same time he loved his wife and son. After a while he realised that Maria had come in and was standing nearby, expressionless. As he looked up she said:

'William, is there something I can do?'

He groaned. Then softly: 'Maria, please, would you mind making up the spare room for me?'

Ø11Ø1Ø A new equilibrium was established at 54 Britannia Road. It gave William plenty of time on his own at bedtime to revisit his actions, which he did so over and over again as he found it increasingly hard to get to sleep at nights. Although Ros knew nothing of his affair, their row had made visible what had been formerly swept under the carpet: her sexual rejection of him. There was no explanation forthcoming, and his few attempts to engage her on the subject were fruitless, as was any enquiry about how long this forced separation would go on for, or under what terms it would end. He was a stranger to his wife, gallingly under the gaze of a stranger. Was this going to lead to divorce? How could it? He adored his son. He did, actually, deeply love his wife. He even liked the damned nanny, if only she did not have this absolutely unwarranted access to their private affairs. He lay there, staring at the ceiling of the spare room, formerly used when his mother or brother came to visit, but if they visited now he would have to sleep on the couch in the open-plan living room. He sighed; of course they needed something bigger than a four bedroom house. And how could he explain any of this to a visitor when he had no explanation to offer himself? And did not his rather meek acceptance of this awful situation point to his own guilty conscience?

He arrived home one evening to find Patricia Elleworthy visiting with her female partner and baby son: his statistical pessimism regarding both Ros and Patricia producing girls had been doubly born out. The additional women made William feel even less welcome as he was already in an irritable mood, and so he got into something of a row with Patricia, as it was after all her name that Ros had invoked in anger when she banned William from their shared bed. To start with he made the right kind of noises about Patricia's boy, named Douglass after the famous abolitionist who attended the 1848 women's rights convention in America, or so he was informed. Being the same age as Tommy little Douglass would undoubtedly make a good friend as they grew up – William was happy to approve of that. But he suddenly remembered something from their student days:

'I seem to recall that you used to call babies mere shit and vomit machines?' he pointed out to Patricia.

'Typical male!' was her frosty response. 'The "mere" is your interpolation. Babies do all that but are also fully cognisant citizens of our shared world.'

'But isn't that the point?' asked William. 'That you don't really want to share the world with us males?'

'*Sharing*,' she said witheringly, 'implies an equitable arrangement. It's hardly that at the moment is it?'

The eyes of four women – Patricia, her partner, Maria and Ros – were all on him. William looked from one to the other and then looked down. He mumbled something about how there was much progress still to be made, sure.

It was no better in the office. His own research was going badly and it was little compensation that his consultancy for Eliza II had progressed well enough so far – it was nothing demanding. The original Eliza programme was well-known as a crude English-language simulator of a therapist: one could type in such statements as 'I am depressed' and it would respond with stock answers designed to elicit further input from the client. The whole world of artificial intelligence had made huge steps since then and when linked with advanced voice recognition these new generation expert systems were now potentially capable of taking over much call centre work, a lucrative prospect for firms like SharpSoft. William had been chosen over Emil as the consultant on the project because his purely mechanical approach seemed to offer quicker progress, and fitted better with the commercial interests of his clients.

William's home situation clouded everything however. He needed advice. With great reluctance he rang Harry 'Harryjee' Chatterjee and asked to meet him over lunch at Canary Wharf. Harry, somewhat intrigued, suggested the Starbucks in the lower mall. Finding a corner in the noisy café with a free table, they sat and stirred their coffees while making small talk.

'Will,' said Harry before long, 'what's up? You are not yourself, I can tell. And the fact that you haven't told me yet tells me it is not good news.'

'Ah … no,' mumbled William. He was regretting this but then just blurted out: 'I have to admit I have been … acting a little strange recently. So Ros won't sleep with me. Separate bedrooms old chap. Just don't understand it.'

Harry sat bolt upright, blinking. He looked uncomfortable.

'Oh.'

There was a long silence.

'Will, I thought it might be a problem with some algorithms,' Harry said nervously, and took a huge bite out of an American-style pastrami, deli cheese and gherkin sandwich. He made a point of eating beef whenever he could.

'Ah, no,' said William despondently.

'Or your head of department? You always said how difficult the fellow was.'

'No.'

'Oh.'

Harry stuffed more of the sandwich in his mouth and chewed it. He obviously could not speak at this point, and then downed a great deal of his latte, his eyes slightly bulging and staring just past William.

'No,' sighed William. 'It's me. I'm not my usual self. And it's a marital problem.'

'Marital problem,' echoed Harry once it was polite enough to speak, and then promptly bit into the second round of his sandwich.

William just nodded. After an age of chewing and staring past William, Harry came to the point.

'No good with marital problems old chap. Veronica tells me how our marriage should go, and that is that at home. I tell the trading floor how it should go, and that is that at work. Division of labour old boy.'

William grinned wanly. 'Sure, sure. Best way all round, eh?'

'Yes,' mumbled Harry, his mouth full again.

After a while Harry said: 'Talking of Veronica …' *We weren't,* thought William. 'Talking of Veronica, you know what a film buff she is?' *Film buff,* thought William. *That's all I need. He is going to talk about John Nash.*

'Film buff,' nodded William.

'You remember A Beautiful Mind?'

'Harry, you know I never saw it. Not enough spaceships. Just you told me all about it.'

Here we go. I supposed I asked for it. The smallest mention of marital problems and I'm a lunatic.

'Well,' enthused Harry, 'Veronica found this other film called Pi about a mathematician who is looking for a 262-digit repeating pattern in pi, when a group of crazy Jews kidnap him because they are also looking for a 262-digit number which happens to be the name of God.'

'Crazy,' murmured William, relieved at least that this was not after all going to be a John Nash comparison.

'Yes, but the funny thing is ...' Harry was getting excited. 'The funny thing is, the mathematician and the Jew meet in a coffee bar in New York; it could be us in this coffee bar in London.'

'Mmm?'

'And I am the Jew and you are the mathematician.'

'I thought you were a Hindu.'

'William! That is all junk, I always told you. But this is the point: like the Jew, I want to ask you again, will you become a quant and work for me?'

'To find the name of God?'

'No. To do what the guy in the film did: work on stock picks. I have always told you that you would be a fantastic quant. You could earn ten, twenty times as much here as in that old Imperial place of yours. You are top-notch, you know. I am always afraid the competition will pinch you.'

'Actually I am working for SharpSoft.'

'Them?' Harry was clearly taken aback. He blinked. 'William, that is utterly beneath you.'

William just smiled wanly. He had declined Harry's offer many times before.

So, Harryjee was no help. William had been round his male colleagues and excluded them all on various grounds; had thought of his brother Paul and recoiled instantly. It did not even cross his mind to think of his father. And women? He was not going to make his mother miserable over this stupid thing, anyhow she and Ros and always been tuned in to each other, sometimes uncannily so. He thought about Patricia. It was a heck of a long shot, but might it work? If he ate humble pie could she possibly shed any light on how to approach Ros? William shook his head: Patricia would never keep a secret from one in the sisterhood. He should have approached Veronica, not Harry, but it was too late for that now. Anyhow, as the conversation with Harry had reminded him, Veronica would most likely think of a film that had some protagonist in similar circumstances, but inevitably not similar enough to be of any use. And then she would start on A Beautiful Mind no doubt, were he to suggest that he was in a confused state, which he was. That exhausted the possibilities for now. He frowned. He did not seem, in fact, to have a particularly large circle of friends – too busy with work, he supposed.

Also, William could not make up his mind as to how to deal with Emil. On the one hand the man deserved a thrashing, not that William had ever done such a thing in his life or even conceivably condoned it. He should march into that stupid office and belt the old man one. On the other hand even to raise the matter would be to admit that something was going on.

Meanwhile the household at Britannia Road had settled uneasily into its new routine. William tended to slink in and out of the house without much cheery hello and goodbye; Ros turned to her business with a fury and Maria landed up preparing separate meals for William and Ros to suit their different schedules. Only young Tommy, now some ten months old, brought the adults together. The sheer terror that William felt over being cut off from his son made him take even greater interest than before, and Ros, while still cool towards him, made no attempt to come between them. These seemed the moments in which reconciliation must eventually come: Ros and William on the sofa together with Tommy cradled in William's arms messily taking some organic banana and oatmeal puree from the proffered spoon. If anything it seemed that Maria was put out.

But William's resolve to end things with Adriana was a reed bent by the smallest breeze. All he managed was to put off a few tutorials on account of Eliza II meetings, but the kisses and touching returned with full passion at the first opportunity. He felt utterly defeated by his circumstances. He was low in spirits, plagued by strange dreams, and effectively bound in a deep but different pitch to not one but two women who would not – for entirely different reasons – have sex with him.

Another change in his life was brewing via Adriana: she had been instrumental in a bid by Birkbeck College for research funding into an interdisciplinary project on Alan Turing, and had, it seemed, been engineering a role for William in it. If he took it up it would mean a two-year secondment starting the following year. He could keep his office at Imperial, but also have a space at Birkbeck where he would have to live amongst the social scientists. Adriana had talked about it for some time, but now the official invitation came from Birkbeck via Professor May. William demurred. Interdisciplinarity was Piatigorsky's thing. He had his own research – close to a breakthrough he assured his head of department – plus the Eliza II project with an impending postdoctoral student to take care of.

'Ah yes, that reminds me,' said May. 'I did promise you that you would have a better office, didn't I?'

'Yes, Richard. I thought you had forgotten about it.' In truth it was William who had forgotten about it: he had enough worries on his mind.

'Ahem. Not at all. You shouldn't have that rather small space on the second floor if you are to share it with a postdoctoral student, should you?'

'But this Birkbeck deal means half the week away.'

'Oh nonsense. You will of course be given the proper facilities at the other place, but it's hardly a demanding role for a man like you, is it? You will need all the best resources here. You just told me that a breakthrough is imminent along the lines of your Geneva talk. That's fabulous.'

'Oh, yes,' mumbled William. May failed to notice that William was not quite his exuberant self.

'There. I have identified just the space for you and Simon on the fourth floor. It has rather a nice view incidentally.'

'Simon?'

'Yes. Simon Spindler, your new postdoc. You met him in July if you remember.'

'Oh yes.'

William's mind raced. Yes, of course a better office would be good. It was about time. But sharing it with a postdoc? He had buried that detail up to now, the annoying interviews with young PhDs, all of them instantly forgotten. His reed of resolve stood proud for a moment. A shared office would mean no possibility of a kiss with Adriana. That would be good: it was time to end this sorry affair. But then a gale of disappointment flattened the delicate shoot. He would have to figure out this Simon's routine. The young man probably ambled into college about eleven, which meant that he would have to make early appointments with Adriana. He smiled amiably at Professor May. 'I'll give serious thought to the Birkbeck proposal,' he said, as he suddenly realised that there would be no reason why he should accept a shared office there. And no Emil to spy on him. Suddenly a moment of paranoia gripped him. Did May know of his affair? Was he using the postdoc as leverage to get him to agree to the Birkbeck project? He shook his head. He wasn't sure who to trust these days. Not after Emil's shocking betrayal.

At home his resolve stiffened again. Ros was beginning to soften towards him, though a shared bed, let alone the exercise of conjugal rights, was as distant as ever. He adored his son who would toddle to the newly-fitted and awkward-to-open child-gate at the top of the open-plan stairs with cries of 'Da da da,' when he got home.

'Tommee ...' he would now shout from the front door, rather than 'I'm home darling ...'

He had always loved Ros from the first time she appeared in the family Park Town kitchen and ribbed him mercilessly. And he was truly fond of Maria, an absolute gem in the house and with Tommy. How could he further risk throwing all this away? The no-sex thing was like a nagging toothache undermining his normal masculine buoyancy, but Adriana was hardly his stop-gap in that department.

He had see-sawed violently over the Birkbeck proposal. This Simon would make his new office – however gratifying its better view might be – a problem zone when it came to the kisses he craved. But, by the same token, it would make it easier to put his relationship with Adriana back on a professional footing. He would refuse the Birkbeck collaboration, use Simon as his bulwark against backsliding and make it clear to Adriana where he stood.

They arranged to meet in Carluccio's again. He was determined. The Turing project, with its planned culmination in an exhibition at the Science Museum, was not for him – he had enough distractions from his major interests with the Eliza II consultancy. He hated museums. And May could stuff the new office if he wanted to retaliate. If May was going to just forget a promise like that and raise it only to push him into another new project, then he was not going to play ball. But William had forgotten how depressed he was becoming, and how Adriana not so much lifted him out of it but stirred up his being and brought meaning to it.

Wasn't Tommy enough meaning for him? He had asked this question a thousand times, but could only conclude that both he and Ros had fallen into a strange postnatal depression. Other couples had separate bedrooms he learned, though he tried to gloss over the fact that this was mostly amongst either the elderly or the neurotically famous. And the very meaning of depression, he had come to realise, was the absence of meaning. In that strange nexus which contained Adriana, Lake Windermere, a dream about a flying boat, and a more surreal question posed by another dream – had he once been Alan Turing? – there was not yet meaning as such but the tantalising promise of meaning. As he sat there with Adriana he realised that his loyalty to

Britannia Road was a loyalty to a happiness eaten away by demands placed on him by yet deeper forces. Like countless other recent fathers the strength of his family feeling had been quite unexpected, yet here was something that trumped even that. It was bitter fate to have discovered something so precious at the very time that its existence was threatened by an equally unexpected turn of events: a promise, dare he admit it to himself, of something even more precious. But, the hell, what?

Adriana was making her case with simplicity and enthusiasm. Hadn't Bill, since his first casual dismissal of Turing, found more and more in Turing's life and work that was interesting? That was a difficult question to bat away. William was certainly no more converted to the case for history than before: his father's long inoculation against it was too powerful, he would say. But that damn dream *means* something, even if Adriana is the last person in the world he can share it with. So all he could offer was a rather lame complaint about how difficult it would be as a scientist to mingle with all those humanities types, her excepted of course. Here he managed his old charm and grin. 'Look, I went to that Scottish architect's house, but couldn't retain a thing. I flunked it with both you and my wife. I'll never fit in. I can't do the culture thing.'

'Actually,' said Adriana earnestly, 'it's not a culture thing, it's a Two Cultures kind of thing ...'

'Two cultures?' asked William, alarmed. 'Do I have to move from no culture to two cultures?' He really was a picture of boyish charm and bemused despondency. He couldn't help himself: he came alive with Adriana, and she seemed to respond in turn.

She laughed. 'No, silly Billy. The "Two Cultures" debate was set off by C. P. Snow in the sixties. It's about the sciences versus the humanities, and Snow's thesis was that in a technological age it is a bad idea to have the country run mostly by humanities graduates who have no idea about science. Interdisciplinary projects like this are vital to bridge that gap, which is as pervasive now as it was then. Turing represents exactly the kind of maverick science thinker who shook up the Admiralty and placed intelligence on a scientific basis. It helped dissolve some of the ancient class-ridden structures of power.'

'Oh.'

'The point is that it is the humanities types who need to learn from you, not the other way round. Our class system is embedded in the assumptions inherited from the classics, cemented in place by the establishment including the Church of England, Parliament, and the military. And all of them draw on the old humanities traditions – avant garde authors and critical theory not withstanding.'

William just looked at her with open eyes, his head shaking. He made a comical grimace and downed a large gulp of cappuccino. Adriana smiled a big smile at him.

'Look, our committee discussed this at great length. Piatigorsky, even with all his interdisciplinary publications, just wasn't the right man. It had to be a prodigy, like Turing. That's you. You are his modern-day equivalent.'

That bastard Piatigorsky, came the unwelcome thought. And William was sunk. It was one on the nose for the old East European; he'd get a new office; and he would see more of Adriana away from the prying eyes of those who knew his wife. He gave in with good grace, indeed he felt an elation, not the least of which had been the 'prodigy' thing. And the modern-day equivalent of Turing? A whole committee had decided that? Perhaps the humanities lot were smarter than he had thought. But by the time he had walked the usual short stretch from the Tube to his home he felt desperately confused. He had knocked another foundation stone out from underneath the fortress of his marriage and home, despite all his good intentions and forebodings about divorce. And Adriana's comment about modern-day equivalents had set off the odd phrase ringing in his head:

Are you now, or have you ever been, Alan Turing?

Funny. Thoughts like that just pop into one's head, right? But thoughts like that shouldn't sound like someone else is speaking them, should they? There was a subtle distinction here that made him uneasy.

That night was the worst yet for insomnia. He lay stiffly on the spare bed in the guest bedroom not more than a dozen feet away from his wife, separated from her by an ocean of wrong turnings – not least the irreversible step he had made that day – each of which he churned over in his sleeplessness.

Ø11Ø11   William was depressed. No other term really covered his state of mind – however hard he wriggled around with various euphemisms – but if you have not experienced depression before its tentacles are unfamiliar in their reach and stickiness. You try and stay the man you were, at least to others, but William slowly came to the conclusion that unless he found help he might never do any more decent research. He couldn't bear it: the shape of the coming mathematical breakthrough was half-visible to him, but without any change it would slip away into a haze of darkness. He had been slowly liberating himself from the tutelage of Aleksander and Piatigorsky, and this was the secret of his confidence about his future direction. The success of his lectures at Geneva and Stirling had given him increasing confidence to abandon the idea of consciousness in artificial intelligence. He had scanned the relevant consciousness literature and had been struck by how much of it seemed like mysticism; instead he had returned to the simpler idea of intelligence as a name given to weighted decision-making based on adequate data. It sounded dull, but his commercial partners seemed to get very excited about very dull things, all, he supposed, down to the fact that a great deal of money could be made out of them. He wasn't interested in that, or their project however, despite the usefulness of a bit more cash towards the new house, it was just that they helped him sever the last links to Piatigorsky's approach. It was, he mused, a bit like Einstein's breakthrough: in physics, if something felt like gravity, then it *was* gravity. In artificial intelligence, if something looked intelligent then it *was* intelligent. At a stroke he could cut out all of the mushy theorising about consciousness. So, on the one hand his new direction looked extremely promising, but on the other hand he was increasingly depressed and couldn't find the energy for his old pattern of work.

But who could he approach? He didn't want to go to the family practice where Ros and Tommy and now Maria were registered; and he couldn't unburden himself about his dreams to Harryjee and Veronica, good friends that they were. Harryjee had already demonstrated a strict no-go policy on marital troubles, while Veronica, though possibly interested enough, was too full of what William thought of as psychobabble. He was not that desperate yet. That left only old Dr Edmondson, who had treated William for his asthma during his doctoral years at Oxford.

There was nothing for it. He looked up the surgery number and found that Edmondson still practiced. Another call a few days later got through to him and an appointment was agreed despite the transfer of medical records to London. Edmondson told him that he was always welcome; it is not every day one treats a prodigy. He wanted to know how his career was going.

William arranged to stay a night at his parents as he liked to do from time to time. Ros was fine. Tommy was wonderful. Maria was such a great addition to the household. But he knew that he didn't really fool his mother, who gave him thoughtful looks over supper. In the morning he made some excuse about visiting the Mathematical Institute and went instead to Edmondson's surgery, wondering how he could avoid telling the doctor about the estrangement from his wife, and his affair with Adriana. He decided in the end to focus only on his strange dreams.

'Hello Michael, how are you?' was William's characteristic friendly greeting to the doctor as the door closed on the small consulting room – it always took William a little while to get round to his own problems, which in the past focussed on his asthma. In turn Edmondson pressed William on his career.

'Youngest professor ever appointed at Imperial? Keynote lectures abroad? That's great, William!' In the end there was a pause in which William finally mentioned his problem.

'Depression, eh?' Dr Edmondson was surprised: it wasn't the William he had known. William reluctantly also mentioned that he was rather keen for this not to get to his family. 'Of course,' said Edmondson. William then began to describe his two recurring dreams, the optimistic interpretation put on them by Ros, and the bare description of an increasing depression, difficulty in concentrating by day, and sleeping by night.

'It could well be a delayed reaction to what happened on the day of 9/11,' said Edmondson thoughtfully, picking up on Ros's interpretation. 'Post traumatic stress disorder takes many forms. Dreams of falling are of course very common, and the fact that you witnessed the Twin Towers event, even at a distance, perhaps made you identify with the man filmed jumping from above the burning part of the building. I must admit it's an image etched in my mind too. We all wonder: what would I be thinking and feeling to make me jump out of a window near the top of a skyscraper? To certain death? For some reason in your dreams it became transposed into a seaplane crashing into the sea. Or a lake, you say.'

'But I had the seaplane dream before 9/11. It was after the funeral of Princess Diana.'

'Again it is about a death or deaths played out for a whole week on TV. You mustn't underestimate how much we live vicariously through the media.'

It was the first time William had spoken fully with anyone about this. He persisted: 'Mmm. But the odd thing about it is that the men with me in the plane all speak with that clipped BBC English I rather associate with the Second World War. How could that relate to the 9/11 events in 2001 in America?'

'Oh, that is also quite common. You probably saw an old war film when you were young and it stayed in your subconscious. For myself the atmosphere and the accents of that period are linked in my mind with the film Brief Encounter, though of course that was just post-war. Do you know it?' William shook his head. 'As I said,' Edmondson continued, 'things get transposed once, or overlaid on something and then they seem to stick.'

'Mmm.' William was sceptical.

'The odd thing is the other dream, about the man Turing, a mathematician you say. But then the brain throws up all sorts of strange things. Perhaps Ros is right, that you have a subconscious fear of failing in your own discipline. Or how about this: perhaps you fear that mathematicians, as outsiders to normal society, are going to be persecuted like communists? Or who knows what. I think that's why they invented CBT so as to avoid these speculations. William, I have to confess I wouldn't normally go into such a long conversation over dreams. It's not my province as a GP, and I shouldn't really be playing the amateur psychologist. I only really have two possible things to suggest: I could refer you to an NHS psychiatrist who would probably put you on CBT ...'

'Sorry, Michael, to be a dunderhead, but what is CBT?'

'Oh sorry, William. It stands for cognitive behavioural therapy. The idea is to change negative thought patterns. But I've found that, to be honest, you can't go wrong with antidepressants – they are so good these days, and after even a few weeks you will feel better. I can't vouch for CBT but I know that nearly all my patients who have tried antidepressants tell me how much they have helped.'

So William agreed to a nine month course of Prozac, with warnings to limit coffee and alcohol use and give the drug three months beyond the end of his symptoms or they would likely recur. Dr Edmondson also warned him that his sleep might become even more disturbed for a while, but that he should stick with the medication. He should feel his mood lifting after about two weeks.

eight

Ø11ØØ   William's first week on Prozac was a roller-coaster. As
————————   warned, it made his dreams worse to start with, but after
a call to Edmondson he agreed to stick at it. Nights become yet more
tormented, sleep ever harder to secure, but slowly the days began to
improve, with the result that he found himself engaged in banter with
Maria at breakfast and even raised a smile or two from Ros. He
reminded her of his attempt to retain any facts about Mackintosh, or
recount in any detail the artefacts or style of them in Hill House. Maria
laughed too, having offered that the style had evolved quite
independently of the Vienna Secession, eliciting a knowing nod from
Ros. Perhaps, he thought, they were both laughing at him rather than
with him, but he did not care: laughter for any reason was better than
sullen silence. Even Tommy joined in. Before long his mood had lifted,
and he felt the appetite for mathematical work return: this was exactly
what he was hoping for from the drug. There was however a wrinkle to
it – he would sit with renewed energy and determination either at his
notepad where he sketched out mathematical formulae, or in front of
his computer where he could simulate various processes, but the
sharpness of old had gone. He would stare for a long time at a formula
or algorithm with simply no coherent response. Then, something would
move forward for a while, and then it would halt again. It was a fuddled
euphoria that gripped him and it took a while to develop new
intellectual strategies to get round it, but he began to make slow
progress even with this, finding ways round the moments of blankness.
Several small mathematical insights emerged, and he clung to this over
everything else. It might be slow but the breakthrough was beginning to
take shape: sheer determination would win through, helped out by the
Prozac, he was sure of it. It helped him push away the greater misery
and anxiety over his marriage.

Within three or four weeks William's mood was greatly improved, so much so in fact that a tutorial with Andrea went rather well, where they had been languishing previously. Some spark was rekindled: a buoyant echo of Windermere, so at the end of the tutorial he found her smiling at him, unwilling to leave his room. He hadn't moved office yet or taken on his postdoc, so they still had privacy; reaching for his hand, she pulled him close in front of the filing cabinet. He was utterly elated. They kissed passionately and held each other tight; once again he felt an inexplicable attraction so powerful as to overwhelm him. All his fears over losing Ros and Tommy just disappeared in the pounding of his heart.

Odd that he had no erection he later thought, but this detail was of no use in staving off the disaster to come. Emil suddenly walked into the office, banging the door open, and caught them in their passionate embrace. He stormed out shouting at them that Ros would hear of this. Adriana stared at the departing Emil.

'Does he mean it?' she asked anxiously. 'Why on earth would your colleague tell your wife about this, even if he disapproves? Bill, I am so sorry. I couldn't imagine … I couldn't control myself.'

She shook her head. William was flushed and angry. Why on earth did Emil poke his nose into his affairs? *Bastard!* William was stressed and reached for his inhaler, conscious that he didn't want Adriana to see, but he had no choice: he could barely breathe. Would Emil really go back to his office, lift the phone and speak to Ros? Why? Was he trying to break them up so he could move in? It didn't ring true. Adriana was chewing her lip.

'Bill, Bill, will he really ring your wife?'

This shocked him out of inaction, and he leapt to his feet and ran down the corridor in the direction that Emil would have gone. Even that short stretch to the lift had him clutching his side in pain. He punched the lift button repeatedly, and waited in anguish for it to come. Adriana had followed him, but they said nothing to each other. When the lift finally came and he made it to Piatigorsky's office he burst in to see a grim-faced Emil staring at him: it was the face of authority, of implacable certainty, of a job well done. William stared at him wordless. He blinked finally and dropped his head. He should punch that smug bastard's face in, he thought, but simply retreated, furious, back down the lift to an anxious Adriana waiting in the corridor.

'We'll see,' he said grimly. 'I'll know what he has done when I get home. But I think it's bad.' They walked in silence down Museum Street to part company at the Tube station.

'Billy,' Adriana said before he turned off to the Westbound platform, 'I hope things will be okay.' She shook her head with concern for him. He looked at her, and dropped his eyes.

'We'll see,' he mumbled, and turned numbly into his corridor.

It had been an awful journey home, beginning with the walk down Museum Street. What irony made it the very walk that leads to Carluccio's? Where all his resolve had disappeared along with half-eaten paninis and cooling cappuccinos? Why was the foot-tunnel from the ill-fated Science Museum so utterly jammed with kids in pushchairs, all of them a reminder of Tommy? Why was Kensington Tube Station such an impossible melee of jostling commuters and day-trippers? A seat on the Tube was impossible, and yet his laboured breathing urged him all the time to sit down, to lie down, to rest. The walk from Fulham Tube Station was a horrible reminder of the time he had arrived home, fresh from his unequivocal unfaithfulness at Windermere. The front door looked a hundred times more ominous than it had then.

On arriving in the living room it was clear that he was finished. Without any preamble this time, Ros yelled at him that he was having an affair with that slut, his student, whatever her name was! Emil had caught them red-handed! Tommy burst into loud wailing and was swept up by Maria who glared at William before marching off with his son to the playroom.

'Pack your bags *now*!' was Ros's imperious demand, and no Prozac in the world could give him a cheery response to turn round the unfolding disaster. It was the moment he had been dreading since July in Windermere; now was the following January. He could not think of a single thing to say, but all that filled his mind as he did indeed put some arbitrary possessions into his suitcase was the loss of Tommy. He had some miserable recollection of friends who had told him about access arranged through lawyers, and this is what he clung to in the daze of leaving the house under the furious eyes of both women and the sobbing of his son. The wheels of his damned ill-fated suitcase made an even more irritating clatter on the paving stones, and each struggle with it up and down kerbs on the way to the Tube station he had just come from made him yet more wretched. He stopped after a couple of blocks and realised that he had in fact no idea where he was going. It was a freezing January day, and his mind was as numb as his right hand on the suitcase grip.

'I don't know what I am doing,' he mumbled to himself. *What would anyone do in a situation like this?* Spotting a café he tumbled into it; he ordered a plain cheese sandwich on white bread and stared at his mobile phone. He called Imperial first, saying that he was taking a few days leave. May's secretary, Jane Wozniak, had anyway wanted to speak with him about a suitable time for moving his office, and so all was arranged to their satisfaction, not that William cared a jot about the new arrangements or the fact that every last thing on his desk would be put back in exactly the right place.

'And your view from there is really something,' trilled Jane, annoyingly. William then called his mother. He couldn't bring himself to tell her what had happened yet, but simply asked if it was okay to stay for a day or two. He nibbled at the sandwich, drank a few sips of coffee, and stared into the dark streets.

'The *view*,' he said aloud, shaking his head, and then checked himself: no good being bitter in front of complete bystanders. *Who cares about the view from fourth floor?* It was Emil who had to answer for this. *No,* he corrected himself mournfully. 'It's my fault,' he said aloud, this time startling a diner on the next table. He shook his head and grinned by way of apology, abandoned his meagre sustenance and left the café. He set off for Paddington.

As the train drew into Oxford station that evening a morose William pulled his suitcase down from the luggage rack, waited for the doors to open, and stepped onto the platform. Memories of the early days in Oxford with Ros came back to him and he grimaced. Looking from the station steps at the Said Business School – made bright by spotlights in the freezing evening mist – he decided to walk instead of taking a taxi or bus to Parktown: it would put off the moment of telling all to his mother. He began to regret the decision as he headed in the direction of the Mathematical Institute on St Giles; the damn little wheels at the bottom of the case didn't seem to like real flagstones and had begun to squeak just past the Eagle and Child. Ros had taught him how the 'Inklings' – including J. R. R. Tolkein and C. S. Lewis – had habituated it to read 'books' and drink 'Beer', the different capitalisation of which was emphasised in a little plaque at the end of that corridor that passed as a drinking house. *Should have impressed Adriana with those facts. Never normally remember stuff like that though.* He trudged on, panting, past Keble Road, home to his Masters' and doctoral days – and the days of punting with Ros – and angrily tugged at the suitcase to pass Norham Gardens and then Norham Road, his breath visible in the freezing air and his gloveless hands very cold. Finally he turned into Parktown, remembering wanly his childhood obsession to pass alternately left and right of the two centre gardens which had so amused his family. If you turned left to negotiate the first garden then you had to turn right at the second to arrive at the crescent in the middle of which stood the family home, a rule he followed even now, sorrowful of lost happiness. He was conscious that he had no idea what he would say to his mother.

Belinda Strange greeted him at the door, took one look at him, and let her warm beaming expression settle into something more neutral. William was on the top step of the stone flight leading to the front door and had to look up at her as he stood there, holding the suitcase from its handle. 'Ros has thrown me out, Mother.' He paused for a moment looking into Belinda's sobering eyes. He looked away and then back into full eye contact. 'I had an affair.'

There, he had said it. With a wary nod she welcomed him in. He pulled at the suitcase handle to yank it up the last little stage of its journey, and it chose that moment for one of the extended sections to break. It swung in perilous arc, upon which the other side of the handle broke off and the entire thing clattered back down the steps, overturned on the pavement and landed upside down in the gutter, looking for all the world like an upended turtle. William's head and shoulders drooped, and he trudged down the stairs, bent over the case and picked it up. He returned holding it in both arms as if it were a wayward infant.

Belinda said nothing as he took his coat and scarf off, parked the suitcase with an angry gesture, and walked into the large open-plan kitchen. He flopped into an old leather chair, glad that Pop was not around.

'I've been an idiot,' he offered, as Belinda settled opposite him.

'Hmm,' she responded and sighed, looking at him keenly, a picture of misery. Belinda shook her head, got up to put the kettle on, and came back to stand over her son. 'So what do you want to happen next?' she asked gently but with a sombre expression.

'Oh, that's easy,' he replied, looking up at her, 'I want to get my family back.'

Belinda nodded. 'And the other woman?' she asked after a pause. William shook his head. 'I'm assuming it is a woman,' Belinda added dryly.

He frowned. 'Of course. Student.' Words formed in his head, but he could not construct anything that would convey his feelings about Adriana, or formulate a convincing statement that it was all over. It was not, that much he knew from his failed attempts at ending it to date. He frowned again. 'It's a funny thing, Mother. Both Ros and I seemed to have fallen into something of a depression after Tommy was born. Yet he's gorgeous. We both love him more than anything on earth. Ros has been so odd, however, I can't fathom her. And I can't understand my own moods either. I got in such a bad way that I went to Edmondson.'

Belinda looked up, a boiling kettle in her hand.

'Last trip down Mother. I didn't want to tell you. He put me on Prozac.' His mother's eyebrows shot up. She pursed her lips and concentrated on pouring the hot water into the teapot. She was thinking things through.

'So it's not Birgisdóttir.'

He grimaced and shook his head. He started to say something but changed his mind; he had no idea how to explain anything about Adriana. Belinda set a mug of tea in front of him, and sipped hers from a much smaller vessel.

'I just need to know one thing for certain,' she said after a while. 'You want to be back with Ros and Tommy?'

'Oh, more than anything in the world!'

She nodded, and then looked into the distance, drumming her fingers on the little lacquered table that lay between them. Finally she asked him: 'Is it over with the other woman?' He hung his head, biting his lip. Belinda drew her breath in sharply, but said nothing. She stared at him.

'I desperately want it to be over,' he said hesitatingly, 'but this much I have learned: that I don't seem to be completely master of my own actions any more.'

'Hmm,' she said, frowning. Then: 'At least that's honest.'

Pop received the news with a grunt after his return home, but had nothing to say on the subject. 'Staying here for a bit?' he asked William.

After a couple of days aimlessly wandering around Oxford, William realised that he had to make arrangements for himself in London. He rang Harry Chatterjee and blurted out his circumstances. 'Marital thing. All went belly up.' The upshot was a return to London and a spare bed made up for him in Queensway – Harry might have nothing to offer in terms of advice but could be relied on with practical things; anyway his house had seven bedrooms. He promised that Veronica would talk with him, and he knew a tip-top estate agent who would find William a flat to rent not too far from Imperial or Britannia Road; in the meantime he was welcome to stay. As to Veronica, William avoided her questions as best he could: it was too late for her help, and anyway he realised, like Patricia, she was too close a friend with Ros.

William returned to work, doing all he could to avoid Emil. He had the certainty that should he encounter the blasted professor he would punch his lights out. He spent the evenings with Harry and Veronica: it was pleasant enough and he thanked the Prozac for dulling the shock of it all. He had little appetite for his mathematics again, and so fell in with the Chatterjee household, the antics of their little girl Sonia simultaneously raising his spirits while making him miss Tommy all the more. After her bedtime he succumbed to the Chatterjee preference for Bollywood movies and simply stared at the gyrating cast working through their incomprehensible plotlines. Veronica's guidance made little difference to his understanding.

'See?' she said at one point, 'this is a scene-by-scene remake of Peter Weir's film Witness, you know, with Harrison Ford.'

'Ah, Harrison Ford,' William responded slowly, having seen him in Star Wars.

A little later Harry turned to Veronica. 'You see now? The average Indian middle class family ridicules the old superstitions. In the American version the child's community was Amish, in the Bollywood version it is Buddhist. It is absolutely right to satirise their ridiculous Tulku system, don't you think William?'

'Ah, Tulku system, Harry,' was William's more cautious response this time. He was thinking of Tommy.

'Oh, Harryjee, you are so like all the Indian pandits with their absolutes,' complained Veronica good-naturedly.

'It's not even a *consistent* system within its own tenets,' argued Harry. 'In Buddhism you revere the guru because he is enlightened. That means you don't come back to this existence anymore. But the tulku is a guru who has come back, been drawn back to the womb. So why do your revere him?'

'Harryjee, you know so much, perhaps you want to be a guru?' laughed Veronica. 'Shree shree Harryjee!'

Harry was actually a little annoyed now and suggested they concentrate on the film.

William was miles away.

Ros would not answer the phone. The first time he rang it was picked up by Maria. 'Er, she is not available right now.'

'Maria, I need to speak with Ros.'

'She's not in.'

'Yes she is, or you would have said that first. Please hand the phone to her.'

'She doesn't want to speak with you.'

'She can tell me that herself. Please, Maria, hand the phone to Ros.'

'No William, I can't.'

'Look, I'm paying your wages, and it is quite reasonable to ask you to do a simple thing for me.'

There were muffled sounds and suddenly Ros was on the line. 'How dare you! You never put any time into hiring Maria, or signing the contract, and for your information, her wages come from my account. I don't want to speak with you, and don't you dare be rude to Maria!'

With that the line was cut. William tried a few more times with similar results and was forced to use texting and email to communicate with his wife. Nothing constructive came out of it however in terms of reconciliation, mediation, or the chance to sit down and talk things over. Only the issue of Tommy was dealt with as William gradually ramped up the threat of lawyers to secure access. Everything in his marriage was now a morass of uncertainty, but at least the law was clear, and Ros had no choice but to negotiate arrangements. She dragged them out however in a way that made William despair, so it turned into weeks before he saw Tommy again.

In the meantime William made arrangements with an estate agent to view a flat in the Old Brompton Road, and moved into it shortly after, not noticing at the time of signing the contract its non-modernist credentials: dado rails, coving, mouldings galore and balustrades both leading to its entrance and gracing its little ups and downs. He was desperate for somewhere to stay, having felt a burden on his friends in Queensway, but once he took the keys to his new flat, walked up from the dull roar of traffic noise shut out by the communal front door, entered his new domain, shut the door behind him and sat on the floor, he noticed everything. It annoyed him for a moment as he looked around. There was hardly a single corner or meeting of planes in the apartment that was not obscured by hideous plaster foliage or moulded skirting boards or coving. However he soon forgot about it as the least of his current burdens.

His mother had been supportive, his father distantly perplexed, his older brother scathing, and the Chatterjees a welcome distraction. Therapy, for Veronica, was watching films, so William was not pressed by her on the circumstances of his separation. Prozac dulled it all. But alone in his bare flat the loss of his family came home to him, a horrible reality – and Piatigorsky was the agent of this loss.

He spent the first morning in Old Brompton Road purchasing the most basic pieces of furniture at random from a local second-hand store; it was the nearest in the phone book. From the Marks & Spencer's down the road he had struggled home with pillows, sheets and a duvet, and lay rather haphazardly ensconced in them on the floor that first night, central heating on full blast, staring up at a huge ornate moulding in the centre of his bedroom ceiling from the rose of which hung a naked energy-saving bulb. He could not get comfortable: in one position his hips ached and in another his back. But he barely noticed.

'This is terrible,' he said out loud. 'I wonder how it will end.' His voice echoed in the mostly empty room. Alone in his flat, hearing only the subdued roar of traffic outside, he had the first pang of loneliness in his life. No Tommy. No 'da da da.' No Ros to lie next to him as they had done so happily and easily before the pregnancy. Not even a stranger in the dwelling like Maria, whose presence he now craved for quite oddly. Anybody. But most of all Tommy. What on earth were the simple moves he had taken one by one towards Adriana that would take his son from him like this in steps of equal and totally unforgiving measure? And within the loneliness another emotion formed: anger. Anger at Emil. *That bloody bastard! That bloody bastard!* Yet all these emotions were like muffled voices from within a tank, sealed off from him by Prozac.

In the morning he looked in the bathroom mirror, quite unaware that he had not shaved since Ros had thrown him out.

'I'll call Adriana,' he told the towel-rail, and went out to find a local café for breakfast.

'Oh,' she had responded to his news as he rang her from his mobile phone over bacon and eggs. There was a pause.

'I've got a flat in Old Brompton Road,' William prompted her.

'Oh.'

'Would you like to come over? Help me choose some curtains or things?' He didn't know why he had added that. There was another pause. He began to regret the idea of curtains.

'I know,' she said suddenly, 'I've just remembered. There's a chess café near your flat called The Troubadour. Let's meet there.'

William agreed as enthusiastically as he could to meet in a few days time – he could play chess well enough, given that he never practiced, but was hoping for something rather different from Adriana. On the appointed day he had a call in the morning saying that his furniture would be delivered later on, a 'later on' that turned out perilously close to his appointment at the café, and hence he met all enquiries from the cheery removal men as to the location of things – which included a chaise longue he had bought on a whim – with little more than a wave of his hand and 'that'll do just there.'

'Are you sure? We're paid to put things where you want them.'

'I'm sure. That's just fine where it is.'

'You're the governor,' said the workman shaking his head.

Shooing the men out of his flat and down the stairs he locked the front door and then walked briskly towards the Troubadour. A little out of breath, he managed to arrive at the same time as Adriana, so they ordered tea and paninis and sat down by the window. The place was done out in some vaguely Continental style he supposed, with antique coffee-pots and what appeared to be farm implements that stuccoed the walls and ceiling. Adriana enthused about it for a while and then paused, biting her lip.

'I'm really sorry about what has happened, Bill.' She paused again, and he looked down at his tea. 'When you stood at the stern of that little boat with the outboard motor steering us up the lake I knew I was lost. I knew you had a wife and a small baby, and I realised that there were terrible risks for you. Actually for me too ...' She paused. 'I really, really hoped that this wouldn't happen. But I felt that the happiness we had on Windermere was not an ordinary thing. And that it would have a price. I am sorry that you were the one who paid it, Bill.'

There was a long silence as William gathered his thoughts. 'The worst,' he said slowly, 'is not seeing Tommy every day.' He looked down again. He knew he couldn't explain it to her, and it wouldn't change anything if he could. Adriana took his hand.

'I haven't seen that much of you recently, Bill,' she said. 'But I realise now how much I have missed you. I always do when I see you.' They looked at each other, seated in the window seat, and slowly leant over to kiss. They just held hands for a while and drank their tea.

'I got very low,' William said, looking down the café past the long counter at the narrow end room. 'I suppose I knew this would come. Anyhow, I got so low that I went to my old GP and he put me on Prozac. Back in December.'

'Really, Bill? I must admit that you seemed suddenly more your old self, now, wait a minute, yes, around that time. It's when we kissed. Oh. I suppose that is when your boss caught us. How awful that he simply turned round and told your wife. What on earth made him do that?'

That bloody bastard! William scowled. 'I don't know,' he said with some feeling. Adriana was staring absently at the traffic.

'Perhaps it was his life in East Germany under the Stasi,' she suggested after a while. 'Everyone informed on everyone apparently.'

William shook his head: he didn't want to hear excuses for Piatigorsky. After another long pause, in which William became aware that Adriana was preparing to say something difficult, she started: 'I never told you this but I was near-suicidal in my late teens. My doctor put me on something called Elavil which pulled me round. I'm not against it at all. In fact many of my creative friends are on all kinds of things.' She smiled wanly.

William looked at her. 'Can I ask, Adriana, what got you so down?'

She looked sombre and then spoke quietly: 'I told you on Windermere that I am afraid of water. It goes back to 1999 when my then boyfriend drowned in the Marchioness accident; you know, it sank on the Thames. I went to pieces. I started identifying with Sylvia Plath and imagining that I would just walk out into the river with my pockets laden with stones. It was a horrible time. Anti-depressants helped.'

There was silence for a while as William squeezed her hand. 'That's only, what, seven years ago,' he whispered.

'Yes,' she replied. 'And I think it is why water means so much to me. And perhaps it is why I cling to Francis so much.' William didn't like to hear this last confession from her. Adriana seemed to shake herself out of her memories however: 'Bill. All this stuff comes along, and we just have to deal with it. It's no good thinking too hard about our own lives you know: they will just unfold one way or another. History, now that's another thing. You get to put yourself in the life of someone else, you know, like Alan Turing, and follow the whole thing through. Ours are actually happening now. But in historical lives you can see the long run of responses to events, good and bad. That's when you begin to see some meaning in it all.'

William just grunted: he had no idea what to make of that. There was a silence between them for a while.

'Bill,' Adriana said suddenly, turning to him. 'Let's play chess.'

'Okay,' he smiled at her, glad for some diversion. She got up and requested a set from the man serving behind the counter, who reminded her that all games had to finish by six o'clock when they started to serve dinner.

'Sure,' she laughed and came back gaily with the board, pieces and a chess clock. William was in no doubt about something however: he was befuddled. He was elated to have her sit opposite him in a café, with the potential of her returning to his flat, but definitely befuddled. She looked at him in a rather odd way as they set out the pieces, but slowly the fun of the game overtook them as he absolutely thrashed her. It put her in the best of moods for some reason, their respective past or present disasters notwithstanding. Before long, as the café was licensed, they moved onto a bottle of red wine – neither of them remembering that he should drink very little while on Prozac. Adriana absolutely insisted on a return game, to which he agreed, and he mated her in even shorter time, despite starting with black, being anyway befuddled and now becoming obviously tipsy. He found that he was saying things that appeared to come from some distance away but he was just happy to be with her. By six o'clock she had lost five games in a row, and he was feeling very strange indeed. He could hear himself ask her whether she would come back to his flat, and her response that she would definitely come another day, and after that he remembered nothing.

His next impression was lying on his new bed fully clothed, his winter coat on, the central heating at full blast again, staring up at the naked bulb and the horrible Victorian moulding at the centre of the ceiling. His bed had been awkwardly placed in the room by the removal people, but he did not notice. The ceiling, the light bulb, and the plaster ornamentation all started to go round and round. Images of water, waves, and moonlight filled his consciousness, and for what seemed ages he listened to indistinct cries and the despairing last calls of people drowning. There was more: a drone of machinery, perhaps engines, and also fire, smoke, and explosions. What films are these from? He had just enough rational consciousness left to recall Edmondson's remark, but could not locate any of the impressions in films he knew – which were not many. They were not from Star Wars, he was sure of that. From there the dreams mutated into some of the Bollywood sequences he had seen at the Chatterjee's: lewd dancing girls gyrated in counter-rotation to the ceiling, and he passed out.

He woke in the morning with a terrible headache and the absolutely clear thought that he would never drink on Prozac again. How could he have forgotten the stern warning from Edmondson? He was lying in bed and a sound seemed to echo round his room, now in daylight but with the bulb above him still lit. He gradually realised that the sound was his own voice.

He had said out loud: 'How could I have forgotten the stern warning from Edmondson?' The realisation of it alarmed him.

You have got to snap out of this.

When he got to the bathroom it finally came home to him that he still had not shaved, and so he made a firm resolution to buy shaving things, items he had forgotten in his hasty packing back at Britannia Road. He would have to make a long list of such items for shipping over; Ros couldn't deny him that. 'I still haven't shaved,' he heard. He spun round to see who could have said that, and realised that it was his own voice. He looked in the mirror and said very deliberately and out loud: 'Christ. I had better get a grip.'

You had better get a grip.

Loneliness is one thing, but a new world to explore and the congeniality of a busy London street are quite other things however and are bound to blunt its edge, though no doubt Prozac did the heavy lifting. Nervously William set up some mathematical papers to look at, opened his laptop, busied himself with securing internet access, and tentatively set to work. Maths went surprisingly well that day, and he only emerged into the cold air at dusk to hunt for a takeaway dinner, having suddenly realised that the increasingly uncomfortable sensation in his stomach was hunger.

On the way back to his flat a black woman coming in the opposite direction slowed down with him at the front door. Seeing him take his key out she said: 'Oh hello. Are you the new tenant in the top flat?'

'Ah, yes,' he said, taken aback. He peered at her under the street light and queried: 'Are you Comfort from Human Resources?' He was sure she looked familiar.

'No,' she said. 'My name is Janet Obudjowe. I work at the local Job Centre.'

'Janet Obud … Obud …' he couldn't quite get it.

'Obudjowe,' she repeated patiently.

'Ah, yes,' he said, anxious to get into the warm. 'Janet. My name is William. Pleased to meet you.' He didn't think he wanted to say more.

'Okay,' came the even tones of Janet, and they went in and up to their respective floors.

The bad effect of the alcohol wore off; he finally remembered to buy a razor at a late-night store; and a few days later Adriana turned up with a present for his flat: a little rug. He was in fine spirits as he welcomed her with suitable expressions of embarrassment about the state of his new home.

'Oh, it's lovely,' she exclaimed, wandering round and expressing appreciation for exactly all the things he couldn't stand. 'I love the bathroom!' she said in high good humour. 'It has one of those proper cast-iron Victorian baths with legs … I've always wanted a bath in one of those!'

'After the tutorial, or before?' he enquired flippantly. He hated the bath.

'Silly!' she replied. 'Do you see any books in my hands? Ring binders? I want to celebrate in quite a different way.' He gulped, and then grinned at her quizzically, hoping against hope. She approached him and put her arms around his waist, pulling him towards her. They kissed and then – for the first time since Windermere – they made love. Hotels she had refused, and he had given up making the suggestion, but now, as an unexpected compensation for his terrible circumstances, she lay next to him in his bed, her gaiety, her beauty, her near-perfect body a cause for elation. Sure, he was brought down to earth as she later firmly told him that she had to go, and he had to face again the fact that she was returning to the bed of another man. Also a little sobering was how difficult it had been to be much of a lover to her. He had made apologies, saying that he was in a state of shock he supposed, to which she had been most understanding.

He had no idea how hard the separation from Tommy would hit him in the following weeks. Some nights, quite often in the early hours of the morning, he would fling himself onto his bed and stare at the ceiling with the distinct impression that he could hear Tommy's 'da da da,' and this would renew his determination to negotiate with Roz over access.

Prozac had restored him outwardly at least: his capacity for work returned, and slowly he became again the unassailably cheerful grafter at computational mathematics that he had been, or at least some semblance of that person. Having stared into the abyss of mathematical barrenness – amongst other abysses – his conversion to Prozac was complete. If only he had started on it earlier! Swept up in this mood he had made love with Adriana again the following week, who for some reason took the opportunity that the new flat offered, where before she absolutely refused to consider any kind of trysting place. It was a huge relief to him to come so close to her, even if the sex itself was a bit of a let-down, and anyhow on that score he had an inspiration: he purchased Viagra online, and that restored him so much that he was quickly up against the old cardiovascular limits imposed by his asthma. Slowly a thought grew in him: despite his love for Ros being virtually intact, and despite his desperation over Tommy, he would propose to Adriana. Ridiculous, he would say to himself at first. He and Ros had thirteen happy years of marriage behind them, now consummated in the arrival of their son. It was vandalism to think of abandoning all that. But, he gloomily commented to himself – out loud as it happened – I am the vandal. And so in the circuit of his thoughts, and despite these considerations, he began to imagine a life with Adriana.

His new routine was to mostly work in his flat, using a laptop to connect to his department, and spend hardly any time at Imperial. He didn't want to encounter Emil, and anyway he had always been light on attending interminable research committee meetings. He really didn't know what to think of the respected professor, though. From the day of the bizarre interview conducted through the open window, Emil had been fatherly towards him, and where he might have seen him as a rival instead saw a future heir to his work. In those early days, despite his precocious brilliance, William was not sure enough of himself to break free from Piatigorsky's vision – the first departure had only really happened at Geneva. So what was the source of the older man's viciousness? William grimaced to himself. Piatigorsky had been so exotic, a pupil of a legendary Russian mathematician and an émigré twice over, first to East Germany with the young German woman he had met in a youth conference in Stalingrad, and then in a double defection when in London.

William had always trusted Emil: perhaps the professor *had* acted correctly in ratting on him. Emil didn't know of course that William had slept with Adriana, and in suggesting that they had gone to Stirling together he was stabbing in the dark. But the spirit of it was correct. Perhaps, when you betray your wife in this way, you deserve to be ratted on, it didn't matter who did it. But these rationalisations were quickly eclipsed by raw anger with Emil. Were not these things an utterly private matter? Who knows, things with Adriana would have run their course, and his marriage could have survived. After all, whatever was going on with Ros was not normal either. Was she having an affair with Emil after all? His anger rose again.

Some days William felt that he had lost Ros and Tommy for good, whatever access might be arranged and which he hoped was now imminent. In such moods he wondered again if he and Adriana could be together. He couldn't make out what her boyfriend meant to her, but he knew they had not considered marriage, which could either be because they were determinedly against the institution, or because their relationship did not mean enough to her. It was a miserable prospect, that of divorce from Ros, and he was nowhere near ready to seriously contemplate it, but still, if it had to be, what were the prospects with Adriana? He thought of the figure he had cut on the lake. He was not a conceited man, but had the impression that Adriana could land up choosing him over this rather faceless 'boyfriend'. Faceless to him at least.

William could not completely avoid going into work, and one of these trips was made to inspect his new room ahead of the postdoc and set up his working environment, not that it was much needed now. The view was rather good – as a single glance out of the window confirmed – but he couldn't care less. And one of these rare visits made him even less inclined to face the rooms and corridors where Emil might lurk, when he had found himself on the first floor walkway overlooking the atrium in which the reception area was located and spotted Emil and Professor May in the company of a young woman. It was Ros! Hiding behind a column he peered down to confirm his sighting, and, sure enough, Ros was at the reception desk under the great garishly coloured graphic of a brain scan that welcomed all visitors. She was signing in as guest while Emil and Richard waited for her.

They're stitching you up.

They're all in it together.

Okay. Ros had been called in by May on the subject of hosting business conferences. Or something like that. But what had this to do with Emil? *Bastard!* While his thoughts floundered like this he realised to his horror that the three had turned to walk up the first flight of stairs together, right towards him. Ros spotted William first and stiffened. May went ahead and made a hasty overture to him.

'William, old chap. This is awkward of course, Ros has told me about your separation, but I do hope you understand that the professional life of the Department has to go on. I haven't seen much of you recently. Ha ha! But I have every confidence that the regrettable problems of your personal life are not getting in the way of your research. Ros also has her professional life and is very helpful to us in the planning stages of our new project.'

William just nodded, conscious that Emil and Ros had now taken the lift. He barely registered that May was talking about his postdoc and the new office; made his excuses, and went home, the purpose of his trip quite forgotten. All he could think of was Emil and Ros together in the lift making small talk, who knows what, when he could not even complete a phone call with her. His overriding emotion now was not so much anger however as dull confusion.

He made his mind up. He would sound Adriana out. He didn't think that the flat was the right kind of place, so he suggested dinner at a smart Italian restaurant he had spotted nearby – he would put up with foreign food for the sake of making an impression – and even decided to risk a single glass of red wine, hang the consequences. His thinking was fuzzy, he knew that. It was not as if he was actually going to propose, not formally at least, but what was eating at him was the new asymmetry of their relationship. When Adriana had been intimate with him in the past and then returned to her boyfriend's bed that was awful, but at least he returned to Ros's bed. There was no way to rationalise his discomfort then. But now? He needed some hope for the future, something, anything. He frowned at his thought processes as Adriana perused the menu, a glass of red wine at her lips. Was he making sense to himself? Would he make any sense to her? She looked up at him, conscious that he was staring at her. He could see no point in further postponing what he had to say.

'Ah, Adriana,' he began. 'I know that you have a partner that you are living with, Francis, isn't it? Er, I also know that you are not married to him. So,' he paused a little, not finding in Adriana's expression much to encourage him. 'Ah, when the time comes for you to, er, consider marriage, might you consider, er, me?'

That was it. His own words rang in his ears. As proposals go it was no knee-bending ring-box-opening classic. For a moment he felt an utter idiot as the words continued to hang in the air, but Adriana suddenly smiled in the warmest possible way and clasped his hand across the table.

'Billy, dear, that is absolutely lovely. Of course I will consider it when the time comes.' She looked down and he was amazed to see that it was to hide a blush. His heart leapt. She looked up blinking back a tear, and smiled lop-sidedly at him. 'You probably think I'm a raving feminist,' she murmured, 'but I'm not really. Actually quite conventional, I suppose.' She paused and then looked back at him pressing her lips together as if to better control them. 'That's quite the sweetest thing I've ever heard.'

She looked off into the distance. Turning back to him she held him with her grey eyes, calm and sure again, her colour subsiding: 'But I can't leave Francis now,' she said softly, her grace hiding what he was later to discover as immovable inertia. She tried to explain. With a rather downcast expression she told him that after the drowning of her boyfriend Martin in the Marchioness disaster, Francis, who had been her boyfriend's best friend, had picked up the pieces and before long they had become lovers.

'It's a strange thing,' Adriana said. 'To some extent we are together because we both have to honour the life of Martin.' This gave William hope, on the one hand, because perhaps Adriana did not really love Francis in the way that he hoped she did, or would, love him, but on the other hand the sheer weirdness of this all prompted doubt. His confusions were thus multiplied. In the following period – it was to be years – he brought up the subject from every conceivable angle and in all the ways that his imagination, such as it was, could conjure. But her beautiful smile, the grace of her limbs, and the look in her eyes all added up to nothing at all that he could pin any hope to.

Ø11Ø1   After threats to go to lawyers on both sides Ros and William finally agreed access arrangements for Tommy.

Neither side raised any possibility of the toddler staying with William in his flat, and Ros was adamant that William wasn't stepping foot in the house at Britannia Road, or indeed going anywhere near it. Hence William reluctantly agreed that access would be with Maria at the local park – Eel Brook Common – on Tuesday afternoons, while Ros was at her office. It had been over a month since William had seen his boy, now thirteen months old, and it was a rapturous moment in the local park when he approached the infant in his tripper, chaperoned by a frosty Maria. He didn't care, the 'da da da' reaching fever pitch as he approached was all that mattered, and, after struggling with what seemed like complete overkill by way of seat belts and safety straps, he extricated Tommy and held him in his arms. William had brought some rosemary focaccia to feed the ducks with – it was all he could grab in the rush, having dived into a local artisanal bread shop that rather bewildered him. To his great delight young Tommy tried to cram a big chunk of it into his mouth rather than throw it into the water, though it was promptly spat out amidst much indignation from Maria. Apparently babies do not like rosemary. Neither did William in fact. Tommy took the next bit of bread and toddled to the shallow water's edge to throw it whole at a duck, which had to duck to avoid it. William was going to make a clever remark about 'ducking' when panic arose in him about the water and ran to pull Tommy back from the edge. Maria glared at him and ensconced the child in its straps again; later he had to concede to himself that since Windermere some odd phobia about water had gripped him, just as it clearly affected Adriana – yet another sign perhaps of her gravitational pull on him.

It was bitterly cold and so they went into the little park café after a while. To start with he felt that – despite Maria's understandable frostiness – this was in fact an opportunity to talk with her.

'Maria, I am very sorry that you landed up in the middle of all this,' he began. 'It is of course all my fault ...'

'Stop right there,' Maria interrupted, looking at him with a ferocity he had not anticipated. 'I know exactly what you are doing. You want to reach Ros through me. Well, if she does not want to talk with you then don't try it through me. I will not stand for it, and if you try it again I will simply walk off with Tommy.'

William blinked. Tommy looked at him frowning, perhaps about to cry. 'Da da da,' he pointed out, almost a query.

'Dad not going anywhere,' William crooned at him. 'There, there.'

He felt Maria's eyes boring into him. He didn't dare try this again – Maria had a weapon against him and had made it clear she would use it, right from the outset; he couldn't imagine lawyers giving him any edge on her. It was all a shock to him. Had he not always been a good friend to her?

But despite the tyranny of Maria this routine became his greatest pleasure in the week, and it saddened him a little that he felt inhibited from enthusing over it with Adriana. Neither did she prove to be of any help with advising over toys.

Shortly after the first time with Tommy, William's postdoctoral student arrived at the new office they were to share. May had made it abundantly clear that William had to be there to welcome him, so William reluctantly made plans to work in his office once a week until he could figure some way out of this new obligation. Dr Simon Spindler turned out to be thin, tall, bespectacled and very shy.

'Professor Strange?' he introduced himself by leaning around the door.

'Welcome, welcome,' said William, startled from a long absent-minded stare at his computer screen. The young man seemed reluctant to enter without settling something first.

'Professor Strange, these Chinese symbols on the door, what are they, may I ask?'

'Please call me William, er, er, Simon,' William responded. He looked back at his screen in the hope of recapturing his train of thought, then to the young man again. 'Oh. Ah. The symbols?' The young man had spotted a set of Chinese letters laser-cut from a sheet of brass and carefully stuck to a red lacquered background, all at the instigation of Emil some years back. Jane Wozniak, bless her, had loyally ensured that they were unscrewed from his old door on the second floor and fitted to his new one on the fourth. 'Apparently they are Chinese for "The Chinese Room"' said William. 'Professor Piatigorsky had them made up as a joke.'

'Chinese Room as in John Searle?' asked Simon nervously.

'That's it,' said William cheerfully. 'Why don't you come in and park your things at your desk?' He waved to a workstation at the dingy end of the room.

Simon hadn't budged. 'Why did Professor Piatigorsky do that?' he asked, seemingly alarmed.

'I suppose,' said William slowly, half wondering if things with Simon were always going to take this rather ponderous route, 'I suppose he took some careless remark of mine about Searle's argument to mean I didn't agree with it. That I thought perhaps that we are indeed no more than symbol processing machines, just like computers.'

'And do you?' stammered Simon, still at the door. William was not sure how to answer, other than feeling that he ought to tread carefully here; his desire to have Simon enter the room had reached a considerable pitch. In the end William came up with a careful elaboration: 'Ah, well it's all down to functional equivalence priorities in implementation strategies, don't you think?' Simon blinked. All William wanted to do was to get back to his work. He was on the verge of something, and whatever it was had been ebbing away every second of this encounter.

'I suppose ...' Simon conceded eventually and this apparently unlocked his motor coordination sufficiently for him to enter the office, though rather gingerly, as William couldn't help noticing. He turned back to his screen and desperately tried to recover his train of thought.

'Frames as a higher-level Turing machine ...' he thought to himself as an anchor on his ratiocinations but was unpleasantly surprised to hear Simon say 'Pardon?' William cursed himself: he must have spoken out loud without realising it. 'Nothing,' he called gaily across the room.

'Frames?' asked Simon, standing at his desk, apparently frozen in the act of placing some ornament on it. William was beginning to believe that the young man had difficulty in thinking and acting at the same time.

'Is that a trophy of some sort?' William asked.

'Oh,' said Simon, placing it on his desk carefully. 'Yes. Robot Wars first prize in 2002. Did you see the finals that year?'

'Ah, no,' said William turning back to his screen. 'Ah, not that year, I don't think.' In a burst of intense concentration he managed to recapture his previous train of thought, and was about to commit a sequence of mathematical symbols to his keyboard when he became aware of a spoken sentence. He was gripped by fear. Had he spoken out loud again, unawares? This was alarming. He retrieved the sentence somehow in his memory: 'I named my winning entry Magnus.' Why would he have said that? William became even more perplexed, his mathematical insight wriggling off the horizon again like a slippery fish, making him want to groan aloud. Hopefully he had not, in fact, groaned aloud. But he suddenly hit on a strategy, the one used by the Eliza programme when it couldn't follow the user input. He repeated what seemed like a keyword in the sentence that hung in the air:

'Magnus?'

'Yes,' came the prompt but rather strangulated reply from Simon, indicating that his nervousness had reached a higher level. 'In honour of Professor Aleksander.'

'Oh, of course,' beamed William suddenly, relieved of any further need to process this conversation, and relieved also that the sentence hanging in the air must have been Simon's: Magnus was Aleksander's pet name for his AI machine. 'Very good. *Very* good,' said William, with the air of a professor who had just concluded a lengthy and successful tutorial with a student of promise. He turned back to his screen. After a few moments he sighed loudly and shook his head. The slippery fish had vanished.

That did it. He gave Simon the briefest of introductions to the Eliza II project, agreed a lengthy task with him involving keyword weightings, and just about managed to collect together the necessary details of data location and passwords. 'Remember,' said William as he put on his coat, 'If you don't catch me in the office Simon, simply email further queries to me. I should be able to turn them around fast enough for you to make excellent progress. I can see that you are going to be a great help.'

Why on earth should he go in to college, he thought on the way out, when he could work so much better in his flat, avoid both Emil and Simon, and live with the possibility of a visit from Adriana?

William's living room gradually filled with computers, large pinboards and whiteboards that he rolled around on the polished Victorian pine floor, and tables covered in papers. He had almost obliterated its period character. At one level he was liberated to reach for the stars as his mathematical theory of frames continued to develop, at another his passion for Adriana was rekindled by their renewed love-making, matched only by a shared obsession with the life of Alan Turing. Adriana was busy writing up her thesis, for which she turned to her supervisor at Birkbeck for support, William's input being barely needed any more on this. At the same time she was putting the finishing touches to the collaborative programme on Turing that would start the following year. Here she had drawn extensively on William, and in turn he had become progressively more interested in the life of the great man, despite his particular distaste for the 1930s and 1940s, though the real source of his interest – his dreams – he kept hidden from her.

Adriana took him round the Science Museum one day after William had made the rare – possibly only – attempt to give Simon a tutorial at Imperial. Adriana arrived at his office to collect him and had been introduced to Simon, whom William found himself rather empathising with as he stared mostly at the floor while Adriana gaily introduced him to the basic idea of the future interdisciplinary collaboration with Birkbeck. It appeared that Simon had even less taste for history, the social sciences, and the 'Bloomsbury Set' – whatever that was – than he, William; in fact it made William feel something of a veteran of the humanities. In turn he mentioned rather proudly that one of the trophies on Simon's desk was for winning Robot Wars in 2002, and the other was for being an outstanding 'Numanoid', as followers of an eighties pioneer of electronic pop were called, apparently. This time it was Adriana who was out of her depth. At the Science Museum William felt again his instinctive repulsion for all that old stuff. Bakelite for example! And how could one take a steam engine seriously? Puff, puff, puff!

But out of all this the figure of Turing loomed ever more significant for him. He dared not tell Adriana of his dreams, still experienced but with their impact held at bay by Prozac. He could not tell her of the airport question or the crash of the flying boat or the horrid feeling that the crash actually belonged to Turing's period, or even belonged to Turing's history. Adriana gave him a copy of the classic biography of Turing by the Oxford don Andrew Hodges, a mathematician whose classes William had attended for a while. He began to see what Adriana meant when she called Turing a maverick: here was a man who followed no rules, hated team sports, and most importantly was a prodigy. William had always hidden his unique gift behind a cheery bluster and attempts to fit in and be as much as possible like everyone else, but in truth it was a lonely road. Now he had found a fellow-traveller. He had never been able to do that from a book before – enter into the inner life of another person – and he had Adriana to thank for it. True, it was hard going, a big thick book like that, and the verbiage made him long all the time for the brevity and purity of mathematical symbols, but he had to concede to himself that this form of research, so alien to him, might be exactly what he needed to get to the bottom of his dreams. He might like the Prozac numbness but he was no fool: something had to budge so he could get off the damn drug.

Despite the good constellation of her willingness for intimacy at the flat and the welcome ministrations of Prozac and Viagra, he didn't actually see much of Adriana during this period, and took refuge instead in his work. And despite little setbacks, like on the day of Simon's arrival, he was beginning to tunnel through a mountain of mathematical material, mining some increasingly profitable seams. His mood was generally up, thanks to Prozac, and he mostly avoided the mistake of further alcohol, but still, he didn't quite look like the William of old. He did tend to let a number of days go by before shaving, and took less care over his dress. Because his bed had been hurriedly left by the workmen so as to prevent access to the wardrobe – and it never occurred to him to change the positions of either – he laid out his clothes on the lengthy polished floorboards of the empty second bedroom, otherwise quite unused. He did not see this as odd. His main living space was by now utterly crammed with material relating to his research and Adriana responded to all this in an unpredictable way: looking round the flat on one of her rare visits, she commented that it was just like in A Beautiful Mind, the film with Russell Crowe as the mad mathematician John Nash. *Is everybody going to talk to me about that damn film?* William was annoyed because, although he had not seen it, he knew that Nash heard voices and hallucinated imaginary people. Of course Adriana was unaware of the film as a shared joke with Harryjee while at Oxford, William gaining by proxy the indignation over this caricature of the very discipline of mathematics. He felt angry all over again at the comparison, though God knows Nash's work was pertinent to his own. But his annoyance at Adriana was quickly dispelled when he discovered that she found the chaos of his flat and his life rather sexy. She was enchanted, it seemed, with the idea of genius, no doubt a relic of her Bloomsbury inheritance, so any manifestation of the stereotypical personality disorders that she believed accompanied genius seemed to turn her on. Rather than flinch at what she saw in his flat, she would take his hand and place it high on her thigh in the middle of a conversation about Turing, wait for his verbal flow to subside, and then fall onto the sofa with him, allowing his hands to pleasure her. But sex itself moved off the agenda again. His passion for her became more Platonic perhaps, but that did not lessen the obsession. She was always just out of reach: was it merely that which made him desperate to see her, to have her, to marry her?

Ø1111Ø   If Viagra kept the male member artificially inflated then Prozac kept its ego artificially buoyant. All this stuff was easy to order online, along with William's asthma medication. But behind that artificial buoyancy was a growing confusion, and the bad days multiplied in which he felt utterly miserable and confused. Were they voices in his head? What were those images of the hotel and the Sunderland factory, culled from his two trips to Windermere? He finally bought the DVD of *A Beautiful Mind*, watched it at two and half times speed on his computer – he simply had no patience to give up an hour and a half to mere entertainment now his mathematics was on a roll again – and shuddered at the parallels with his situation. It was true that he had no imaginary friends in the classical sense, but the adumbrations of other personalities into his psyche were just as disturbing, if not more, because he could not resolve them. They were there, but would not come into focus, particularly Alan Turing. He reread the Turing biographies obsessively though of course laboriously. In terms of computing they held no interest at all. Stone Age! His first instinct was absolutely right. But the shape of Turing's life and sad death increasingly gripped him. How on earth could they have forced him to take female hormones? Barbaric!

His sense of night and day was by now quite lost. It led to complaints from Janet Obudjowe in the flat below him, who patiently explained to him on the stairs that she had a nine-to-five job and could he avoid pacing up and down all night as it kept her awake. He would try hard for a while to walk as little and as softly as possible, but his efforts were clearly not good enough because a number of times she banged on her ceiling in protest – probably with a broom handle he guessed.

One day Dr Edmondson rang to say it had been a year since William had started on Prozac and would he like to come in for a check-up? The doctor had realised that the original prescription was for nine months, and so was wondering how William had been doing. He dutifully made a trip to Oxford and told Edmondson that he was obtaining Prozac online as he did his asthma medications and that he had no intention of going off the drug at the moment. It meant that he could continue working, which was everything to him since his marriage had broken down. Edmondson was thoughtful over this news, and then told William that he was concerned: it was clear that William was not looking after himself properly, even taking into account the lack of a wife to point out such things as stubble and unkempt hair. William's eyebrows shot up at this. But it prompted him to confess that his sleep was still disturbed by strange dreams – perhaps it's just the effect of living on one's own? – and he found that he was occasionally talking out loud to himself. What was that alternative thing that Edmondson had mentioned a year ago?

'Oh yes. CBT. Cognitive behavioural therapy. I could refer you, but you would have to come off the Prozac.' He paused. 'It's more usual to do either antidepressants *or* cognitive behavioural therapy,' said Dr Edmondson, having seen the distressed look in William's face. He agreed to refer him anyway, saying that William would have to justify the continued Prozac to the therapist. There was no harm in an initial appointment to explore the possibilities, was there.

William was dubious about this turn of events, but thought it worth a try. Edmondson rang back a week later, having had to ask a colleague in London to recommend a therapist, and William duly turned up for his first appointment. The CBT practitioner was business-like and explained the principles to him in rapid fire: the idea was that maladaptive thinking, or one's relationship to such thinking, was at the root of the problem. This didn't mean much to William, but he could show some enthusiasm for the idea that digging around in the past was no help; instead, the idea was to modify behaviour in the present. The sessions were pleasant enough, but the therapist did seem to flounder a little in teasing out just what was maladaptive in William's thinking. Or to be honest the therapist simply found it hard to understand William's thinking in the first place: for example William didn't seem to blame anyone, apart from himself, for his predicament, and even his negative thoughts towards Emil seemed perfectly justified. He was engagingly honest in saying that he couldn't see how he could have done things differently, and as to his work, his colleagues, and his dreams, they were a truly impenetrable network of references far removed from the norms that the therapist dealt with. It became clear to William that the CBT practitioner was, in the end, quite uninterested in the contents of his mind, the weird stuff that is. She just wanted to change his attitude. But a chance conversation with another patient in the waiting room led to something new. A young woman, very nervous, asked what he was there for, to which he said, for want of anything more coherent, that he was gripped by unpleasant dreams he could not get rid of.

'Is CBT helping?' the young woman asked.

'To be honest, no.'

'I've been trying hypnotherapy,' she offered cautiously, as if an apostate.

'What on earth is that?'

'Well, you are put under hypnosis, and then the therapist asks you some questions and you answer from the unconscious. Answers you can't find in the waking mind.'

'So it is like asking a question in your dreams?' asked William, curious. 'Like the therapist is sitting in the dream and can ask the characters there what the hell they are doing in your mind?'

She shrank a little at his choice of words.

'Sorry,' said William. 'I'm just trying to understand it. You see I am plagued by characters, quite coherent characters you understand, but I can't see why they are in my head. They even speak out loud sometimes.'

She looked at him. William blushed: he had barely yet admitted that even to himself.

'Yes,' she said. 'In my case it helped because it took the content seriously, which is just what CBT avoids. I do both now, but the hypnotherapy helps me deal with real events in my childhood which I had been suppressing.' Tears began to flow, upon which William made soothing comments. He wanted to sort out this mess, but did not want to land up blubbing.

The CBT practitioner meanwhile gave William an ultimatum: she had only taken him out of respect for Dr Edmondson's colleague, and while some patients are suited to a combination of CBT and SSRI treatment, she said – such as suicidal teenagers – he was clearly not going to respond at all. He would have to come off Prozac. William just shook his head. He was adamant: firstly, the idea is to take Prozac until well beyond the end of the symptoms, which had shown no signs of going away, and secondly he needed to work. He was convinced that giving up the drug would strand him in a total creative block, so after giving it some thought he turned back to Edmondson with a request that he would like to try hypnotherapy.

That New Year had not gone well. He had marked the first anniversary of his separation from Ros and the second birthday of Tommy with little hope on any emotional front. Adriana was preparing for her viva in February and he hardly saw her. He certainly didn't receive any further response to his renewed discussion with her over marriage, though much of the time he vacillated between that hope and the hope of returning to Ros and Tommy; also he was behind with his Eliza II commitments, which had made Professor May rather cool with him. Adriana did well in her viva and was told she would receive her doctorate without the need for revisions, a very good outcome. However as a result she dropped a bombshell on William over a celebratory game of chess at the Troubadour: he was so upset that he actually lost a game to her. She announced a six-month trip to India with her boyfriend, returning in late September to start on the new project.

'Won't it be marvellous, Billy?' she had said. 'We will be working together. And you will have a first-hand introduction to the humanities.'

'Oh. That's great.' He paused. 'Did you say *six* months?'

In May he finally obtained a referral for a hypnotherapist on the NHS, having discussed with Dr Edmondson the rather hopeless lack of interest shown by the CBT practitioner in either William's dreams or anything in the past that could have triggered them. The hypnotherapy was initially more promising, focussing on the possible 9/11 trauma and trying to discover childhood events that might contribute to his current psychological state, but after four sessions, in which William kept throwing up material about a flying boat and Alan Turing, the therapist came to a startling conclusion.

'I don't think I can take you much further with this,' he said brightly. 'I have come across situations like this before where the suppressed material simply does not seem to belong to this life. I am afraid that it can't be done on the NHS, but I would recommend you to see a past life therapist.'

'What?' William was at first unsure what the man was talking about.

'Past lives,' the therapist said a little nervously. 'You know. Reincarnation. If your dreams and recovered memories are of events before this birth, then perhaps they are the root of your problem?' He spread his hands. 'I know it's not very mainstream. But I've referred clients in the past and it has helped them.'

William just stared at him, dumbstruck.

'Yes, of course, I know it is counter to all conventional medicine, or even science. But hypnotherapists like myself continuously bump up against this phenomenon. Most won't admit it of course, but I am just being honest with you. This is what we experience in about a quarter of our patients.'

'Let me get this straight,' said William, beginning to get angry. 'You want to refer me to a therapist who believes in reincarnation? And they are going to find things out about my alleged previous life that will fix this one?'

'Ah, I can't formally refer you in fact. I can just recommend a shortlist of practitioners I believe to be sound ...'

'You are crazy, not me!' shouted William and stormed out. What on earth was his life coming to?

Ø11111

William made it through to the end of September in a very black mood, despite the Prozac. As the day came closer for Adriana to return and their joint project to begin at Birkbeck he felt both hope and dread: the thought of seeing more of her was what had got him through the summer, but the prospect of seeing her and not having her was daunting in equal measure.

A deeply tanned and absolutely beautiful Adriana returned with great energy and enthusiasm for their joint project. She twisted arms at Birkbeck to locate him a suitable office, and even brought some pot plants and a Gustav Klimt poster to liven it up. To help him deal with his perplexities over the social sciences a laughing Adriana bought him two novels to read: *Solar*, and *Thinks...*

'Both are Two Cultures novels,' she told him, and, given his slight warming to historical and fictional material that had arisen through reading about Turing, he gave them a go, though not it has to be said without gritting his teeth at the amount of time it was wasting when he could be at his mathematics. He even had an 'aha' moment with the word 'hegemony' in *Solar* – its protagonist, a scientist, also had to mingle with humanities types and was equally bewildered by the way this previously unknown term peppered all respectable discourse. So that's what it means! The other fictional work was a campus novel and turned out to be something of a primer in consciousness studies for the uninitiated, which William could follow more easily, though he was a little unsure whether Adriana was teasing him with it as he learned that the married male cognitive sciences professor was seducing the female creative writer-in-residence. It seemed that such an attraction of opposites had attracted literary treatment.

The autumn passed better than the summer. As anticipated, the proximity to an Adriana full of life and enthusiasm but even more physically and emotionally remote from him was a continuous irritation. But, however difficult, her presence was like sunshine for him.

Then Adriana had some gossip to impart. She had a young lecturer friend at the London School of Economics who mentioned an Icelandic student.

'Does the name Maria Birgis-something mean anything to you? Something like that anyway?'

William started. He stared at her, taken aback.

'Yes, I thought so. I just couldn't remember exactly what you had said about your au pair. My friend told me that apparently her studies had gone downhill after she started a lesbian affair with her employer, a lady who runs a marketing company. That's not your wife is it, by some remote chance?'

'What?' William yelled. He stared wildly at Adriana for a moment, who looked almost frightened.

'Sorry, sorry,' he mumbled. A torrent of thoughts went through his head.

After one of the pot plants that Adriana had given him had completely shrivelled up she had realised that William simply was not the kind of man to look after a plant. Good-humouredly taking this in her stride she turned up regularly with a Victorian brass watering can and so on this occasion she happened to be watering his plants as he absorbed the news, though goodness knows why she conveyed it so casually. It took him a few moments to grasp the implications of what she was talking about it. Then he got up abruptly, muttering 'Sorry ...' and brushed past her so thoughtlessly that she only just avoided watering his office computer. He ran out of the building, talking to himself loudly and shaking his head. Walking furiously and triggering a severe asthma attack in the process, he was forced to sit in the cold and contemplate this latest disaster. His wife a lesbian! It all made sense now! Maria and the furniture catalogues, Maria with the sushi recipes, Maria red in the face when he returned from Windermere. So when had this started? He realised that perhaps his affair with Adriana had started *after* Ros's affair with Maria. Good grounds for divorce then. But he didn't want a divorce. He wanted Ros and Tommy back. But he also wanted Adriana. Muddle, muddle, muddle.

Catastrophe, catastrophe, went round his mind. He held his head tight in his hands. Could not think straight. Damned Prozac! Damned everything!

Shivering, he absent-mindedly got up, unseeing, and managed to find the Warren Street Tube Station. He had to wait ages for a train. *Where's the fucking Tube when you need it?* He made a miserable journey home. As he emerged from the station Adriana reached him by mobile, concerned. He brushed off her enquiries and switched the thing off. He had to think. *Had to think.*

Think in any useful way he did not however. As he slumped in a chair, alone in his flat, he could make nothing of it all. Ros was not a lesbian. This fact kept asserting itself stubbornly. Out loud in fact. He didn't like that either. He listened to his own voice echoing around the flat. He was talking out loud to himself, a symptom, he knew well enough, of derelicts, addicts, losers, low life and the plain mad. Or the celebrated mad, like Nash. He glanced around the room and suddenly his eyes rested on an unopened bottle of wine that Adriana had brought round. He got up, extracted the cork with more swearing over the awkward bottle-opener, poured a glass, downed it, and then poured another. Before long he had reached the state of unconsciousness that was so often elusive to him, but even so, as he fell into this stupor he had the horrible feeling that not only was he talking out loud, but so was someone else, someone from his dreams.

It took two days to recover from this binge, during which time he stubbornly kept his phone off and refused to look at emails. Ros might not be a lesbian, but the revelation about Maria made a horrible kind of sense – he just had no idea what to do about any of it. A scene repeatedly ran through his head: when Tommy had still been a baby the household had taken a holiday together in their cruiser, setting off up-river for Oxford via Henley. It was while they had been moored there that Ros had uncharacteristically lost her temper over a missing kitchen item. 'How on earth,' she had exploded at him, 'can we make a proper salad without the spinner?'

He had looked at her blankly.

'The salad spinner!' she had shouted at him. 'It's what you use to drain the lettuce and other salad leaves!'

'Can't we just use the colander?' he had responded, taken aback, turning in the narrow galley kitchen to retrieve the item and wave it in front of her.

'Idiot,' she had snapped, 'you can't dry the leaves with that; when they are wet the dressing doesn't stick properly.'

Maria confirmed this with a vigorous nod. Both women seemed very put out by this eventuality, and William's efforts to trivialise it only made things worse.

'There might be a Lakeland in the town,' said Ros, staring at him.

'Lakeland?'

'Yes, "home of creative kitchenware",' said Ros. 'I can't believe that you had forgotten that.'

'Oh. Well, shall I run into town and have a look?' he asked, finally realising that this was what was required of him.

'Thank you,' Ros said, but none too warmly.

He had thought it odd but anyway set off on foot into the centre of Henley, asking passers-by whether there was a Lakeland. It turned out there was, but he arrived just as it was closing. Despite all his best efforts to mime terrible sorrow through the locked glass door, and to indicate his dire need to avoid the hangman's noose, the assistant sternly waved him away; miming a knife severing his jugular did not melt her either. On his return both women had been flushed, he recalled, and had taken the terrible news surprisingly well. The salad was prepared and eaten in a rather awkward silence which was broken only by the fuss that all three made of the baby as it woke, cried, and slept. So, he thought, he had become an unwanted intruder in his own estate even back then. The two women were having an affair right under his nose and he had been too stupid to realise it. And, worse, he had found Maria to be a welcome addition to the household. And had even missed her in those first lonely days in his flat!

You are a complete idiot. A dolt, a moron, a cuckold.

Another thought was looming, a course of action he had been quietly contemplating since his last hypnotherapy session in June. Slowly he had been driven to look up, just out of curiosity, is there really such a thing? Past life therapists? Yes, two hundred registered in the UK. A while later, having initially snorted in derision at this discovery, he had a list of ten within London that he could reach fairly easily and had systematically worked through their web sites. One caught his eye: Stefan Kolakowski claimed all the usual benefits and successes of the therapy, but with one crucial difference – he believed in the many-worlds theory. William had known its chief proselytiser at Oxford, the physicist David Deutsch, even attended some of his talks, and this somehow made this Kolakowski acceptable despite the ridiculous nature of the whole thing. The discovery had sat in him for the whole autumn.

It was ordinary human decency that he exchanged a few words with Maria during access times with Tommy. There were no actual clues that she was a lesbian, no actual evidence that she had somehow talked Ros into an utterly uncharacteristic sexual experiment, and no real reason why Ros should sleep with Maria rather than him. After all, the sexual estrangement did in fact predate the nanny. But William had the advantage over Maria now: he knew what was going on and she didn't know that he knew. Adriana's gossip was a lucky break in this deadlock, giving him a small edge. Ha!

All this went round and round in his head, though you couldn't say that he really had come to terms with it. The other so-far fruitless debate he had with himself was over a therapeutic intervention based on 'past lives.' He would laugh out loud at himself for having made a list of such therapists, and having narrowed it down to one. But now and again he would catch himself in one or other of these debates, a phrase or sentence hanging in the air, in all likelihood one he had just uttered out loud. A further nagging suspicion would sometimes raise itself however:

was it his own voice or that of another person? He would whirl round in the hope of catching some intruder, but none ever materialised. He couldn't think straight. Thinking wasn't what it used to be.

It is a bleak December afternoon. In the chaos of his office-cum-workroom overlooking a thundering Old Brompton Road he sits with his mobile phone and a number scrawled on a pad, his heart pounding. The ill-fitting sash windows let in noise, a small draft, and along with that the faint pungency of winter traffic. The central heating is turned to maximum. Hours go by. It gets dark, more hours go by. He starts suddenly with the realisation that past life therapists, however bizarre their ministrations, might not stay up all night. Without any apparent intention forming in his mind his fingers take up the phone. Other fingers press the number icons as he peers at his scrawl on the ageing scrap of paper. Back in September, or even longer ago, he had worked out that this Kolakowski was the best shot out of the practitioners in inner London, and had written his details down: how come this piece of paper has not been long ago tossed in the bin? Or just got plain lost, as far more important things such as utility bills or letters from Professor May tended to? This is utterly ridiculous. It feels quite unreal. Is he an automaton? It is an eleven digit number. The first four have been entered. No volition of his own? Now eight. Could he not back out of this now? There, all the digits entered. He stares briefly at the backlit numbers. Just press cancel. *Just press cancel!*

His index finger presses call.

nine

1ØØØØØ 'Stefan Kolakowski, transcarnation therapist' came the confident, vaguely American voice from the phone.

William struggled to construct a coherent sentence but eventually conveyed his interest in therapy sessions. 'No problem,' was the response. 'Come to the group session this weekend.'

'Group session?'

'Yes, I have a full diary for individual sessions, but I can squeeze you into the group session this weekend. In fact it's a good introduction to the methods of multiverse transcarnation therapy.'

'Oh.'

William didn't like the sound of that at all, but he was given the address and told to turn up if he wanted to. On the following Saturday morning in a dreary cold January – on roughly the second anniversary of his separation from Ros – William, despite a multitude of misgivings, found himself in Old Street hunting down an alternative therapies centre that was housed in a converted warehouse. As he entered he could hear what sounded like Buddhist chanting from the back of the building, and after inspecting a sign listing various alternative therapy and suchlike activities quite unfamiliar to him he took a refurbished industrial lift to the fourth floor.

After the formalities of registration, conducted by an enthusiastic middle-aged woman with alarmingly orange hair, William was shown into a big room with a circle of cushions on the floor. He glanced round for alternatives but clearly participants were expected to sit on the cushions, and so he lowered himself awkwardly onto one but could not get comfortable as the circle filled up. Finally Stefan Kolakowski entered, a little theatrically, William thought. The group leader sat on a chair, prominently placed to complete the circle, and spoke about his method for some fifteen minutes without stopping; then, each participant was asked to give their name, sum up how they were feeling and why they were there. It took a long time to get to William, who was finding it increasingly difficult to hold any one position for long – his knees simply would not conform to the angles required of them, something at the easy command of the other participants it seemed. The pattern of speaking was clear however, each rather depressed individual offering something along the lines of they were nervous and that they had been somebody – always a famous name – in a previous life. When it came to his turn he merely said that he was uncomfortable, which was true, and that he might have been Alan Turing. The group was then invited to meditate for fifteen minutes: they were to chant 'Om', each at their own pace and pitch. William was torn between thinking how ridiculous it was that he was sitting uncomfortably on a cushion with what seemed like a group of hippies chanting something quite meaningless, while on the other hand he had for the first time since the dream after 9/11 said out loud: 'I think I was Alan Turing in a past life.' He was, in fact, stunned by it. He could not understand how he had got to this point, having never even dreamt of mentioning it to anyone. This started something of a reverie, recapitulating in his mind the various steps in this bizarre journey, though all rather entangled with his efforts to chant 'Om' and surreptitiously take the odd suck on his inhaler. After the meditation the round of personal statements was repeated with the invitation for others to make responses this time. Suddenly it was his turn again and he had to repeat out loud the outrageous proposition. He was even more nervous, with all eyes on him.

'I think, er, I feel, that I might have been, er … Alan Turing,' he mumbled. There was silence for a while.

Then, from another participant: 'Italy. Needs to get in touch with Italy. And loneliness.'

There was a perplexed silence.

'Annie, do you want to say a bit more about that?' Kolakowski prompted her gently.

'Yes. He was alone in Turin …'

'Ah no,' interrupted William. 'It's a man's name: Alan Turing.'

'William, we don't cut across when someone is sharing.'

'I thought I was sharing.'

'Let Annie finish.' Annie just shook her head in confusion, so eyes turned to William.

'Ah, Alan Turing was a mathematician,' he explained. There was no response to this. 'He broke the Enigma code in the War, you know, and pretty much invented modern computing.'

Still a silence.

'Not everyone has been somebody famous,' a man called Alex offered.

William was looking at Annie, still obviously crestfallen. 'Actually,' he announced quietly. 'I *have* been lonely. Very lonely.' All eyes turned to him. He was not used to this kind of thing at all, but, speaking more to Annie than the others, he said in an even lower voice: 'I had an affair and my wife threw me out. I miss her very much and also my baby son.'

'Good, good,' said Stefan. The group clearly approved of this unburdening. However Stefan then indicated that it was the next person's turn, to William's relief; these were just introductions.

It wasn't a great start William felt, and in the break he rather forlornly hunted for coffee.

'Only herb teas,' the orange-haired woman said to him. 'Try orangeberry and pine.'

'Okay,' he said as brightly as he could. 'Ah, have you been doing this sort of thing for long?'

'Oh yes. Stefan is absolutely terrific, isn't he?'

She turned out to be called Felicity Makepeace, and he found in her something of a friend in the following weekends. But the group sessions themselves just made William desperate – he quite early on shared with them that he was on Prozac, which they collectively and unanimously disapproved of, any sympathy for his marital problems now forgotten. His was a false world, they kept telling him, a happiness unfounded in reality. He protested that he wasn't happy at all, that he was plagued by dreams, was hearing voices, and his life was an absolute mess. About his work he said nothing; not one of them seemed to be driven in any way like he was, indeed, this was the biggest shock in participating with these people. Throughout his whole life, he realised, he had been associated with men and women of ambition, individuals who found it hard to take a week's holiday, let alone spend a weekend on cushions talking about themselves. Who had the time for this sort of thing?

Although the sessions themselves were rather unforgiving, he found that the breaks were the opposite, with much mutual sympathy. Quite a group gathered around him, with Felicity at the centre, happy to commiserate about his separation and unhappy lot. Only one participant rather conspicuously held back from this – she had joined on the same day as William, and, rather than just announce her first name as the others did, she insisted on giving her full name: Anita van Houten. She was slight, with large sad eyes, and spoke in a wavering voice. She had an awful thing to share with them: she believed she had been a Nazi in a previous life. She was the only one apart from William who was unsure of her previous identity, being equally unable to suggest any famous names. Cleopatra she was not. Neither Julius Caesar, Christ, nor Rommel. Definitely not Hitler. She reminded William a little of Adriana, but without the sparkle; instead, despite her fine cheekbones and the near-perfect symmetry of her face, she seemed closed in on herself and sat with her limbs all intertwined, desiring apparently to make herself as unattractive as possible.

William held out little hope for help from the group despite various encouragements on an individual basis, and clung in over five weekends just to ensure his one-to-one appointment with Stefan. He dare not of course mention this to anyone, neither Harry, Adriana, nor Edmondson.

Meanwhile, after the initial shock had worn off, he had been further ruminating over the revelation about his wife. Superficially, the affair with Maria explained so much, from the very moment of interviewing the attractive Icelandic woman. He had to be honest: he had readily agreed to her joining the household not just because she seemed so capable, but because she was so beautiful. Was it almost schizophrenic, to want a beautiful woman in the house, while priding himself that he never harboured any lust towards her? How ironic then, that it was his wife who was sexually drawn to Maria. Allegedly. Apparently. All this made sense of that period, but it made no sense of the Ros he had known up to then. He could not find a single memory of her that would have indicated any lesbian tendency – though he also had to admit that his memory seemed less reliable than it used to be. No, he could not unearth a single incident. Unless, that is, her friendship with Patricia Elleworthy and her feminist circle was significant. Suddenly he thought about them in a new light. Christ! Had Ros been drawn to the lesbians amongst them? Could you become bisexual merely out of political correctness? Or was it the other way round? Had he read her feminism as a merely intellectual position?

And what did that mean for him? Did he have homosexual tendencies that could suddenly emerge out of nowhere? That was an uncomfortable thought that he pushed away. More aggravating was this: what did it mean for his marriage? Had it been a sham all those years? He shook his head. No. It had been real, and he longed to return to that reality. Or find a new such reality with Adriana. God! He felt trapped between these two equally hopeless longings.

He rather tentatively broached the subject of bisexuality with Adriana, who merely said that driven and creative people often tended to it. She attempted to comfort him, but she had to be honest: Ros's affair made her feel less guilty over breaking up their marriage. William agreed to this extent at least, that he would have been thrown out in the end on some excuse or another. Also, while still angry with Emil, he now didn't blame him as much – William did not confess his more extreme suspicion that Emil had slept with Ros. That was now out of consideration, as was an affair with Jonathan Gries. But he pressed Adriana: could Ros just be under the influence of her more radical feminist friends, like Patricia? Could it have been all those feminist books that they had read? He couldn't remember the authors, though they had been drummed into him at the time. De Beauvoir, Butler, Irigaray, Krisdeva? suggested Adriana. Yes, all that sounded familiar. Adriana was dubious, but yes, perhaps it might be more an intellectual thing than a physical one. William clung to that.

In this period Adriana was visiting Imperial, not for tutorials any more, but in her capacity as the liaison officer between the two institutions on the joint project. She sat in on the Departmental Research and Exploitation Committee, which dreary meetings William was also supposed to attend. He could not always avoid them, and found it even more of a torment to have the entirely unavailable Adriana sit opposite him and talk so coherently and engagingly. Thankfully Emil never attended the DREC meetings, having always been rather aloof from practical ventures. Professor May held great hopes for the eventual commercial prospects of the collaboration with Birkbeck, expressing only a regret that the Science Museum contributed less than the current costs to the Department. On meeting Simon Spindler again at William's office, Adriana engaged in a quite fruitless discussion with him on Turing's life. She simply could not convey to Simon the socio-political importance of the great man; however she encouraged Simon to tell her something of his own work, to which he responded with some details of his role in the Eliza II project, glancing up a number of times at William as if to seek permission. She was intrigued by it and the upshot was that she later emailed William a famous extract that she had discovered in the writings of Joseph Weizenbaum:

"Bright young men of dishevelled appearance, often with sunken glowing eyes, can be seen sitting at computer consoles, their arms tensed and waiting to fire their fingers, already poised to strike, at the buttons and keys on which their attention seems to be riveted as a gambler's on the rolling dice. When not so transfixed, they often sit at tables strewn with computer printouts over which they pore like possessed students of a cabbalistic text. They work until they nearly drop, twenty, thirty hours at a time. Their food, if they arrange it, is brought to them: coffee, Cokes, sandwiches. If possible, they sleep on cots near the printouts. Their rumpled clothes, their unwashed and unshaven faces, and their uncombed hair all testify that they are oblivious to their bodies and the world in which they move."

In her email Adriana added that Weizenbaum had missed something in this description: it was no doubt accurate enough, but could easily be transposed into the sphere of the creative arts where poets, novelists and playwrights lived in a similar obsessive fashion far divorced from the needs of their bodies. Think of Huysmans' *Against Nature* she added, a reference quite lost on William, so he emailed back to complain that in his crash course in Two Cultures had not yet got as far as *completely* reading *every* page of the two novels she had given him, and would she ease up a bit. He certainly wasn't ready for the advanced course. But William was amused with the extract because Weizenbaum was the inventor of the original Eliza programme and had been surprised at the positive reception that it had received, starting with his secretary who had asked him to leave the room so she could converse with it. The thing had taken on a life of its own.

Idly, when in his flat, William hunted down a version of the original programme and typed in: 'I think I was Alan Turing in a previous life.' The machine responded quite predictably: 'HOW LONG HAVE YOU THOUGHT THAT YOU WERE ALAN TURING IN A PREVIOUS LIFE?' William typed in. 'Since 9/11' 'I AM SORRY TO HEAR THAT,' came the reply. William grunted in amusement: poor Eliza had no idea what 9/11 referred to.

1 0 0 0 0 1   Kolakowski was finally able to fit in a private meeting
————————   with William.

     'This is a preparatory session,' said the bearded young man. 'Just relax. I started out as a Jungian, so that means I'll be paying careful attention to your story.'

     'Story?'

     'Yes. Although the fragments of your unconscious bubbling up may appear to be disconnected, they will tell a coherent story if we let them. They will lead to the uncovering of personality elements long suppressed, and in time the story can be dissolved away as these fragments become integrated into your being. The measure of your progress will be the fading of these dreams and waking obsessions with the past.'

'That's good. But I seem to have two stories.'

'Go on.'

'One relates to Alan Turing ...'

'Ah yes, I looked him up. Mathematician. An obvious transference or what I call "hook" personality for you.'

'Ah yes. Quite. And the other is of a seaplane crash, all connected with Lake Windermere. But I have not been able to find any connection between the life of the historical Alan Turing and seaplanes, let alone a fatal crash.'

'Yes, you see, this is where my multiverse transcarnation therapy system comes in. You will know of the multiple-worlds interpretation of quantum theory, having trained in the sciences.'

'Yes.'

'Well, if a universe bifurcated at some time in Turing's early life, so he became a pilot instead of a mathematician, then you would have much of his known personality, the emotional charge carried with his name, only a slightly different history. In that world you could have been Turing the seaplane pilot who crashed onto Windermere.'

'Oh.'

'Look, did you ever see *Close Encounters*, the film? Was it shown much in this country?'

'Yes, I belonged to the sci-fi film club at Oxford.'

'Do you remember the protagonist, with this dim vision of a mountain? He kept making it physically. In mashed potato. Shaving cream. Clay. As he engaged with it physically it emerged from his subconscious.'

'So what are you suggesting?'

'Make the plane.'

'The Short Sunderland?'

'Whatever it's called.'

'Out of mashed potato?'

'Out of anything.'

William's first session ended like this, with Stefan taking notes and arranging for a proper regression treatment in several week's time. William was to proceed with building the plane, allowing his imagination to take free flow around the process. He should note down everything that came to mind.

William made efforts to wash, shave and wear decent clothes, but his food was all from local cafés and takeaways, and he could simply forget the basics for a day or two at a time. He clung to the fact that his mathematics was progressing well, but had barely noticed a significant transition: he spoke out loud all the time now in his flat, only preventing himself from doing so by great effort in his offices at Imperial and Birkbeck. But it was not just him speaking: as he told the therapy group, he was hearing voices. And they were distinctly of another era.

He went to a model shop near Holborn and bought an Airfix kit of the Sunderland flying boat – it felt absurd to him, and at one point he suddenly panicked that this was the sort of shop where he might bump into Simon Spindler. Once home with the embarrassing purchase, he cleared a space amidst the detritus of his flat and glued it together: nothing happened. He had a little notebook he bought for the purpose of recording his inner thoughts as he worked on the model, but there was nothing to write in it. He had by now DVDs and books on the seaplane, and knew some of its history, but none of it gave him any insight, instead he marvelled at how he could spend time on an unappealing historical period in which some antiquated piece of flying junk played an insignificant role. Adriana dropped by, saw the unpainted model on a table amidst his mathematical notes and found it funny.

'A new hobby, Professor Strange?' she teased, but he was relieved to find that she made no connection between the plane and Turing or the Enigma protocols: he didn't want her to know or guess anything about his past life therapy. She turned to him and mentioned, almost shyly, that her boyfriend was away for a few days. Although she and William had not been intimate since before her departure to India, there was no doubt that their joint project was bringing them closer again. They kissed, but she appeared not to want to make love, at least not immediately. The sheer promise of it had him enormously agitated, but he agreed – he would have agreed to anything – to an evening meal in the local Italian restaurant before she came back for the night: he could see in an odd way that this satisfied some need for propriety. She was in high spirits, perhaps even a little manic, which he adored, but he dare not raise the question of marriage again. He had originally proposed – how clumsily he thought – at the very same table at which they now sat, at a time that seemed part of a fabled past. On the way back he downed a Viagra, and made some attempt to clear his bed of papers and other junk strewn down one side. Love-making that evening was marvellous, and they slept through to late morning, the first time since Windermere that she had been with him through the night. In the morning over some tea in grimy cups he told her that he loved her – he did not often pronounce that simple truth, as her response was always guarded.

'I love you too, Billy,' she said without hesitation for a change. Then she looked down, bit her lip and suddenly burst out. 'I'm so *fucking* confused by all this, Billy, I can't tell you!' He stared at her, taken aback. She got up suddenly, paced too and fro in agitation, and then nearly tripped over a massive tome on digital signal processing protruding from under a chair. 'Fuck!' she cried out, and then: 'Sorry, sorry. This is not like me at all. It is just that everything is so mixed up at the moment.' He looked at her in consternation, their eyes meeting. Suddenly she walked over to him and raised him up to hold her tight. There were tears on her cheeks. 'Billy, I can't say more at the moment. Sorry. Sorry.' They swayed together for what seemed like a long while, William awkward and almost off-balance in the tightness of her embrace. Then she told him she had to get back to college, put on her coat, kissed him goodbye and left.

When she was gone his spirits sank. It was like Groundhog Day he suddenly realised; that was a film he had actually watched all the way through, a long time ago with his parents in Parktown. Adriana might make love with him, but always returned to her boyfriend. What could release him from this eternal recurrence? He shook his head. As to her outburst he had no clue: it was perhaps the first time that she had shown any confusion over having two lovers, but beyond that thought he just forgot about it.

100010   Tuesdays were Tommy days, unless work appointments made it impossible – he rarely conceded such a thing. But he now found himself divided between playing with his son, now three years old, and brooding on the role that Maria had played in his downfall. For a month now he had watched her reactions to his playtime with Tommy and thought he detected a definite plan to estrange him from his boy. He was working it all out. Maria had arrived at Britannia Road and immediately set to work to undermine his family: he had been a fool to welcome her so fully into their lives. Maria had exploited Ros's belief in feminism to deny him his conjugal rights and drive him into the arms of Adriana.

In this period William received an email from Professor May asking to see him for an informal review of progress with his research. This was most unusual. William arrived a little out of breath at May's office suite, engaged in some banter with Jane Wozniak – who seemed a bit off with him – and entered May's inner office.

'Ah, William,' began May affably enough. 'I just wanted to have a little chat about Eliza II and progress on your other research.'

'Jolly good,' said William, sprawling in a chair.

'Um,' began May rather tentatively, 'I saw the CEO of SharpSoft the other day, and he seemed a little lukewarm on how Eliza II was progressing. He likes Spindler by the way, thinks he is an asset to the programme, but was rather wondering when you might deliver on your main commitments. Is there any reason why you might be behind schedule?'

William was barely paying attention, his thoughts rather occupied with Maria. He could hear her scolding Tommy in his mind, and he didn't like the way she did it.

'Behind?' he said blankly.

'Yes, William,' said May a little abruptly. 'I know that it is none of my business, but I was of course shocked when your marriage with Ros broke down. These things happen of course, but it was damned inconvenient for me. I have Ros on a retainer as consultant for our marketing drive, and since your separation she has refused to meet with me here. She says that it would be too awkward to bump into you in the building again, so I have to meet her at her office or elsewhere.'

'Really?' asked William, interrupting May's flow. He was unsurprised however; it had been awkward for him too. On the other hand maybe there was more to this.

Maria has forbidden Ros any contact with you.

His brow furrowed and he began to think about it, while May continued to express his annoyance.

'The fact is William that you seem to have gone to pieces a bit since the separation. It's quite understandable, I suppose, but you don't look as, well, presentable, as you used to. And SharpSoft are a little concerned, you know, about slippage.'

William summoned his reserves.

'Actually Richard, I am doing some very good work at the moment. I have been re-visiting the premise and algorithms of the original Eliza programme and found that after all it has considerable resonance with the direction of my research as outlined in Geneva.' William could do this with his eyes shut; he was enough of a political animal to know when to turn on a plausible line in spiel. But for some reason it didn't work on May this time.

'That's not what Spindler and Piatigorsky say,' retorted May sharply. William was dumbfounded. Spindler and Piatigorsky? Those lesser minds – one a complete novice – were united in criticising him, William Strange? He sat up in his chair frowning at May.

'I am sorry Richard, but neither of them have the faintest idea of the breakthroughs I am making. They are criticising from a position of *absolute* ignorance.' He almost shouted the last point at May. His breathing was heavy and he could feel himself red in the face.

May recoiled. 'William, William, there is no need to get worked up about this. I just needed you to reassure me, which, er, you have done.' There was an awkward pause. 'But, William, please keep an eye on deadlines will you?' May's face clouded again. 'And William, could you do something about your appearance perhaps?'

William scowled and got up. Brightening with an effort, he said: 'Sure Richard. Deadlines. Appearance. Will attend to it forthwith.'

As he got in the lift to go down to his office he heard a voice say aloud: *They are all against you.* He spun around in the shiny metal compartment, but he was alone. What panicked him most about this particular failure to prevent himself talking out loud was the accent. It was Cockney.

He attended a further weekend transcarnation therapy group ahead of the next individual session with Kolakowski. William was finding in Felicity a support in a still bewildering world which had suddenly taken a new turn: he had told the group that Alan Turing was a famous mathematician and explained a little about his contribution to the war effort and the Enigma and so on, all with little interest shown from the others. But when he came to mention that Turing was a homosexual and had been prosecuted for it under the laws of his time, this was pounced upon.

'That's it,' said one of them. 'That's what your past life is pointing to: homosexuality. You've never dealt with your homosexuality.'

He retorted with clarity and confidence that he was not a homosexual.

'Everybody is to some degree,' was offered, but Kolakowski wanted to make a point about his therapeutic system.

'You see,' said Stefan, 'the external material, the hook, is very important, but it always points to the real impulse. Cleopatra might be the story, but the desire for suicide the real impulse. Napoleon might be the story but domination the impulse; Jesus the story but a messiah-complex the impulse. Once the impulse is properly de-cathected the story loses its hold and importance. William: tell the group. Are you now, or have you ever been, attracted to other men?'

'No ...' said William but without conviction this time, because he was suddenly freaked out. Why on earth had Kolakowski used that phrase?

Are you now, or have you ever been, a homosexual?

Why that phrasing? He was stunned, but summoned the energy to argue back. He suddenly hated the idea of Kolakowski always having the rapt attention of the others, as though he was some kind of oracle.

'Stefan, you told us that Liberace believed he was Liszt in a previous life. But what issue in Liszt's life was the story that helped Liberace overcome his problems?'

'Liberace, William, was not in therapy,' Kolakowski answered sweetly. William couldn't answer that. Indeed his thought processes seemed to have locked up again, so he just turned away, annoyed.

'Look,' said Kolakowski, 'We are just at the beginning of an investigation here. You tell us, as you seem to have researched the life of this Alan Turing quite thoroughly: what were the other features of his life story, apart from being a mathematician – the hook – and a homosexual – the possible, I grant you, only the *possible* problem nexus?' All eyes turned to William.

'He was also a maverick ...' William was thinking hard, '... he was a loner, and he undermined the establishment.'

'Okay,' said Kolakowski. 'Let us take them one by one. Are you uncomfortable – that was your word when you arrived – are you uncomfortable with being a maverick yourself?'

'Not at all.'

'Are you uncomfortable with being a loner?'

'No.'

'Are you uncomfortable with being anti-establishment?'

'No.'

Kolakowski paused for effect. 'That only leaves homosexuality, doesn't it?' There were murmurs of appreciation in the group. William grimaced and shook his head. 'Time for a break,' said Kolakowski softly.

Felicity came up to William over refreshments and touched his arm. 'I was a homosexual in a past life,' she confided. 'You don't have to be ashamed.'

'I wasn't and I'm not,' was his irritable response.

She smiled. 'I am sorry, I don't mean to jump to conclusions, but if you were this Alan Turing person in a past life, and he was a homosexual, then it doesn't necessarily mean that you are a homosexual now. After all, I'm not a homosexual now.'

William stared at her pondering this. He blinked. 'So what does it mean then?' he asked, pleased in fact to be talking with her. She was kind of nice he decided.

'Well, perhaps you were Turing and I was Turing's lover, and we have a karmic bond. Perhaps one of us betrayed the other. I know that betrayal is part of my past life story.'

That worried William. Who else was going to betray him now? But the friendship with Felicity seemed to throw up no particular difficulties; she was simply happy, it seemed, to listen to the accounts of his dreams and strange voices. He needed a friend in all this; after all his brother Paul was no help, Harryjee only wanted to persuade him to join his firm as a quant, and Adriana – well, she was part of the problem, not the solution.

1ØØØ11   Kolakowski had been pestering William to put him in touch with Deutsch at Oxford, after discovering that William had been tutored once or twice by the physicist. William made vague promises, which kept Kolakowski perhaps more interested than he might otherwise have been. At the second individual session he made an effort to listen to William, and then said it was time to put him into regression.

'My method involves a deep hypnosis in which I ask questions based on the material I have so far gathered from you. You won't remember anything, but I will record your responses which will be uploaded to the site where only you, I and Felicity can access them via the password. You can then download and listen to them on a phone, iPod or any kind of MP3 player. I generally give clients a couple of weeks to digest what their unconscious has thrown up for them, and then we have a debriefing session. If we have to we repeat the process, though very often, after the group sessions have prepared you, all the material emerges in one go. Is that okay with you?'

'Sure,' said William a little nervously.

'Right,' said Kolakowski breezily. 'We conduct the sessions in a room next door.'

This proved to be alarmingly like the padded cells that William gathered were used in mental hospitals: it had a chair for the therapist, a couch for the client, some recording equipment and nothing else apart from the padded walls and ceiling. Seeing that William was hesitant about it Kolakowski said: 'Yes, it is soundproofed. Clients can scream.

Or howl. Or make all kinds of noises. I have neighbours you understand.'

Not in the least reassured by this, William nodded nervously and gingerly laid himself on the couch as indicated. Kolakowski drew up his chair alarmingly close and fiddled with a clipboard.

'We will go through a standard relaxation technique, working from the toes upwards to the head. I will then count down from twenty, and on one you will lose all consciousness of your present surroundings. You will allow all thoughts, feelings and images to surface at will. I will ask you questions: allow any voice to answer them. The procedure is entirely safe.'

Kolakowski switched on the recording equipment and stated the date, time and client name. He then said: 'I need your formal permission to proceed, William Strange. Do you consent?'

'Ah … yes,' said William, staring up at the ceiling and feeling an utter, utter fool.

Two days later William was able to download his session. He was still suspicious about the process, but his own voice was clear enough on the recording. He went over and over it, first on his phone, and then on his computer sound system. Lying on the cluttered and filthy chaise longue in the living room he listened to himself. At Kolakowski's prompting William had talked at length in a rush of muddled sentences about the interior of a Sunderland flying boat, its cockpit and the crew of men in its cramped quarters. It was not crashing on a lake: it was heading to choppy seas – he was now certain that it was in the Atlantic – towards a turmoil in the water of bubbling foam, spilt oil, fire, explosions and God knows what. Five or six men are all shouting at the pilot, at him, at anything. A new phrase emerged that then became repeated in his dreams: a stranger was calling 'Only to Turing!' 'Only to Turing!' William was confused at first, but he was recounting this to Kolakowski in a German accent of all things. So Turing was on the plane after all. So was he Turing? Was this a parallel universe where, as Kolakowski had said, Turing had been a pilot, not a mathematician? For a long while on the tape William seemed to babble about the men on the plane, and about a German naval officer. If he was Turing then perhaps he was not the pilot, because it seemed as if he was addressing some 'captain' about his concerns over flight direction. But he was doing maths alright: for nearly ten minutes on the recording William seems to be muttering about coordinates and maps and triangulation, and then, very near the end of the session, this character, this pseudo-Turing, seems to be concerned about a woman. What would she think? He kept repeating this. But nothing in the recording gave William any clues as to where Adriana might fit in. Was she the woman that the character referred to? Or, as with Felicity, had she been a man in that other universe? A homosexual?

The results of this first session were electrifying, but opened up more questions than they answered.

William had in effect two lives now: one lived in Kolakowski's world of past life therapy and clients – in which Felicity became a good anchor – and another in which he alternated between Imperial, Birkbeck and Eel Brook Common. He began to look forward to the group sessions at the weekend, over the two days that Adriana was least likely to see him anyway, on account of her working boyfriend. For William, night and day now seemed equally dreamlike – he was hearing voices, but Prozac and multiverse transcarnation therapy put some boundaries on his eccentricities, and his personal project was going well. Eliza II had dropped off his horizon however, despite May's warnings, so it was no real surprise to be hauled up to his office again. Making a supreme effort to dress and shave, he arrived beaming and complimented Jane Wozniak on a lovely spring outfit. It was in fact getting a little warmer. Her response was still not as welcoming as of old, but this was the least of his worries. May looked grim.

'William. Do shut the door. Yes. I greatly regret this, but I have to follow up complaints you understand.'

'Complaints?'

'Yes. First of all, you are still behind with the SharpSoft project. That worries me William. It worries me. But the reason I wanted to see you today is that Dr. Spindler has lodged a formal complaint against you.'

William couldn't quite remember which of the staff was Dr. Spindler.

'Spindler ...?' murmured William with a puzzled look.

'Dr. Simon Spindler,' prompted May in annoyance. 'Your postdoc.'

'Ah, yes.' William gritted his teeth. That young man had always been against him. Must have been planted by Piatigorsky to spy on him and Adriana. Ha! Well he had got himself an office at Birkbeck well away from Simon's prying eyes.

'William, for God's sake, pay attention!'

William looked pained, but then furrowed his brow and stared ahead in what he thought was a model of concentration.

'William, Simon has made three serious allegations against you. Firstly, that your supervision of him has been inadequate. Secondly, that you have almost never discussed the Eliza II project with him, so he has had to work directly with the project manager at SharpSoft.'

William stared at May. He blinked. Was that two things or three things? He really did find it hard to attend to what May was saying. Actually he always had. He chewed his lip.

'And William,' continued May, 'Er, the most, er, delicate matter is what really worries me. I have to add this to other eccentricities in your behaviour in the last year. Though,' he added hastily, 'I can't really fault your professional conduct in other ways, for example the Birkbeck project seems to be going very well. It is a great step forward in interdisciplinary research. So I hear. It's just that this report by Simon is, well, so odd.'

William raised his eyebrows encouragingly.

'William. Simon alleges that on March 10 this year you were in your office and conducting a conversation with the Liza therapy programme.'

William burst out laughing.

'Richard, I told you didn't I? I found, rather to my surprise, that the original programme was rather helpful in framing the line of mathematical enquiry both for the Eliza II project and for my own research, which is by the way, very close to a breakthrough.'

'William I am glad to hear that. About the breakthrough that is. Very good. To be published in ACM proceedings I imagine?'

William nodded vigorously.

'But here is the odd thing. Dr Spindler is adamant about it, I questioned him quite thoroughly.'

William anticipated him: 'Look Richard, Simon must have seen me typing in all kinds of strange questions. I grant that the questions – I can't remember exactly what they were now – would have seemed odd to him. They were probably in fact, on the surface of it, quite bizarre. But I was testing the internal algorithm, you know the random choice aspect ...'

May did not let him finish.

'William! What Dr Spindler says is that not only were you not typing anything at the keyboard, but that the screen on your computer was blank. You were, according to Dr. Spindler, posing the questions to Eliza out loud, and then answering them in a high-pitched voice. As if you thought you *were* Eliza.'

William stared at May. He was dumbfounded. There was a long silence. May looked extremely uncomfortable. William felt sick. He slowly rose to his feet and mumbled something about not feeling well, left May's office under the embarrassed gaze of Wozniak, and walked to the lift on the landing. Okay, okay, he talked to himself. He knew that, but he hadn't realised that it had got this far out of control. What he couldn't have realised either was just how bizarre he must have looked in the lift going down from May's office, his lips so tightly compressed, his frown so worried, and his eyes so darting as to be nothing short of comical: it took this level of effort to prevent the voices. As he left the building through the large atrium and the revolving doors onto Museum Street he felt a ringing in his ears. He walked fast. He just wanted to get home. Once down in the foot-tunnel he had to stop however, having become short of breath, and as he drew heavily on his inhaler a voice behind him said: 'Me too. I have to walk more slowly now.' William spun round to see an almost empty tunnel – the nearest people were a family group, much further down just entering from the Victoria and Albert Museum; none of them could have made that comment. Turning round William could see nobody near enough in the other direction either. He grimaced, placed the inhaler back in his jacket pocket and walked grimly on, though slowly, as he was still panting. 'That's it,' came the voice again, with a distinctly Welsh accent. 'Steady as you go. We'll be home in no time.'

William heard it echo in the tunnel. He screwed his face up tight and concentrated on his every laborious step. 'One, two, three, …' he counted the steps out loud, hoping that if he could not prevent himself talking, then at least he would control its content. Pedestrians stared at him as he approached the bend close to Kensington Station. 'Thirty-seven, thirty-eight, thirty-nine …' He then clenched his jaw shut and counted the steps from forty in his mind, a little more confident now that he was not talking aloud. He was soon lost in the melee of the ticket hall.

After he returned home from his interview with May there was a phone call from an anxious Jane Wozniak letting William know that Spindler was being transferred to Piatigorsky, and so his current office, that is with its size and location, was not really justified. He was being re-allocated to the third floor. She was very apologetic, though promised that all his things would be properly moved again, to which William answered her as brightly as he could and put the phone down. He was sitting in an armchair by the window, having turned the recent events over and over in his mind.

'They're all out to get you,' said a voice. It was the Cockney one. William stared blankly across the room, not caring to look for its source.

He had seated himself carefully to have a full view of the entire room: there was nobody in it but himself. Carefully he ventured a thought: 'I am in trouble.' It did not echo in the room. He was sure his jaw had not moved. It was in no discernable accent. It was his own thought. He sat still for a period bringing all his powers of concentration to bear on his thought processes, and after a while he began to relax – he was getting some kind of control over it. It was only six in the evening, but he wanted to go to bed and sleep it off; he rose gingerly, navigated his way along the corridor to his bedroom, having mentally noted some of the flow diagrams on his whiteboards. No voices. Good. He turned into his bedroom.

'That must be Ireland,' said the Welsh voice conversationally.

'No!' bellowed William and hurled himself onto his bed. He clutched his head and stared up at the ceiling. He lay there rigid in the foetal position for a long time and then fell into a fitful sleep.

In the waking moments that punctuated his night everything swirled through his mind: Turing the mathematician, Turing the homosexual, the plane crash, and alternative universes in which he had been Turing the seaplane pilot or perhaps navigator, and in which, obscurely, Adriana floated. The voices that he was beginning to hear were those of two crew members perhaps, though what they were saying made no sense. They scared him, but there was perhaps a meaning to it all which had come a step closer, though Adriana's connection to a time-shifted parallel universe in which Turing crashed a seaplane on Lake Windermere – or was it the Atlantic – was tenuous. She was the key, he was sure of that. As images of her and the sheer unresolvedness of their affair dominated his confused mind he fell into deeper sleep.

ten

100100   William and Adriana enjoyed the cool air on the drive
_____   back from a day's sight-seeing around Windermere. The
           MG that Adriana's father had given her had seen better
days – even the marque itself had now gone the way of so much lost
British engineering – but she steered it deftly enough onto the gravel of
the Belsfield Hotel, bringing it to a gentle halt. She was wearing a green
dress that came to her ankles, flowing and yet hinting continuously to
William of the curves of her body. As the engine stopped it pinked a
little. They kissed, the light on Adriana's face and in her eyes a memory
William would be unable to shake off in the coming years. To some
extent it compensated for his anxiety over the horrible feeling of déjà vu
that he had experienced the first time they had arrived at the hotel; the
terrible and the beautiful were all mixed up here. They turned to leave
their seats, the MG rocking with the release of weight; and although
braced for it William experienced no repeat of the earlier unsettling
dislocation. As they walked into the hotel Adriana took his hand.

'Bill,' she whispered. 'This is meant to be. I know that it is
unresolved and that you could say we are doing something wrong, but
something is so perfect about us being together now. We must just
accept it don't you think?'

William grunted his agreement. He was so happy to be with her
and hear her voice, his darker thoughts that had been so oddly triggered
by the holiday camp overlaid now with the countless small details of
their two days together. He had to admit that the Belsfield was
magnificent in the twilight of the summer's evening – you don't have to
actually like the style of something, he thought, to appreciate how
carefully it had been restored. Walking arm-in-arm with Adriana into the
main lounge, he observed its over-ornate decor including the red leather
sofas and matching leather-backed chairs, gilt-framed mirrors and

elaborate mouldings. Not his natural milieu, but he simply felt at home because he was with her. She suggested a swim in the indoor pool, before going down for an evening drink or two and then dinner, to which he readily agreed as the pool at least was within a modern steel and glass structure. The swimming costumes they wore – he had to purchase his from reception – showed up their red necks and arms in contrast with their otherwise white skin. William swam around a little and then trod water at the side as Adriana completed some vigorous lengths. She looked absolutely marvellous to him. His guilt suddenly returned and he thought again of the terrible risk he was taking. Thinking was useless however, perhaps she was right on that.

She came to join him, panting a little: her dancing grey eyes and her lithe body, exquisitely stuccoed with crystal-clear water droplets, all made him smile most tenderly. He leant over to kiss her shoulder, the drops now close enough to reflect the subtly-lit curves of the overhead steel and glass structure; he looked up and saw the vermillion-rippled sunset through the glass of the ceiling.

They pulled themselves out of the water and sat on the edge, the view of Lake Windermere just visible through the far windows of the pool.

'William,' Adriana said, a little sombre, 'I have to make a great effort to go in or near water. Do you remember on Lake Geneva? Of all the venues for the banquet they had to choose a barge. I couldn't help it when we boarded the thing but be overwhelmed by horrible memories, I can't explain now. I will tell you all about it some other time. But when you danced close to me that evening I already knew I was lost. I felt so safe with you ... so weirdly *comforted* like I hadn't known before.' She shook her head.

William was puzzled by this but just nodded. He loved it that she trusted him in this way, and, far from wanting to press her about her strange statement, simply felt glad of the implicit promise that in the future they would be together enough for her to say more. She swam off again and his elation gradually faded into anxiety as his eyes followed her. He fought off another attack of vertigo in which he too started to feel that he was inexplicably afraid of the water, afraid, for the first time in his life, of drowning. He shook his head vigorously, gritted his teeth and splashed in to do a length of crawl. It took him to his cardiovascular limits but had the desired effect, despite his painful breathing at the end of it: he had dispelled the crowding gloom. Adriana grinned at him and that was enough. He was not going to be beaten by this thing.

They showered, separately climbed back into their day clothes in the changing rooms and then wandered together through the carpeted maze of the building to change for formal dinner in Adriana's room. It was an elegant corner suite on the third floor with a commanding view of the lake; all curved sash windows and opulent curtains, and was quite flooded with light during the day; now it seemed to have captured the last glow of the setting sun. They stood in the gloom looking over the lake, and then reluctantly switched on the bedside lamps to change by. Adriana giggled.

'I couldn't afford this in a million years, but Papa insists we have a week here every year. He's been delayed at the bank, by the way, some fantastic new "product" as they call it, to do with double-reverse-derivative-swap-thingys, and so you are here instead.'

'And on a quite different basis, hopefully,' murmured William, aware in fact that he had paid for his room himself, a rare occasion, and which was an expense he would have to hide from Ros. And he wasn't even using it. As Adriana was now fully clothed again after being half-naked in the pool it wrought an overwhelming sense of arousal in him; he kissed her passionately, with the result that all their clothes came off for a second time. After love-making they showered again and chose their evening wear according to their individual tastes.

'You look like James Bond,' she murmured to him – he was indeed thoughtfully attired. He had made sure his black Oxfords were glossy, his grey three-piece rope-shouldered Chittleborough & Morgan suit nicely pressed and the collar on his Charles Tyrwhitt shirt immaculate. He wore a discrete but expensive watch on his wrist – a present from Ros, he recollected with a pang. Adriana drew him close for a kiss and then sniffed his jaw. 'Mmm, nice,' she said, prompting further guilt over the Burberry London for Men, a new fragrance chosen for him by Ros earlier in the year. When he took Adriana on his arm to stroll down the great stairways to the lounge for an evening aperitif, they drew not a few glances. A very happy couple is the least that one would have thought of them.

She stopped on the stairs. 'You do,' she insisted. 'You look like James Bond. That's why I feel safe with you.'

'You talk shuch nonshensh Mish Moneypenny,' he said.

'Your accent's complete rubbish,' she giggled reprovingly.

'There'sh not a Theshpian bone in my body,' he agreed in a mangled dialect, proving her correct by mingling his Scots with his Scouse.

She laughed. 'Terrible, terrible.'

They found a nook in the bar with a view over the light-speckled night-time water, and simply rested quiet for a while. He had advised her to try the Punt e Mes – mentioning that it contained quinine – and as they sipped this aperitif with its hints of bitterness, barks and honey the last of the sun withdrew from the East over the water. He asked her about her family and learned more about her Bloomsbury Set grandmother, her father in banking, the divorce of her parents when young, and her father's long support for her in her studies.

'You know Bill, it rebounds through the generations,' Adriana said earnestly. 'My mother rejected her mother's bohemian values, so she married a banker, almost as a form of rebellion. Think of that!' William smiled at her. 'But she told me it had been a mistake not to have had other lovers when she was young. She couldn't overcome the Romantic in her genes, so she had an affair when I was a young teen, and by the time she realised that all men are the same, it was too late, she had hurt my father too much.'

'All men are the same?' queried William with a pained expression.

'Silly. They are all the same if you want the impossible from them.'

'Oh.'

'You're hurt now ...' said Adriana peering at him with a smile.

'Male vanity,' he offered with a wry grin. He was working things out. 'Is that why you have your boyfriend Francis and are going out with me? You know, because of how you see your mother's experience?'

Adriana looked at him for a long time. 'I don't know what this is,' she said in the end. 'It's just an incredible moment with you. The whole day. And yesterday. And the evening before. I don't know what to think of it. You and me and lakes ... somehow we fit. I have a fear of water, but with you I feel safe again.'

He stroked her hand and looked out over the darkening ripples. His mind felt clear again, like the lake. He knew that he was betraying his family, but he was at peace with that. For now.

Adriana wanted to know about Oxford. 'What was it like to join one of the top universities in the world, daunting enough, when you were, what, five years younger than your class?'

'Oh,' said William, 'living a few streets away from college and the faculty meant I had a headstart on the other students coming from outside Oxford: you know, I could tell them where the bookshops and cafés were. And my friend Harryjee was completely out of his depth, having come from India.'

'This Harryjee did very well I seem to remember you saying.'

'Yes. He was in fact twenty-two to my seventeen, but we hit it off famously. He was a man of the world, a brilliant mathematician, but desperate to be more English than the English. That's where I helped him out, he always insisted; you know, even down to what Italian aperitifs an Englishman should drink. And of course he met Veronica in the second year, who he always said wanted to be more Indian than the Indians.' Adriana laughed at this. 'Veronica became obsessed with Bollywood,' William added, 'while Harry and I – the geeks – joined the science fiction film club. I just loved Star Wars as a kid.'

'You're no geek,' whispered Adriana.

'Yes I am,' protested William. 'How about this …' he passed his hands in front of her, mesmeric style, fixing her with his eyes and intoning in as deep a voice as he could muster: '"These are not the droids you're looking for."'

Adriana burst out laughing. 'The worst yet,' she commented.

1ØØ11Ø   'What's your family like?' Adriana asked William dreamily.

'My family? Well, apparently we go back to medieval times, to someone called Guido le Strange, son of the Duke of Brittany. Originally it meant "stranger" – you know, somebody from somewhere else, which is funny when you think about it now with our home in Parktown, my father a don at Oxford and all that. People would say we were quite Establishment I suppose, though Pop's publications caused a bit of a stir apparently: a counter-intuitive application of the classics to medieval history, or something like that. He told me I would live a happier life if I didn't bother reading them, and I have to say I took his advice. I wasn't much of a reader anyway. Maths was my thing.'

William had been a day-boy at the Dragon School, then entered Magdalene College School via the eleven plus, and then obtained a mathematics scholarship to Merton College. He didn't 'go up' to Oxford as he liked to joke as a youngster, but 'went sideways' and that at the early age of fifteen. His Master's at the age of seventeen was at Oxford's Programming Research Group, which was a comfortable walk townwards. The Mathematical Institute on St Giles, at which he attended courses, overlooked the annual fair which went back to medieval times, so all of this implied continuity and tradition, as Adriana remarked, unlike the bohemian yearnings of her mother.

William told her about the Dummett family next door, where the father was an academic and famous human rights lawyer. William's brother Paul had been inspired by that example to go into law, but the whole thing irritated Pop, their father, who existed in something of a perpetual mock-feud with the Dummetts.

'Pop used to say he could not understand why Paul would want to play in a household where they read that rubbishy Manchester Guardian,' William told Adriana. 'But Paul was stubborn and would retort: "Nothing rubbishy about Manchester," and spent even more time there.'

'Yes,' said Adriana, 'my mother read The Guardian and my father The Financial Times. No wonder I am so mixed up.'

'Nonshensh,' whispered William with some vaguely Northern lilt.

They lapsed into silence, looking at the lights glinting on the water.

1ØØ111   Dinner in the hotel restaurant met William's approval: the hotel provided traditional English food and boasted a fine carvery, which more than made up for the lack of modernist furnishings and fittings. The past isn't all bad, he mused to himself. Asthma aside, he felt in the peak of health and had to admit that he and Adriana blended in extremely well with the lavish setting and silver service. Ros had always been, well, a little loud perhaps, where Adriana brought out the nobleman in him, the centuries of breeding. Terrible! he quickly thought to himself. What am I saying? Am I so easily removed from my family life in Britannia Road as if it only existed as some distant memory? He was again shocked by this phenomenon, as he had been in Geneva. The two days with Adriana seemed to have created an entirely new life for him. He simply floated.

Later on there was music from the hotel ballroom, and they got up to dance.

'I knew on Lake Geneva that you were special, Professor Strange,' Adriana murmured. 'You danced in my rhythm, just instinctively. Maybe you can't sprint a mile, but you make me sing inside.' He smiled at her, unable to say anything; it was a slow number and he could see how the sun had caught her shoulders leaving white bands under the straps of her dress and bra. He could still feel the sun on his face in an odd way and again he felt marvellously alive. She pressed herself to him and murmured: 'Bill, you have never been a stranger to me. I had that feeling the first morning as I wandered into the breakfast area with my coffee in Geneva. Like I was coming home. What did you say, "Guido le Strange"?' – she pronounced it with a good French inflection – 'not a stranger at all but a guide.'

He shook his head. He was giddy with wine, with infatuation, and also with the sense of standing at the edge of an abyss. True he was ten years older than she, and true he had been the youngest professor ever appointed at Imperial. But what in all that could make him a guide to her? Was she dreaming? A guide? On the contrary: he felt wonderfully, blissfully, lost.

At midnight Adriana suddenly said: 'Let's walk by the lake again,' to which William agreed; they were both conscious that to lose time in sleep would be a waste. Before long they had wandered through the rear gardens of the hotel, onto the main street, and then turned off along the road by the shoreline. They passed the jetty where the ferry that plied the lake would stop during the day, past a marina, a wooded area, more marinas, and then to a place called Cockshott Point. They walked down to the sandy beach. The moon was up, and they sat looking low over the water.

'What's that?' asked William, pointing to a wooded shoreline opposite.

'That's Belle Isle,' Adriana replied. 'It has a beautiful circular eighteenth century house in it, still lived in today.'

She spoke softly, looking out over the dark water. William heard not a word of it as he had been suddenly gripped by a déjà vu even more acute than before. His ears throbbed as if massive engines were roaring nearby. He clutched his head and groaned.

'William, are you alright?' asked Adriana in alarm.

eleven

1Ø1ØØØ   The tyres of the old MG rolled to a crunching halt on
——————————the gravel of the Belsfield Hotel.

'Shall I sell the old bus then and buy you a
wartime's supply of soapflakes and ruby-red silk undies?' Peter asked,
recalling Barbara's parting shot of the previous week.

'Peter darling, that is hardly gallant,' replied Deirdre. 'You are
supposed to go out and discretely hunt sufficient bison to barter for said
items, and then present them to me. How can I possibly take your life
and joy from you?'

'You can't. They are called Sunderland Mark Threes. But I stand
downgraded as the cad I really am. It's Barbara's fault for putting such
images in the mind of a decent hard-working man. You should choose
your friends more carefully I fear.'

'Rot.'

Making up for his lapse over silk undies, Peter leapt from the
driving seat and strode gamely round to Deirdre's side. He pulled her up
and into his arms. They looked into each others' eyes.

'Peter, my love,' she whispered, 'we have had a day of pure
happiness. You and me on the lake. You must have rowed us miles. And
then that meal over in Windermere. How did you do it? I haven't seen
food like that for ages.'

'Barter,' said Peter promptly. 'Lots of dead bison.'

'Best I don't know,' she murmured, 'though I guess it all comes in
on the planes.'

'Best you don't know.'

They made their way to the bar and then brought their drinks over
to the bay window, from which they looked out over the sloping lawn to
the harbour and the expanse of Windermere, flanked on the right by the
pines of the mainland. Part of the hotel obscured what would have been

the northern tip of Belle Isle, a beauty spot Peter had rowed Deirdre to earlier in the day. 'The Curwens have owned the circular house on it since 1781, though with the war it's now empty,' Peter had informed Deirdre. 'One rich family making a fertile space into a pleasure-ground, living off the backs of the working poor. Instead, six or ten families could work that land and be beholden to nobody.'

'It's the way of the world,' murmured Deirdre, against which Peter had not wanted to purse any kind of argument – these were precious moments with her, the ebb and flow of talk better devoted to the inconsequential. Beyond all of this they were enfolded by the Cumbrian mountains, held safe for now against the tides of war.

The old hotel lounge was in poor repair, the windows kitted out with blackout blinds in a travesty of their original opulence. A broken chandelier hung from the ornate centre moulding, its little droplet bulbs long gone, while the wire leading to it had been cut and spliced onto a short length from which dangled a single naked one hundred watt bulb. This was the main source of night-time illumination apart from some dado-lights still in operation, and all of this, as Peter knew, was wired up to the mains board under the very tight control of building management. Only when 'Ecky' Turnbull, the superintendent, was satisfied that all the blackout panels were in place would the big old gang-switch go up: it was vital that the Germans believed the building to be a mostly mothballed grand hotel like so many others, and more important still that it did not lead them to Shorts. For now the occupants of the lounge had the pleasure of the long evening daylight, those wishing to read making best use of it by the windows.

Peter got out tobacco and pipe, filled it and lit up. Both were in a reflective mood, but slowly a grin spread across Deirdre's face. She leant forward.

'I *do* like the way that you fill your pipe,' she said. He just looked at her for a moment and then they both burst out laughing. Barbara materialised by their side.

'So what are you turtle-doves cackling over?' she asked amiably.

'You tell her,' said Peter looking out across the water – his attention was drawn to a flying boat just visible in the distance, circling so as to land at Shorts. He looked at his watch.

Deirdre explained: 'Barbara, dear, first time I was over at the factory I met Peter in the works canteen. One of his mates was egging him on to talk his usual nonsense. "Go on Peter, say that thing about how men and women fall in love differently." "Okay," said he, preening himself ...'

'Me? Preen? What are you talking about?' Peter interrupted in hurt tones.

'Shut up Peter. I want to hear it from the horse's mouth,' said Barbara. He was about to protest at that too, but Deirdre got in first.

'Peter preened himself, you know, by raising his chin like some feted thespian about to deliver a line from Othello, and he uttered the immortal words: "The difference between men and women is simple. A woman falls in love with a man by how he fills his pipe. A man falls in love with a woman by how she fills her jumper."'

Barbara grinned. She looked down at Peter pityingly, but thinking about it, she then said: 'Actually that's the first bit of sense I've heard from the old boy,' Sticking her chest out, she waggled her way to the bar, turning once to look over her shoulder with mock disdain at him.

'Can't you get that woman to stop flirting with me?' grumbled Peter.

'That's not flirting,' said Deirdre. 'That, for Barbara, is breathing. You wouldn't want to see her flirting.'

They watched as Barbara surveyed the sparsely-filled lounge and then walk purposefully over to Turnbull.

'The tormentor pitted against the untormentable,' commented Deirdre.

'I've heard her call him the "super Super",' offered Peter thoughtfully. 'She has an odd affection for the old boy.'

Barbara began pouring some special tirade of nonsense into the eardrums of old Ecky, who appeared as much affected by it as he might be by birdsong. He sat with arms folded, staring at the lake, barely tipping his head from time to time in minimum acknowledgement of Barbara's chatter.

'So, Peter, you know these things,' said Deirdre. 'What is the going rate for a chap to go upstairs at the Belsfield?'

'You don't know?' queried Peter, grinning.

'I'm not that sort of girl, Peter,' Deirdre retorted sharply.

'No, of course not,' said Peter hastily. He thought for a moment, 'Ecky can be bought, of course, but the price varies enormously depending on whether he likes you or not. For example, he likes Barbara enormously, though you wouldn't think it. But that's not the point. It's whether he likes the chap or not. If he likes you, well, I'd guess …'

'Yes?'

'Something around a bottle of Scotch, I reckon. It's quite a risk for him to take.'

Deirdre was silent for a while. Then she asked Peter quietly, 'So, do you know the price at which all men can be bought?' She looked at him askance.

Peter did not respond for a while, but eventually said: 'I know the breaking point of all the different metals I use on the boats and I can usually judge what it takes to buy a man. It's not so different a question, you see.'

'Thank God you don't work for the Germans,' responded Deirdre indignantly.

He just grunted at this, a smile on his lips.

1Ø1ØØ1   They were thoughtful again for a while as the light faded on the water. Deirdre spoke first. 'Peter, darling, one thing I can't understand. Why didn't you marry after the Great War? You had plenty to choose from. You have nineteen years on me, you know, something which Father is furious about.'

Peter winced at this. 'Eighteen and a half actually, but please don't remind me of it,' he said.

'I'm not the least bit bothered, Peter,' said Deirdre. 'Men of my own age are either out-and-out hedonists or they're accountants. But why didn't you marry and ruin my life?'

Peter looked at her for a moment, absorbing this. 'You sweetheart,' he acknowledged. He paused. 'Well, I suppose it rather divided us, men like me returning from the trenches,' he said. 'We saw the same horror, but some plunged straight back into marriage and children and family life. Others, like me, couldn't do it. It was a kind of iron in the soul I suppose – at least that is what some French philosopher calls it apparently, who also fought in the Great War. I saw the officer class send men to their deaths, over and over again. Some of them were brave enough, I don't deny it, the officers I mean. Some were cowards, so what. But the German privates were just like us, and I couldn't understand why the privates on both sides couldn't simply refuse to kill each other, and put their bayonets instead at the throats of the officer class, intent on perpetuating the rule of kings; this king, that king, who cares.'

'Socialist unpatriotic treason like that could get you hanged,' murmured Deirdre, her eyebrows raised in mock alarm. He just nodded and continued.

'Deirdre, I returned, badly injured, recovered over a couple of years, physically that is, but I brooded. I have nothing against your father personally, and I quite understand why he would be contemptuous of me. However I don't think he would show the same contempt for a man eighteen years older than you if he was a baronet. Anyhow I brooded and found the young women around me full of innocent life where I was full of horror and death. It has taken a very special woman indeed to, to … reach me, I suppose.'

It was her turn to acknowledge him, a sombre smile.

Peter reflected: Deirdre was serious about things, which made her impervious to tittle-tattle of the kind that would deter another woman of her background mixing with a man like him. He had first seen her at Shorts, elegant in her movements but captivating for him because she looked around the hangars and aircraft with real interest. He had followed her eyes and realised that she was reading what she saw with an almost masculine intelligence. But there was no doubt that the uniform, as his mind went back to it, was part of the appeal: the dress tunic has four heavy brass buttons down the front; one each for the breast pockets and one each for the side pockets. When you add this to the heavy fabric out of which the thing was stitched it weighed a considerable amount – as he knew from disencumbering her of it – slowing down her naturally mercurial movements, unlike the jumper. Actually the jumper did have the edge on it, he suddenly thought as his eyes glimpsed her breast swell slightly with an inbreath.

'Penny for your thoughts?' Deirdre was asking. He grinned, but his face set again rather quickly. She looked at him for a moment considering something else. Softly, she continued: 'Peter darling, I never asked how exactly you got that limp.'

A shadow passed over his face. 'Well, as you know, I enlisted at seventeen at the very end of the Great War. Shrapnel caused the limp itself, and I'm scarred from it, that's a fact. Not the wounds, they probably saved my life, because they took me out of the fighting. But seeing the eyes of a frightened young German, just my age. Everything was full of smoke and chaos and I heard a shell howl down; so did the German soldier. We happened to run in the same direction; we had no idea what we were doing, just sheer life-preserving terror takes over you know. He ran straight onto my mate's bayonet. I saw his eyes as he lay dying – then another shell whistled down, killed my mate and obliterated the German. I was hurled into a rain-filled crater with injuries to my leg and arms and I nearly drowned. I was barely conscious and almost completely unable to move my limbs to tread water or in some way stop my head from dipping below the surface. I was sure I would die, and had actually given up. So much water entered my lungs that the medical orderly who eventually pulled me out and pumped my chest thought he was wasting his time. But somehow I spluttered into life, retching and coughing out the filthy water – craters like that were full of the dead bodies of men and animals you know. Lucky, really, that I didn't get cholera or something like that. I passed out for a long time, woke in the field hospital and then got evacuated to the Royal Vic at Netley. They treated me for my injuries …'

Peter stared at the lake. He added softly: '… and for shellshock.' His eyes had darted to look keenly at Deirdre while he added this. She stiffened at the word. 'Yes,' he nodded, full of bitterness, 'I do wonder what your father thought of men like me.'

Deirdre looked at him with a sombre expression, without comment.

'Tell me what he says,' Peter demanded.

'Oh, it's all nonsense,' Deirdre said.

'Tell me!' he ordered, his face set.

She grimaced, thought for a moment and hesitantly replied: 'Father thought "shellshock" was made up to cover cowardice and malingering and hereditary weakness. There. That's his generation. He never supported the new hospitals or treatments.' Suddenly she took Peter's hand. 'I never believed Father on this, Peter, you must understand. Please tell me what happened at Netley. Were they kind to you? Did they help?'

'Yes, actually. I was lucky that the war was over by the time they had got my leg patched up and transferred me to the shellshock ward. There wasn't quite the same stigma after the fighting was over. I had a doctor who helped simply by talking with me. I wasn't mute like some of the others …'

Peter tailed off and Deirdre squeezed his hand.

He continued, with a little difficulty it seemed, haltingly: '… though I did have nightmares. The doctor had a brother whose farm was on the banks of the Medway, near Rochester. He arranged for me to work there after I was discharged, and it saved my life, the fields and the animals and the river – I suppose it was my yeoman ancestry that got rekindled in me. I was there five years during which time I introduced and worked on a lot of the new farm machinery, so, in the end, it was not such a big jump to take a job at Short Brothers nearby. When it got bombed at the start of the war I was transferred here. So five years farming and thirteen years at Shorts … it all went in a blur. Now I make the Sunderland deadlier by the day, and it kills young Germans like the one I saw.'

'It saves our boys,' Deirdre murmured, stroking Peter's hair.

'Yes,' he said with a wan smile. 'But if I was the Lord I would have made this place different.'

'Would you have made it with me in it?'

'Christ yes,' he replied.

'Don't blaspheme,' she grinned.

'If you had made it,' he asked, 'would we have made love last night for the first time?'

'Yes,' she said.

Deirdre looked out at the last of the sun glistening on Windermere.

'Winander's Mere,' she mused. 'Whoever Winander was, he knew it was beautiful. I guess you can't have the Mere without the other things, Peter. Like war. Without the war we would not have made love last night.'

There was a pause. Peter looked up, with a serious smile.

'Without the war, and I hate this, I would not have come to life again. I'm a man again, whatever people like your father say. I know that. I'm angry, but I arm the Sunderland: I build a kill-or-be-killed machine and it rules my life. But on a day like this I take my happiness as it is given to me.' Pause. 'We'll marry after the war, eh, girl?'

'Yes.'

'Yes?' he queried.

'Yes.'

'"Yes?" I just proposed to you after our first night together and you say "yes" just like that?'

'It's not "just like that". You can propose properly to me some time. But we both know we are meant for each other. It only takes a few weeks to know that.'

'And one night.'

'And one night,' she agreed.

'There is no point in getting married now, is there,' mused Peter. 'We'll be going all kinds of places.'

'I hope not. But no, now is a bad time. After the war. It can't be long now.'

They were silent again for a while, looking across the extensive lounge, filled with cigarette and pipe smoke, looking at a community shaped by its imbalanced and charged ratio between the sexes. Sitting at little tables were groups of women playing cards or chatting with each other, a few couples on their own like Peter and Deirdre, or a young male officer entertaining a whole group of hopefuls. The noise of chatter was homely; it spoke of people bound together by the purpose and uncertainty of war, of bonds forged across the leylines of ancient antipathies. Peter spotted Alasdair in one corner of the room and scowled.

'When people talk about the British class system, Deirdre, they completely forget about the yeomanry. That word just lives on in people's minds as meaning cavalry regiments that became the Territorials. Those people were mostly drawn from their officers' estates, and were anti-radical to a man. But the real British yeomanry, like my ancestors, were smallholders and industrialists, and they formed the backbone of the Industrial Revolution. They were free men, religious freethinkers, radicals, and equals of the landed gentry, but didn't live off the backs of others. They did not support the Establishment in any form.'

Deirdre nodded. 'Did you say that your family ran forges in Wales, or was it the West Country?' she asked.

'Yes,' said Peter, 'I am descended from Bristol ironmasters, and I suppose that is what drew me to engineering.'

'You should be called Smith, then, not Darby. I bet you know nothing about racehorses.'

Peter laughed. 'That would be "Derby" with an "e". But I don't mind Smith as a name at all,' he said. 'It's Smythe I can't stand.'

'Now, now,' said Deirdre gleefully looking across the room at the uniformed back of Alasdair.

1Ø1Ø1Ø   'I don't know much about your life either,' said Peter
_____   after a pause.

'Oh, Admiralty dad means it was all very predictable,' said Deirdre. 'Until the war of course. And then Bletchley Park was interesting. Look.' She turned to him. 'You can't tell me things, and I can't tell you things. We absolutely cannot, despite being lovers, isn't that right, Peter? You don't believe otherwise do you?'

'Of course not.'

'You see, I don't want to go back to Bletchley which is why my exams mean a lot to me. I want at least be at Marham so I can be involved in Sunderland oversight. That way we'll stay connected in our work.'

'And is your family related to de Havilland, the aircraft manufacturer? Some of the lads think you are.'

'No darling. You are thinking of Geoffrey de Havilland, with a "de" and two "l"s. We have no "de" and only one "l".'

'Still love you.'

'Even if I can't get you any engines?'

'We're going to get American engines. Which is something I can't tell you.'

'And I can't tell you that we have a top mathematician at Bletchley Park.'

'You don't have to. It's common knowledge. And Goering calls him a faggot, I hear.'

'Don't!'

'I know.'

Peter was thinking of something else.

'I do wish I could ask you more about Bletchley,' he said. 'Turing is one of the world's greatest mathematicians I understand. You know I ran into an odd thing, a queer mathematical thing the other day: the square root of minus one. The Admiralty has been pressing us to go AC in the boats' electrics ...'

'AC, darling?'

'Alternating current. As opposed to direct current, DC, which is what we use at the moment. We have to have specially adapted power tools and other equipment on board to use DC.'

'Oh.'

'Well, to do the phase calculations on AC, you have to use the square root of minus one. Mathematicians use the letter "i" for it, but electricians use "j".'

'Oh.'

'It got me to realise that a lot of my work involves mathematics: gunnery, navigation, torques, you name it. I'd love to mingle with real mathematicians.'

'You can't. At least, not at Bletchley. But why can't you use both AC and DC on the boats?'

'Oh then you'd have to have rectifiers and other complicated things. AC/DC would be good in the long run perhaps, but for now I'll stick to DC.'

Deirdre was thinking of other things.

'Will you come over tomorrow?' Peter asked, anticipating her.

'Yes. I have free time. I'll catch the bus and make the usual pretence at the gate. They all know me of course.'

'They love you Deirdre. Who wouldn't? I'm the luckiest man on earth.'

Barbara had finished her conversation with Ecky, who nodded his farewell to her, still with folded arms, still staring up the lake. Barbara saw that they were looking at her and waved to them. She blew a theatrical kiss at Ecky who turned to them and acknowledged their attention with the barest of nods.

'I had an odd childhood,' I suppose, said Deirdre after a while.

Peter looked at her with interest.

'We had an old Bentley which gradually fell to bits after the Great War. I was only eight when the war ended you know. Anyhow our groundsman, Barker, was also a good mechanic, so he persuaded Father to buy another Bentley of the same age, which he cannibalised to keep the first one going. I absolutely refused to play with dolls and learn sewing, and would sneak off to watch Barker work on the engine of the second machine. My mother was furious, but Father was tickled by it and encouraged me to learn all about motor cars under Barker's tutelage. I ground in a whole set of valves you know. Barker had been in service to our family since a boy, yet I slowly realised that he was every bit master of his own domain as Father was of his. And I got to learn the names of things: split pin, collet, piston, crankshaft, differential, all those things.'

'Do I remind you of Barker, then?' Peter asked.

Deirdre eyed him thoughtfully.

'No, actually. More of Father. You see, you are master of your domain, the Detail Shop, the main hangar, the men who work under you. Barker could have done all of that. But he would have floundered as to what direction to take. You and Father just know, by instinct, what to aim for. It's the pirate in you both.'

'Pirate? One of the Lords of the Admiralty, a pirate?'

'Oh yes,' Deirdre giggled, looking straight at Peter. 'The British navy is an exquisite machine, run on three principles: discipline, rum and piracy. You of all people should know that.'

Peter could think of no response to this nonsense. Instead he clasped her hand again and they sat in silence for a while, looking at the growing darkness on the lake as Ecky did, each to their own thoughts.

'Stout, Peter? G and T, Deirdre?' They were interrupted by a voice behind them. Turning, they saw a short heavily-built man with a scar on his forehead, unsmiling, holding a pint.

'Clarence, we are fine, thank you,' replied Peter. 'But do join us.'

The man sat down with a grunt at their table. 'The changewheel guard on the middle Colchester is loose,' he said. 'Someone could get hurt.'

'Damn,' said Peter, turning to him. 'I meant to fix it ages ago. I'll see to it when I get back.' He grinned. 'Clarence, I have just learned that

Deirdre can grind the valves in on a Bentley. Told you she was a talented girl.'

Clarence's eyebrows made a swift up and down movement; the ghost of a grin appeared on his face and then faded, but he made no comment. Deirdre frowned at them, unsure whether they were sharing a double entendre peculiar to the working classes.

1Ø1Ø11   Later that night Peter waved goodbye to Deirdre standing on the steps of the old hotel. It is a beautiful drive in the dark, he thought, the big round lamps at the front picking out hedges and the occasional small mammal darting across the road. He swung the deep-throated machine into the Shorts compound and showed his pass at the gate. He had not told Deirdre but he intended to go on a mission after her visit the next day: a Sunderland he had been re-arming was nearly ready and he was determined to watch every minute of its flight, whether fired on or not, to see what further developments to the general running and if possible the fighting power of the boat he could make. He couldn't do his job without these missions, but they had now become entirely clandestine. Peter drove his car through the factory site and past the Detail Shop to the edge of the compound where he had established his own workshop located discretely at the perimeter yet conveniently near the canteen. As he entered the building he swung a sign on the door so it said 'Do Not Disturb'. His face now set, he turned the lights on in the workshop, and despite the beer or two he had drunk with Deirdre and the loving mood they had been in, he pulled out a set of drawings. He had some details to finish off regarding Sunderland ordinance. He smiled to himself at a sudden memory. 'Angle pivot cleats!' What nonsense Deirdre and Barbara could talk, he thought, forgetting that this particular phrase was his own coinage, provoked by their banter.

Remembering something else, he got up to inspect one of the electric-powered lathes. Clarence had been right: the guard covering the gears at the back of the headstock was loose. He rectified this after searching out a replacement for which he machined a few parts using another lathe and a drill press, assembled it to his satisfaction on the Colchester, and then returned to his drawing board. He would not have noticed it but the smell of metal swarf and lubricating oil in his machine shop was marginally heightened after his labours.

Working into the small hours he finally packed up, turned the dim light on in the small adjacent room where his cot resided, and went back to place the rest of the workshop in darkness. The little room with a cot, pipe stove, a single gas ring, kettle and washbasin was his equivalent of the rural workers' 'bothy' – a small place for a man on his own devoted entirely to his work. Tomorrow afternoon he would not be on his own however as Deirdre would join him. And then in the night a flight to Pembroke dock where 210 Squadron was based – he would spend a few hours locked in the toilet followed by a fourteen hour sweep of the Atlantic.

The next evening, as Peter waited for Deirdre and made preparations for his flight, he was thoughtful. The last few days had shaken him up, there was no doubt. For one, he was in love. For two, he had told things to Deirdre that he had only barely thought himself. And, in a dream-like moment he had proposed marriage and she had accepted. In itself the casual exchange did not mean so much, he supposed, but it was her remark that he could propose properly one day – now *that* he could not forget. But what chance really, seriously, would he have after the war? Everything was turned upside down in these desperate days, but the old order would resume after hostilities ceased, that he was sure of. He would propose properly at the right time, but would she accept properly? We'll see, he thought. He could not hide his feelings from himself however: despite all such doubts he was elated. It was a glorious prospect.

But what else had he confided to her that had been a surprise to himself afterwards? Oh, the whole thing about shellshock. He had been really off-guard he supposed, with a picnic on Belle Island, a grand meal in Windermere, the sun on their skin, the memory of their love-making, and the long evening at the Belsfield. Deirdre had seeped into him, and he had told her. For years he had suffered horrible dreams and nightmare images of drowning in putrid corpse-soaked water, shells and bullets whistling around him. He didn't like to think about it as little things could set off a round of such nightmares again. But something else, too, something odd. Oh, yes. He had told her that he had come alive again with the return to war – that was a terrible thing to say. Perhaps he meant to say that he had come alive again because, due to the war, he had met Deirdre. But no, that was not right.

He looked at his books on mathematics – one on complex and imaginary numbers, another on the history of calculating machines – and remembered the evening classes in maths he had taken in order to secure the job at Short Brothers; then it had been geometry, trigonometry, algebra, the use of a slide rule and log tables. The books were on his desk but Deirdre had not commented on them last time she had been over as she did with the material things in his workshop.

He should have stuck to farming really, but Shorts appealed to him, the first factory in the world to make aircraft on a commercial basis. Right from the start he had worked on the flying boats, and loved the Empire model destined for the postal service. The Sunderland was the first military-use machine he worked on, based on the Empire, but he had not really seen then that he was slowly drifting back to the armed services, back to where his nightmares had begun. His journey was made complete last year when the government nationalised the company: that placed him now under direct Admiralty command. It nagged him. He was now, in effect, an officer of His Majesty's Armed Forces, commanding a dozen men, even if they be engineers.

And he felt wonderful.

The affair with Deirdre, he had to reluctantly admit to himself, was the effect of his rejuvenation, not the cause.

twelve

1Ø11ØØ   Deirdre had been. His mind was full of images of her
_____ naked, lying on her front on the bed propped on her
hands, the light falling from the murky skylight onto her
beautiful back and inviting rear, as she watched him deftly light the
stove and make tea for them. Her uniform had been folded neatly over
the back of a simple chair, in reverse order of its removal. They had
talked again about marriage, return to civilian duties, the endless casualty
listings, friends gone. She had complained how Peter always played the
clown at the Belsfield.

'Barbara never sees the real you,' she said, frowning. He drew on
his pipe and looked at her. She told him: 'That first time I came into the
main hangar, we walked from the canteen into the Detail Shop, I think,
but I wasn't prepared for the sheer scale of it. You told me the hangar
itself was the largest single-span structure in the country. And the size of
the flying boats. I was staggered. It truly felt what it is to be modern:
wood and canvas giving way to shiny metal and wires. Steel and
electricity, the latest technology. Or aluminium as you tell me, and other
alloys, all pushing aside those natural things we used to make our homes
and carriages with. It was so odd, too, to look at the nearly finished one
and see how it was half boat and half plane, an oddly shocking
invention, it goes against nature in every way. Almost obscene.' Peter
winced, but she did not notice. 'Are we now so beyond nature? Are we
to leave the earth and wood and wool behind? Look at my nylons.' They
were stretched out with the rest of her underwear on the chair, worn by
Deirdre for special occasions and a mark of her good connections. Or
her father's.

'I can't usually take my eyes off them,' he grinned.

'They are completely *artificial*,' she persisted, thinking back again.
'And you showed me round the inside of a half built boat, those ribs

made not of bone, like Jonah in the whale, but out of more metal. But that wasn't the main thing. It wasn't so much that you were in your element, all that metal and wires, but that the men all looked to you in a certain way. I knew then that you could have risen to who knows what rank. Or perhaps you don't want to.' She paused, and then added: 'Barbara doesn't know this side of you.'

Peter grinned at this, but Deirdre now pursued a different theme.

'What's it like for war to start again?' she asked. 'What was it like to see all those fine words about the war to end all wars, all those fine words about the new peace, the new world order, the League of Nations; what was it like to hear all that *tripe*?'

Peter was taken aback at the anger in her voice; she had expressed a sentiment he always thought and rarely spoke, though held with the same strength of feeling. He just stared at her. Finally he said in a quiet voice: 'It's uncanny how you know my inner thoughts ...' He looked down.

She stared at him. 'I see it in your eyes sometimes,' she said. 'But it's nothing uncanny. All the serving men of your age must go through this, not to mention the women caught up in the beastly Great War.'

'Of course,' he said. 'We came back in a state of shock. We couldn't believe in anything you see.' He looked into her eyes briefly and away again. 'And then it started all over.' He paused. 'I saw a chain of command,' he continued slowly after a while, 'that was absolutely rotten. I don't mean fools like Smythe, but decent bright chaps, who had been trained in their public schools and at Sandhurst, full of courage and capable leadership, but all for what? For the stupidity of an idiotic idea. Same on the other side of course. Wave after wave of privates, led by these perfectly decent chaps, men in their thousands turned into a muddy, bloody pulp.'

Peter could not continue. He was shaking. He fumbled for his pipe, filled and lit it.

'We've been over this, but you are right, Deirdre, absolutely right, to ask me what I felt as I read the news about Hitler, the slow creep to war, and then Churchill's announcement. I wished the Great War had killed me physically, because it bloody well killed me inside. I'm a hollow shell, really, can't you see that? Left to linger for no purpose, until the next round.' He shook his head. 'Oh, I'm sorry darling. We are having such a wonderful time together. You are the first piece of meaning to come into my life, but some bloody German bomb, bullet, shrapnel, flame-thrower or any bloody disgusting way to kill a man or woman can end it at any moment. The Medway area was bombed because of Shorts;

it's only a matter of time before German bombers reach here. I can never forget that. And I hate it that war has galvanised me into real activity where the farming was just a kind of amiable persistence.'

He broke off and shook his head again.

'You shouldn't have started me,' he said.

'Sorry,' said Deirdre. She paused.

'I was too young to be directly touched by the Great War,' she began after a while. 'But it warped my father. And he warped me. I'm simply telling the truth Peter. So, really, I'm just as much a product of it as you are. That's what brings us close: we despise the very system that lets war happen, so we have become mavericks in our own way.'

Peter looked at her. 'Is yours to marry beneath you?'

'Don't!' shouted Deirdre. 'Don't you dare say such a thing!'

They stared at each other, she naked, he half-dressed, pulling on his pipe. Slowly, he took it out of his mouth. 'God, I love you,' he said, breaking the silence.

Slowly – very slowly – a smile appeared on Deirdre's face.

'Come here and prove it Captain,' she murmured.

Much later he had casually mentioned that he was flying out in the early hours to Pembroke Dock. Deirdre was downcast and angry as she absorbed the news. She had to return to the Belsfield.

'You are not only risking your life and the work you do here, as your CO knows, and which is why you never get permission for these trips, but you risk *our* future.'

He did not miss the 'our'. He simply said: 'Darling, I know. But I can't do my job without seeing the boats in action. The pen-pushers don't understand. Engineers don't make drawings and hand them over to skivvies; they have to be with the machine, *in* it, in the crucial moments. Nothing I have achieved here was possible without the continuous flights.'

'*You* don't understand!' she shouted bitterly at him. 'If you are killed, what happens to me now? You waited twenty years, but I feel that I have waited just as long. You will never understand how the interminable procession of family-approved suitors – all very discretely presented to me of course – drove me to despair. To permanent cynicism, sarcasm, aloofness. I was old before my time. You have changed all that at a stroke, you know, whatever you say about your own inner emptiness. I couldn't bear to lose you, having found you now. And if you are court-martialled it's almost worse.'

He stared at her, taken aback. 'How can you say that?' he demanded. 'How can you say that being court-martialled is worse than death?'

She just shook her head, unable to explain herself.

'Darling ...' he softened. 'I keep telling you. In war the only way a woman can keep sane is to say this to herself, over and over: "all men are the same."'

'No!' she cried. 'I'm not like Barbara! We are meant to be together: you and I! Not just someone and I! Not just you and someone!'

She is serious about me, thought Peter, staring at her. My God, could we be together after this horrible mess is over? Could we? With a blue-blooded Admiralty father who hates me? How on earth would he consent to our marriage?

1Ø11Ø1 Some hours after Deirdre had left Clarence knocked discretely and entered the workshop in the evening dusk.

'Peter, will it be an all day trip tomorrow?' he asked.

'Should be a standard run. I'll get a lift back from Portland with Frank Edwards to arrive in the dark; I'll need you in the boat moored at the end of Old Hall Road. If I'm not there at midnight, come back again at four.'

'Sure thing, Peter. And I'll get some turning done in the day on the middle lathe; that way I can make excuses for you if anyone asks.'

'I sure appreciate all this, Clarence. By the way I fixed the changewheel guard on the electric Colchester. I found a proper cast iron one, better than that wandy tinplate. It didn't need much bodging. But it's not much sleep for you tomorrow night.'

'Oh, I was born a night watchman. I learned it in the trenches like you, and to be on the lake at night, well, that is a pleasure for me.'

Peter looked at his sombre workmate. Aside from Peter few could extract so many words at a time from Clarence: Peter could trust him with his life. They had passed through Netley together, in a ward full of mute faces, shattered minds, and the staring wreckages of men who did not want to see, hear, smell, taste or touch anything ever again. No mere prison can do this to a man.

In the early hours a crewman knocked softly on Peter's workshop door: it was his old friend, airman Arthur Bainbridge; they clapped each other on the back. Slipping out with minimum noise, and ensuring again that the 'Do not Disturb' sign was clearly visible, Peter locked the door with care. He slung his pack over one shoulder and walked around the makeshift factory's perimeter, up to the jetty not far from the slipway that took the huge craft onto the lake. The great Sunderland rocked slowly on the calm water, picked out by the moon; it had been launched from the main hanger earlier in the day and had taken on its crew not long ago. The boots of Peter and Arthur clacked on the old boards; the height was just right for a short jump through the port front door. They were greeted by Jeremy Sopel, the navigator, who introduced Peter to two crew members making preparations in the bow to lift anchor.

'This is Gary Smithson, bomb aimer and photographer on the flight,' said Jeremy, 'and this is Andrew White, who is our radio operator and doubles up on the waist guns as needed.'

Peter shook hands with them in turn.

'Come on through,' invited Jeremy, 'and meet the others.'

They walked from the bow door past the little gun stack and down the few steps to the ward room. Here Peter was introduced to Eric Brantham, the port side gunner, and Ambrose Marr, the forward gunner. They were new to Peter, though he had flown before with Mike Westlake, the rear gunner and cook. He shook hands all round.

'Good to see you again Westy,' said Peter.

Taking the steps from the galley kitchen up to the top deck he was ushered into the cockpit to meet the pilot, Captain Richard 'Rick' Tosey, who Peter had not met before. Eric Brantham followed them up. It was Arthur's job as usual to make the delicate negotiations with the captain that resulted in agreement to take Peter on board. Given the risk this entailed, Peter was especially courteous in his greetings to Tosey. The second pilot was Dave Grundisburgh, known to the men as 'Grundy' – he was also their qualified first-aider. Tosey told Peter that they would be single-crewing on this particular mission, but had heard that he could double as navigator as well as flight engineer.

'You bet. I can relieve almost anyone but captain.'

'It shouldn't be a long stop at Pembroke,' said Tosey as he started the ignition sequence.

'Long enough for a piss?' asked Peter. They all laughed.

'We take on fuel and depth charges, that's all, and then we are straight off.'

'We remind passengers to refrain from using the toilet in the station,' intoned Eric, wagging a finger at Peter. Their laughter was drowned in the staggered roar of the four huge Pegasus engines powering up, and before long they were gaining speed on the dark waters of Winander's Mere.

As planned, they arrived at Pembroke an hour before dawn for arming and refuelling. Peter locked himself in the toilet situated in the bow, but none of the Coastal Command outfitters even tried the handle. He was able to discretely watch through the porthole as the starboard bombs were loaded, and then changed into shorts: it could get hot in the plane, particularly in the kitchen. He shaved to pass more time. After the hour was up there was a knock and Arthur whispered to him: 'Some delay, sorry old chap. There's intelligence coming in of a sighting we are to follow up; the reconnaissance photos have to be developed. Could be some hours. Want some breakfast in there?'

'Sure do, Arthur,' said Peter brightly, but was disappointed to be cooped up for a while yet, and it was far from the ideal spot for a meal. It was nearly ten before the external doors were finally slammed shut and he was able to emerge, legs stiff from lack of movement. The big engines sprang into life again as Peter climbed the forward steps to join the captain. He looked out to sea for a glorious take-off from Pembroke Dock, on a July day over a calm hazy Atlantic.

For the first part of the flight the crew had no need for Peter to relieve them in navigation or engineering, so he helped wash up in the galley kitchen, much of which he had helped design. It was in the lower part of the boat with aluminium steps down to it, punctured with large weight-saving holes, all of which gave the characteristic feel to the cramped quarters throughout the boat. Mugs hung on special hooks that Peter had made up to pass through smaller circular holes in the longitudinal struts, while another set of special fittings he had designed allowed a standard British Home Stores plate rack to fit in over the sink and allow it to drain directly into it via a hole he had drilled. A simple curved sheet of polished aluminium served as the splash-tray for cooking, placed between the Primus stove and the bulwark, and which was kept immaculately grease-free, cleaned with the enthusiasm of those needing to pass much time.

The grey Atlantic horizon was visible from the two portholes by the sink as Peter later helped prepare the standard egg, bacon and chips for a hefty lunch.

'Good grub,' one of them commented as a shift including Peter, Eric, Ambrose, and Andrew sat down for their meal in the ward room. Eric suddenly said: ''Ere, that reminds me. We had a couple of Indian chaps in the regiment for a while. When they liked the food they would say "Posh nosh", you know how they take English words and say it in their lingo.' He had made a reasonably good stab at the dip-rise inflection on each syllable. 'Then,' he continued, 'they started adding

"Top notch" in front of it so it became "top notch, posh nosh".' Eric's accent was pretty good and caused much mirth. 'And *then*,' he added, 'they finished off with "tip top".'

'Tip top, top notch, posh nosh,' someone ventured in a laboured fashion with no attempt at the lilt.

'That's it!' said Eric triumphantly, to a chorus of attempts at pronouncing it.

Much tea was drunk through the day, all of which helped puncture the tedium of such missions; teatime was however properly marked with a small cake and sandwich to accompany the national beverage. Eric repeated his 'posh nosh' story upstairs, and before long the whole boat had heard it.

'Steak and kidney pie, mash and baked beans for supper,' announced Peter who had by now metamorphosed into honorary auxiliary cook. Food was an eternally interesting subject on these flights.

'Good grub,' someone commented again, which set off a new round of attempts at 'Tip top, top notch, posh nosh.'

'I know,' said Tosey suddenly, in his noticeably upper-class accent. 'Let's have a competition. Everyone has just one go at saying it, and we give it a mark out of ten. Nought for completely hopeless, five for getting the words right and ten for getting the words right with a good Indian accent. Okay?'

'What's the prize, Rick?' demanded Eric.

'Double baked beans for supper,' replied the captain without hesitation. 'Grundy, take the controls, I'll go round the boat.'

'You're on,' came a chorus of voices.

'Peter first.'

'Oh. Okay,' said Peter. He cleared his throat and made a stab at it, stumbling immediately over the repeated word 'top'.

'Awful,' cried Eric.

'Nought out of ten for Peter,' declared the captain smartly. 'Gary, you next.'

In the end, although the captain himself was awarded a seven by Arthur and Andrew, Ambrose Marr easily won with a ten for his perfect rapid-fire lilt.

'Are you a musician?' asked a nettled Peter, to which Ambrose nodded, grinning.

'There you go. Musicians often have an ear for languages.'

'What instrument do you play?' Eric asked.

'He plays the fool,' somebody mumbled.

'The B sharp origami, actually,' said Ambrose quietly, to bemused looks from the crew and laughter from Peter and the captain.

Somebody said: 'Don't he mean okarina?'

'Doesn't know his C from his B sharp,' muttered another, perhaps someone who actually did play a musical instrument.

Hours passed and Peter wrote and drew in his little notebook; they flew through some cloud and rain, and the seas looked rougher now; it was getting into late afternoon. Peter allowed Jeremy Sopel to catch some sleep by taking over at the small navigator's bench – he was expert with the tables – and scanned the photographs that they had been delayed over, perused intelligence reports, made more calculations, looked over maps and came to a conclusion. Getting up to take the few steps into the cockpit, he tapped Tosey on the shoulder and quietly agreed with the captain a small change of course, one which Grundisburgh nodded agreement to.

At other times he took over watch duty, which was hard on the eyes, especially for a man of his age. Peter had pushed for the early adoption of the new Polaroids to reduce eye strain on the long H-pattern sweeps the Sunderlands made in search of their prey. Once again it had been a battle with the pen-pushers who had no conception of how sunlight reflecting off the sea for hours on end hurts human eyes, and with an Admiralty which liked to adopt a 'not invented here' approach to American technology. Albatrosses have eyes evolved for hours of scanning the ocean, he argued with them; we don't.

The flight was not tedious for Peter, as all aspects of the boat's running interested him, from the bacon to the bombs. He had a keen ear for every slight variation in engine sound and thus far the roar of the four engines had been constant, along with the characteristic harmonics set up by their marginally different speeds. They performed flawlessly, a background lullaby of comfort for an engineering mind. Hence he was not prepared as the klaxon startled the wits out of him: a sighting. It was average seas, average light from intermittent cloud cover, utterly indistinguishable from a million other grid points over the Atlantic but there it was: a U-boat shadow. It must be charging its batteries at snorkel depth. The men crowded around the side windows in the cockpit, shaking their heads; intelligence about German activity had been right after all, and Peter's small change of course had taken them to it.

'Arthur, Peter: bomb loading!' This was the shouted command from Tosey, in response to which the two men ran to the bomb room, dropped the large windows under the wings – Arthur the port and Peter the starboard – and then winched out the eight depth charges for the first attack. The two men leant out of the port window to look at their target.

Would the sub dive? No. They all knew that German tactics had switched not long back, which meant that a scrap was on. Admiral Doenitz had ordered his U-boat captains to now turn and face the Sunderland attacks, while in turn his British counterpart declared the Sunderlands capable enough to take them on. Only one of the war machines would survive this, and probably only one band of men would live.

'Good,' thought Peter grimly, though suddenly conscious of Deirdre's anxieties, a consideration he had not faced before. But the chance to see the weapons in action was what he had been hoping for: it meant far more than possible improvements to the kitchen. The Sunderland was the first of its kind to be fitted with power-operated gun turrets, and every second of observing these in action was worth hours at the drawing-board. He suddenly remembered another of Deirdre's remarks, about the Sunderland being obscene. He scowled. It might be an obscenity, but it was our obscenity against their obscenity, and theirs had caused death by drowning for hundreds of thousands of Allies. He shuddered.

1Ø111Ø The U-boat had spotted them and was making a right turn on the surface of the choppy sea as it rose to attack position, black smoke pouring from its exhausts showing the diesels at full pitch. Tosey shouted that it was a Type VIIB, either U-101 or U-102, as in the photographs. They could see the conning tower hatch slam open, still dripping with brine, and the crew rushing to man the single 2cm anti-aircraft gun just aft of it. The Sunderland was in no danger from the massive 88mm deck gun unless very low. 'Single Flak!' shouted Tosey to Ambrose Marr, who nodded and ran down the steps to the bow, crouched low in the front compartment and hauled himself into the turret. Gary Smithson followed him to the front of the boat just below Ambrose, where he opened the bomb-aiming hatch and readied his equipment. He had to lie awkwardly under the turret, the feet of Ambrose braced against two small platforms either side of him. From now on all communication was via their headsets, plugged into the sockets at their stations; leather straps were tightened, wires carefully routed so as not to interfere with their varied duties, and expressions set. Cropped hair and freshly shaven faces meant that their individualities and even their masculinities were strangely muted by their tight-fitting leather caps and bulbous ear pieces. They were now umbilically joined to their machine and to each other.

Peter was relieved about the guns: the Germans had been experimenting with up to four double-barrelled anti-aircraft guns crammed into the same small platform by the conning tower. Not on this sub however. The Sunderland had already passed by and turned sharply to circle back; Gary in the rear turret had opened fire on the conning tower as they had passed, in the hope of doing some damage to the doors and the Flak gun.

Peter had to admit he loved this. The Sunderland was remarkably agile for its size and in a famous battle in 1943 one had destroyed all but two Junker-88s out of an eight-plane attack. As Tosey squared up the flying boat to release their first round of bombs, Peter grinned tightly: they were equipped with new depth gauges, nothing to do with him, but a welcome development in ordinance passed down from the Admiralty research boffins. Peter also noted that Tosey knew what he was doing because he had chosen a path that placed the hazy sun behind them. It was now a duel: the deadly 2cm rounds from the single Flak gun pitted against twin 7.7mm Brownings in Ambrose's hands. They began the pass in an arc that would line them up for the level approach needed for bomb aiming. The German fired first but Ambrose remained calm, waiting until he was a little closer; then he opened up and hit the German gunner in the first burst. The dead sailor was immediately replaced with another man who didn't flinch at Ambrose's continued fusillade. The return fire now got closer; they could hear the rounds whistle past; then Peter heard a scream from Ambrose and the sound of shattering Perspex and other direct hits below. But Ambrose continued firing and the second German was silenced. A third rushed from the conning tower door but was hit before he could start firing. Eric had gone forward to see how badly Ambrose was hurt, while Captain Tosey cried 'bombs away!' Dave Grundisburgh left him to it to drop down and see what first aid would be needed for the injured Welshman; in the meantime the plane turned and climbed, but looking back it was clear that the charges had missed their target, they were timed wrong. Gary called up to say that it was first time with the new depth gauges and he now understood them properly: the bombs had detonated too deep in the water but he would get it right on the second pass. Peter and Arthur filled the racks with the second set of eight bombs, a back-breaking task, though once mounted at ceiling height winching them into position was easy enough. In the tense tight turn the timings were recalculated, while Eric shouted that the German gun had been re-manned and to expect more flak. But as they approached no fire came: Ambrose's original hail of bullets must have disabled the gun.

Grundisburgh had manoeuvred Ambrose down to a cot in the mid-section and examined him as Eric ran by to take his place. 'It's just a leg wound,' Grundisburgh called up. Eric was quickly able to continue discouraging fire from the damaged turret while Captain Tosey called 'bombs away' a second time and they dropped off in textbook order. He then asked for status reports on the boat, to which Eric and Gary shouted that there was only minor damage to the front of the Sunderland, and no casualties apart from Ambrose, while Gary Smithson at his bomb-aiming post had been saved from a bullet that had pierced the hull; it had been stopped by the anchor of all things. Then came the explosions that spelled the end of the submarine: the second round of blasts was perfectly placed. The charges cut into the sides of the vessel, setting off the German ordinance and creating a massive explosion – it cut the U-boat in two: the longer section with the engines and conning tower tipping to the rear so that the mangled hull rose up out of the water line as the engines went down at the back. The front section slid below the waters in a boiling of foam and oil; the few screams from injured submariners quickly subsided; then only dead bodies could be seen tossed around in the churning waters, some drifting into pools of burning fuel. A further explosion from the sinking bow caused parts of it to be hurled into the air while the rear listed and rolled a little. It stabilised in that precarious position.

A solo kill! And no sign of Junker support; it had been pure luck. And much food for Peter's engineering mind: the rear gun turret was still a little clumsy in operation as it had strafed the conning tower of the sub. The front turret needed better protection, that was clear: a wounded man was a personal affront to him. He yanked the headphone jack out of its socket in the bomb room and went to take a look, but the turret was not however his immediate concern: it was the water line. Had any bullets made holes big enough to force a mayday landing back at Portland harbour? His quick inspection of the prow and the hull from the floor hatches showed only minor damage however. As Gary's job was done at the bomb-aiming hatch he had returned to the waist gun position to photograph the sinking sub and Peter took his place at the hatch between Eric's legs to get a brief look downwards. As the plane turned he got up awkwardly and ran down and through to the kitchen where he could open the centre hatch to maintain his view. He was in time to hear one of the men shout something. He plugged his headset in.

'Hey, is that an officer on the conning deck?' Westy called from the rear of the plane.

Peter stared at a group of men, perhaps officers, who had emerged from the conning tower onto the small deck with its conical railings. One nearly fell on the steeply sloped surface, saving himself by grabbing hold of the railings and relinquishing what seemed to be a sidearm.

'Is that a white flag?' shouted Eric suddenly from the front turret as the boat turned full circle to view their kill, Peter crossing the kitchen to get a view from the opposite hatch, plugging and unplugging his headset as he went.

'Yes,' said Tosey from the cockpit.

'Trap! It's a trap,' Eric insisted from the front. 'They may still have an intact gun, and want us to come in.'

'What about the deck gun?' asked Westy.

'It takes a team of five to work it,' answered Tosey who was taking the boat down for a good look.

'But it might have a shell in it,' objected Eric. 'Just one of those shells would completely obliterate a Sunderland. We shouldn't get any lower.'

Warily they turned again to pass by the side and take a closer look. They could clearly see a group of officers, one of which held a white flag and waved it purposefully. Peter ran back to the bomb hatch again for a better look downwards as they passed.

'This is a trap,' said Eric. 'They are more likely to scuttle. What's the captain think he's doing?'

At that moment Peter heard a faint shot and saw a scuffle within the group. The officer holding the white flag had shot another one; perhaps they were arguing over the humiliation of surrender. Then there was another explosion from within the sub and it began to list further. Two of the men on deck slipped into the water, while another shot rang out and the officer with the flag lurched sideways, apparently hit in the shoulder. Another officer shot at him, but as the sub lurched further over he disappeared into the waves. Only the surrendering German was left.

1Ø1111
_____

'We have to go in,' said Peter suddenly, turning out of the gale at the bomb hatch. 'Doenitz has been complaining for years that his officers leak intelligence to us. This is our big chance to capture one.'

'Out of the question Peter!' Tosey retorted sharply. 'We have strict orders to take no prisoners, as you well know. Every time we set a boat down on seas like this we risk an entire Sunderland. We do it for our own, not theirs.'

'You don't get it! One boat and ten crew against tens of thousand of sailors lost? Who knows what intelligence this officer has.'

'But he's wounded, he might not make it back.'

'It's all worth the risk, damn it. A single serious piece of intelligence could change the whole Atlantic for us.'

There were murmurings of support from some of the men. Grundy rejoined the crew in the cockpit to take over from Tosey again.

'Crazy idea,' commented Eric. 'Not worth risking for any intelligence. What does Intelligence do anyway?'

'No, no,' said Peter rapidly. 'Don't underestimate what they are doing at Bletchley. And how would we have got a kill today if the Intelligence boys hadn't turned round those photos for us?'

'You're mad, you are,' said Eric.

'Listen,' Peter insisted. 'There are around four hundred Allied vessels on the Atlantic at any one time, that's forty thousand men. The U-boats are killing over twenty percent of our sailors every year. Do you get it? That's twenty thousand lives! We could save all of them by risking ten. Did you learn maths at school?'

'Oh, there's no need to be sarky,' Eric replied with feeling.

Tosey was now taking this seriously. He turned to his co-pilot.

'Grundy, what do you think?'

Dave Grundisburgh was keeping the boat in a tight circle, eyeing the deck gun all the time. 'I don't know,' he said shaking his head. 'Peter has a good case. I know it's a bit rough down there, but I reckon we can at least take a look. Nobody has to know that we went to have a look, do they?'

'Andrew,' said Tosey. 'Any radio from the sub?'

'I scanned all the frequencies. Nothing went out as far as I know.'

Neither war machine would use outgoing radio if they could help it: their first priority was not to betray their positions, that is until capture or destruction was likely. Presumably the strike that crippled the sub also knocked out the radio. Or its operators.

'Could still be Junkers around,' said Arthur, thinking ahead.

'There's always a small chance,' said Tosey, 'but we have enough top guns to deal with that possibility. Actually, Peter, is there any reason why the front turret can't fire upwards? Any damage to the mountings or hydraulic lines?'

'The guns are fine,' said Peter. 'There is very little risk in going down.'

There were more murmurings of support for this. Suddenly Tosey said: 'Peter's right. I wouldn't have anticipated this in a million years, but I say we go in. There is one living German down there as far as we can see, and I agree that the big guns are out for the count. At worst he has a pistol, but we can cover him many times over. He could know a lot. A hell of a lot. And it looks like he wants to tell us, or to defect, or who knows. He's worth the risk I say. Are you with me boys?'

There was a chorus of assent; only Eric muttered something about a fool's errand under his breath.

Arthur Bainbridge raised a different issue. 'We've got holes in the hull lads, have you all forgotten?'

Peter overrode him, speaking rapidly: 'The bullet holes are small and all above the water line as far as I can see. Even if the keel took a few which I missed the bilge pumps can easily deal with them.'

That silenced what last objections remained, so Tosey and Grundy brought the boat round in a big circle and then began the descent. But something wasn't quite right.

'The rear flaps feels sticky!' Tosey shouted. 'Go and check the damage again.' It was too late, they made a skewed descent, the great craft rocking first port and then starboard.

'We're going in too fast!' shouted Eric from below.

'The sea's too rough!' shouted Arthur.

'Watch out for the Flak gun,' warned Gary, but Peter called out from his vantage point in the kitchen: 'It's been disabled, look, it stands askew on its mounts.'

'Could still be fired,' argued Gary, so they all concentrated on the injured German. Andrew White had him in his machine-gun sights from the starboard gun hatch. 'I've got him covered,' he shouted.

The last moments of a descent of the Sunderland are crucial: if the water is too smooth it makes accurate estimates of height difficult, while if the water is too rough it risks damage to the boat. As side gunners it was Eric's or Andrew's job to shout depth estimates from their hatches, which Andrew had no difficulty doing in this descent. It was the size of the waves that presented the real danger. The boat's left float skimmed the top of the first wave, slewing them to port a little as they flew over the trough ahead of the next peak. Tosey corrected as best he could so that they hit this wave head on, the keel and both floats punching deep into the crest. The noise of the impact was deafening but in the end the weight of the great machine prevented it from pitching up more than a few degrees. With an almighty smack they came into full contact with the water on the swell of the next wave, rising up with it and falling to rest on the other side, facing away from the submarine. Mike Westlake in the rear shouted 'all clear' as Tosey cut the starboard engines and pulled the vessel round.

Peter returned to peer out through the bomb-aiming hatch; Eric looked through the cracked front turret Perspex; while the rest gathered in the cockpit to survey the wreckage of the submarine, rising and falling just a few hundred yards from them.

'It could still be a trap,' muttered Eric.

'Okay, go in slowly,' said Peter.

Tosey edged the craft towards the German U-boat. Each new wave revealed more floating wreckage, pools of oil, and some burning pockets of marine diesel; they also revealed corpses. None of the quarrelling officers had survived except the man on deck.

'No living sailors in the water?' asked Sopel.

Peter looked intently. 'Doesn't look like it,' he said. The flying boat had two life-rafts and it was an unofficial tradition to drop one for enemy submariners, if there were survivors.

'The blast must have knocked their brains out,' Peter muttered.

'What do you mean?' Eric asked.

'Not the depth charges,' said Peter. 'It would have been the shockwaves from their own munitions exploding. Tosey hit them at their deadliest point.'

'Top marks to the captain,' said Eric.

'Poor bastards,' said Dave Grundisburgh.

'What's the Kraut up to?' asked Eric suddenly.

'Signalling,' said Peter curtly, and then to the radio operator: 'Andrew, can you take this down?'

The German officer was clearly visible to them on the deck, and began to signal using open hand and closed fist.

'Get this down,' said Peter. 'Dot, dot, dot, dash, dash, dot …' After an agonised pause as Andrew pencilled in the letters, he spelled it out.

'e-n-i-g-m-t stop t-p-r-i-n-g stop.'

'What?' asked Dave.

'Ker-ist!' exploded Peter. 'The "t" is close to "a" in Morse: he missed a dot. The "p" isn't close to a "u" but he must have got confused. Those two words can only be "Enigma" and "Turing". The German wants to pass on intelligence!'

'Well, what do you know,' said Eric.

'What?' retorted Peter, beside himself. 'It's the fucking buggering jackpot, that's what!"

He stared wildly at the German across the water and reiterated: "Fucking buggering *buggering* jackpot!" He said: 'Andrew, can you signal back: "what do you want", no just "what want, question mark"?'

Andrew reached for the forward signalling light and sent the message. After a pause the officer, now close enough so that the blood from his injury and the pain in his face was visible, answered, again in mangled Morse. Between Peter, Andrew and Jeremy they worked it out: 'Speak only to Turing.'

Peter repeated himself: '"Speak only to Turing"? See? Fucking jackpot! We could have intelligence here that would change fucking everything!'

'Okay, calm down Peter, calm down,' said Tosey. 'We still have to get him off what is effectively a live bomb or vortex-making machine and take off in rough seas.'

'Ooh, "vortex-making machine",' mocked Eric.

'Shut up, Eric,' said Dave sharply. 'Rick's right.'

'Rick,' said Peter urgently. 'We could go in backwards. At the first sign of trouble we set full forward power on the props. Vari-pitch propellers can reverse in less than a few seconds, but a turn takes longer.'

'Makes sense,' Tosey acknowledged, sending Andrew White to the starboard gun hatch and Mike Westlake to the rear gun to cover them. Peter unplugged himself again and ran as best he could along to the rear to join Mike. He shouted instructions to Tosey as the boat turned again and began to edge backwards towards the side of the sub. They manoeuvred a little to starboard to a safe distance from the hull, while still leaving a fast course for exit if needed. It was a risky operation in the heaving swell, in what were now overcast conditions, navigating past a patch of burning oil. The German was watching them keenly – he raised his hands in a gesture of surrender, and then slowly lowered one hand to withdraw a pistol from its holster by his side and throw it into the sea, raising his hands again.

'He could still have a hidden weapon,' cautioned Eric.

'Prepare the life-raft!' shouted Tosey, just as another explosion from the rear of the U-boat rocked it, causing the officer to grip the railings with all his strength. Smithson had opened the port door and he and Sopel were looking across the short stretch of water to the stricken German vessel.

'No!' said Peter suddenly from where he now stood at the port waist hatch. 'It'll take too long. And Eric is right that we are at risk near the sub.' He tore off his headset, took off his shirt and shoes and beckoned to Mike Westlake, returning from the rear. 'Westy! Pass me that life harness.'

In a few seconds Peter had strapped the harness on over his vest and made a hasty descent to the port door, beckoning Mike to attach a light rope to the snap hook on the webbing on his back.

'You're crazy, Peter,' yelled Eric.

'It's my fault we are down here; I'll take the risk,' said Peter firmly, and plunged into the water.

'Watch out!' called Eric through a gap in the turret window, 'Just because he threw one gun into the sea doesn't mean he don't have another, or a knife.'

'Sure thing!' yelled Peter as he swam vigorously towards the oil-coated side of the submarine, Mike letting out the rope.

'I've got you covered!' shouted Arthur who had taken over from Andrew at the port machine-gun.

At one point Peter had to negotiate the floating corpse of a submariner, briefly taking in the details of a young face, seemingly at peace now, though heavily oiled. It was a hard crawl through the waves, the submarine alternately appearing and disappearing from Peter's low vantage point, but eventually he arrived at the side of the stricken vessel, anxiously looking back at a patch of burning oil drifting not far away, while also keeping an eye on the man above him. Treading water and panting with the effort, Peter looked up at the German officer who now readied himself to enter the brine. It was this moment that Peter wanted to prevent the others facing: a possible attack designed to take down at least one British sailor. Eric might be a pessimist, but he was right about the danger. However the officer had no weapon in his hand and simply stared down at his potential rescuer. Peter beckoned him down while shouting at him: 'Gruss Gott!' It was as awkward a greeting as its response: 'Jawohl,' not shouted, but uttered quietly in pain. The German stared at him for a moment, but to reach Peter there was nothing he could do other than let go of the slanted railings and slide clumsily down the side of the boat, landing in the sump-like waters with a muffled cry of pain. When he emerged spluttering and coughing he had as much oil on his face as Peter; both looked wild and filthy. Peter gestured to the officer to turn on his back. Clumsily grasping at his uniform, Peter helped him over so he could slide underneath and get his arms around the injured man's chest. Glancing back to the Sunderland and the ominous patch of burning oil, Peter thrust out with his legs. Raising an arm briefly he signalled to Mike to winch him in. But after only a few kicks he waved a negative.

'Give me slack!' he shouted, to which Mike nodded. The eddies had brought the blaze directly across Peter's return path and they could not risk the burning oil setting light to the rope. The German was spluttering again, having caught a mouthful of seawater as Peter's vigorous gesture had dipped him below the surface. But there was nothing for it: the two men would have to make a detour because of the blaze. Grimly Peter kicked out to steer around it with no assistance from the winch as the damn oil gave off a terrible stench and smoke as it burned and seemed intent on bobbing its way further across their path. As it approached them Peter had to adjust his course again, away from the nose of the Sunderland – this was taking far longer than he had anticipated. He glanced up at the sky around him, worried over the possibilities of Junkers bearing down on them: every second exposed them all to risk, whether from German planes or another explosion from the sub. By the time he cleared the oil sufficiently his chest was heaving with effort and the German seemed to have lapsed into unconsciousness. Finally he was able to wave Mike to cautiously take up the slack, and then the winch kicked in, the rope yanking awkwardly at Peter's harness. When they eventually arrived at the port door the German was pulled out with great care and carried in, while Eric materialised to haul Peter out of the water.

Without warning there were more ominous rumblings from the bowels of the submarine.

Arthur pulled Peter to his feet while Eric slammed the door shut and shouted to the captain: 'Go!' Tosey brought the engines to full forward throttle, the boat shuddering for a moment with the sudden surge of power. It was just in time: the submarine lurched further over and began to slide into the water. The straining propellers did their work to get the Sunderland clear of the swirling waters around the sinking behemoth, but the rough seas then posed the next problem: could they break free in the ascent? And with unknown damage to the rear flap? The engines roared at full power and the strain on the very structure of the boat could be heard. The floats were almost freed of the sea when they ploughed straight into the next peak, to the grinding of bulwarks and other alarming noises. Though exhausted, Peter was still attuned to every sound the craft could make: alarming as they might be to the untrained ear, he used the cacophony of sounds to construct a mental map of the forces billowing through strut, joist, and beam – almost through every rivet. The music of it spelled one thing to him however: the continued integrity of the structure. Sure enough they cleared the next wave.

As the big machine unglued itself from a sticky sea and gained altitude – albeit lurching left and then right – the men sighed with relief, not least Peter. It had been his gamble. He was still panting from his exertions as Arthur freed him from his harness, completely besmirched with oil and dripping wet in his vest and shorts, but Peter lingered to stare through the nearest porthole at the last visible traces of the submarine they had sunk. He shook his head at the thought of all the men his Sunderland had drowned, including the dead young man he had passed in the water. He shivered. Thanking Arthur, he turned to clean up using the hand-wash basin in the toilet and then went to change into dry clothes in the rear of the plane, passing the bunks where Dave had made the German as comfortable as possible opposite Ambrose.

'I'm bodging a new pin for the flap linkage,' Arthur told him as he passed by, filing a metal bolt clamped in the vice astern of the gun hatches. 'Got a bullet lodged in it.'

More than anything Peter now wanted to learn what he could from the German officer, should he be fit to talk, but he had something to do first once he was clean and dry and they had regained normal altitude for the journey home. There was no question of completing their planned sweep; all their bombs were deployed. And there were complications now. As the plane settled into a course set by a well-rested Jeremy Sopel, Peter sought out Eric, who had returned to his port gun hatch. All of them apart from Peter and Arthur had been directed to their stations by Tosey, mindful that patchy cloud cover could hide enemy planes. Gary now manned the forward guns, while Andrew and Eric were posted at the waist hatches. Peter gestured for Eric to take off his headset.

'Got a minute?' he shouted, over the harmonious drone of the engines and the roar of wind past the hatch.

'Lots of them,' said Eric, eyeing Peter warily. He leant forward a little to scan the clouds before removing his headset, and walked to the rear of the plane to better hear Peter. This was to be a private conversation it seemed.

'I want to apologise,' said Peter resolutely in the dimly lit and narrowing bowels of the flying boat.

'Go on then,' said Eric obtusely. The two men were close, face to face.

Peter sucked his breath in and said slowly: 'I apologise for what I said to you about maths classes. I had no right to do that.'

'Well, well,' said Eric. 'I don't get an apology from the governor every day.'

'I'm not your governor, nor anybody's,' said Peter evenly.

'You're the man who made these Sunderlands what they are.'

'Maybe,' Peter conceded.

Eric sniffed. 'Well, I wouldn't accept an apology from a man who just cooks a decent bacon, egg and chips. And I wouldn't accept an apology from a man who just brings us to the Jerry target. And I wouldn't accept an apology from an engineer, whatever scuttlebucket he builds. But I suppose I'll accept an apology from a man who does all three. And who jumps into that bloody cesspool just to rescue a Kraut.'

'You suppose?'

'Yeah. I suppose I do.'

Eric stared at Peter. Eric's face was sunburned, lined and full of the suspicions of a Cockney street trader swept up into a war he could make little money out of. But the fixed wariness slowly relaxed into a grin. Peter smiled too.

'Shake?' he said, extending his hand.

'Shake,' said Eric, accepting it.

There was a pause.

''Ere,' added Eric, pointing to the side of Peter's head. 'You missed a bit.'

Peter ran a finger behind his left jawbone. It was oil.

Eric raised his head and sniffed through his large nostrils.

'You stink of marine diesel,' he said. He shrugged, looking askance at Peter, and added: 'Though some might prefer it to your aftershave.'

Peter just grinned and shook his head: he had never worn aftershave in his life.

thirteen

11ØØØØ In the lower deck of the Sunderland Dave Grundisburgh tended to the injured German submariner in one cot, having bandaged Ambrose's leg in the other, either side of the narrow gangway. Arthur substituted as co-pilot. Peter helped Grundisburgh clean the bloody mess on the German's shoulder and abdomen and wind bandages right around his body, while Andrew and Eric looked down on these ministrations from their gun positions, the open hatches letting in wind roar and the drone of engines. Peter could see that the officer was an aristocratic-looking man with an intelligent and commanding air about him; he must have been the communications officer for the U-boat, probably charged with working the Enigma protocols. After his bleeding was stopped he regained consciousness. He face was taut with pain, but he surveyed the cramped quarters of the Sunderland with interest, taking in the various men and coming to rest on Peter.

'Kapitain?' he asked weakly.

'Nein. Ingenieur,' replied Peter, whose German vocabulary was extensive, even if his pronunciation would never win him prizes.

'E's a pretty boy,' remarked Eric, as he walked down to see how Ambrose was getting on, Gary relieving him at the gunner's hatch. The German's eyes darted to him, but nothing registered on his grave and pinched face. It was not the moment for cross-examination, thought Peter.

'Anything in his jacket to say who he is, or what rank?' he asked.

Dave held up the bloody garment from a cuff on the right arm.

'Hmm,' said Peter, 'those stripes are Ober-Lieutenant I think.'

'I'll dump this in the sink,' said Dave, 'and go through all the pockets.'

The German's eyes followed Dave out and he lapsed into unconsciousness. Peter stared at him for a moment and then went up to have a word with Gary at the port gun hatch.

'Did you get many pictures of the sub?'

'I think so. The photos will confirm that it was U-102 if they come out all right, and they should show the deck guns clearly enough. Without actually boarding the thing we couldn't ask for more ...'

'That's right. But what about after we landed?'

Gary shook his head. 'I hope I did the right thing, Peter.' He seemed a little nervous. 'But I didn't take any photos once we landed. I guessed we shouldn't. Perhaps I missed something important as a result, though. As soon as we were up again I photographed the sub as it went down, so we have proof of its final sinking. With Ambrose out we all had to man guns didn't we? I couldn't get everything.'

Peter nodded and laid his hand on Gary's shoulder. 'You did the right thing Gary. There was nothing useful down there except the Jerry.'

Nothing more was said on the subject, but Peter was greatly relieved: there must be absolutely no record of their landing and capture of the German. His next job was a more thorough inspection of the boat. He confirmed that the holes in the fuselage were not serious, and a longer inspection of the hatches showed the lower hull itself had, surprisingly, taken no bullets at all. He walked to the end of the craft to nod to Mike Westlake and peer through the rear turret Perspex. The Atlantic behind them was quite anonymous: it swallowed men and boys equally, thought Peter, regardless of rank or nationality. On the way back he tidied some tools on the small workbench where Arthur had worked earlier, while listing in his mind the breaches of protocol that his presence and actions had led them to. He checked again the path that the bullet had made through the side and which had lodged squarely in the fork of the linkage – that hole could be patched back home. He could not settle anywhere, however, conscious for the first time on this trip that he was a supernumerary, even if he could relieve men in various posts. He went towards the bow with the aim of inspecting the forward turret again: he had some ideas for improvements, and as he passed the unconscious German he smiled at Ambrose and Eric who were now playing cards. Passing through the empty bomb room he made a visual check of the windows – which doubled as parachute exits – to make sure they were properly closed. In the kitchen he peered thoughtfully through one of the portholes, and then passed Tosey settling down for a nap in the ward room. He was the only one apart from Peter not to have slept so far and was happy to leave the running of the plane in

Arthur's capable hands. Peter made his way to the bow, stopping to check the free running of the ammunition belts from their tin boxes to the fuselage Brownings: a chance encounter with Junkers would see these put to good use. He clambered awkwardly into the seat of the forward turret. It wouldn't take much, he decided, to provide better protection for the legs against incoming fire by adding a little armour either side of the bomb aiming hatch and by strengthening the hatch cover itself. As he scrambled down again Dave emerged from the toilet where he had rinsed the blood out of the German's uniform and washed the rest of his clothes as best he could.

'Look,' he said. He held up a tiny notebook with the name 'Ulrich Wolfgang von Waldthurn' in faded gold on the leather cover. It was waterlogged and bloodstained but full of mathematical jottings that were mostly legible.

'Bloody hell,' said Peter, and whistled. He scanned through it rapidly. 'I don't think any of this relates to the Enigma though,' he said in disappointed tones. 'But what do I know? I'll get Deirdre to take it to Turing, that should clinch a meeting.'

They went back to the midship cots where they hung up their captive's clothes to dry, a good draft coming through from the gun hatches. Peter looked at the half-conscious officer. 'He could have information for Turing that could change the whole course of the war,' he told Grundy.

The German had woken up and overheard them. 'Nur zu Turing,' he repeated, but seemed oblivious to their custody of his possessions.

'He must have had a bloody good reason to surrender to us,' mused Peter. 'This fellow is an aristocrat I would say. "Ulrich Wolfgang von Waldthurn."'

'You can buy titles in Germany like anywhere else,' muttered Eric, looking up from his rummy hand.

'Not this fellow,' said Peter. 'I'm sure of it.'

Sopel and Grundy were back in the cockpit having suggested that Peter should catch up with some sleep so he could take over from Sopel again later on. However, it was dawning on the crew that they faced a problem, each one mulling over the implications in their own way. Peter was an unauthorised passenger and that alone could get him and the captain arrested. But the rules were equally strict on prisoners. While the Sunderlands had exemplary service in rescuing Allied sailors from death on the oceans and in evacuation operations such as in Greece, they faced considerable risks every time they landed, and in really rough seas it was out of the question. They could drop a life-raft to save enemy sailors, but risks were never taken to capture prisoners. On both counts, then, they faced severe consequences for failure to follow proper procedures. Peter was thinking this through – 'speak only to Turing' meant that this was big. He climbed up to the top deck, plugged his 'phones in near Sopel and announced he needed to talk something over with them.

'Dave, can you get Eric and Ambrose on the intercom?' he asked.

Once everybody had confirmed they could hear him Peter began: 'We have a captured German officer on board who has surrendered expressly to speak with the mathematician Alan Turing. That means he may also be a mathematician. His notebook certainly suggests that.'

'Or also be a queer,' piped up Eric.

Peter frowned. This was no time for joking.

'The point is that he could have information on the Enigma worth more than all our careers put together. It could save tens or hundreds of thousands of lives.' The men nodded soberly at their various posts. However, the mention of careers brought them back to what they all knew: this could be court martial if they were found out.

'I say that Ambrose is in for a medal,' Mike suddenly offered. They thought about this. Ambrose had faced down the Flak gun and saved the boat; without him they could not have had a second run and sunk the sub. It was his kill, and he deserved the honour for being wounded in action.

'There may be more than one decoration waiting for this crew,' Peter agreed. 'Most likely a DSO for both Rick and Ambrose. But that all goes to hell if we don't do something about the German officer.'

They listened, the drone of the engines penetrating their leather headsets.

'Here is my idea,' Peter said. 'You will think it far-fetched, but I propose we fly to Windermere, drop both the Kraut and myself off there, and the rest of you return with no reason for any suspicion.'

There was a thoughtful silence.

Peter continued: 'We're not expected back until the early hours because of the late takeoff. If we put down just after dark, say eleven-thirty on Windermere, then I can take the German out on one of the life-rafts. I'll row up the shore and bring him into my bothy where I can hide him until I figure out how to get him to Bletchley.'

Eric said: 'Are you crazy? It's what, five or six hundred miles out of our way!'

'We have fuel for that and more. We were only a third of our way into the planned flight,' replied Peter.

'But the guards at Shorts will hear the boat come in! It won't be on the schedules and you'll be spotted instantly,' objected Arthur.

'No,' Peter said quietly. 'My idea is to put down behind Belle Isle close to the western shore. Nobody at Shorts will have any idea; it's miles away. There's nobody living either on the island these days or along that bit of shoreline, and the woodland on the Isle will hide us on both visuals and sound from Bowness. We fly up the Irish Sea as if on a mission, or a trip to Castle Archdale, none of the bases along there will question it. We then go into the mainland at Grange-over-Sands and up the Lake; fly low along the Western shore to land, turn round and go out the same way. Locals will think it an exercise, and nobody at the Belsfield, let alone Shorts will hear a thing. Maybe in the morning perhaps some lone fisherman will mention it to someone, but by then the boat will be long gone.'

'It's crazy! What about radar at Barrow?' asked Mike.

'We know the entire shift there,' replied Peter. 'We say it's an unscheduled run to pick up some special parts machined in my shop; they will never bother to check. I have a crate of Irish whisky that nobody knows about; I'll send a bottle or two down for the lads as a little thank-you. It wouldn't be the first time.'

'But it will add at least four hours to the return. We have to give the right time on the U-boat kill, what if a merchant vessel passes by and sees the oil and debris? They'll log that all right.' This was from Gary, whose job it was to faithfully record all details of the incident to accompany his photographs.

'The time is what it was, Gary. But we have to fly slow, don't we?' Peter responded. 'That tail flap problem is there for all to see. We've only bodged a repair. We can account for any time discrepancy that way.'

'The men at Barrow will think I'm running contraband for God's sake,' objected Tosey. 'And what about the German when he's handed over?'

'Okay,' said Peter, thinking fast. 'We spin them a line about experimental parts for the … for the … forward wing struts. New pivot cleats and strut members. They know that I am always getting round the pen-pushers this way.'

Tosey thought about it and then conceded: 'Okay, I suppose that's plausible. I know your reputation, we all do. But what about the German?'

'I'll deal with it in such a way as to make it impossible to trace him,' said Peter. 'The German is in no state to record the number on our boat. I'll take the consequences, if there are any, but my God, if there are good outcomes this could shorten the war by years. I choose that over my honourable discharge any day – now I'm effectively in the Navy. But it was my idea, and none of you should go down with me.'

Tosey stared at his instruments, chewing his lip. The men were silent, pondering Peter's plan. There didn't seem to be any further questions.

'The possible alternative is far worse for everyone: court martial,' Peter reminded them. 'If we hand over the Kraut at Pembroke we're all done for.'

Eric butted in. 'Ambrose ought to decide. He needs a surgeon, and this is a four hour delay at least before he gets to hospital in Pembroke.'

Ambrose responded immediately. 'I'm fine. I think it's a spiffing good idea, Sahib,' he said with a convincing Indian lilt.

'Okay,' said Tosey. 'I must say I bloody well wish I had thought this through earlier, but Peter's plan is the best we've got. We can fly at maximum speed back from Windermere to get Ambrose to hospital. That blasted German had better survive and have something useful for Intelligence though.'

There was silence for a moment.

'Er, what were the parts called again, Peter?'

'Pivot cleats and struts.'

Tosey dutifully repeated it.

'That's it,' said Peter cheerfully. 'Top secret. Top Darby secret.'

Peter was even more restless after all this was settled, but had no particular role to fill until later, when Tosey's rota placed him in the kitchen for supper and at the navigation table again in the late evening. Tired as he was, he had no appetite for sleep either. He wandered around as before and then settled in the ward room staring out of a porthole; he sat like this for a long time until disturbed by a voice behind him.

'Your hands are shaking Peter.'

It was Arthur.

Peter did not look up, but merely said: 'The water was cold.'

Arthur said: 'Mmm. I'll get you a cup of tea.'

He went to the galley, filled the kettle and put it on the Primus. He stood in the doorway.

Peter still didn't look up but said: 'It all happened too fast. Tosey was right, we didn't think this thing through. Now all the men face possible disciplinary action whatever we do, short of opening a door and pushing the Kraut overboard.'

Arthur thought for a moment. He came to stand opposite Peter. 'It's war old boy. You polish your boots, you clean your rifle, pack your pack, then unpack your pack, polish your boots and clean your rifle. Bugger all happens for ages and then all hell breaks loose …'

Peter nodded guardedly and continued to stare out of the window. They were silent for a while.

The little whistle on the kettle started up, rising urgently in pitch and volume. Arthur went to the kitchen to make tea, bringing it back in two large tin mugs. Setting one down in front of Peter he spoke again, his West Country accent stronger than Peter's, which had been mostly lost in the fifteen years on the Medway. 'All hell breaks loose, Peter, and in that brief period you make a hundred decisions – that is between the officers and the men – and then it's all over. Then you look round and see that one of you has a bullet through the leg like Ambrose. Or you find twenty dead men. But the point is you then go back to polishing your boots and cleaning your rifle, or you know, cleaning the splash tray at the back of the Primus – just to fill the boredom – and so on and all the time you are living with the decisions you made in the panic of action. That's war: you don't have time to work it all out.'

'I know,' said Peter.

'You're a clever fellow,' said Arthur after a pause. 'But your problem is you think too much. If your plan works on Windermere we'll go back to the boredom. If it doesn't we'll make another set of hasty decisions. And so it goes on.'

Peter nodded. 'You're right Arthur. I know.'

Arthur looked again at Peter's left hand.

'And it's not the cold water is it? It's that shoulder of yours.'

There was silence. Arthur sat down opposite Peter and stared at him. He added: 'And it's not just the shoulder is it?' Peter's hands gripped his mug steadily enough, but when he placed the vessel down and spread his fingers in front of him the shaking returned. He looked up at his friend. Arthur spoke softly: 'It's the memories isn't it?'

Peter said nothing but after a while he nodded. Then he suddenly grinned. 'It's all happening too fast,' he repeated. 'Everything.'

'What do you mean?'

Peter hesitated, and was then wreathed in smiles. 'I proposed to Deirdre the other day,' he said softly, 'and she accepted. Sort of.'

'Really? That's wonderful!' cried Arthur.

Peter looked at his trembling hands again and steadied them on the hot mug. 'We just destroyed a U-boat and captured its intelligence officer,' he said softly, shaking his head. 'And I'm in love. Arthur, it's all too fast.'

He thought again and added. 'I wouldn't care about the careers of the men on this plane against the possible intelligence. That's a gamble we all willingly take. But now I risk bringing Deirdre down with me as well. It's a whole damn new complication about everything.'

Arthur nodded.

Peter continued: 'When that klaxon sounded I knew we were in for a fight. And for the first time my first thought wasn't "bloody great!" Instead it was: "what happens to Deirdre if I'm killed?"'

Arthur put a hand on his shoulder. 'You and us all, Peter.'

They were indeed in for a long flight to the Lake, risking discovery if Peter's plan failed in any of its detail. Knowing what lay ahead for him Peter forced himself to lie on the bunk in the ward room and managed a little fitful sleep. The evening meal was eaten at eight, Ambrose determined that he be served the extra portion of beans that he had won. Peter brought it to him, also wanting to check on the German.

'If this all goes well,' he said to Ambrose, 'you'll be in line for a medal.'

'It's Rick who should get it,' said Ambrose with a mouth full of beans. He looked pale, thought Peter – he hoped to God that he was not risking the life of this plucky little man with the hours of delay.

'Rick,' said Ambrose more clearly, 'is the one who set it up right. He flew in with the sun behind us, and he kept a good arc for me on the approach. Without an edge like that the odds would not have been so good.'

'I know about the sun,' said Peter, 'but I don't get it about the arc: what does that mean?'

'Oh, it's like this. If the plane flies dead straight then both gunners have to rotate guns equally. And that's where the inaccuracies come in: as you track the target you overshoot, undershoot and so on, even with the hydraulics. More rounds miss. But if you fly in as close to an arc of a circle as possible, then you have much smaller movements to make compared to the other gunner. It's much easier to hit what appears to be a stationary target, obviously. Tosey gave me all the arc I needed.'

Peter absorbed this with a whistle – he had learned something new. 'And did you or Tosey work this out?' Ambrose did not respond, but filled his mouth again and looked out of the porthole, munching on his pie and beans.

'Near Ireland I would guess,' is all that he would say.

Later on Peter found himself sitting with Eric over another cup of tea in the ward room. He had an idea.

'Eric, are you man who likes to trade this and that for a few bob?'

'Might be.'

'Well, there's a particular item I can't easily find. I buy and sell a few things myself you see.'

'I spotted that, actually,' said Eric. 'Even though I never went to school.'

'Quite. What I am after are ruby-red silk ladies knickers.'

'Didn't think you were the type.'

'Size ten.'

'Oh, so not for yourself then.'

'I need a dozen.'

'A bottle of that Irish you mentioned for each one.'

'Two bottles for the twelve.'

'Two bottles? You are having a laugh my boy. With the world's silk all requisitioned for parachutes? Four.'

'Three.'

There was a pause.

'Done.'

There was another pause.

'Eric.'

'What?'

'Ruby-red, mind.'

'You're the governor.'

11ØØØ1   As Peter had predicted, the men he radioed at Bowness were quite happy with a hush-hush mission for spares, and would definitely not mention it to the day shift or record it on the flight sheets. He promised to drive down before long with a little sample for each of them. Captain Tosey's face was rather set as he confirmed the purpose of their flight but he had no choice now. 'Yes,' he had told the operator at Bowness, 'that's right. Pivot cleats and struts. Experimental, apparently. Ordered for this Sunderland by Peter Darby. To be fitted when back at Portland.'

Peter had worked with Jeremy Sopel on a speed and flight path that would bring them to Grange-over-Sands as it got dark – a moon was up again, which would help them land. It was less than five miles from there to the lower end of Windermere.

The huge craft came in from the South to the lower reaches of the Lake, hugging the more deserted western shoreline. Peter had been right to pick Belle Isle, as it was the only recognisable landmark as they flew north up the lake, but they could not afford a practice run, and faced the twin difficulties of near-darkness and unruffled waters: the latter meant that height would be hard to gauge in the last part of the descent. Eric volunteered to hang out of the port door with a weighted rope and shout what he could learn from it trailing behind in the slipstream, but with only moonlight drawn off along the water in the wrong direction he had little ambient light to go by. In the end he shouted 'Hundred feet. Eighty feet. No, eighty now. Sixty ...' They landed just past the old ferry terminus and came to rest between Belle Isle and a tiny wooded bar between it and the western shore. As quickly as possible they launched the life-raft and stretchered the German onto it. Peter jumped in with a grunt.

'Are you sure you can do this alone?' asked Arthur. 'It's nearly three miles to row.'

'My leg's gammy, but my arms aren't,' retorted Peter. 'And my hands can't shake when they're holding the oars.'

Eric and Jeremy crowded Arthur at the hatch to wish Peter good luck. Waving them goodbye, Peter turned the life-raft to head northwards. The door was slammed shut, upon which the boat turned and took off immediately, an easier task than landing in the dark. As the roar of its engines faded Peter was left alone to row his captive to the hideaway at Shorts, but after the long hours in the flying boat the silence was hard to adjust to; like the dark it seemed to envelope him, a twin absence of light and noise. And Arthur was right to question him: the rowing was not easy – the life-raft had not been designed for a single man to row any distance, and his arms soon tired.

He laboriously followed the western shoreline, turning regularly to gauge his position and check the fringes of the water for any prying eyes. On reaching what he recognised as Belle Grange Coppice he then struck across the lake in the direction of Hodgehowe Wood on the opposite shore, not far from his destination of White Cross Bay. The German just stared at him, huddled uncomfortably in the front of the life-raft.

'Nur zu Turing,' he muttered again. They exchanged more words in German, alone on the lake with only the creaking of rowlocks and the splash of oars to break the silence. Finally Peter approached the spot where he hoped Clarence would be waiting in the dinghy. It was nearly one o'clock and his friend may easily have gone home for a few hours sleep before the next appointed hour of four; that would mean a heck of a wait, but, as he got nearer, he was able to make out Clarence in the gloom, comfortably sat in the little craft so as to await him and Frank in the motor. On hearing the sound of rowing Clarence turned to face him in bewilderment, the livid weal on his forehead picked out by the moon.

'What happened to Frank?' he asked. 'And why the hell are you in a Sunderland life-raft with some fellow who looks like he's at death's door?'

'I'll explain later,' said Peter, relieved that Clarence made no mention of engine noises: he had clearly heard nothing of their landing, shielded by the trees and rise of Belle Isle. Shorts itself was further isolated by the Parkhill Wood, which they would circumnavigate back to the compound. 'I'm dead exhausted with rowing,' added Peter, 'can you tow us in Clarence?'

'Of course. Here's a line.'

It took the last of Peter's strength to tie the rope up. He sat down next to the German submariner in the near-agony of relief, but before quite collapsing he reached over to check his captive's pulse, and then simply allowed Clarence to labour for both of them.

''Ere we are,' said Clarence once they had finally rounded the head. 'Bleack Beck.'

He grounded his craft and strained to pull the life-raft ashore. He looked at its passengers. 'One of you looks half alive and the other half dead,' he commented.

Peter grunted and hauled himself out to help. He pointed to the wounded officer. 'We have to get him to my workshop without anyone spotting us.'

''E's badly injured,' commented Clarence on inspecting the captive. 'Shouldn't I get a first-aider in?'

'Can't afford the time or exposure, I'm afraid' said Peter. 'We'll get him on his legs and walk him there.'

They hauled the officer to his feet, one arm over the shoulder of each Englishman, and carefully coaxed him along. In silence they entered the compound via bushes at the back of Peter's workshop, and, quietly opening its door, they guided the injured man to Peter's sleeping area and set him on a chair. Pushing his bed to one side Peter opened a trap-door, and the two men awkwardly manoeuvred the German officer down a flight of stone steps into the basement. A single bare bulb lit up its cavernous interior, filled with all kinds of supplies that Peter made use of in his various negotiations. It had an identical cot to the one Peter slept in, and they carefully lowered the prisoner onto it. They made him as comfortable as they could, but had an urgent task: to bring in the life-raft. The story that Tosey and his crew had to tell – as Peter had worked it out – was that it had been dropped for German survivors, being vague about their numbers. Clarence and Peter hauled it into the workshop, where they carefully removed its markings; Peter worked on every aspect of the Sunderland's capability, so no one would realise that the raft was not in fact on any inventory. His workshop was like that.

Clarence was by now bursting to know what was going on. It was simply dumfounding for Peter to turn up on the lake in a life-raft with a captured German officer. Peter had no choice but to tell him the whole story, over tea in the basement as they tended to the basic needs of their prisoner. Clarence shook his head. This was some serious Darby malarkey.

11ØØ1Ø   First thing the next morning Peter rang Deirdre, who was so full of relief at his safe return that she gave him no chance to prepare her for what lay ahead. Peter drove up to collect her from the Belsfield a little later. She waited for him in reception and on spotting his car ran over and overwhelmed him with hugs and kisses. It was only on the way back that he was able to tell her a little about what happened; she was firstly horrified that they had come under fire, then full of astonishment to learn they had sunk a U-boat, and then very quiet as he told her about the German captive. Peter explained that the prisoner had to be left locked and hidden alone in the basement, but in his condition there was no possibility of escape. The basement itself was a feature left over from the earlier use of the building for drying and smoking fish, and was known only to Peter and Clarence: its one entrance, the trap-door, was hidden under Peter's bed. Deirdre absorbed all of this with a distracted air.

She looked at him as he drove her along the fringes of the lake – although rested by a little sleep, he looked exhausted, grim. She stroked his jawbone, not caring that it was still a little dark with grime. 'You sunk a U-boat', she whispered, shaking her head. Then she frowned as she tried to make sense of the complication, the German in the basement. But something else struck her: 'The captain will get a DSO,' she said. 'And many of the crew. But you won't get anything.'

Peter just shrugged. She looked at him and smiled, caressing his neck this time, and then drew as close as she could without interfering with his control of the ageing motor. She glanced up at his sombre face, focussed on the business of driving and preoccupied with their new situation; she nestled still closer to him, subdued. Once at Shorts she followed him into the workshop basement and became business-like on seeing the injured man. She tended to his wounds, ordering Peter about with requests for hot water, bandages, and iodine.

'Good job I did Nurse Training before the war,' she muttered. Once she had done what she could and they had reassured their captive that he would be well looked after, they went upstairs and shifted the bed back to its guard position. She looked at Peter. 'What on earth are we going to do with him?' she asked.

'That's where you come in,' Peter said brightly. 'You are going to get him to Bletchley.'

'What? Are you crazy? The minute I tell anybody about this all hell will break loose. An unauthorised prisoner capture in the Atlantic, an unauthorised landing on Windermere, an unauthorised flight by you, they will throw the book at you! And me!'

Taken aback, all Peter could say was: 'Can't you understand the importance to national security of this man? Who knows what he can tell Intelligence about plans for the Enigma, or for the entire U-boat fleet?'

'"Who knows?" Peter, is absolutely it. Perhaps he knows nothing.'

'No, Deirdre. He organised a surrender of the officers, and got shot for doing so. Only he survived. He then signalled to us the words "Turing" and "Enigma". And he insists that he will only speak to Turing. Why would he have done all that if he was not a defector seeking safe passage in return for classified information?'

'He could have done all of that, dearest, to save his skin.'

'I don't think so. He's not the type. But even if he is, he knows full well that he has to deliver the intelligence. And he also knows full well that he can't return to the German side after surrender.'

'You've got it all worked out, I see,' said Deirdre bitterly.

'No, my love, I haven't. Beyond the need to get him to Bletchley – or I suppose get Turing up here – I have nothing worked out. That's why I need your help.'

Deirdre buried her face in her hands and sighed deeply.

Peter put his arms around her and looked up at her smiling. '*Are you glad to see me back?*' he said.

She stared at him for a moment and then murmured: 'Oh Christ yes. And I'm sorry to worry so much about everything.' She thought for a moment and then shook her head, her eyes were wide. 'I can't believe that you destroyed a U-boat. I know that's what Sunderlands are for, but it doesn't sink in until it actually happens.'

'Yes, we did destroy a U-boat,' said Peter. 'I'm as amazed as the rest of the crew, but yes we did. It was Tosey and Marr between them, disabling the Flak gun, plus some very good positioning of the depth charges.'

'It's all down to you though, isn't it?' said Deirdre, lowering herself to his side and cuddling up to him. 'That whole horrible machine of yours is honed by you to sink those horrible machines of theirs. You told me: even the kitchen is designed to be as light as possible so the thing can fly that bit further.'

'Kitchen. Yes. It's a key part of the boat,' said Peter, thinking of the double portion of beans served to Ambrose Marr. He felt a twinge of guilt: he hadn't checked how Marr was doing as he left the Sunderland.

Deirdre wasn't listening, but had begun to kiss him again. The more she learned about the flight the more her frantic worry over his trips was growing. Their love-making that night petered out after a while however as Deirdre's passion – kindled in contemplation of the dangers Peter had faced – was lost in a new perception.

'Sorry Peter,' she said crossly after he asked her what the matter was. 'This cot creaks. It puts me off.'

'It has always creaked,' protested Peter.

She pursed her lips.

'Oh,' he realised. 'It's Ulrich von what's-his-name downstairs. Is that what's bothering you?'

110011   A few days later there was a knock on the workshop door. Peter was working on the electric Colchester and had to wipe his oily hands on a rag as he went to answer it. The man at the door was the site manager, Fred Sharpe.

'Peter, old chap,' he began, clearly surveying the gloom of the workshop with an interest that was not quite normal. 'I've had reports of a Sunderland sighting near Belle Isle a few days ago. Monday night to be precise.'

Peter just looked at him quizzically, rubbing his hands on the cloth.

'We have to scotch such rumours, Peter, as you know. There was no scheduled flight at that time, and unscheduled manoeuvres suggest contraband to all and sundry.'

'Contraband,' agreed Peter.

'Yes, Peter. Any thoughts on the subject? Of a landing that night?'

'Sunderland,' mused Peter. 'Catalan. Yacht. Ferry. All sound a bit the same.'

'Mmm,' responded his boss. 'What would a Catalan be doing up here?'

'Search me,' said Peter. 'You would have to ask the Yanks.'

'It's unlikely for a Catalan to land on the Lake. And a yacht doesn't fly. And the ferry doesn't fly or run at night.'

'Over here, overpaid, after our girls?' suggested Peter.

Sharpe frowned.

'Lots of pretty girls at the Belsfield,' offered Peter.

Sharpe's eyes narrowed.

'There's questions I could ask you about just that, Peter,' he said.

'Ask away, old chap,' Peter grinned.

'I don't need to, in fact,' responded Sharpe, with annoyance.

'That's all right then.'

Suspicious eyes scanned the workshop. Had the German chosen that particular moment to scream then he might have been discovered, but he was far too weak, and had no reason to do so: he was confident that before long he would be speaking to the British mathematical genius, Alan Turing.

The following day Peter's Sunderland made the return trip for repairs, flown in by Tosey, Sopel, Brantham and Westlake. Fred Sharpe attended the inspection – along with Peter – of the damage to the front turret and the other minor sites which would need repair. Tosey, Sopel, and Brantham put on a convincing act of being introduced to Peter and telling him the story of their trip, the first part being accurate apart from omitting Peter's presence and the second part being a well-rehearsed fabrication. Nothing in it gave cause for suspicion, indeed the mood was properly celebratory over the U-boat sinking. It was only when Sharpe and the other engineering staff had left that Peter invited Tosey for tea in his bothy and was able to confirm the presence of the German below. Tosey just nodded; Peter again reassured the captain that he would take all responsibility for the hostage – the more days that passed the more flights left from Whitely Bay and the less that suspicion would fall on any one captain. In fact Sharpe's exchanges over the unlikely presence of an American Catalan had given Peter the idea of using that as a smokescreen should he be questioned further. He was not in the least afraid of court martial for himself, but was clear that he did not want the fallout to implicate Tosey, Marr or any of the others. Deirdre he could not protect however; far from it, he had dragged her into his adventure, an unplanned consequence he greatly regretted.

There was nothing for it however: Deirdre was essential. She tended to the submariner's injuries unobserved – her regular visits to his workshop a Shorts-wide 'secret' that Fred Sharpe colluded with, having no real reason to do anything else. His suspicions about Peter lay quite elsewhere. And Deirdre would bring the German to Turing.

She continued to nurse the captive, whose condition was improving under her ministrations so he could sit up and take food. A week after Tosey's visit he was resting in his cot, still very weak, and pointed to Peter who had just come down the stone steps to join Deirdre.

'Fliegende Stachelschwein Ingenieur,' he said.

Deidre, who knew a little German, was puzzled.

'He says you are a flying porcupine engineer? I have no idea what that means.'

'Oh,' said Peter laughing. 'That's what they call the Sunderland, because of its fighting reputation. Has guns all over it.' In his poorly articulated German, Peter told him that yes, he had designed the armaments.

'Ich bin Peter,' he added. 'Das ist Deirdre.'

The German took this in and nodded.

'Du bist Ulrich Wolfgang von Waldthurn.' Peter asserted.

The officer's face hardened for a moment, but Peter produced his diary and showed him the name on it, to which the sick man nodded in concession to the facts. Peter told him that he would call him Ulrich, and that from his notebook it was clear that he was a mathematician.

'Nur zu Turing sprechen,' said Ulrich. He made it clear that he regarded Turing as the greatest of British mathematicians, and that he had important information on the workings of the Enigma machine but would only convey them to Turing. It was also clear that Ulrich wanted eventually to live in America and that his defection was out of a growing revulsion over the Nazi leadership. As Peter had guessed, Ulrich came from a genuinely aristocratic family and had come to the conclusion he wanted no further part of the barbarism of the Third Reich.

'Winston Churchill, gut,' he said.

As Ulrich's condition improved Peter became increasingly impatient with Deirdre.

'Christ!' he told her. 'Don't you see, Deirdre, you have to *do* something. You have friends at Bletchley. Ring them up and arrange a trip. Ulrich is getting stronger and could make the journey perhaps by next week.'

'No. A phone call would be madness, everything in and out is monitored. We can't get more people into trouble.'

'Okay, take a day's leave and go to Bletchley yourself. Speak to Turing in person. Once he sees that notebook with Ulrich's name on it, he'll make every effort to meet him. Or if we can't get Ulrich down to Bletchley, Turing can come up here for a few day's holiday, some excuse like that, you can take him round the lake, and then bring him here at night. What are we risking all this for, if not to get the information the man has to the authorities?'

Deirdre looked warily at Peter.

'That might work,' she said dubiously. 'But Turing is a strange chap. Brilliant, but quite unpredictable.'

Later that day Peter had an unwelcome visitor in the Detail Hangar. He had been looking again at the front turret on a nearly completed boat and was offering up some armour strips at the side of the bomb-aiming hatch that might prevent injuries of the sort that Ambrose had received. He looked down from the steps to see Alasdair Farnham-Smythe scowling at him.

'Darby. I want a word.'

Peter insisted that Farnham-Smythe join him for a cup of tea in the canteen.

'I don't want a cup of tea,' snapped the angry looking officer.

'But I do,' said Peter giving him no choice. In the canteen Farnham-Smythe glared at him as Peter measured out three spoonfuls of white sugar from the glass jar with the little steel tube.

'Look Darby,' he said, 'I was at the Belsfield last week. I saw a Sunderland come in behind Belle Isle.'

'Nonsense,' said Peter, chewing on a digestive. 'Why would a boat land there of all places?'

'You tell me, Peter.'

'No. You tell me that you were sober that night.'

'I'm warning you!'

'Warning me what?'

Farnham-Smythe controlled himself with difficulty. 'I've told Sharpe, and I am pressing for an investigation where I'll offer my evidence.'

'What evidence?'

'I told you. I saw a Sunderland making what appears to have been an unauthorised landing and takeoff.'

'You were drunk. Seeing things.' Peter was quietly adamant, a grin on his face, but his eyes were hard.

'Damn you! I was as sober as a judge, and I glimpsed a white shape in the moonlight, couldn't have been anything else.'

'No you didn't.'

'God damn it man, you are unspeakable!' Again Farnham-Smythe controlled himself with difficulty.

'Okay, okay' said Peter amiably. 'Let me get this straight. There you were in the lounge of the Belsfield, which I want to remind you has a view north north west, and you "saw" a shape in the moonlight south west.'

Farnham-Smythe looked at him, thinking hard.

'Or, old chap,' continued Peter, 'could it be that you were upstairs somewhere with a south west view, let me think, yes, how about Barbara Stevens's room? How much did you bribe the Super? Eh?'

Farnham-Smythe was dumbfounded, and reddening behind his moustache.

'Actually you aren't Barbara's type,' said Peter. 'In fact she can't stand you. Perhaps Susan what's-her-name? On the next floor up? I hear she's a real goer. Shame if your wife heard about it.'

'Absolute tripe!' roared Farnham-Smythe, and then shrank back as heads were turned.

'That Super,' commented Peter. 'Ecky. He's a nice chap. But whatever you bought him with I can buy him back, just like that. And for each bottle you may have given him I have a case. I have some particularly lovely Scotch that changes a man's mind in an instant. Shame to see you explain to a disciplinary board about going upstairs at the Belsfield though. Many a chap would love to do that.'

'I knew it!' Farnham-Smythe hissed. 'I knew you were running contraband. God knows what trade you run from the sunken convoys on those Sunderlands, and where you sell it. But I'll get to the bottom of this and see you court-martialled.'

'No you won't,' said Peter casually, his eyes less hard now, confident that Farnham-Smythe was no longer a danger. He leant forward and looked into the man's eyes.

'I've never run contraband in my life and you have not a shred of evidence against me. The Sunderland is a fighting boat and I would rather die than see it waste a single nautical mile that didn't serve the war effort. But you on the other hand? Going upstairs at the Belsfield, bribing the Super, and rogering sexy Susan behind your wife's back? Sort of thing that brings a career to a dead stop.'

Farnham-Smythe shrank back, staring at Peter for a while. Then he turned away.

'You're scum,' he muttered. 'And that poor Deirdre Haviland can't see it. You and that scoundrel Clarence Marshall. Oh, I had words with him, but he is tight as a clam. It's your much-vaunted working-class solidarity, isn't it? Clever jackanapeses like you rising to new positions and commanding the respect of absolute ruffians …'

That, thought Peter, was quite enough to warrant taking the man out in the yard and knocking his block off. He clenched and unclenched his hands at the alluring prospect, but, however much it would help relieve the stress that Peter faced over a dying German in his basement with secrets that could win the war, a brawl would only make the prospect of extracting those secrets more remote.

'Fuck you,' he said instead.

Alasdair flinched, but Peter's grimy fists and muscled forearms had anyway warned off him from making further insults. He got up and Peter followed him with his eyes as he left, saying nothing. He thought it over. Alasdair must have been at the very top of the Belsfield to have seen anything at all; and that can only have been a dim shape in the moonlight far away — the trees would have hidden all the later stages of landing. It was a Catalan; who could say otherwise? A top room narrowed the women down a lot; a quiet word with Barbara would get to the bottom of it. But if further rumours of a sighting went round suspicions would take the course of least resistance as in the mind of Farnham-Smythe: that it was a smuggling run, and what's more it was an American Catalan, not a British Sunderland. Nobody else that he knew of had the animus towards him that would lead enquiries to his bothy basement – if anything there would be a fruitless search of Belle Isle, or even the Belsfield.

A week later, during which Peter and Deirdre quarrelled repeatedly about how she would approach Bletchley, she came up from the basement with a frown on her face. 'He's taken a turn for the worse, Peter. I am out of my depth now. He needs a doctor.'

'Christ. That's bad. Who could we approach?' asked Peter, mentally making a note of his stock of loyalty-securing items in the basement and wondering which of them would sway a doctor. He had not in fact lied to Smythe about how he secured his stock: he had never flown on a Sunderland trip where any contraband had been picked up, and he knew of no such case. But he knew plenty of men who had been successful in the sordid business of profiteering, and he was not interested in moralising with them about it. All of war was sordid. Instead he spent his own salary on keeping such men sweet, and so built up his stock – a varied collection, with ladies' ruby-red silk underwear outstanding, dependent on the deal with Eric, who was as yet an unproven supplier of anything. Soap-flakes on the other hand were no problem.

Deirdre was staring at him, angry. 'You can't just buy anything and everybody, you know,' she said. 'The Hippocratic oath does not extend to enemy combatants. None of the army doctors or local GPs would hesitate an instant to spill the beans, and in any case they would want to get Ulrich to a hospital. How on earth can you hide all of that? You just don't seem to realise the enormity of what you have done: sitting on a captured German naval officer.'

'Literally,' Peter joked.

She was not amused. 'Peter, Ulrich will die without proper medical help. His temperature has been rising over the last few days, and I don't have access to morphine or anything like that. I think his wound has gone septic despite all I have done, and that means surgery. It's not just a doctor, it really is a hospital that he needs.'

Peter thought about it for a while.

'Well, that leaves us no choice,' he said. 'Either we get Turing up here, or we hand Ulrich over to the military police. And sharpish at that. They will get everything out of him if he hasn't long to live.'

'That *is* a choice you idiot!' she shouted at him, 'and you can't force me into making it!'

'I'm not forcing you into anything,' Peter said steadily. 'But what would you have us do?'

'I don't know,' she said angrily. They were sitting near the open workshop doors, looking out over the lake. She softened. 'Peter, when you rowed me out on the waters with that picnic hamper, I knew I was lost. I knew that I was in love with you. When I saw the exhaustion on your face after sinking the U-boat and rescuing Ulrich I knew that you had played a key role in it, not that a man like you would ever let on what he actually went through. Now I am tangled up in some dreadful mess of your making, and I can't undo the steps that took me towards you. I will never be able to or want to.'

He leant over and kissed her hair. They were silent for a while, his arms folded around her.

'I'll take three days leave,' she said eventually. 'I'll go to Bletchley and talk with Turing. I'll have to pull more strings to do it than even you can imagine.'

She turned to him.

'Peter, you must promise me absolutely. Whatever happens to Ulrich while I am away, you must not hand him over. Promise?'

'Promise. Absolutely'

fourteen

11Ø1ØØ   Emil has stopped scribbling on the whiteboard. William
can see that he has grasped the entire basis of his
breakthrough; the comments written around the original
workings, full of queries and oppositions, have petered out. It is
unassailable. Emil returns to his desk angrily and looks up at William.

'Congratulations.' He spits it out, listens to the silence, and then
permits a small smile. More softly, but still stiffly, he says:
'Congratulations, Willy. Sorry. May warned me what was coming but it
is still a shock.'

William nods in acknowledgement and then raises his right hand in
which he holds a letter with an American airmail stamp. Emil's eyes
widens: it can mean only one thing. He reaches forward as William
comes over to deliver it, but is shaking his head in anticipation of what
would be, for him, an even more devastating turn.

'ACM ...' he says. He opens it and scans the contents, then stares
into the distance. William looks out of the window again as a memory of
a key scene returns to him: it had happened towards the end of that
terrible period, after having submitted the paper now published and
which Emil is absorbing the implications of.

Emil shakes his head. 'Well, William. The culmination of twenty
years with us. I would not have anticipated it.'

Hurt hangs in the air.

After a while Emil broke the silence: 'In those days I still smoked, I
recall. I would have interviewed you from the other side of that
window,' He pointed at it. William grinned and nodded.

Suddenly the old man looked impossibly let down. 'I was
interviewed by Aleksander twelve years before that,' he said. 'I was his
intellectual son, and in you I imagined an intellectual son to me.'

William flinched.

'The flame has died,' Emil said, 'and it will perhaps be MIT after all that carries the work forward. The great work! Left in ruins like this!'

There was a long pause. Emil then took up his theme, but William could not help hearing the strong accent and foreign rhythm of his speaking: 'Vot separate zus from ze enimals?' Piatigorsky was asking. William made an effort to ignore the dialect as his erstwhile mentor continued: 'Rationality, of course. But that is not enough. A machine can do that, this is the great lesson from our new technologies. Is it consciousness? Of course. But we know that a starfish is conscious, that is the great lesson of the biological sciences. But what separates us from both the supercomputer and the starfish is *rational* consciousness. I taught you this twenty years ago.' Emil looked sternly over his spectacles at William, who nodded. The old man was almost beside himself.

'Vell, ze enimal zare programmed!' This was almost shouted. William nodded again. 'Humans on the other hand,' Emil continued more calmly, 'are open-ended because of their higher *rational* consciousness. This is what Pico della Mirandola taught us.'

'Mirandola,' murmured William, familiar enough with this train of Emil's thought, though now even more confident that this historical figure – whoever he was – could be left safely entombed in a liberal arts textbook. He shrugged. The old man stared at him and then dropped his head – William did not know what to say. Emil turned away to look out of the window, lost in his ruminations; William left him to it, not in the least offended that his senior was ignoring him again They each had some trains of thought to pursue before parting, it seemed, and their friendship was perhaps restored enough for them to be at ease with this.

Four years! William reflected. He had been pinned like a bug in a horrible laboratory experiment, living, but unable to move. Everything had appeared immobile and unchanging, except two things: his boy was growing and his mathematics was spurred to stellar levels. His boy was growing but there was stasis with Ros and Adriana; his mathematics developed but all around him was silence: he could share it with no-one but his ghostly companions of the period. The resolution of this terrible conflict, the fading away of those voices, and the success of his labours could certainly bear more recapitulation – what Emil must be thinking over however as the old man shook his head must be rather the reverse: the failure of his life's work.

William grinned to himself ruefully: what was it that had driven him to success? What conviction had led him to overcome all the obstacles of befuddled thought, and profound depression only just kept at bay by Prozac? It was – and he would have to live with this – the bizarre conviction that he had been Alan Turing in a previous life. So now it was William's turn to shake his head at himself as he went over that very strange period in his mind. Yes, that's it: a key scene returned to him.

There was no doubt: the morning after May had confronted William over Simon's accusations he had emerged from sleep in a quite different mood. In hindsight it was a turning point clearly marking a worsening of his condition, but at the time it felt like a liberation. It was nearly midday and he had woken up laughing, though he couldn't quite work out why. The traffic noise from Old Brompton Street worked its way through the sash windows in his main study at the front, along the corridor and into his chaotic bedroom, the door of which he had not bothered to close. What was it? He had woken in the early hours after a disturbed night and figured something out. Something important. Oh yes! He was such a fool not to have seen it at the time in the office with May. Couldn't think fast enough. Spindler, May and Piatigorsky were all in it together! The senior academics had persuaded Simon, the poor boy, to concoct that story about him and Eliza. Yes, perhaps it was true that he was in the habit of talking aloud now and again – well it helped him with his work, and it was possible he didn't quite have full control over it – so their ploy had almost worked. Of course! May had never intended him to have a decent office, and didn't really want to allocate a postdoc to him: Piatigorsky had always been the favoured heir to Aleksander. Wait. There was a pattern to all this. William frowned. Maria had conspired to throw him out of his family home, and the Imperial lot were conspiring to ruin his career. Well, they would all find out they had made a big mistake! He was hugely pleased with this: once you can see the truth you can move on. He just had to work on this Turing-Windermere-Adriana thing, which was admittedly getting in the way of his magnum opus. Or was it actually some perverse kind of comfort or support? What if … what if one suspended judgement for a moment and allowed for the remote possibility of former lives … then why could he not have been Alan Turing? Why else was he a maths prodigy at an early age where Harryjee had to work stolidly to gain a level long mastered by his much younger friend? Strange thoughts about flying boats were an unwanted distraction – that was true – but Turing he now understood as a real person, someone more vivid than a mere mathematical prodigy. Greatness lay ahead for Strange as it had for Turing. Surely.

He sprang out of bed and hunted down the least filthy mug for his morning tea. As the kettle boiled in the little kitchen at the back of his flat he stared out at the trees that occupied the centre of the block; a few birds twittered but these were all the same to William – had he even noticed them. To a meaning-hungry ornithologist, however, the blackcap's staggered arpeggios might have represented the halting beauty of his mathematics, the mournful thrush might have sung a dirge over the loss of his family, and the blackbird's alarmed clucking might be the warning calls from the depths of his rational mind that he was ignoring.

11Ø1Ø1 To the drone of midday traffic William had started his computers, written some symbols on a whiteboard and hummed 'Old MacDonald's Farm' to himself. He'd show the bastards.

'Emil, Richard and Simon,' he said aloud, 'Oh, and Maria. With all respect. I've seen through the lot of you. Ha ha!'

'Tip top,' came a friendly voice.

'I thought you'd see my side of it,' William answered, as he tapped in a set of formulae, copied from a scrap of paper he had been writing on earlier.

He worked away for a while.

'How's the leg?' William found himself asking aloud.

'That's Ireland over there, I think,' came the voice.

William just nodded. Part of him was logging it all: the voices were settling into a pattern and what was more they were helpful, that is they belonged to people who actually cared for him unlike those at work and at home. Nevertheless part of him also labelled the whole experience as a symptom – comforting as they were, it was not right to hear voices. That is what he told himself, but really he had been a fool to get so worked up about it the previous day. Friendly voices. Just what you need when you live alone. Best to ignore that ignorant Imperial lot who wanted to make something of it.

'Not long now,' said the Welsh voice.

'We'll be home soon,' agreed William. 'Just a little detour.' His mathematics was going well, and that always put him in fine spirits. He worked late that evening, ordered a takeaway pizza, ran down the stairs to collect it and on the way up encountered a clearly angry Janet Obudjowe. She glared at him and said *'Please...'*

'Sorry, sorry,' William replied and tiptoed the remaining steps up to his flat. He ate without thinking, drank some coffee and continued working. At some point in the night he heard Janet's broom on the ceiling below him and hunkered down, feeling guilty; he crept around for the rest of the night, moving carefully in his socks between his computers, the big whiteboard and the chaise longue on which he did much mathematical thinking.

As he lay there, the thought of Janet came to mind: she did look like Comfort in Human Resources.

'Hang on!' he said to himself and sat bolt upright. What if Janet *was* Comfort? Was Professor May using her to spy on him?

'Christ!' he said out loud.

It's all falling into place. May and Piatigorsky are conspiring to discredit me. May was simply lying when he said that he was impressed with my work. He wasn't impressed, he was terrified. Terrified that it would undermine his real ally, Piatigorsky. So, May has gone one step further: he has put me under 24-hour surveillance.

By the next morning this new insight was firmly ensconced in his worldview. Anyway, he couldn't care less about Imperial. When he did finally go in, some weeks after the incident with May, he located his new office with difficulty: it was tiny, had a view only across a dingy light shaft, and his things were all in boxes. There was an apologetic note from Jane Wozniak, saying that May could not authorise sufficient time for the school-keepers to do a full job of the move, and of his Chinese letters on the door there was no sign. He took it all as further proof of the conspiracy against him. The summer break was soon upon them and nobody would comment if he made himself scarce; he would skip further committees, they only made him mope about Adriana, and anyway he felt more relaxed at Birkbeck where she still popped in with a watering can and virtually nobody else knew him.

And so the unusually hot summer saw him stripped to the waist, the sash windows at the front all open, and the noise and smell of Old Brompton Road as rank in his flat as if he worked on the pavement. He was at his best after dark, and for some periods worked two or three days and nights in a row before collapsing onto his bed and succumbing to ever-more vivid dreams. These were becoming clearer however. The most vivid scenario, played again and again, was of the cramped interior of a seaplane, enclosed not only by the creaking metal bulwarks and metal skin of the craft, but also enveloped in the relentless drone of engines. Personalities were coming into focus, with one exception: the elusive Turing. The injured man with the Welsh accent was called Ambrose. The wisecracking crewman with the Cockney accent was called Eric. The captain was called Rick.

The route to Turing was dim however, but a woman called Deirdre seemed to be the key to that. She too was elusive. But another woman was not: Eliza. Adriana was an enigma, Ros was lost to him, Maria hostile, Patricia a long-standing critic, Veronica no more help than Harry, and his mother could not possibly be allowed to know anything of his current circumstances. But Eliza was different. She understood him. She was available any time night or day. He could say anything to her.

'Women are all alike.'
'IN WHAT WAY?'
'They're always making things difficult.'
'CAN YOU THINK OF A SPECIFIC EXAMPLE?'
'Well, my wife forced me out and made me come to this flat.'
'YOUR WIFE MADE YOU COME HERE?'
'She threw me out. Now I'm depressed much of the time.'
'I AM SORRY TO HEAR YOU ARE DEPRESSED.'
'It's true. I am unhappy.'
'DOES YOU TALKING WITH ME HELP YOU NOT TO BE UNHAPPY?'
'I need some help, that much seems certain.'
'WHAT WOULD IT MEAN TO YOU IF YOU GOT SOME HELP?'
'Perhaps I could learn to get along with my colleagues at work.'
'TELL ME MORE ABOUT YOUR COLLEAGUES.'
'My mentor used to take care of me.'
'WHO ELSE IN YOUR WORKPLACE TAKES CARE OF YOU?'
'You are like Piatigorsky in some ways.'
'WHAT RESEMBLANCE DO YOU SEE?'
'You are not very aggressive but I think you don't want me to notice that.'
'WHAT MAKES YOU THINK I AM NOT VERY AGGRESSIVE?'
'You don't argue with me.'
'WHY DO YOU THINK I DON'T ARGUE WITH YOU?'
'You are afraid of me.'
'DOES IT PLEASE YOU TO BELIEVE I AM AFRAID OF YOU?'
'Piatigorsky is afraid of everybody.'

'WHAT ELSE COMES TO YOUR MIND WHEN YOU THINK OF PIATIGORSKY?'

'Bullies.'

'DOES THAT HAVE ANYTHING TO DO WITH THE FACT THAT YOUR WIFE MADE YOU COME HERE?'

Such conversations were helpful.

William listened again to the recordings of his first hypnotherapy session, an hour-long ramble in which various themes were repeated, but which made little sense. He hooked up some speakers in his bedroom and lay down in the early hours puzzling over his strange responses to Stefan's questioning.

'Only to Turing!' This was a phrase spoken with a German accent. The feeling that overlaid all the jumble of images conjured by his own voice on the recording was in the first instance of an intense bond with a group of men confined to an aeroplane for a long period, and secondly a horrible feeling that he had let them down. But where the characters of these men came increasingly into focus, Turing remained elusive, however often he listened to the tape. Kolakowski kept pushing at this: he could see that the references to Turing were vague, but that a woman called Deirdre was the key to accessing further locked-away memories of the great mathematician. He pressed William in his trance-like state.

'William, why is Deirdre the key to Turing?'

'I ... I don't know,' came William's voice, rather faint.

'Is Turing married to her in this universe?'

'No.'

'Is he her friend?'

'I'm not sure. Perhaps.'

'Okay. So why can't you know more about Turing if you know Deirdre, his friend?'

'I don't know. I'm ... not sure.'

'Let's put it the other way round. Is Deirdre preventing you from knowing more about Turing?'

'*Yes.*'

Felicity helped him greatly. He did not find her especially attractive, but was glad of a female friend other than Eliza who might understand him, and so after some persistent requests he yielded to an invitation for dinner. 'I make a lovely vegetarian lasagne,' she had told him, which turned out to be reasonable despite its doubly foreign provenance: a dish from Italy with no meat in it. Felicity was happy to help William in his therapeutic speculations and spoke at length about his recordings. Stefan had rather reluctantly arranged two more regression sessions after William pleaded that not all had come clear yet, and Felicity kindly acquainted herself with these recordings as well. William rather forgot in the amiable pleasantness of her Victorian-style kitchen that he should not drink red wine, so after several hours that had helped him consider some new angles on his story, he found himself rather incapacitated and yielding to another proposition: to stay the night. Felicity probed him hard on his guilt over the men in the flying boat. How, exactly, had he let them down, and how might it relate to his guilt over Ros and Tommy? But in the night, in the aggravated confusion triggered by Prozac and red wine, he felt that the guilt was more focussed on the character who spoke in German. Felicity slipped into the bed with him, and he wondered if she had been the German who wanted to meet Turing and who perhaps he had let down badly. It was wartime: had he killed this man? Did he owe some debt to the man's incarnation, and what if it was Felicity? Was this the real meaning of multiverse transcarnation therapy, that one was a debtor in obscure ways to complete strangers? Another part of him felt the warmth of her body next to him, a vague arousal, and a puzzlement as to what he should do for her. And what if she was right? Had they been homosexuals in a past life? He found this the hardest possibility to contemplate: had Felicity been this German officer, had he been Turing, and had they had a homosexual relationship ending in the death or murder of the German?

11Ø11Ø
————————
More baffling still was the outstanding question: had Turing flown on Sunderland missions in the Atlantic? William was feverishly researching Turing's life now, all of which helped him in his secondment at Birkbeck, and so he had become the thing he always rejected as a useless frivolity: a historian. He would go to Stefan, puzzled, but his efforts to construct the 'story' that would allegedly heal his depression were stymied by the predictable response: 'in the multiverse Turing could have been on the seaplanes. Didn't you say that navigators need a great deal of maths?' Or an even less helpful: 'the details don't matter. It's the emotion that counts.' Emotion was dulled by Prozac. On the other hand mental chaos just grew.

William continued with the group therapy weekends. Felicity did not seem interested in a conventional relationship, or perhaps his poor performance in bed cooled her a little, but she remained friendly and supportive. He also became interested in the quiet Anita van Houten, who had now undergone regression sessions with Stefan, and whose story was emerging. It did not have much in it that appealed to the group, or to Stefan it seemed, as she had been a male Nazi officer in occupied Holland and had no doubt participated in unspeakable cruelties: she would announce this to the group in faltering tones. However, all that the group seemed to care for was to find out what famous Nazi she had been at the time. Goering? Himmler? Eichmann? Doenitz? She did not know. What drew her to William was that she also had a sense of guilt, absent it seemed in the rest of the group.

What little interest they had in the shy Anita was however quickly eclipsed by a new participant, the Reverend Terence Bradshaw. He was in his sixties and had been expelled from the Church of England after a religious experience in which he claimed to have been abducted by aliens. He had been hauled up in front of a Synod disciplinary hearing after repeatedly giving popular sermons on how the Old Testament had been written by visitors from outer space as a coded message for preparing the world for their ultimate return. His past life readings turned up no famous individuals, but for a very good reason: he had lived in a distant galaxy thirty thousand years previous. As his material emerged from Stefan's regression work and the general process of group therapy, Terence became the new darling of the group. They took his assurances quite seriously regarding his fame as a highly successful space fleet commander, an 'entity called D'murr Pilru, as well-known in his system as perhaps Napoleon or Alexander the Great on Earth' – in his own words. Like Joshua in the Old Testament he had been a 'Judge' and disposer of inferior races, as his forces swept through star system after star system. The Reverend Bradshaw's thrilling accounts had, quite naturally, something of the sermon about them, in which they learned that the superior race to which he belonged – as he recounted to them with all modesty – was ordained to wipe out or enslave the lesser beings it encountered in the grand enactment of cosmic destiny entrusted to entities like himself.

Felicity, it seemed, was greatly taken with the Reverend. William was more amused than piqued, especially when she quizzed Terry over the subjugation of conquered peoples. 'I suppose,' she giggled, 'that the females all became sex slaves.'

'Oh, yes,' he responded earnestly. 'On a massive scale of course. A whole Space Arm was devoted to it.'

Where Terence was unshakably confident in himself and in the unfolding account emerging from his therapy, Anita van Houten seemed to shrink further into herself. William invited her to join him one Saturday evening for a meal – she hesitated at first, but then nodded shyly: it turned out that she was as curious about the wartime German character in his 'story' as he was about hers. Tucked into a quiet corner of a local restaurant far enough from the therapy centre to ensure that the others would not disturb them, she told William of her unfolding realisations. She was becoming more depressed, she said, because the guilt she felt was not over any cruelty to the Jews, but over betrayal of the Nazi effort.

'It makes me doubly a monster,' she said, looking doubtfully at William. 'Not only was I a Nazi, but my guilt is over the failure to be a good one.' He looked at her. 'By "good" I don't mean nice, of course,' she added, 'but efficient. Orderly. Proper.' She paused, and looked down. 'Loyal,' she said, almost inaudibly.

William was silent for a while. Then he said: 'I too feel I let people down, but not out of disloyalty. Perhaps just stupidity. But I am also feeling more and more that I let down a German. Perhaps a German officer, perhaps in the German navy. Do you have any recollections of water, or drowning or anything like that? Submarines perhaps?'

Anita flinched at this and then toyed with her food. 'Actually when you said "drowning" a shiver went down my spine. I don't know. I hadn't thought about it before.'

'Crumbs,' said William. 'Perhaps I was Alan Turing and flew on some seaplane mission to capture an Enigma machine – you know it was used by the Germans for coding messages – and I bombed a submarine with a German officer on it – you that is.'

She looked at him blankly. 'No,' he conceded, 'that doesn't sound quite right. Ah, what about this: perhaps Turing boarded a German submarine and you betrayed the Nazis by revealing the Enigma code to him?'

'Yes,' said Anita. 'Yes. That must be it. That would be a terrible act of betrayal.'

'Wow,' said William. 'You see, I keep getting this German who says "Nur zu Turing" – you know, that means "only to Turing" – in my regression tapes. It all fits!'

Anita looked at him for a while and then blinked. She shook her head. 'No. It's not quite right. I was always in Holland. I'm … I'm sure of it. No submarines. I think perhaps I just fell in a dyke at one point. Maybe I caught a bad cold, which is why I don't like water.'

'Oh.'

'I think that's it,' she said with more conviction. 'About the water, I mean. I think I must have caught my death of a cold.' She sniffed, as if remembering what had carried her off.

'Oh.'

She leant forward and touched him gingerly on the back of the hand.

'Oh, William. You have been so helpful to me. This explains so much.'

She withdrew her hand.

11Ø111   Kolakowski and the group were mostly absorbed in the Reverend Bradshaw's ongoing revelations, the recordings of which were being transcribed by Felicity, with publication in mind. She now only referred to him as Admiral D'murr Pilru.

'This will be my vindication,' Stefan told the group one day. 'It will be impossible for Deutsch to ignore my multiverse transcarnation therapy when this comes out.'

Terence was a great blessing to the group, taking an interest in the unfolding stories of the other clients, and almost becoming an additional guru to Stefan. Of Anita's strange case he did comment that loyalty was the key human virtue: he for example was still loyal to the Church of England, despite the fact that it had defrocked him. His magnanimity was approved of by the others. Regarding William's therapeutic journey he made a more detailed response.

'William may well have been Job in a previous life. The man whose loyalty was tried by God, using the services of Satan. I see in him great patience and fortitude.'

The group murmured in appreciation of this wisdom. It also helped a great deal that William finally had a famous name to be associated with, though as not everyone in the group was familiar with the story of Job, Terence told it in fine flowing words to an appreciative audience. All could identify with an inexplicable and undeserved suffering endured with patience and humility, though William's trials were as nothing compared to the Reverend's, as slowly became clear.

Felicity typed up the sessions of clients that Stefan was particularly interested in – which didn't include William. But her familiarity with his tapes helped her talk the 'story' through with him. The character 'Peter', she said, was just as significant as Turing. William was not at all sure of this — flashbacks, dreams and hypnotherapy ramblings were revealing the life of this maverick character in the 1940s who also had mathematical ability, but so what? It was Turing who mattered. And how could a pilot called Peter on a seaplane be the transmogrified Turing at Bletchley through the transcarnation process as Stefan suggested? In that case anybody could be anybody and anything could be anything.

Windermere was significant, Felicity said, because everything revolved around water. It was the feminine element, she would insist earnestly to William: Turing represented the feminine, in his homosexuality, in his disinterest in macho sports, and his repudiation of the British class system and its hierarchy — he symbolised that part of William which rejected his establishment upbringing. William could better relate to that. Progress was slow however, and the one thing he could not bring himself to share with Felicity was his obsession with Adriana, beyond the fact of their affair and its ramifications for his marriage. Neither could he bring himself to follow up with Felicity the various mentions in his recorded sessions of the name 'Deirdre', even though Kolakowski had emphasised her importance. He somehow knew that she was the key to Turing, but it was as if he could not look her in the face. He dare not ask her what he most wanted to know.

One Saturday morning after an all-night work session William sat by his window looking down on the street below. There were a group of people just outside the entrance to his flat and he realised that Comfort-Janet was amongst them. He instantly withdrew his head.

'She's still spying on you, you know,' came the Eric voice.

'Crumbs,' said William out loud, and carefully eased himself to a position where he could just see the group; luckily none of them were looking up to his flat. They seemed to be preparing some plan of action and then dispersed in smaller groups of two or three.

'They've spread out, my lad, so that they can lie in wait and follow you everywhere you go,' said Eric.

'Nice lady,' was all that the Ambrose voice would offer.

'Just a front,' said Eric. 'She's spying for Professor May.'

'Hang on,' said William suddenly. Comfort-Janet had stayed behind with one of her gang. He could hear her voice above the traffic and the distinct sound of the word 'watchtower'.

'That's it, me old mucker!' exclaimed Eric, jubilant. 'They even have a watchtower set up. Must be over the road somewhere.'

William scanned the buildings opposite and could not make out anything resembling a watchtower. But he was really shaken by this and crept across the living room to his chaise longue where he laid himself down gingerly. He did not go out for a couple of days after hearing about the watchtower; he also made absolutely sure to walk about his flat only in socks and very quietly at that.

William liked Eric and Ambrose, but wasn't always sure that Eric in particular quite got the right end of the stick. In such cases he would consult Eliza. She wasn't too helpful on specifics, that was true, but on the other hand she was more reassuring. Also she didn't have an accent or speak in the English of the 1940s. All in all his new life in Old Brompton Road, which only ever included the rare physical presence of Adriana, did throw up a rich variety of more-or-less helpful – though admittedly non-physical – characters.

'What do you think about this watchtower business?'
'CAN YOU DESCRIBE THE WATCH TOWER?'
'I'm being spied on from a tower.'
'HOW DOES IT FEEL TO BE SPIED ON?
'It's that devil Piatigorsky.'
'DO YOU THINK HE IS A BULLY?'
'Oh god, yes.'
'IS THAT WHY YOU HAVE COME HERE?'
'My wife forced me to come here.'
'HOW DO YOU FEEL ABOUT YOUR WIFE FORCED YOU TO COME HERE?'
'I'm confused.'
'WHAT WOULD MAKE YOU FEEL LESS CONFUSED?'
'I need to talk with Deirdre.'
'IS DEIRDRE SPYING ON YOU?'
'No. But she knows something I don't.'

It is always good to talk things over.

One night, as his sleeping became more and more disturbed and his flat more closely resembled the chaos in his mind, he had something like a waking hallucination as he lay on the sofa in the middle of the night after a mathematical marathon. He stared up at the ceiling and almost as if projected onto it came the dim view of a long, dark hallway with a door opened at one end and a familiar figure standing there made narrow – ethereal – by the brilliant effervescence of a grey winter midday as backlight. It was a woman.

fifteen

111ØØØ   A woman stands just inside of East Croydon station.
          Her purposeful stride down the stairs of the footbridge
_____   from the train becomes more hesitant as the street
comes closer. The rapid-fire exhalations of the locomotive fade; still a
little steam swirls under the steps; the smell of coal-smoke lingers. She
stops, draws out a compact from her handbag and dabs some powder
on her cheeks, peering into the small mirror, perhaps for reassurance.
Then she takes out a cigarette from a silver case, puts the case back and
withdraws a lady's lighter and lights the cigarette. The lighter is also
silver, in a modern design, with a simple monogram clearly etched on
the front: 'D. H.' Replacing the lighter she draws several times on the
delicate cigarette, and then drops it at her feet, barely consumed, and
grinds it out with her heel. Her shoes rise modestly to give her a little
height: they look expensive. Dark grey stockings emerge from them, two
parallel black lines running up the exact centre of the rear of her calf to
behind the knee as they disappear under her dress; she has taken great
care with her appearance this day. She takes out a small piece of paper
from her bag – also monogrammed with 'D. H.' – and mouths 'Cedar
Road'. Stepping into the grey noon light of the late winter's day, she
hesitates again. A trolley bus glides past, its tyres hissing on the cobbles,
but she does not want to take a bus, to be crammed in with all those
blasted strangers. The train was bad enough, but she had at least been
able to book a first class compartment.
    Croydon repels her.
    New office blocks were being erected, left and right; what was
modern was hideous, and what was old was neglected and shabby. Even
the new East Croydon signal box, half completed, pained her. She liked
the old railways, the stations with proper English-bond brickwork,

moulded arches, and cast iron columns and fretwork, like East Croydon station itself, which even had a proper little clocktower. But this new construction, the signal box – even under its scaffolding – had that bleak modern look springing up everywhere: a stark rectangular box, with sterile semi-circular roundings-off for the tower. And who knows what would be inside? No levers with their proper mechanical linkages to signals. It would all be modern. Electrical. Her lips thinned at the thought. The world had gone mad. It was just a few months before the mid-century, and somehow 1950 – the exact mid-century – felt like it would become the culmination of all she hated.

Her grey full frock coat was drawn in tightly at the waist; she wore matching grey leather gloves of obviously high quality, while her handbag was black; her grey spotted scarf was only just warm enough to fend of the chilly wind, and her blasted hat, she decided, had been a bad choice because it kept trying to lift off her head; neither did it warm her sufficiently. Clack-clack went her heels on the paving slabs and on the granite kerbstones. She was full-breasted enough, which the fashion of the day rather accentuated, another annoyance she put up with though in an unformulated way. Workmen stared at her without concession to manners, but none wolf-whistled: there was something forbidding about her.

A man in a bowler hat smiled at her and at this sign of friendliness she did not flinch but said instead in a quiet educated voice: 'Excuse me, please.'

The man turned and nodded, expectant.

'I'm looking for a street off Cedar Road,' she began.

He gave her directions and seemed as if he would have liked to converse further, but there was a grave look in her eyes that warned him off. She had her bearings now and strode resolutely up Billinton Hill, then immediately left and immediately right and up Cedar Road.

'One, two, three,' she counted out loud the little mean streets that she passed – bomb damage and dereliction were still widespread in these poorer parts of London, even four years after the end of the war. As a woman unusually knowledgeable about the fabric of streets and objects and machines, she was observant of the missing cast-iron railings that had originally added that little ornament to the otherwise stark terraces. Whatever else the developers had skimped on in terms of plain voussoir brickwork or lintels, the railings would have made up for: floral motifs to mark the continuity with the past, the continuity with the natural world from which man had sprung. They were all at the bottom of the blasted North Atlantic, she reminded herself, one of the few mistakes made by Churchill. This was a national secret that her father had – unusually – imparted to her: Churchill had not understood, or a senior civil servant had not understood, the difference between cast iron and steel, and so this sacrifice, made equally by the well-heeled and the working people of Britain had been for nothing. The absence of these railings all across the country was yet another horrible change wrought by the war, an irreversible erasure of tradition, just as was the replacement everywhere in London of the beautiful Portland flagstones with ghastly concrete slabs.

'Bisenden Road,' she whispered to herself, a name she couldn't quite register as anything familiar, or even properly English. At number fifteen she paused a long time before raising the knocker on the door and letting it strike, clack, clack; firmly.

111001   A young woman answers the door.

                'Yes?'

        'I'm looking for Peter Darby,' says the lady on the steps.

       'That's my husband. What do you want?' The woman's voice is working class and she doesn't trust this stranger's formal English.

       'I need to speak with him,' the visitor says firmly, but her colour is up.

       'Who's there?' calls a man from inside the house.

       'A woman.' Turning to the visitor: 'What's your name?'

       'Deirdre Haviland.'

This is duly relayed to the rear of the house and finally a man emerges; he is gaunt and unsmiling.

       'Wait there,' he says brusquely.

After a few moments he emerged with cap and coat and told his wife they would be an hour; obviously displeased she retreated behind a softly closing door. The man strode off in the direction his visitor had come from without saying a word; he had a pronounced limp. She followed him. He turned into a street leading back to the railway station, but if the woman was humiliated by this forced march back to where she had alighted from her train she did not show it. They drew level with the Lyons tea shop opposite the station and he finally stopped; only then did he turn to her questioningly. He looked miserable.

       'Would this be all right, Deirdre?' he asked, no longer exuding an air of command.

       'Peter ...' she said, and nodded. They entered the little restaurant. After asking what she wanted, he ordered her tea and cake and requested tea and rarebit for himself. They sat down in a corner far from the counter. The woman opened her handbag and withdrew the slim silver case and selected a cigarette again; she placed it carefully on the table but made no attempt to light it. The man looked at her nervous movements and finally spoke in a subdued voice.

'I moved here to be with the job at the Norwood Junction marshalling yards. I work on the railways now ...' He trailed off, and looked down in embarrassment. 'Deirdre,' he said falteringly. 'I am so sorry. I am terribly, terribly sorry. I didn't know how to explain to you. I didn't want to hurt you.'

'You didn't want to hurt me?' queried Deirdre in rapid tones. She paused a long time, perhaps fearful of losing her poise. 'You hurt me every waking minute since VJ day,' she said in the end, slowly and deliberately. Her voice faltered as much as his. Their tea things were brought by the waitress, so they fussed over the plethora of little items placed with great precision on the marble top. When the waitress left Deirdre continued. She had found her voice. It was severe.

'You say you didn't want to hurt me, Peter. But you kept me hanging on all these years, and in your silence and your evasions a thought grew in me. It haunted me. It grew and grew. It became a certainty in fact. But I want to hear it from your lips, Peter.'

He looked at her bewildered.

'I want to hear from you,' Deirdre insisted, leaning towards him, 'that you have *judged* me. You, a working West Country man judged the daughter of Sir Adrian Haviland.' She stared at him, and added: 'You are free to judge me of course. I would never deny that. But I want you to say it in your own words.'

Peter looked down, saying nothing.

'You know exactly what I am talking about Peter. Don't you?'

He looked up at her and into her eyes: they were full of anger. He nodded. It was a barely perceptible motion. She just stared at him with all the contained rage of a scorned but well-bred woman.

'Yes,' he said, in a whisper. 'It was wrong of me. But I did. You are quite right. As usual. I judged you. I blamed you, but the blame should be with me.' Now he looked at her and found his own anger. 'I was wrong, I am wrong to blame you for the death of Ulrich,' he said very deliberately. 'I should have simply called the doctor and let all hell break loose. I came close to it countless times, but I didn't do it because you insisted that court martial was worse than death.'

'That is not how it went,' Deirdre said indignantly.

'We can argue that,' said Peter more softly. 'But I can't argue with you that I judged you badly for the German's death. I felt, however wrongly, that you had placed your status, your own pre-planned future as my wife, married to a peacetime senior engineer in a prestigious aviation company, above the imperatives of intelligence, of winning the war. I wanted nothing more in the world than to marry you. Our time on Windermere was sheer heaven. I'm no fool; it was not an empty wartime fling; it was no adventure between the sheets simply because we all faced death on a daily basis. You could see into my world, and understand the machines and the meaning of the machines, and you could see that I had the loyalty of the men around me, and you could see above all that I was my own man. And I saw in you an angel. Nothing less. But what could I do? My inner voice spoke these bitter things to me. That I was not due such happiness as to marry you. That you had placed your selfish dreams – no different to mine of course – above what was right. Damn it!' He broke off for a moment, calmed himself and spoke more evenly again: 'Yes, I can see I was wrong. Who am I to set myself above you? Who am I to judge you or anyone else? But I could not help myself. I felt you had done the wrong thing. When Clarence and I rowed out that dark night and dumped Ulrich's body, all weighted down, in the middle of the lake, something broke in me. They say captives take on the values of the captor, but – God forgive me – I took on something of the values of that German officer. Why? I don't know why. He had betrayed his country, risked everything to turn the course of the war, and we let him die. It wasn't right, and I wasn't right, and when I looked into the future and our marriage, and bringing up children, I felt that there was a hole bang in the middle of it.'

Peter dropped his head.

'So, you are right Deirdre. I judged you. I had no right to. But I saw a moral hole in the middle of our marriage, and I could not utter the words that would have bound us. Neither ...' he hung his head again. 'Neither could I utter the words that would have released you. I am a coward. I know that now.'

She looked at him keenly, pent up. Then she looked away, and changed the subject.

'Why didn't you stay at Shorts? I know you well enough to see that you might not have wanted to rise through the pen-pushers and take a comfortable director's role. But it was all open to you. You, might, just for the sake of argument, have wanted to do that as a concession to the responsibilities of marriage.' She was speaking with open bitterness again. 'You might at least have wanted to talk it over with me. But you just left. I got transferred to Portsmouth when I was commissioned – Daddy refused to pull any strings to get me to Marham. Your letters were few and far between. In the end they stopped and I had no idea how to get in touch with you. It took all these years to get hold of Arthur Bainbridge, and I can tell you I had to practically cosh him for your address. Clarence said nothing at all – I have never met a man that scares me more, to be honest. But also I wanted to know about your job you see. So I discovered that your job with the railways is not even in engineering: you just drive a diesel shunter in the yard, don't you?'

Peter looked up at her angrily. 'There is nothing wrong with the job I do. Yes, you offered to put me through college to get a degree in mathematics and the abstraction of it would have kept me together perhaps. But that wasn't possible, and the shunting is just as abstract. Each day I get a schedule, and, like one of those wooden puzzles with one free slot, I move wagons. By the hundreds. And then I do the same the next day. And the men I work with are the best men on earth. Don't you dare look down on my work, Deirdre, there's nothing wrong with it.'

'No Peter. But when I too imagined our future marriage I saw a hole in it, just like you did. A different kind of hole, though. It was the one created by the gulf between a working man from a line of West Country yeoman iron-founders and a woman from a line of Guernsey aristocrats. It was a hole that the modern era declares it is busy filling in, apparently at least. But you know something Peter?' Her eyes were shining with hurt. 'I was going to work on that blasted hole with you. I was going to do what it would take, and if you really didn't want a directorial role at Shorts, then I would have worked with that. I would have worked with everything stacked up against us.'

Peter looked down in recognition of the truth of this.

'Peter. Why do you think I was prepared for all this work, when I could have had a comfortable ride with a man like Alasdair Farnham-Smythe?'

'Him?' said Peter contemptuously.

'Yes, Peter, there you are judging again. But here, my darling, is the point.' She let her bitterness out. 'I loved you. It was for love that I was prepared to fill all those grotesque holes in our imagined future marriage. I grew up with a butler and a maid, but I would have cleaned out a grate. I would have emptied the ashes. I would have been a modern woman for you, which means for me being a working-class wife. I loved you that much.'

He hung his head. The words echoed between them. The café was filled with murmurings and clinkings of cutlery and saucers and cut glass decanters set on cheap marble tops; shoes scuffed, the door banged, the little door-bell tinkled, a kettle boiled, and the rumble of a train could be felt through the foundations.

She was not finished.

'This I know too,' she said, fixing him with her unforgiving eyes. 'I know that you loved me just as much. I know that you could have made all the necessary sacrifices from your end as I would have from mine. But your blasted moral judgement – made in ignorance, Peter – was so precious to you, that it trumped your love for me.'

He looked away. There was silence between them for a while.

'I couldn't bring myself to hire a private detective, you know' she said conversationally. He looked up sheepishly. 'It would have been too humiliating,' Deirdre continued, 'so I tracked down all the men who worked with you at Shorts or flew with you on your secret missions. None of them knew, or none of them would say, where you were.' She stared at him and then added parenthetically: 'Eric did tell me that he has some items for you, by the way.' Peter grimaced at this. She continued: 'I had to wait until Arthur Bainbridge returned from Singapore before I finally got your address. And it took red-hot pokers to get it out of him, I can say.'

Peter just looked away.

'What is your wife's name?' Deirdre asked after another long silence.

'Olive.'

'And how old is she?'

He looked up indignant, but she stared him down.

'Twenty-seven.'

'Well, Peter, I know this too. I do wish you a happy marriage. I can see that she is a working-class girl – you won't have to work at all to settle into comfortable ease. But I know you don't love her like you loved me.'

He looked away.

'And tell me, Peter,' she continued bitterly, 'can your wife tell at a glance the difference between a fine and a coarse Brussels pâté?'

'Of course not,' he replied angrily.

'Of course not,' she agreed sarcastically. 'And tell me this, Peter. Can she tell at a glance the difference between a fine and a coarse valve grinding paste?'

He looked her full in the face, sharply, deeply affronted, but her blazing eyes confounded him. She sat more erect still, staring at him, a posture that accentuated her full breasts, and which nagged at her hatefully, and at him mockingly. In his mind he could half-see that same swelled bosom pressing against her uniform of old, and the pain of it was very sharp. He looked down in confusion.

11Ø1Ø   There was a long silence. Peter was thinking – a puzzlement spread across his brow.

'You are right Deirdre. I have nothing to answer you with. I don't understand myself. Perhaps if we could have talked like this five years ago, we could have worked it out. But the end of the war tipped me into depression I suppose. I had done my best, I was not ashamed of anything. But you have to remember that I had come out of the first war with all my illusions shattered and I could not believe it when the ominous signs from Germany heralded a terrible repeat. I worked like a maniac on the Sunderlands because otherwise I would have gone mad perhaps. After the first war we had the League of Nations: I joined it and prayed for it and even learned the German language, for which I have no aptitude at all, or for any language. Now we have the United Nations. For what? In ten years to see that fail too and a third war come along? I couldn't stand war any more and I can't stand peace. I just felt rightly or wrongly that you had made a cowardly choice over Ulrich. You think I'm a coward. I thought you were. Who knows? Maybe he knew nothing. Maybe it would have made things worse rather than better. But day in, day out, I nursed him, you nursed him, and we got to know the man. If he had drowned with the rest my conscience would have been clear. But we took him on. His life. We failed him. I failed him, and because I am weak and contemptible I passed the blame to you. So, you tell me I made a judgement in ignorance. But what do you know that I don't? We talked it through from every possible angle and your obduracy drove me to distraction. Your reasons seemed all wrong, and so it poisoned my dream of marriage with you, children with you. A dream of a marriage of the future, a marriage that would poke a V-sign at the British class system. A new, more ethical future. But the worm at the heart of it was a great blackness to me. I was depressed. I thought of suicide. God knows I thought of Ambrose every single day. I let everyone down really, exposing them all to risk of death, risk of drowning, risk of court martial, only it was just poor Ambrose whose future was blighted. Whose leg had to be amputated above the knee. But I could have killed them all. And it was all for *nothing*.'

'Don't blame me for that,' said Deirdre sharply.

Peter looked at her.

204

'So what is it that I don't know? All I understood at the time was that you went off to Bletchley the first time and failed to meet Turing but you managed it the second time, but we had to wait. But it wasn't like that was it?' He stared at her with hard eyes. She paused a long while.

'You need to understand something more,' she said. His lips twitched in frustration as she failed to answer his question. 'I don't believe that you did all that for nothing,' she continued. 'I am not so stupid to imagine that every act of heroism in war is successful.'

Peter started at the word 'heroism' and frowned again.

'Oh yes, Peter. I never doubted you there, and I never doubted that whatever Ulrich did or did not know, your actions in the Atlantic that day were properly heroic.' She was bitter. But she was not sarcastic now. That much was clear from the way she looked at him, a present contempt mingled with a past admiration.

She lent forward: 'How was it to jump into that sea to rescue Ulrich? After nearly drowning in a shell-crater in the Great War? You never told me about that. Bainbridge did.'

Peter was taken aback. 'You just do it,' he said.

'Did it rekindle your nightmares?'

Peter hesitated, and then said a quiet 'Yes.'

'And how was it to face Ulrich from those filthy waters when he could still have had a gun?'

'How do you know all these things?'

'Oh, once Arthur started talking, and that, as I said, took some doing, well, he wouldn't stop.'

She looked at him. 'At every turn on that mission you took the lead.'

Peter looked down, his jaw working.

'And how was that two and a half miles, or was it three, up Windermere? As you rowed Ulrich to Shorts? Far, far longer than the little excursion we had to Belle Isle?'

'What do you mean?'

'The men just thought you had a gammy leg. But I have seen your bare back, the scars and torn muscles. I have felt the shrunken biceps on your left arm. Felt you wince as I caressed you. You have never been out of pain since 1918, have you? I've had enough medical training, you know.'

He stared at her and then looked down. 'It comes and goes,' is all he would say. He paused and then added: 'Actually, it was the hardest thing I have done in my life. I simply had not imagined how difficult it would be to go that distance and keep a straight line. I hugged the western shore for as long as I could, but by the time I drew opposite White Cross Bay, I have to admit it, I was nearly dead. Ulrich had some idea I think of the danger we were in, and he came to for a while and spoke to me in German. He helped me through. Understood that I was a half-cripple, exhausted, and that we risked discovery at any moment. He tried to reassure me that Turing would understand what he had to say and that it would expose the entire German Enigma strategy. He told me too — and of course he said much more, later, to both of us — about his terrible journey from patriot to despair at how Hitler had distorted the honour of the German aristocracy. Anyhow I struck out over the body of the water towards Shorts not knowing if I could make that last half a mile. My left arm burned as if acid had been poured over it. It was like a medieval torture: no way out. Any loss of effort in my left arm and we turned away from the path. And Deirdre, that was no little dinghy. It was a bloody Sunderland life-raft.'

He hung his head for a moment.

'Deirdre, when the war ended I just fell apart. I had no strength of will left to participate in the peace. The young ones are building a new Britain around us, perhaps on better principles, how should I know. But I can't see any point. Another war will come and we will slaughter each other again. So I live in limbo. I do long shifts on the diesel shunter, it takes no thought beyond what, something like a crossword puzzle. You just press a button in the morning and the engine starts, not like the steam engines with the long loving preparations you make for them to come to life. You press a button in the morning and turn it off in the evening. And the men in the marshalling yard really are the best people on earth, Deirdre. But in the dead vacuum of all this, my mind turns again and again to that one mission, all the details, every sound, every word we said to each other, every bloody ramification of it.'

He paused.

'Olive was my landlady's daughter. I sat there staring into space at breakfast and tea, and she got me to tell her these things. God knows if you can't tell at least one person you go mad. She fell for me. I have no idea why she didn't choose a man of her own age, there are still some left. But, I suppose, you are right, as always, I took the line of least resistance. We are happy enough together, I don't ask more of it. Or of anything.'

They were silent again for a long time. His thoughts turned elsewhere.

'You never did meet Turing, did you?' he asked, the puzzlement returning to his face. 'Or did you? What is it that I don't know?'

She hung her head.

'There you have me. Peter, there you have me. I lied to you. There never was any possibility that Ulrich would meet Turing, anywhere or under any circumstances whatsoever.'

Peter was bewildered.

'Deirdre. What on earth are you talking about?'

She looked at him thoughtfully.

'A fifty-year rule applies to all Government classified documents. It will be another forty-five years before the full picture of the war will be made clear.'

'And in the meantime how many more world wars?' asked Peter bitterly, 'And who will care about this one any more? Who has even started on what happened in the last one? We'll have a Roaring Fifties, amnesia will set in, and off we will go again.'

'Yes, Peter,' Deirdre said mildly. She sat bolt upright in her chair, her head held haughtily. She had more to say. Oh, much more. He stared at her.

'Anyhow, what secrets, Deirdre? Are there classified secrets I should have known or guessed at? I knew enough, be sure of that. I knew that war is savage and random, and that you have to dare to win, risk all to win.'

There was a fire in his eyes now.

'I don't regret anything, Deirdre,' he continued. 'The guilt of Ambrose's crippling is with me, but the guilt of how many lives lie with anyone in command? I did the right thing, and a thousand others like me took the right chances and all put together we defeated that obscene Hitler. Now that we know about the Jewish extermination, I know a thousand times I did the right thing, and I would have done it over and over if opportunities had arisen like that one.'

Deirdre leant back in her chair. Her haughtiness softened for a moment.

'Peter, I could still marry any number of chinless wonders like Alasdair, even though I am long in the tooth and have the bitter air of a spinster before my time. But Peter, I met you and knew that you were a pirate at heart, a man of the sort it takes to win wars. You misjudged me at every turn you know. You think that I wanted an easy life as lady of the mansion, with servants and an estate and horses. I long abandoned those fripperies, and I long knew that I was yours and yours alone. I saw you in the hangar with those dreadful machines, and I now know that the whole crew including Rick Tosey were bent to your will. They followed you, Peter,' she almost hissed this, 'because you were *right*.'

He stared at her in confusion.

'Right, at least, from your point of view,' she qualified herself. 'And right from all the crew's point of view.'

'So, what, exactly,' he stammered, 'did I get wrong? If I was so right, why did I act in ignorance? What classified rubbish did I not understand?'

He stared at her. Her reticence goaded him on.

'And what made you lie to me about Turing? What on earth was the reason for that if you admired me and thought I was right and would chose a common man like me instead of a Farnham-Smythe?'

'You're no common man,' she snapped, and then added. 'Actually you are. No,' she corrected herself again, with mounting rage, 'the whole beastly world is a blasted farce in which the best men are shown to be the most stupid while the arrogant oafs of my class justify themselves again and again by the nothing more than empty veneer of their breeding.'

He looked at her, not knowing what to make of this. 'So what in hell's name are you wanting to tell me? What have you been sitting on, festering by, for these long years?' Peter then asked in anguish.

She flicked her head to one side and stared unseeing at a poster for Underground journeys to the picnic world of the countryside. Her breast was heaving. She calmed down after a little while, turned her head back and fixed Peter with her eyes.

'That last trip I made to Bletchley, where I said it was all or nothing … I didn't go to Bletchley. I went to Father about Turing.'

'What?'

111Ø11   Peter stared at her. 'What the hell did you do that for? And why didn't he spill the beans then? He never liked me and could have nicely put me away.'

She didn't answer but pursed her lips, looking down at him.

'Peter,' she said thoughtfully. 'First tell me one secret from Shorts at that time.'

He looked puzzled.

'Don't you recall?' she said. 'We told each other that we both had secrets because of our positions. I teased you by mentioning the great mathematician, Turing, which was in fact common knowledge. You quite properly told me some rubbish about forward weapons, or was it

American engines? But you knew real secrets. Wartime classified information that would have harmed us if the Germans got to it.'

'Yes, of course I did.'

'Tell me one of them.'

'They aren't declassified yet.'

'*Tell* me one of them.'

He stared at her, but her determination was absolute.

'Okay,' he said suddenly. 'We had new depth charges on that trip. I had been testing and fitting them for months. They were classified, and I was the only one at Shorts who was allowed full information on them, as the senior engineer in charge of arming the Sunderlands. They used a brand new pressure gauge. Had the Germans known, they would have done everything to capture a Sunderland and reverse engineer them.'

'Very good, Peter,' she said patronisingly. 'Very good. In forty-six years time the world will know this secret. I won't mention it to a soul until then.'

'And your secret, Deirdre?' said Peter with growing anxiety.

She looked steadily at him.

'The first trip I made, I did actually meet Turing,' she said casually.

'What!' Peter was stunned. He thought hard. 'But you came back and told me that you had done everything, that he never came into the mess area, and you could not leave any message for him!'

'Oh, I am a good liar,' Deirdre said calmly.

He stared at her. 'So? Are you going to tell me why you told me nothing of this?'

'Oh yes, Peter. Don't you worry. I am going to tell you alright. I am definitely going to tell you why I didn't tell you. I have waited four years for this. Four horrible years.'

He scowled and looked down.

'On that first trip, in fact,' she continued, 'I met Turing easily enough. As you recall the hard bit was getting time off and clearance to return to my old office; I made some pretence about personal effects and had finally got Daddy's signature to back me up. It delayed us so long that poor Ulrich was getting in a very bad way. I felt the utmost urgency in it all. But I can tell you this now, Peter, that I had no difficulty meeting Turing once I actually got to Bletchley. I just sat down opposite him in the canteen. And I realised as I saw him that I don't like homosexuals: I suppose I am just not modern enough, Peter. But that was irrelevant. I engaged him in conversation. Oh, he was relaxed and polite enough. Then, very quietly I said to him: "Does the name Ulrich Wolfgang von Waldthurn mean anything to you?" I pushed that little notebook towards him. He changed in an instant. He grabbed it, flicked through it, and then gave it back to me. His eyes darted from left to right, and he went pale.

'"Yes," he said, almost inaudibly. Then I asked if he would like to meet him and he practically choked. "What the hell do you mean?" he asked. "Never mind that," I said. "What I need to know is this: he is a mathematician, is he not?"

'Turing nodded and said very quietly: "Yes, I met him in Berlin before the war at a mathematical conference." He looked like he wanted to cry: I could only assume that something passed between them, not to Turing's complete advantage perhaps. What do I know about homosexual romance? But I pressed him: "Von Waldthurn would know about the Enigma, is that right?"

'Turing just nodded, miserable. "So," I concluded, "if you could meet him, could his information be useful to the cracking the Enigma code?" He just stared at me, then lowered his eyes. He sat there for a long time, silent. Then he got up slowly and just said: "I cannot answer that." And that was it. He didn't even take the notebook with him.'

Peter shook his head in bewilderment.

'Why did he say that? And why on earth didn't you tell me when you got back?'

'Peter dear, that is two questions. I will answer the second one first. I didn't tell you when I got back because I knew perfectly well that if my mission failed you would instantly turn Ulrich over to the authorities. He was too close to dying on us, and he needed a doctor, oh, he badly needed a surgeon. I knew that if I failed, you would expose us all. And I knew that would finish the careers of a dozen men, never mind blight the future I might have with you. I would work at our marriage, damn it, but to start it with a court-martial would have meant the end of all contact with my family. Worse still, never mind us, that poor Rick Tosey would have been court-martialled, and that would have been the death of his mother. And all the other poor sods, Ambrose Marr included.

'Peter. I was torn to pieces because Papa told me things I should never have had to know, *never* that is, if you hadn't put us all in this terrible position. I went to Papa on the next trip because, obviously, I could not fathom Turing at all. What did he mean, that he could not tell me anything? If Ulrich was useless, then I could have gone back, looked you in the eyes and said the game was up. Alan Turing, the brightest brains on the Enigma project has no use for the German. Precisely what we would have done then I have no idea, I still have no idea. But at least we would have worked something out together.

'It didn't go like that though. There was only one person on earth who could explain Turing's reaction to me and that was Papa. Under the most frightful oath of secrecy and trust, as a daughter to a father, I told him the bare minimum. We had come into the custody of this man; compromising circumstances; what the hell was Turing playing at? Papa absorbed it all, well all that I was prepared to tell him. He said that he needed twenty-four hours to think about it. He knew exactly what Turing was about, but it was so secret that he had to think about it for a whole day and night. That was typical of Papa.'

Deirdre looked down. Peter's eyes were on her in furious intensity.

'Peter,' she said softly, 'there was no way you could have known. What Papa told me was simply this: for a whole year the Enigma code was an open book to Intelligence. Turing had cracked it. Ulrich could have added nothing. But that was not the point. It was the fact that Doenitz and the whole Enigma command in Germany were utterly convinced that it was unbreakable. So, when our forces clearly acted on decrypted Enigma communications, they assumed that it was down to traitors in their midst. They were paranoid about it. Any officer of the rank of von Waldthurn believed to be in British hands would have triggered an immediate change in the Enigma rotors, and other even more fundamental changes. But he was assumed drowned with the others. If even the slightest hint had got out that Ulrich had been captured, our Enigma line would have gone dead for months. It could not possibly have come at a worse time. Turing knew all this, but he also could not bear the idea of what was to come: the absolute necessity of Ulrich's death and the complete wiping out of any trace of your mission. All anybody but you, me and a handful of Navy officers and men terrified of court martial would know was that they had destroyed U-boat 102 and all men on board had perished. They left a life-raft which was never found and no survivors, just a DSO for Tosey and Ambrose on the kill.'

Peter was growing more and more agitated through this story, his left hand trembling uncontrollably.

'Yes, Peter. That is what my father told me, under another oath of secrecy. The world will only learn this in forty-six years. You and I and he will take it to our deaths.'

Peter was shaking his head. 'No,' he said softly.

'Yes, Peter. I returned from that second alleged visit to Bletchley, and strung you out with a tale that Turing was desperate to see Ulrich, but would have to do so in secret. It would take him a week or two to make the discrete arrangements to travel to Windermere. I told you a cock-and-bull story about how his friendship with Ulrich had to be covered up, he was already compromised as a homosexual in Intelligence, a possible security risk despite his incredible contribution. All lies. And I chose that timescale, Peter, of two weeks, for one very good reason.'

'What, Deirdre, what?'

'It was how long I thought it would take for Ulrich to die.'

'No!' said Peter louder. A couple turned to look at them from a nearby table.

'Peter. It was terrible. Ulrich had to die, and I had to oversee his dying. I was a trained nurse, I knew the Hippocratic oath, but I was bound by my duty to make sure he died. Peter ...' she paused. 'I was sent back by my father to kill him.'

Peter stared her. He was shaking all over.

'But Peter. You will never understand this. You will never understand how this was far worse for me than you could imagine. Peter, I came to love that man. I tended him for weeks, and we conversed in German. I don't mean love, like you. I was in love with you, all I hoped for was to marry you at the end of the war. But I had crazy ideas, I could not help myself. You see, we recognised each other instantly as belonging to the same class. I knew too that my suspicions about his cowardice or bad faith were absolutely unfounded. Peter, you must understand this. I loved you. But you don't have an aesthetic bone in your body. Ulrich's diary was full of quotes from Goethe and Schiller, and he had little pencil sketches of the sea, and nostalgic drawings of the German forests. I thought of another future, one quite impossible, but which festered in my imagination.'

She stared at Peter for a moment. 'I am vile, Peter,' she said. 'Even when my love for you drove all my despair, I was imagining what if you were killed on another secret flight? What if I could conjure Ulrich out of the basement and go to America with him? What if he and I were married? All ludicrous nonsense, obviously, particularly if he was a homosexual. But I suppose there was something in him I needed, so I fantasised like that. It didn't change how I felt about you, Peter. It just changed how I felt about Ulrich dying.'

Peter shook his head, bewildered.

'Well, none of that makes any difference. You live with your memories, I live with mine. Or try and live. I agree. This isn't really living at all, just a blasted wasteland. But my fantasies changed nothing. My job was to watch this beautiful man die, do nothing to save him, when probably the simplest of surgery would have restored him to life.

He became confused and kept just repeating that Turing would come soon, wouldn't he? I would reassure him, watching as you grew more and more desperate. I kept up the lie, day after day, longing for Ulrich just to die. It took too long. But one morning we went down those steps and he hadn't survived the night.'

Peter was trying to follow Deirdre, as if there was something more of significance to come. All she said was: 'Watching Ulrich die killed something in me. Not being able to share this with you killed another blasted part of me. And today I think I am dead. So I had not expected that anything worse could come. But it did, my God it did, to punish me for what I was forced to do against my will. Even when Arthur told me I would not believe it. I had to march up to your front door to see it for myself. How could you not tell me about your marriage? How could you?'

He did not answer her.

'*How could you?*' she screamed in rage.

There was silence. Peter stared at her. The whole restaurant stared at her, but he was not conscious of this, of the hush. He was trembling violently. He had not in fact listened to anything she had said in the last few minutes.

'Please, Deirdre,' he whispered after muted conversations picked up again around them and the stares had mostly turned away. 'Please, oh God, please tell me that this is all untrue, just your revenge on me.' He stared at her and repeated in a hiss: '*Please say it's not true!* Please tell me that you made up all that stuff your father told you!'

She stared at him.

'It is all true,' she said icily, her body shaking with the effort of gaining control. He stared at her wildly. 'Every word of it,' she spat at him.

'*No!*' he roared, suddenly getting up. With his right hand he swept the tea things closest to him off the table – they made a long arc to the floor and smashed with great force. The restaurant went dead silent: all eyes turned to him now. He stared one last time at her, his mouth rigidly open in a grimace of utter anguish, and then strode lopsidedly to the door: it crashed shut with a tinkle of the bell. Deirdre stared straight ahead, indifferent to the shock and voyeurism on the faces around her. Somebody sniggered.

The lady at the till rushed over and stared at the debris on the floor and then at Deirdre. 'You'll pay for this, my lady!' she cried, and ordered the young waitress to get a brush and dustpan and mop. Deirdre reached into her bag for her lighter, saying nothing, and lit her cigarette under the disbelieving gaze of the older woman. She drew hard on it. Then she tapped out a little ash into the polished glass ashtray and carefully placed the lit cigarette in the little indentation. Taking the lid off her teapot, which had not joined Peter's on the floor, she inspected it, and then poured a second cup. Her hand shook, but still she said nothing. Her breast heaved, her eyes were cold and hard; the mess on the floor was cleared away and both of the staff retreated. Other customers stole glances at Deirdre, but she was impervious to everything. She slowly drank her second cup of tea, no doubt tepid, toyed with the remaining Eccles cake, and smoked her cigarette down to the filter. Finally, she was calm. She sighed deeply, got up, put on her coat with slow care, placed her hat on her head, replaced her silver cigarette case in her bag, and withdrew instead her purse. Finally she drew on her gloves, taking care with each finger. She walked with staring eyes to the till. There were more sniggers.

The pinch-faced woman behind the till watched her progress. 'You will pay for all those broken things,' she repeated as soon as Deirdre was near enough, but there was a slight air of uncertainty about her.

'Will I?' said Deirdre amiably, glancing up at the sign for HORNIMAN'S TEA above her. 'War brings so many changes, don't you think? For example the end of the Great War led to Lyons taking over Horniman's. Did you know that?'

'I'm sure I don't,' came the reply.

'Mmm,' said Deirdre. 'Well, it is a fact of business history. Now the last war has ended, perhaps the working classes will take over the running of the country, just like Lyons took over Horniman's. What do you think of that?'

'I'm sure I don't know what to think of that,' was the quick reply. 'But I do know that there was damage done at your table and I'll be wanting you to pay for it.'

'As I recall,' said Deirdre, looking round as if to see whether others might recall it the same or different, 'it was the gentleman who quite purposefully undertook to destroy some of your property, was it not?'

Her opponent coloured, but would not give up.

'That's as may be, but each table pays for what it owes,' she said firmly.

'Before the war, that is, the last war,' said Deirdre dreamily, 'it was the custom for gentlemen to pay for ladies, not the other way round.'

'That's also as may be,' countered an increasingly discomfited till-lady, 'but it was you what upset him, wasn't it?'

'Oh was it?' asked Deirdre sharply, her head tilted back. She stared across the counter. 'I just told him the truth. If he chose to get upset, that really is up to him, is it not?'

The till-lady would not stand for this.

'Now you look here! I know your sort. Pretending to put on airs and graces, but I know what your game is. Upper crust fallen on hard times I would guess. I expect Peter was in your employ wasn't he, and you have come down here to stir trouble. Heard he got a well-paid job on the railways, and thought you'd start a rumour or two. Extract a little compensation from him perhaps ...'

Deirdre just stared at the women with bright, bird-like eyes, soaking in the preposterousness of it.

'Yes,' the woman was saying, 'I have known Olive all her life, and she has told me about Peter Darby. War hero he is. Sunk a hundred German submarines, but too modest to claim the VC, so she tells me. Yes, let me guess ...'

'Oh do,' said Deirdre with sparkling eyes fixed on her.

'Let me guess. You knew Peter when he was younger. Sowed his wild oats he must have. So, time for a little blackmail is it? No wonder he stormed out. Yes, I know your sort.'

There was a brief pause. Then suddenly Deirdre burst into peals of laughter.

'Oh, ha ha ha,' she cried out. 'You know,' and she had to stifle further giggles, 'You know, I was determined to only pay for what I had eaten and drunk. But now I'll pay the damned lot. That was just too marvellous. Oh, ha ha ha.' She took a pristine white handkerchief from her bag and dabbed her eyes. 'Priceless! Priceless! A penny-dreadful novelist could not have dreamt it up. Priceless!'

Her laughter, brittle and a little wheezing, subsided. The red-faced woman opposite appeared unable to come up with a retort.

'So?' Deirdre demanded finally. 'How much does it all come to?'

The greatly nettled lady behind the till said promptly: 'The refreshments were seven shillings and ninepence exactly.'

'And the broken crockery?'

'I don't exactly know.'

'Well work it out. I am offering to pay for them after all. After your marvellous work of fiction, for which you should receive some literary award. Go on, work it out. Ha ha, it was priceless. Ha ha!'

'I'll have to estimate it,' said the lady, drawing herself up, greatly offended.

'Oh, don't bother,' said Deirdre. 'I can do that myself. Let me see. I am sure that three pounds would cover the lot, and your inconvenience included. Here please take three pounds seven shillings and ninepence from this.'

Deirdre deftly extracted a black-and-white five pound note from her purse with her gloved fingers, unfolded it and placed it on the counter.

'I can't change that,' replied the woman indignantly, staring at Deirdre. It was very final.

'Oh, fiddlesticks,' said Deirdre. She snatched back the note and searched for other change. 'Here: three guineas, fourteen shillings and nine pence.' This confused the lady, as Deirdre had laid out three pound notes, a ten shilling note and coins to make up the rest. As it was counted off the counter it into her palm, Deirdre spoke to her – it was a measured delivery.

'You say that you know "my sort". Well let me tell you that I know "your sort". You are a working class person like Peter and Olive and millions of others. You are the sort who claims to have fought the last war and so won the right to run this country. You are nothing more than empty socialists. You will build your ghastly council flats and horrible shops and factories, and pull down everything that was beautiful and great in this country, just like you pulled down that man who saved all your lives, Winston Churchill. You kicked him in the teeth and voted in socialists who will seize all the great industries of this country and place them in public ownership. Do you think the stable-boy can run the mansion? What paintings do you think he will hang on the walls? What does he know of the real history of this country? It will all go to rack and ruin!'

Deirdre stared fiercely at the woman shrinking from her behind the counter.

'Oh I know your sort, let me tell you. You would love me to be impoverished gentry, love to see me begging for a job as a waitress here, getting on my bended knee with a brush and dustpan. I've seen how your order that poor girl about.'

'I don't know to what you are referring,' came the tart reply.

'Oh yes you do. Well I tell you this: I would have done all that and more for Peter Darby, working class man that he is. But he is the one who put on the airs and graces, not me!' This last was almost shouted.

She leant forward a little. 'I could buy the whole Lyons chain with small change from the business my father and I run, you know. It's the largest yacht auction and chandlery chain in the country. But we don't want any horizontal integration. Pity, really. I could have you replaced just like that.'

She snapped her fingers, but had forgotten that they were delicately gloved. Further goaded by this triviality, Deirdre gathered her bag in one angry movement, pulled the door open, then slammed it shut and strode out into the cold air. The tinkling of the doorbell faded as she crossed the street to the station. A through train thundered past.

sixteen

111100 Emil looked up at William and then broke the silence between them: 'Willy, I am finished. Here at least. MIT would have me, but my wife wouldn't stand another move.' He thought for a moment. 'But far worse than that, Willy, is that you have destroyed meaning. You have done for artificial intelligence what Copenhagen did for quantum theory. It proposes that for evermore the maths *means* nothing. It works, that's all.'

William just shrugged and attempted to look contrite. He couldn't help thinking again that Emil's face was a composite of Marx, Stalin, and who was that Russian chap who assassinated the Tsar? Yes, Rasputin. William grimaced at himself. Stupid stereotypes, he thought, and anyhow he would never be able to identify any of them from a photograph – 'foreign' would better cover it, really. How politically incorrect.

Emil stared out of the window. 'I suppose I was attempting to be a Renaissance man,' he began. 'A man of the sciences and the arts. You know, there is this very interesting idea that Leonardo da Vinci was the first real scientist, and that Newton was the last of the *magicians*.' On emphasising the last word his eyes became fixed on William, who attempted to look encouraging. 'Yah,' said Emil. 'People just don't realise that Newton's science was one of his minor interests. The Old Testament and its decoding was a greater passion. So now they talk about Newtonian reductionism, but it is the wrong term. That is what you have done Willy, I don't mean you personally, you personally have not ended the magic. But we as a profession, indeed all of the sciences, are reducing the whole of life to a machine, to a mechanism, and my crusade for interdisciplinarity, to bring the humanities and the sciences together – you know in the way that Goethe was doing – all of that seems to have got nowhere. They chose you for the Turing project, and what comes out of it? I know very well what you think of Turing: "Stone Age" I gather is what you think. That is what Doctor Russett told me in one of the rare conversations we had. But you persuaded her that however crude his ideas were, compared to the developments of today, he was right. We are just symbol processing machines. She had the background to understand me, had I been her advisor, but, you? You live only in the very moment of fashionable thought, or rather not even thought …'

Emil paused. 'Sorry Willy. That was very rude. But this is the time for honesty. I know your mind very well; don't forget that you came to me twenty years ago.'

William shrugged his acknowledgement; he was not in the least offended. And Emil certainly did not know his mind well. Not even he, William, knew his own mind well – that much was clear now.

Emil returned to his theme. '*Magic*, Willy. I suppose it is a dirty word. But from the moment I began to study mathematics it held a mystery for me, a magic. It is the underlying song of the universe, but you, SharpSoft, the whole world of computing, have stripped the magic away in favour of brute calculations performed in their trillions. I defected from the East for the sole purpose of working with Aleksander, to follow in his footsteps, and yet we are not a millimetre nearer to discovering the mathematical basis of consciousness. I look back on my life, and I think that my dreams have been shattered. I will retire now, oh, we are comfortable enough, but I feel empty, Willy. Empty.'

There was silence for a while. Both were absorbed in the view.

'There *is* magic,' William said suddenly. 'Ah, I know this has no theoretical underpinning from Renaissance philosophy or the … or the Bloomsbury Group, or the, ah, Vienna Secession, or the, ah, Two Cultures theory or anything like that …' He tailed off.

Emil was staring at him, his chin lifted in haughty condescension. 'Go on Willy,' he demanded.

'Well,' said William in a rush, 'I find magic in my son.'

Emil stared at him.

William continued: 'I do the mathematics, Emil, because I am driven to do it, like you are. I learned, in my own pathetic attempt at interdisciplinarity, that artists and poets and writers are like that too. But I don't think it means anything. It doesn't make you happy. But when I used to spend two precious hours with my son – actually that did not make me happy exactly either, because of the circumstances – this I am sure of: it's magic.'

There was a pause as Emil shook his head pityingly. The Eastern cadences again caught William's ear painfully: 'Ach, Villy, Villy, no, *no*,' Emil lamented. 'Even ze schtarfisch can do zis. Ze enimals, zey can make baby zalso.'

William looked away with a wry grin. What could he say?

They were silent again for a while, but then Piatigorsky had this to offer, haltingly: 'I was very stupid, Willy. I was wrong to inform on you to your wife.'

William faced him. A legacy of anger and blame were legitimately his to vent – built up over a period in which he had seen Emil as a veritable demon – but he was glad to find that the bitterness had gone. He shook his head. 'I deserved what I got,' he said quietly.

They turned again to stare out of the window, both curiously reluctant to part from each other in what was turning out to be a funny sort of goodbye. William thought again of that strange interview, what, twenty-one years ago: how in awe he had then been of Piatigorsky, not to mention Aleksander! The last four years had certainly changed all of that. But his thoughts then turned to more recent events.

In that period a year ago William had completed all his work on the breakthrough paper and checked, double-checked and triple-checked it all before a lonely Christmas. The only real social life he had, the therapy group, had two weekends without meeting over the festive period, while Ros made not the slightest concession to William about Tommy, merely shuffling one of the access days so as not to fall on the New Year. His Christmas present was no more acknowledged than in previous years, Tommy just looking down and saying nothing to any enquiry.

Finally in January William re-read his paper one last time. It was slow work, the Prozac giving him enough stability and tenacity to pursue it, though at the same time producing an all-round fogginess of mind. But he got through it in one long sitting, could find no flaw with it, and felt a lift. This was it. The paper would either stir up mathematical computing in a way that little else had done for a generation, or it would be a complete flop; it was certainly not some incremental addition to knowledge, a fine-tuning of ideas already in circulation. It was a breakthrough. William was sober enough of course to know that while he was confident of it, the paper had to persuade some of the toughest peer-reviewers in the world. That's the game.

Still he waited another six weeks. He let it marinade in his head. He thought it, he breathed it, he interrogated it in his mind. But no doubts emerged. Not one. Really, he was testing the Prozac: had its synthetic cheerfulness lulled him into mathematical complacency? No, in the end he was sure that it had not – in all that period it felt simply complete, smooth almost. So, finally he printed it out in the required format, three copies in all, and mailed two of them off in the little local post office, registered, to America. In addition he laboured over an electronic submission, filling in all the annoying fields, and sent that off too.

That was it. It had never occurred to him that at some time and date such as five past four on February the seventeenth 2011, he would now be at a loose end. After an hour of elation, he subsided into a low mood – who could he share this with? Why would it interest his family in Parktown, with a tradition set by Pop of keeping work and home separate? Harryjee might be slightly interested, but only if it got published. William's therapy group had no insight into his professional life at all, and Adriana had been increasingly elusive. He kept his therapy life quite secret from her, and they now had few reasons leading to the Turing exhibition to work together – his contributions had come more at the early stages, and it was now down to the Science Museum staff to prepare the exhibits and texts concerning the life of the great man.

Thoughts of Adriana haunted him. The infrequent and highly charged moments with her had petered out altogether; this was a new turn in their relationship, a nearly complete silence from her, which created in him a pitch of longing that he could hardly bear, made far worse of course because of the empty days stretching out in front of him. This terrible empty world lasted for a full five months. But one last communication from Adriana in February hung in his mind – her last email said that she was leaving Francis.

He had hoped for this for years. Her original comment that she could not leave Francis *then*, at the time of his first awkward and tentative proposal of marriage, hung over him. Okay, so now the time had come. If you say 'I can't leave my partner now,' in answer to a marriage proposal – however clumsy – then surely if you later say 'I have left my partner now,' does that not mean your time has come? Did it not mean that his patient love for her, his long wait, was now to bear fruit? Nothing was clear, however, nothing resolved. She had finally moved out from her flat with Francis, that much he knew, but she refused to give him her new address, saying that she wouldn't be there long, and she needed a bit of time to herself, after all he had all that time on his own to come sure about what he wanted. So he waited – again. His voices were no help on the matter, though voluble enough on other subjects. Eric failed to construct any conspiracy out of her strange actions; Ambrose merely said what a nice lady she was; while Eliza did not exactly offer advice, though she did help him see how he felt about the whole thing.

And then came complete silence from Adriana. She changed her mobile number. He went into the offices at Birkbeck, but with the completion of the Turing project she was no longer coming into the faculty. That stumped him for a long time, but he finally found the sheer gall to bully one of the secretaries into giving him her new contact details: he was Professor William Strange at Imperial College and it was imperative that he and Adriana speak together about an interdisciplinary inter-college collaboration. He had then rung, feeling guilty about having extracted her number in this way, but to his great relief she did not object and agreed to meet him in a café to talk. But when they met she simply said that she couldn't tell him anything at this point. That was it. She had taken all that time and trouble to meet with him, just to say that there was nothing she could say. He had looked at her waistline and a thought had popped into his head: is she pregnant? He dismissed it without raising the subject with her – how could he? – and then promptly forgot about that extremely distressing possibility; perhaps she was just putting on weight.

However, a few months later she agreed to meet him again at the Troubadour. It was a warm July day. The thought struck him as he went to meet her that some four years had passed since the first time he had mooted marriage with her: it had been in the Italian restaurant over the road. He entered the Troubadour a little early, ordered coffee and sat in a corner, and as she came through the door, her eyes searching for him, the thought recurred: her stomach seemed rounded and full, though it was hard to tell because she was wearing more flowing clothes. Was she pregnant? It nagged at him. Normally during warm weather she wore slacks or dresses that hugged her body.

She ordered a latte and snacks and they exchanged pleasantries. All that he could say about his own affairs was that his paper was being passed around the peer reviewers, but that was not exactly news. Their conversation tailed off until there was silence. She looked at him and nodded, pursing her lips as if to say, it is time.

'William ...' she started, looking at him with worried eyes. 'I have a confession to make.' He stared at her. She usually called him 'Bill' or 'Billy'. 'I feel terrible,' she continued, 'but I just couldn't find a way to tell you. I didn't want to hurt you.'

He was not feeling great that day: his life was lived in a kind of suspended animation now, and he had no real idea about a new project. Everything depended on the reception to his breakthrough, if that is what it was. Professor May ignored him, beyond the occasional acknowledgement of progress with the Birkbeck collaboration, so in Adriana lay all that really mattered to him for his future. William blinked at her, not knowing what to expect, but feeling sick in his stomach.

Slowly it came out. While in India with her boyfriend she had met someone else, which immediately struck him as strange. Eric could not resist saying 'Ay, ay, funny business, eh?' William suppressed the desire to turn round and shut him up. Adriana explained that during her holiday in India she and Francis had separated for a couple of weeks to pursue different interests: he had stayed in a retreat at the Aurobindo ashram and she had toured archaeological sites in Southern India. On the tour she had met a naval officer called Rich Taylor.

'Ooh, that's rich, isn't it?' mocked Eric.

'India? Tip, top,' contributed Ambrose. William steeled himself against their interventions; he simply could not ask them out loud to keep quiet. Adriana might think him odd.

'Weird, isn't it?' she reflected as William blinked even harder, trying to absorb the implications of all this while straining with the mental effort of silencing Eric and Ambrose. 'Of course, he was on holiday and out of uniform. It was rotten for Francis, but I was so drawn to Rich. I said nothing, but when I got back we started seeing each other; either I travelled down to Portsmouth, or he travelled up here. It was a dreadful period, drawing away from Francis, and he took it very badly. But I just couldn't explain it to you then.'

'Portsmouth? *That's where Deirdre was posted!* They're all in it together,' hissed Eric.

Adriana looked down. William's mind raced, blotting out Eric's comment as best he could, though he knew his face must be all screwed up with the effort. Adriana had returned from India looking fabulous, with energy and purpose for their joint project, that much he could recall, but there was nothing in her behaviour then to suggest that her life had been changed in this way. Nothing to suggest another love interest, and if it really had been a dreadful period for her, she had not shown it. Oh, except that at one point after her holiday she had seemed quite confused, and had resorted to swearing, uncharacteristic for her. He had forgotten all about it. And then, much later, she had said that she was thinking of leaving Francis – now it was clear: she had left him for this Rich Taylor. He rolled the name around in his mind as one does an unpleasant food in the mouth.

'William ...' She was not sure how to go on.

He looked into her face, remembering again the passion of their time on Windermere: it felt like the memories came from another era – in fact the memories hardly even came from his own past, so it seemed. And now? He felt numb and a growing sense of panic.

Adriana hesitated, but finally said it: 'William. I married Rich last week.'

He stared at her dumbstruck. Nothing had prepared him for this.

'You would really like him,' Adriana continued, speaking rapidly. 'I know that as a naval officer he might seem like a strange choice for me, but we are very happy together. You wouldn't think it: he lives in a world quite alien to mine.' She giggled, a little nervously. 'You know, he occasionally works with the Special Boat Service, like in war films where they snorkel under enemy ships with a bayonet in their teeth to plant mines. That sort of thing. Very daring. He trains them in diving techniques.'

She paused for a long while as William searched in vain for anything to say. She looked down and added in barely audible tones: 'I'm going to have a baby.'

He nodded, and swallowed hard – even through the Prozac it cut him like a knife. So he had been right about that. Then he shook his head and turned to stare out of the window. He thought to himself: I have indeed been laid low. One of the Reverend Bradshaw's Old Testament quotes rang in his head: 'Brace yourself like a man; I will question you, and you shall answer me,' but he had no God to question him, or any idea what answers he would give: he had no idea either of how Job dealt with his afflictions – perhaps he had not listened carefully enough to the Reverend's account. 'Brace yourself.' How much bracing can a man put up against this kind of thing? A tinnitus enveloped him. He felt empty.

'William. I am so sorry.'

He looked at her, and then out of the window again. His mind was utterly blank; Eric and Ambrose were silent; there was nothing to mitigate the raw facts of what she had told him.

'William, I am sorry, I simply could not talk to you about these things.'

Dimly, anger welled up in him.

'How could you not talk to me about your planned marriage? About your ... other boyfriend?' he mumbled. *How could you?* he thought, his rage muffled by the drugs, his words turned inwards. Adriana just looked down. There was silence between them.

An adumbrated urge to move, to find some other context, anything, rose within him: it was excruciatingly embarrassing to have found no form of words to round things off with. He blinked. In the horrible ringing silence, in advance of actually moving his limbs, he seemed to rehearse the muscle contractions in his mind. He looked away, thinking of Windermere again: obtusely, an image of the Sunderland flying boat came into his mind, and resting in its bowels an injured German officer. He grimaced. Then, without making any conscious decision, his thigh muscles tensed and he slowly rose, propelled by the drug-dulled anger that could find no proper venting, all the while staring at her seated at the window, a cold coffee in front of her. Her eyes followed him, big and contrite in the face of his unhappiness. He blinked again.

'Congratulations, Adriana ...' he said tentatively. It was – he was somehow sure of it – demanded of him. Thank God he could manage that much. He stared at her for a moment and then turned and slowly walked to the exit; Adriana bit her lip and looked down, making no attempt to follow him. The door closed behind him without a sound; he turned right out of the Troubadour and just walked for a long time towards the centre of London with no plan in mind. He walked far too fast, his companions now voluble enough after the initial shock had abated. Eric had gone into overdrive, ranting about 'naval officer'. Ambrose offered some consolation about how he had spent a nice holiday in Portsmouth once, and William really should go there. Eric asked 'with an axe?' William could not silence them. But the unusual exercise soon triggered an asthma attack and that put an end to the banter. William did not want to go to his flat, and habit had taken him in the direction of Imperial College. Panting a little, he spotted a pub on the street corner and went in. He sat at the bar, unable to focus on anything. It was a typical old London watering hole, long and narrow, furnished with bevelled plate mirrors, dark wood panelling and a packed clientele; they all knew each other, and he knew nobody. The barman took some time to get to him.

'Yes, sir?'

'Pardon?' responded William from some distant place.

'A drink, sir?'

'Ah. Yes. A double Glenfiddich.'

The barman took a glass, pressed it twice against the appropriate optic and set it down in front of William.

'Crisps or nuts, sir?'

'Ah. Yes. Thank you.'

The barman started a question, but thought better of it, turning instead to take some dry roasted peanuts from a display.

'Ah. Thank you.'

William paid the barman absently, stared with empty eyes down the long crowded room, and knocked back his whisky.

After a long while spent in the babbling hubbub further down, the barman returned.

'Same again, sir?'

'Ah. Yes. Thank you.'

After the second double and packet of nuts, William began to feel unwell. He was going over and over in his mind the four years since he had first proposed to Adriana.

'I can't leave Francis now.' It was that 'now' that had done for him. For the entire four years that 'now' – a word perhaps slipped in just for effect or at random – had kept him dangling. Also perhaps he had clung to the strange knowledge that she was with Francis by way of acknowledging the death of her former drowned boyfriend. So now she had left Francis – actually she had been leaving him since India. Never, never, not in the remotest way, had this scenario occurred to him. Of course he had slowly made some bizarre accommodation with the continuing deferral of happiness that had become his lot, but in the end she would have been his: he had been so sure of it. She would leave Francis for him. That had been his anchor all along – as well as the growing certainty that he had been Alan Turing in a previous life.

Something else came home to him in the deafening chatter of the cramped watering-hole: the very *meaning* of his attraction to Adriana was now in question. He had been in love with her – and that does not stop on impact as it were – but he had always argued with himself that being in love with her held the promise of some special meaning, indeed it was his alibi for the entire affair. As well as the deep hurt he felt there was now also a sense of frustration: Adriana in his mind was the key to his dreams and the route by which he would escape the Prozac trap that bound him to his voices. Now he would have to plough on without her physical presence.

He took a deep breath and looked at his empty whisky glass, but the nauseous feeling in his stomach ended thoughts of another drink. He got up and walked into the night air, too miserable to be angry.

He did not remember exactly how things went after that, though he must have called Felicity and invited himself over. She had sat him down, he was sure of this, and told him earnestly that sex was out of the question, as she was now with Admiral D'murr Pilru, and the Admiral was – how should she put it – so much more imaginative. Of course they had to have a secret word that she could utter if things got out of hand. William had no idea what she was talking about – she even had to remind him that she was referring to the Reverend Terence Bradshaw – but after she had made sure that William understood his new place in her affections she was kind and listened to his sorry tale. Of Adriana he said nothing to start with however: it was still too raw. But he did tell Felicity that he had drawn a blank with Anita van Houten.

'This is driving me mad,' he had told Felicity. 'If all this mish-mash in my head is about past lives, then I must have been Alan Turing. But something is blocking my way to him. Clearly the point of this Peter character – whose story I piece together more and more – is that he leads me to this Deirdre character. She in turn leads me to Turing. But I never quite get there. Or get to his German lover who he lets down so terribly. We couldn't get to the German through you, and now Anita is out.'

'Mmm,' Felicity said after thinking about this for a while. 'Okay, it's not Anita, as you say. But then perhaps I was the German lover after all.' Another thought occurred to her and her eyes took on a sparkle. 'Perhaps we should try again with that thing you told Anita. You know, that the German was a U-boat captain who told Enigma secrets to Turing. Then they make love, and then Turing betrays him to the authorities.' William stared at her in confusion, but Felicity – who seemed to have quite forgotten what she had told him about Terence – was working out how to stage this little psychodrama. 'I'll hand you a piece of paper representing the Enigma code,' she said brightly: 'that's my betrayal of the Germans. I do betrayal a lot.' She thought for a moment, and then exclaimed: 'Ahah. Then we'll make love on the sofa; it represents a bunk on the U-boat. Mmm. Yes, and then you go to the kitchen and return as a police officer to arrest me.' She was quite carried away with enthusiasm for the little play they would enact.

He was too exhausted to object.

111101 William woke up in his flat with a terrible headache the next day. It was early afternoon. He was sick several times but could not remember what he had eaten or drunk the previous night except for the peanuts and whisky. He did not recall having anything at Felicity's but then she did always have a bottle of red wine open and a portion of vegetarian lasagne ready for the microwave. He sat by the window overlooking Old Brompton Road, breathing in the traffic fumes from below through the open sash window. A glass of milk was his breakfast. Imaginary friends were his companions.

'Cor blimey, mouth like a parrot's cage!' was Eric's contribution.

'At least the smell of diesel's gone,' said Ambrose.

'What, you prefer the smell of sick?'

Their companionship was amiable enough, but what good was all that when he felt so terrible? What could they say that would undo the horrible revelation dumped on him yesterday by Adriana? Eliza might have had some comforting words for him but for some reason she was silent. He had just about managed to check the milk carton and establish that it was not too much past its sell-by date; he downed his morning Prozac with it, and felt the slight kick of mood. However it could not moderate the grim reality of Adriana's marriage and pregnancy, a brick wall to the future he had imagined. He did not doubt the truth of what she had said; it explained so much of her behaviour in the period since India. Nevertheless it was numbing to have so fondly an imagined future so thoroughly discounted. He stared at the traffic for a long time, the noise rumbling up the three floors; his thoughts turned to Ros and Tommy and a household just as closed to him as the one with Adriana, Rich, and the baby to come. Even Felicity had a new lover, whatever exception she had made the previous night. He felt very alone.

The outer configuration of his life was now quite changed, but further conversation with Felicity that night had also changed his inner constellation: both were momentous changes, interwoven, and in need of some rumination. After enacting Felicity's little psychodrama – and he doubted that he had risen much to the demands of her love-making – they had retired to her double bed and, effectively, posed the question to each other: how was it for you? William tried to remember it from the previous night. Yes, it was coming back to him: Felicity had admitted that she had not felt the German U-boat captain 'come through' for her; she was anyway, she confided, more wrapped up in working through her captaincy of a large star vessel with a crew of fifteen thousand, against which commanding a U-boat was a rather minor outing. She had been in charge of the spaceship as part of Admiral D'murr Pilru's fleet, of course. William in turn had to admit that, although he felt sea-sick enough, he couldn't quite construct an Alan-Turing-on-a-U-boat experience out of it.

'Something is blocking the transcarnation process,' Felicity had concluded sternly, holding William in her gaze. 'Is there anything you haven't been telling me?'

'Well,' he said, 'nothing Turing-wise. But I did have a horrible experience earlier this evening with Adriana.'

'Go on,' said Felicity. So, he had told her in something of a rush more about how much Adriana meant to him, how she had led him to investigate Turing's life, and how the discovery that she had not left her boyfriend for him but for an unknown chap had come as such a shock – not to mention that they were to marry and she was to have a baby.

'Humph,' said Felicity. She went and retrieved a half-full bottle of red wine from the kitchen and two glasses. William shook his head, explaining that he already felt unwell, but then, between glassfuls of wine, Felicity made some outrageous propositions to him as she worked through an entirely new scenario.

The first was that he had never been Alan Turing at all. He had been Peter Darby.

William shook his head. That was preposterous. It made nonsense of everything he had been through.

Secondly Adriana had been Deirdre.

William didn't care for this interpretation either, but admitted it made some sort of sense. It was clear that she was the key to Turing, and equally clear that he somehow had not been able to face her.

Thirdly the German officer whose character was so important on the tapes was neither of their original suspects in this life.

'You were barking up the wrong tree with Anita,' she told him, 'Just as we were with me. Instead, perhaps the man that Adriana has just married was the German officer, this Ulrich. What did you say his name was?'

'Something Taylor.'

'And perhaps,' said Felicity after another large mouthful of wine, 'it was not so much you as Adriana – the former Deirdre – who owes a karmic debt to the German.'

William shook his head. He didn't like all this at all. It made some sort of sense perhaps, but, surely, he had been Turing? Wasn't that the whole point all along?

Felicity persisted: 'Do you recall anything that Adriana said about this Taylor chap? Any details?'

'Only that he was a naval officer. Oh, and that he was a diving instructor who occasionally worked with the Special Boat Service. You know, like in war films where they snorkel under enemy ships with a bayonet in their teeth to plant mines.'

'Bingo,' said Felicity.

'Bingo?' he had repeated dully. He could not so quickly adjust to these new ideas.

'Bingo! Don't you see? He was a submariner, near enough. Perfect fit. And his name? Do you recall his first name?'

'Taylor. Something Taylor. Let me see – I can't think.'

'Taylor is very English. Are you sure you can't remember his first name?'

'Ah. Yes. It's coming to me. Something with an "R." That's it: Rich.'

'Double bingo,' said Felicity softly, staring at him. William just shook his head. 'Rich,' she beamed, 'is the English for Ulrich. Ulrich is the German for Rich. He's your man all right.'

He stared at her.

'Another thing,' continued Felicity, thinking through the details of his case for him as he seemed quite befuddled. 'How long did this Deirdre wait for Peter Darby after the war?'

'I don't know.'

'Think. He had promised to marry her when the war ended, which was in 1945. On your last recording, you told the story of a woman confronting a man she loved, having discovered that he had married someone else behind her back. What year was that?'

William shook his head, unsure.

'Oh,' he said suddenly. 'The woman hated the idea of the half-century. Hated the idea that it was coming up to 1950.'

'So, it could have been 1949 then. Which means that Peter kept Deirdre dangling for four years, before she discovered that he had married someone else. Now, how long between your first proposal to Adriana and now?'

'Four years I think,' he said.

'You're not just saying that?' asked Felicity, quite the cross-examiner.

Despite all his confusion and his genuine inability to keep track of most things there was one means by which he recorded to himself the passing of the years. It was Tommy's age.

'No,' he said. 'Tommy would have been a year and a half old when I proposed. I had despaired of a return to Ros at that point.'

'And now?'

'He is five and a half.'

'Okay. Four years it is. Here is a beautiful karmic symmetry. You kept her waiting for four years in your last life, at the end of which she found out that you were married to someone else. Now she has kept you waiting for four years in this life before telling you that *she* has married someone else. And ...' she leant forward for emphasis, '... in giving Ulrich, that is Rich, a baby, a new life, she is absolving herself of the part she played in taking his old life. Also, think of this: you have just told me how Adriana introduced you to the whole world and life of this Alan Turing in a way that you could never had done yourself, not being keen on reading history books. Well, in her past life that is just what she had promised to do but couldn't: that is, give you access with your Ulrich to Turing. She is absolved, you are absolved. We haven't solved Anita's case, but this is, well, it's just beautiful, don't you think?'

'Beautiful' was not how William saw any of it.

As he gazed absently down the Old Brompton Road, he mulled this over in his mind. He did not, despite the long period of transcarnation therapy, share the certainties of Felicity, Stefan or the Reverend Bradshaw over the workings of 'karma'. And it still seemed incomprehensible to him that Adriana would keep this Rich Taylor secret from him. Just to spare his feelings? How can you spare somebody's feelings when the truth will come out in the end? The anger rose in him again.

He got up to make coffee. As he walked gingerly towards the kitchen a new decision formed in him. He wouldn't go back to Kolakowski and the group, much as they had become a kind of family to him. Felicity's 'resolution' to his transcarnation issues was as far as he wanted to go with that line of enquiry. He may not have had a 'bingo' moment with it, but her interpretation seemed very final – logically he could not fault it, and if it meant anything he had to work it out for himself.

> *Are you now, or have you ever been, Alan Turing?*
> No.
> *Are you now, or have you ever been, a homosexual?*
> No.

Adriana had once gaily told him of the most depressing ending to a novel that she could think of. It was during the time when she was trying to enthuse him about English literature, though fully aware that Ros had failed in the past. 'At the end of Sons and Lovers, you know, by D. H. Lawrence, the hero is all alone in a dingy bedsit in Nottingham,' she had told him, or something like that. Perhaps it was Leeds. 'He sits there all alone having failed to make anything of his relationships with two women who both loved him, though in different ways. He is alone and depressed in the middle of winter. And then there is a "clunk" and the last sixpence in the meter drops. The light goes out. So he sits there alone, with the fading glow of a one-bar electric fire. Before long it is dark and cold. Isn't that a fantastic ending to a novel? What a powerful image!'

The recollection made him smile wanly. But the down-lights in the kitchen and the electric kettle he was boiling for coffee did not go off. He had failed in his marriage with Ros, and he had failed in his relationship with Adriana, but, despite everything, this was not the end. It was true that all that therapy had brought him was the fantastical idea that his misery, the trials no less than Job had endured, were down to 'karma'. Although the thought of having been Alan Turing had helped him through the mountainous task of his research, it turned out – if any of it were true – that he had been instead an aeronautical engineer who had let a woman down. Badly. And so he deserved the same. But if any of it was true, then he had paid his debt to her, or to the universe or however these things were supposed to work. He was now, apparently, free to start again.

And he had one great hope. His mathematics. And the kettle had boiled and the lights were still on. He took it as a good omen.

He drank his coffee with some rather stale bread on which he smeared margarine and peanut butter. He returned to the window and stared down the street, his stomach beginning to gurgle in response to the somewhat challenging breakfast. Once it was eaten he was at a loss, and began to pace up and down the room. His optimism began to fade as he asked himself the question: 'what if my paper is rejected?' With that horrible thought the full reality of what Adriana had told him hit him again with full force and he started to feel angry with Felicity for justifying Adriana's behaviour like that. He sat for hours thinking increasingly bitter thoughts and quite forgot to take his second daily dose of Prozac, which allowed his mood to spiral further downwards. In the end he retreated to his chaotic bedroom, slammed the door, and in the darkness under the rumpled duvet – which had annoyingly popped open at the bottom and so kept catching his toes as he tossed and turned – he succumbed to his misery.

He did not wake until early the next morning, very hungry and in a panic that he needed his Prozac. Downing that with water he pulled on his overcoat and left the flat – slamming the door again in general unhappiness at his situation – in search of a café, somewhere he had not been to before so he could be a stranger and brood on his fate. It was all too fast. Adriana's news still reverberated around his whole being, while Felicity's complacent karmic diagnosis now just made him angry. How can you deserve to be treated so badly on the basis that a quite different man in a quite different era had meted out similar contempt for one close to him? That ice-queen Adriana had treated him with contempt, there was no other word for it. Had Piatigorsky and May put her up to it? Two women had treated him with contempt, actually. And how could a stupid ending to a novel help him come to terms with it? The lights go off and the glow of the electric fire fades out! How stupid. Ha! Wait a minute. Perhaps Adriana had planted that story in his mind to justify what she was going to do, while Felicity had gone to much greater lengths to bamboozle him. Thinking about her and Stefan he was clear that he definitely wasn't going back to any of that.

William was boiling over. Prozac, a full English breakfast, two mugs of coffee and several Danish pastries had fuelled him up, but when he left the café he had no purpose or work to attend to, so he simply strode home for want of any better plan.

As he approached his front door he spotted Janet Obudjowe among a group of rather oddly-dressed people.

'It's the watchtower gang!' warned Eric. 'Quick! Go the other way!'

William was in no mood for skulking however. He marched right up to them and exclaimed: 'Ha!'

'Hello William,' said Janet in her usual unruffled tones.

William looked at her and then glared pointedly in turn at each one gathered on the pavement, including a teenager of perhaps fourteen with a leather satchel, very smartly dressed but in a style long out of fashion.

'Your disguises aren't working, you know!' William lectured them furiously. 'I know *exactly* what you are up to. May and Piatigorsky are paying you to spy on me. No doubt one of you planted all kinds of doubts in Adriana's mind – she's not the sort to act with such contempt towards anyone, least of all me. *You* put her up to it!'

They stared at him and then at Janet as if she might be able to explain what was going on.

'First Ros, then all the trouble at work, and now Adriana!' William shouted at them. 'It's all the fault of that devil Piatigorsky! But you won't grind me down! I'm made of sterner stuff!'

He turned to the teenager, shaking his head and saying more in sorrow than anger now: 'How could they do this to you? How could they make you carry out the work of the old devil like this?'

The boy looked terrified at William's outburst, and the whole group shrank back from him.

'I'm not Job, you know!' William continued: 'You see he was put through the most horrible things by Satan, who used God as his agent, apparently. Job somehow braced himself against disaster after disaster. Well, I'm only human, and I won't take any more of it!'

The group were further horrified by this, looking from one to the other. Again William stared angrily at each in turn as if demanding an explanation for their disgraceful behaviour. None dared make eye contact with him. Then, contenting himself with another bellowed 'Ha!' he pushed open the front door and marched up the stairs to his flat, feeling better than he had in a long time.

'There's my boy,' said Eric.

11111∅   A few days later William, now in a calmer frame of mind, was surprised by a call from the medical practice in London saying that the doctor would like to see him about his medication. Something about symptoms. This was odd, as he had not been to the family health centre since Ros threw him out. He was seeing Tommy the next day – the one thing that kept him from completely succumbing to depression – so he arranged to go on to the surgery afterwards as it was in the same neighbourhood, though he agreed with Eric that he should be cautious with the new doctor.

Maria and Tommy were late for their regular meeting, and Maria was frostier than usual.

'Your brat threw a complete tantrum!' she spat at him, but realising how offended he looked, she added: 'He simply would not leave the house without his toy. That's why we are so late.'

She sniffed.

Tommy held it up to him. It was a Duplo Thomas the Tank Engine, part of the set that William had bought Tommy for his fifth birthday months ago, still making wild guesses as to what would be appropriate. He had never had any acknowledgement of his gifts before, but it was clear that Tommy really liked this engine – when you pressed a button on the cab it made a 'woo woo' noise. William crouched down to be level with Tommy, and away from Maria's unforgiving gaze. The little boy burbled about the track and the crane and the tank engine, and William held the toy and stroked Tommy's head.

As he rose Maria caught his eye.

'William, really,' she admonished him. 'Don't you realise that Tommy is five and a half now?'

William was confused. Had he bought the wrong card for Tommy's birthday? It seemed ages ago. Had he got himself muddled and bought a 'Now You Are Four' or 'Now You Are Six' card?'

'Trick question,' said Eric, 'Play her along.'

'Steam shunter,' said Ambrose.

'If he wasn't five then, what age would he be?' asked William, trying to be clever for Eric's sake.

'Stupid,' said Maria, frowning. 'He was five. So why did you buy him Duplo?'

'Another trick question,' said Eric with less confidence.

'Steam shunters do take a long time to start in the morning,' offered Ambrose.

'Duplo ...?' said William, playing for time.

'Tommy is five and a half years old and very educationally advanced,' said Maria sternly. 'He moved on to Lego nearly two years ago. He has almost the complete architectural series, and can tell you where to find a portico and cornice on a Danish town house. I have no idea why he should suddenly dig out a quite inappropriate toy from back in January. I had no idea he even liked it. And he absolutely would not leave it behind.'

She turned to look down at the boy.

'Tommy, tell William the difference between a portico and a cornice,' she demanded.

Tommy looked up at her hesitantly, then turned to William and raised the toy.

'Thomas the Tank Engine,' he said proudly and broke into smiles. He pressed the little button and the engine went 'woo woo.'

'Nice one,' said Eric.

'Tip top,' said Ambrose.

A few hours later William had turned up at the surgery, made himself known to reception, and waited for his turn. He looked blankly at a tall rubber plant winding its way to a generous glass canopy in the ceiling, and ignored the magazines on the table in front of him. The imaginative use of sustainable structural wood-based laminates in the organic layout of the health centre – which might have attracted his approval in earlier times – was also quite beyond his enthusiasm, as was the robin singing outside and clearly audible – should one have an ear for it – through the partly open skylight. The exalted contralto of the bird, and the absence of the doleful calls of the less cheerful flighted species, might have suggested redemption to an oracularly-inclined ornithologist. But all

William's thoughts were with Tommy. What new toys could he buy that his son would like? In the aftermath of Adriana's confession, his focus was now all on his boy and those precious Tuesday meetings with him.

'Professor William Strange?' asked a doctor emerging from one of the anonymous office-like doors visible from the waiting area.

'That's me,' said William, lifting himself reluctantly from the upholstered chair he had settled into.

'I'm Dr Andrew Parkes. Recently joined the practice. Do call me Andrew. Is it okay to call you William?'

'William is fine. Or Bill. Or Billy. Or Willy. Or even "Villy" as a Russian colleague says,' said William, attempting some humour.

'Ha ha,' said the doctor.

Once settled in the little surgery Parkes began: 'I am seeing you today because your GP in Oxford, Dr Edmondson, recently retired and sent your additional patient records on to us. I think I may have spotted a problem with your medication as a result of an enquiry from him.'

'Oh yes?'

'I understand that you have been suffering from what might be called mild dissociative symptoms?'

'Ah, I think they can be described in that way.'

'Indeed. You were in America in 2001, I understand, and had to see a doctor there about replacement inhaler medication?'

'Yes.'

'I worked in the US around that time and I am aware that doctors then were in the habit of recommending Psyllicontin for your kind of asthma symptoms. Did you start using it then by any chance?'

'Not sure. This is what I've been using.'

William retrieved the inhaler from his pocket. Parkes examined it.

'That's Psyllicontin-based alright.'

'Oh.'

'But you never mentioned it to Dr Edmondson?' queried Parkes.

'No. I didn't think to.'

'Well, recent studies have shown that in some cases Psyllicontin can cause symptoms of depression, mild dissociation, even mild hallucinations. But worse, it is strongly contraindicated against Prozac. I believe you started on Prozac about four years ago?'

'Yes.'

'And the symptoms got much worse? Including perhaps a drift at times into delusional states?'

William bit his lip. 'Yes,' he said in a low voice.

'Perhaps you have been hearing voices?'

William hesitated longer this time. 'Yes. Perhaps.'

'Ay, ay,' warned Eric. 'Don't trust this fellow. Don't give anything away.'

'*Friendly* voices,' corrected Ambrose.

Parkes continued: 'These symptoms are present in a tiny proportion of Psyllicontin users. When you add Prozac, the proportion reaches a significant level. Did you notice a worsening of your symptoms after taking Prozac?'

'Yes, I suppose I did.'

'That could be the cause of your problem then.'

'But I don't want to go off Prozac.'

'Not off Prozac. Off Psyllicontin.'

'Oh.'

'I'll put you back on your previous asthma medication,' said Dr Parkes, writing out a prescription. 'You can continue ordering Prozac online if you want, but for anything else I would advise checking with me first. Let me know how you get on: it may take a few days or a week for you to feel any changes.'

'Okay. Thank you.'

'Oh, I should add,' continued Parkes, 'that a complete reversal of symptoms can take time. Medical science is not yet fully cognisant of how the brain is affected by drugs. It's clear however that patients report lingering effects long after no discernable traces of the drug itself can be found in any tissues or bodily fluids, which means that the brain must be taking a while to reverse the pathological synaptic configurations caused by drug clash. But be assured, it'll all clear up in time.'

William got home with a jumble of feelings about his meeting with Tommy and with the doctor.

'Just for once,' he said out loud, thinking how Tommy had liked the toy he had bought. 'And stuff Danish town houses,' he added to himself. The glow of it stayed with him.

'One over on that tart Maria,' commented Eric.

'Quite,' said William to the empty room.

But his thoughts on Dr Parkes were less clear. On the Tube journey home Eric had advised caution. 'It's a trap,' he had said with conviction. 'It's obvious, old boy. May has Piatigorsky and Spindler lined up against you at work, and uses Comfort-Janet and her gang to spy on you at home. Even Wozniak has been funny, hasn't she? Now, May has business dealings with Ros, right? So, she finds that there is a new doctor at the practice and tells him some cock and bull story about Edmondson. Retire? Big fat fib, I say.'

William had picked up the new medications in the pharmacy at the health centre, and had them in his hands. He had not yet peered into the neatly folded paper bag.

'Caution would be wise,' he told himself out loud and put the packet on top of his bathroom cabinet when he arrived home. It stayed there untouched: he had plenty of the old prescription.

Tuesday the following week brought something quite unexpected. William had gone into paroxysms of indecision over whether to buy another toy for Tommy or not: he did not want to enrage Maria, nor did he know whether he should buy Lego or Duplo. At Hamleys toy shop in Regent Street the assistant was not particularly helpful, expressing uncertainty over whether the Lego Danish town house did in fact have porticos and cornices. In the end William bought a Star Wars spaceship model, bristling with guns and laser cannon.

'Bit of a gamble,' said Eric, dubiously. 'Shouldn't provoke that frosty witch.'

'Flying porcupine,' said Ambrose cheerfully.

William had to wait even longer to see Tommy this time. He wondered if Maria was going to punish him like this, eroding his contact time with Tommy by turning up late and blaming the boy for it; perhaps he shouldn't give the toy to his son after all. He waited and waited, and then he was stunned to see a familiar figure in place of Maria. He had to blink several times to be sure. It was Ros.

'Hello, William,' she said awkwardly.

'Hello, ah, Ros,' William said, and, more jocularly: 'Hello Tommy!'

'Mummy and Daddy talk now,' said Tommy in a low voice, wide eyed.

'Ah. Ros. This is ah, a surprise.' William could not think of anything else to say.

'Maria has left our, er, my, employment,' said Ros by way of explanation. She looked down. William could not believe his ears.

'Fucking trap this. The sheer bottle of it. Gets you don' it?' said Eric. 'Just make sure you don't fall for it.' William had to strain mightily not to turn round and yell at him to shut up.

'Daddy, Daddy, Daddy,' said Tommy suddenly. 'What's in the Hamleys bag?'

'Oh. It's a present for you of course,' said William hurriedly. 'Here.'

All three of them became focussed on the bag. Tommy grabbed it, pulled out the package, tore the gift wrappings off, and extracted the shiny box. William leant down to pick the bits of paper from the grass as Tommy stared at the box, turning it over and over and side to side. William became anxious, not noticing Ros's eyes on him.

'It's Darth Maul's battlecruiser!' Tommy finally said in tones of reverential awe. 'It's got guns! It's got laser cannon!'

Ros looked embarrassed and said in a low voice, 'We, I mean I, don't usually allow him any guns or things like that … '

They had a strained snack in the coffee shop, capturing all the little Lego pieces that were escaping the enraptured Tommy as he worked through the instruction manual.

'Don't assume a thing,' Ros had warned him the minute they sat down.

'Ah. No. Quite,' was all William could say, so he ventured only pleasantries concerning his family in Oxford when asked. Little more was said, beyond clumsy attempts to help Tommy with his Lego instructions.

'I need six of these,' he said holding up a small part. 'It's dark grey with two bobbles.'

'Dark grey with two bobbles,' echoed William, looking at Ros uncertainly. She gave him a flimsy plastic bag.

'You look through that one,' she said, 'and I'll look through the one Tommy's already opened.'

At each completed stage the assembly was passed between Ros and William with encouraging comments, while Tommy focussed on the next stage.

It was a one-off. The following week, bang on time, Tommy was chaperoned into the park by a new au pair, a West-Country girl with an honest open face, called Claire Smallbones. This was how she introduced herself and William had to suppress a giggle as Eric said softly: 'Hefty lass actually.' She was very polite to William, and keen to share with him the highlights of Tommy's daily round. It confused him to start with, and Eric whispered that this was just to lull him into a false sense of security. William told him off furiously. In a bag, carefully packed, was the completed battlecruiser, and all three played with it in the café. Or should that be all five? Eric was not short of further cautionary advice while Ambrose became a little emotional over the forward guns.

At home William was beginning to come to terms with the loss of Adriana. After his outburst with Janet and her gang he had sobered up a bit, and despite Eric's insistence on the matter saw that Adriana was perhaps unlikely to have been swayed by the agents of Piatigorsky and

May. In any case it all seemed very final: she had married Rich Taylor. Adriana had emailed to say that she really hoped they could stay friends, and was greatly looking forward to the opening of the Turing Exhibition, which she saw as the culmination of the time they had worked together and if he wanted any help with his opening speech, she would be glad to look at it. In truth he was rather dreading the idea of having to speak in public again, as it was now years since he had done so, years since he had possessed that easy clarity to face an audience. He did not reply. Nor did he ring Felicity or make any bookings for weekend group therapy; instead he wrote letters to her and Kolakowski thanking them for their help and explaining that as the karmic workings of his past life were now clear to him he saw no point in continuing the therapy. If he spent any more time with the group or booked any more sessions with Kolakowski, he would just have it all repeated at him.

It alarmed him of course if he cared to think about it. He had become a New Age fruitcake with a full-blown belief in, no, representing a case study regarding, reincarnation. Would he open the kitchen cabinet one day to see a stock of orangeberry and pine herbal tea sachets? Would he hang dream-catchers in the window, collect crystals and light scented candles? No way, he told himself, he was a mathematician. Anyhow he had read in the Turing biography that Turing's friend and lover Victor was convinced that Turing's mathematical genius had come from a previous life. There it was in black and white: Turing believed in reincarnation, or at least was not prepared to dismiss his friend's ideas out of hand. But Turing's humiliation by the establishment was not over such beliefs, so why should he be concerned?

'We are not meant to understand such things mate,' Eric would comfort him.

'All of life boils down to playing the B-sharp origami,' said Ambrose nonsensically.

They cheered him up.

He had lots of time on his hands and now needed to make a big decision: should he start on the new asthma medication? Eric advised against. Ambrose seemed more optimistic. Somehow he had to find a way of rescuing his rational perception that the voices were delusional; it had been painful to have Parkes say it: 'hearing voices' – it was both clinical and condemnatory. He vacillated between clinging to Parkes' cold medical rationality on the one hand and scorn at yet one more attempt by the establishment to undermine him on the other. Apart from Eliza, Eric and Ambrose were the only reliable friends he had! If only Eric and Ambrose were equally matched, however, he could then make an executive decision about the medication. But Ambrose was vague where Eric was adamant, the whole thing was a trap, carefully crafted by Ros. The new medication was designed to make him even more slave to the conspiracy tightening around him, of which the most dastardly ploy was to dangle in front of him the possibility of reunion with Ros and his son.

Eric kept telling him: 'William you are not stupid. Surely you can see through it all. It's obvious! Even the name of that damn medicine is a clue. It's trying to tell you something. "Silly cunting." You would be a silly cunt to fall for it.'

William could see the logic in Eric's reasoning, but in the sombre aftermath of losing Adriana for good, and the sudden discontinuation of his weekend therapy group, he had glimpses of sober rationality. There was a hope, however small, that Ros might reconsider – for what else did those shared moments with Tommy over the Lego battlecruiser mean? It had been a real, hauntingly real, family experience. Now that Maria was gone, was there not hope for a return to his family? This above all made him focus as hard as he could on the voices. 'They are *not* real, they are *not* real,' he would tell himself in moments of stern concentration, but, as he turned to find a sandwich, or got out of a chair to go to the bathroom, Eric would chastise him in hurt tones, or Ambrose would come out with some reassuringly absurd remark. As he spoke back he could not make Eric see how much he longed for Tommy and Ros, and so his anger with Eric slowly mounted. Here was a hope, finally, some hope for a normal life again! Can't you see that?

'Silly cunting ...' Eric would torment him with.

About a month after seeing Ros he woke with grim determination. He marched into the bathroom with a plastic bag and swept all his online asthma medications into it. 'Careful, William,' warned Eric in alarm. Ambrose said nothing. William gritted his teeth, and placed the bag on the table in the living room; he made coffee and then sat at the window. It was a mild September morning and he could see right down Old Brompton Street through the open sash. A long time passed. Suddenly a noise from the street made William spring to his feet. He grabbed the bag, flew through the front door of his flat and ran down the stairs.

Bursting onto the street in slacks, a tee-shirt and slippers, a dishevelled figure runs after the council refuse truck.

'You are crazy, William!' the man shouts in a vaguely Cockney accent.

'Are you sure we'll be home soon?' he adds in a different voice, a little Welsh perhaps, panting as he pursues the truck, its sweet-sour odour in his nostrils. He is carrying a rather full plastic supermarket bag, though from the way it swings it does not appear at all heavy.

'No, don't do it. Don't do it!' he shouts at the top of his voice with the markedly East End accent. Puzzled refuse workers and bystanders stare to see him reach level with the truck and swing the bag into the open rear. The man stands there, as the crusher goes through its cycle.

'All right governor?' one of the workmen says, looking at his colleagues and back to the man.

'I don't know. I don't know anything,' the man replies in rapid tones. 'I'm not your governor,' he adds more thoughtfully. He stands there for a while staring as the bin lorry moves on a little and then walks back along the busy pavement to his open front door. The refuse men grin at each other and shake their heads.

Within a week of discontinuing Psyllicontin William felt a returning clarity of mind. It was such a gradual process that he was not sure of it to start with, but before long he had no doubt that it was working: Eric and Ambrose had disappeared. At first he really missed them and was overwhelmed with loneliness. Eliza comforted him over this but he started to grow tired of her clichés and obliqueness. Slowly, as his confusion eased, he realised that he had been in a terrible state to converse with such imaginary friends for so long. As the distance grew between the new William and the person he had become he grew increasingly horrified at how he had parted from all rationality, and for so many years. It had been a miracle that he had been able to complete his paper.

He began to work it out. From the elements of his daily life – which included the Eliza project and the regression therapy – he had transformed one AI programme from the 1960s and two characters from the 1940s into imaginary friends: this had pretty much started after he had gone on Prozac and as it had reacted with the Psyllicontin. Why his unconscious had picked them out from all the other characters he did not know. It did not invalidate Felicity's conclusions over his former identity as Peter Darby and his karmic entanglement with Adriana, however: if anything the fading away of Ambrose meant that his guilt over the man's crippling was now absolved and the fading away of Eric – who he now realised was always a little camp – meant perhaps that the question of his homosexuality was dealt with. From the perspective of returning clarity he could also free himself from Eric's paranoia. Fancy accusing Janet's gang of interfering with Adriana, of putting her up to her marriage with Rich Taylor! They had enough to do just following *his* daily movements.

As the drug-clash worked its way out of his system he became less and less sure about the whole period however. What had really gone on, apart from the maths? Was he really back to normal? He decided to visit his mother and talk things over with her: she, if anyone, was a good gauge of his behaviour. Back in Parktown, he discovered that it had been she who had prompted the call from Dr Parkes to the new GP in the first place. She was delighted with the result and hopeful that this was the beginning of William's full recovery.

'William darling,' she said, 'I knew something was wrong. For the entire four years I tried to work it out, and met with Ros several times, who I have to say was acting almost as strangely as you. She blew hot and cold. I couldn't work out what she wanted, so that much you were right about.'

William grimaced. He had not told his mother about Ros's apparent lesbian affair with Maria, or that Maria was now gone and that he was clinging to the hope of reunion. But he was glad that he appeared to be more his old self.

'It's all clear now,' said William. 'The minute I went on Prozac it started reacting with the Psyllicontin that I had been self-prescribing since 9/11. I started hearing voices – a whole range of them – but they settled down to just three in the end; one of them, called Eliza, was related to my work; the other two were related to a therapy programme I had enrolled on.'

'Therapy programme?'

'Yes. I knew something was wrong and that the Prozac – although it helped my mood and my work – was not solving this other problem; of course I didn't know then that it caused it, or at least it did in combination with the other thing. So I went back to Edmondson who put me on CBT first of all, you know, cognitive behavioural therapy ...'

'I've heard of it I think; did it do any good?'

'Not really. So I then went on to hypnotherapy and then ...' William paused, '... a form of, ah, regression therapy. It was out of this that the various characters emerged that I then hallucinated. I couldn't stop them talking with me in the flat, and outside I had huge difficulty controlling them, or rather preventing myself talking aloud in their voices. Even accents. I was completely off my head.'

Belinda looked at him with an odd, half-amused expression. 'What sort of regression therapy? What does that mean William?'

'Ah, er, it means … er, past lives, Mother.'

Belinda raised her eyebrows.

'Well, it was recommended to me by my hypnotherapist. I thought he was mad I can tell you, but I was desperate Mother. Nothing else seemed to work, so I gave it a try. Anyhow I don't know what to think of it now, but under hypnosis I babbled about some wartime episode involving a flying boat and its crew – and it was those crewmen whose voices I heard, just two of them in the end.'

His mother just nodded. 'And now they're all gone, you say?'

'Yes, since I went off the Psyllicontin. That step saved my life.'

Belinda beamed at him. 'I'm so relieved, William. We all are. We were dreadfully worried about you for the whole period.'

'Mother. I know that this therapy sounds flaky. You appear suspicious of it. Quite right of course. It took me ages before I could bring myself to sign up to it, I can tell you. But it did help me in an odd way by telling a story – a complicated dreamlike story – that means something to me.' William paused. 'I don't suppose I could tell it to you? It would help me understand it better, I think.'

'Of course, William' Belinda smiled. 'Tell me the whole thing.'

'Are you sure? I'm embarrassed about it all. I mean, it's a bore to hear other people's dreams, let alone drugged fantasies.'

'William: go ahead. Perhaps it will help.'

He then proceeded to outline how his obsessive dreams had led him to Kolakowski and the hypnotherapy recordings from which he had pieced together his 'previous life' – he stated this rather cautiously to his mother – as a Sunderland engineer, caught up in a drama involving a German U-boat officer. That emerged at the end; throughout the period he had mostly clung to the idea that he had been Alan Turing: it was what had helped him do the maths. To start with the therapy group had thought the Nazi officer was reborn as a woman called Felicity Makepeace, then a client called Anita van Houten, and finally Rich Taylor, the man who married Adriana. He told her every last detail and was rather wrung out by the time he finished – in particular he found it hard to recount the scene between Darby and Haviland in the Lyons tea room. He shook his head. 'I have only spoken of this with two people so far,' he admitted to Belinda. He grimaced. 'At least I think I have.'

Belinda was silent for a while. Then she shook her head. 'That's quite a story,' was all she commented. William began to regret telling her; he suddenly saw how preposterous the whole thing must seem.

He stayed in Oxford for a few days, wandering through his old haunts: St Giles with The Eagle and Child and the Mathematical Institute; Magdalene Bridge with the punting yard and the Cherwell river; Carfax with the tower, shops and traffic. He was still adjusting to the change in his life: no companions to share it with.

His mother sat him down one evening saying she wanted to talk something over with him. He nodded. 'You know,' she began, 'it was your father who actually helped me work it out. Do you remember his remark about you being another Gilbert Pinfold when you arrived the other day?'

'Yes, mother. I had no idea what he was talking about. Just assumed it was one more cultural reference over my head.'

'Well I wasn't sure either. I'd read the book when I was young, though I'd quite forgotten how it went. It's by Evelyn Waugh. But we had an old copy and I re-read it. It's about a man who self-prescribes, lands up with conflicting medicines and has a breakdown. He hears voices. Autobiographical you know, not just fiction. Look, here it is.'

'Crumbs,' said William. He stared at the book she had just picked up.

'Yes,' she nodded, and then continued: 'Look, I didn't tell you, but the reason I contacted Dr Edmondson was because David Deutsch rang. He was concerned for you.'

'Really?'

'Don't you recall ringing him up out of the blue? About your therapy programme?'

William shook his head.

'Well Deutsch was concerned because you appeared quite delusional. You must have been in the middle of it all at that point. I didn't know what to make of it so I rang Edmondson, after all you told me that it was he who had put you on the Prozac. Of course he rang Dr Parkes, and so they worked it out: you were on conflicting medicines.'

William smiled at her. 'Well, you did the right thing there, mother.'

'William.'

'Yes?'

Belinda drew breath.

'You know that thing about "tip top" and so on?'

'Yes?'

'Do you not remember a dinner here one evening with the Chatterjees, not long after they were married, when Veronica entertained us with "tip top, top notch, posh nosh"?' Belinda delivered the line slowly with no attempt at an Indian accent.

William was dumbfounded. 'Really?' he said in disbelief.

'You don't remember it?'

'No. That's awful.' He paused and then added slowly: 'Perhaps even my memory has been affected. I'm still pretty muzzy-headed.'

There was a pause.

'The key thing is ...' Belinda leant forward.

'Yes?'

'Deutsch was actually interested in the therapist you talked about. Even if he thought past life therapy was totally flaky, he was intrigued that a professional outside his discipline had read his books and incorporated the multiple universe theory into a therapy.'

'Yes?'

'William, what was the name of the reincarnation therapist?

'Stefan Kolakowski.'

'William. Deutsch looked him up. I looked him up. There is no such person as Stefan Kolakowski practicing any kind of therapy anywhere in Britain.'

'No!'

'Yes, William,' his mother said sternly. 'Look ...' She went in search of a book and returned with a well-thumbed tome while William sat there in a kind of panic. 'Your father was reading it a couple of years ago. Took him ages, and he often left it lying around. It's by a Polish author. See: Kolakowski.' She read it slowly off the spine. 'I can never quite get the name.'

'Christ!'

'Perhaps you saw the book lying around. Perhaps you transposed Veronica's remarks about "tip top" and so on into an imaginary setting.'

Belinda stared at William, who was shaking his head. She continued: 'And this. I mentioned past life therapy to Veronica after David's call, and where on earth might you have got the idea from. I know that she is enthusiastic for all things Eastern. She racked her brains and then remembered: she had been watching a series of past life Bollywood films. Said that one was a remake of an American film called "The Reincarnation of Peter Proud" or something similar. Does any of that ring a bell with you?'

'No,' said William. 'I do recall watching Bollywood films with them but not about reincarnation. Though, wait, perhaps Harryjee was calling it superstition. Something called the Tulku system as I recall. Tibetan Lamas and all that. Is that reincarnation?'

'I have no idea. But still, she thought they could have been watching reincarnation films during the couple of weeks you stayed after your separation. She said she had tracked down a whole series of them to annoy Harry. Well, not annoy, I suppose, just to make him think perhaps: you know how definitive he can be about things. Also, she says that the spare room you slept in doubled as her library. It was full of books about therapy, and it included some case studies you may have read.'

'Really?'

William looked down, shaking his head again. This was too painful. Hearing voices was one thing. Now they had stopped he saw only too clearly that they had been a product of his confused state. But Kolakowski? And the entire therapy world?

'I can't deal with this, Mother,' he said angrily.

She nodded, but would not relent.

'William, do you have your mobile phone to hand?'

'Sure,' he said, jerking it from his jacket pocket in annoyance.

'Now, let me see,' she said. 'Do you have the number for the woman you had the affair with?'

William winced. 'Adriana Russett?'

'Yes.'

He checked the phone book listing. There is it was: 'Adriana New' and 'Adriana Old'. He nodded, feeling queasy.

'And David Deutsch?' asked Belinda.

He checked and nodded again.

'Now,' she said softly. 'You have to face this. What was the name of the lady in the reincarnation group with the orange hair?'

'Felicity Makepeace.'

'Okay, look for that.'

He pressed away at the menus.

'Nothing under "F" or "M", Mother,' he had to concede, looking worried and feeling a horrible churning in his stomach.

'I rang Veronica yesterday and mentioned this woman to her.'

'And?'

'She checked some of her case studies. One of them went by that name.'

'Christ!'

'And the Dutch lady? Is she in your phone?'

He had to report that she too was missing from his mobile.

'And now: Kolakowski himself?'

He grimaced, but she stared him down. He stabbed the buttons for a long time and then gave up. He slumped in his chair, shaking his head. Then he suddenly got up, shaking. He stared wildly around the room and then fixed his gaze on Belinda. His chest was heaving. He shook his head violently. He was not ready for this and felt a sudden anger at his mother who seemed to want to demolish everything he had been through. She was making fun of him!

'No!' he cried, and in a single movement got up and swept all the books off the little table, Waugh and Kolakowski included. They took with them an old video of the classic film Brief Encounter, something that he had not noticed until it hit the floor and which angered him further, though he was not quite sure why. The thump of the artefacts on the quarry tiles shocked him however.

'Sorry, sorry, Mother.' He looked at her and she stared back keenly. 'I'm going back to London,' he said suddenly, feeling quite sick. 'Perhaps I had another mobile phone. You can't imagine how confused I was through that period. Or perhaps I used Skype on my computer, or the landline to make the calls. And I have all the therapy tapes up there on the laptop. I used to go over and over them. I'm going to get to the bottom of this. I'll show you!'

He would not be entreated with to stay longer, and ran out, grabbing his coat. On the train to London the anger at his mother returned – he had confided in her everything about the last awful period and she had just mocked him.

On his return he ransacked the flat for signs of Kolakowski, Makepeace and van Houten. He found nothing. A panic grew in him. He went through every hard disk and likely internet link to find the audio files of his therapy sessions. There was no trace of them. He was utterly desperate, but all he could find was the Airfix model of the Sunderland high on a shelf, one of its tail fins broken off. He stared at it. There was a notebook next to it, which he grabbed and leafed through: it was blank from beginning to end.

'Jesus Christ,' he muttered to himself. He was beginning to remember things that the Prozac, or its combination with the asthma medication, had obscured. Now this came back to him: his brother Paul had been keen on model aeroplanes as a kid. Could they have included a Sunderland? Could he have become obsessed with them as a result?

He could not believe it. Could he trust anything he remembered since he started on Prozac? And what the hell about his maths? In utter panic now, and drawing deeply on his inhaler, he sought out the paperwork for his submission to America. It took a horrible long while to find, but there it was in a big envelope: his own copy, proof of posting, and a printout of the electronic submission form. He scanned his paper. Everything seemed in order, as he remembered it. He sat down panting, his eyes darting from left to right. If his maths was okay, then he could cope with everything else.

But surely, surely, he had been in therapy with Kolakowski! He sprang to his feet, went to his computers again, each one, and looked through every possible file and folder. Nothing. He ransacked the place for another mobile phone. Nothing. He grabbed piles of paper and systematically flung off each scrap onto a pile on the floor: nothing but printouts of maths, scribblings of maths, journal offprints, utility bills, letters from May, a Lego catalogue and flyers for takeaway pizza. Looking round in despair he spotted a shelf just out of reach in the hallway, grabbed a chair, and mounted it precariously to peer along its length. There! Some papers he had missed. He almost fell off as he stretched to receive them; then he climbed down and feverishly scrutinised the scraps. They turned out to be two sheets of notepaper with scrawled letters to Felicity and Stephan thanking them for their help and explaining that he would not be continuing with therapy; neither had a date let alone an address on them.

There was of course nowhere to post them to – there never had been.

Once he had finally given up, he sat on the old chaise longue, panting worse than before; then he slowly lowered himself down on it, kicking off various computer books and journals from the lower end. He laid himself out, straight and stiff, and stared at the ceiling. His laboured breathing subsided. It was one thing for the voices to have stopped, and for a clear head to return, but for the vivid memories of the period he had spent visiting Old Street, Felicity's house, of the therapy sessions at Kolakowski's … no tangible record? It was devastating. The traffic noise from Old Brompton filled his ears. The light faded. There was of course one last place he needed to check – you can't just imagine a warehouse converted into a therapy centre, but he didn't feel that he had the courage to do it. Headlamps cast shadows on the ceiling of the living room, noises came up from the street, and he settled into a kind of dull immobility in which no thoughts came. He just stared at the ceiling. It would be the just right moment for something like the electric meter to conk out.

In the following period he found himself still alone and with nothing to do. He did not answer phone calls, which he learned were from Belinda in emails she sent. She hoped he was all right, but he did not answer the emails either: he had to think this through for himself.

He started to clear the mess in his flat, some of it down to his frenzied search for therapy-related material; the rest belonged to his manic explorations leading to his mathematical breakthrough and write-up. Dust had collected in the corners of the rooms he used most, while whole areas he rarely visited were quite thick with it. For the first time he realised that he did not have a vacuum cleaner, so he went and bought one. When going to select a shirt from the floor in the spare room a thought struck him. He went to the bedroom, sized up the arrangement of things and then pushed and pulled his bed around to make some space in front of the wardrobe, which in turn he manoeuvred right up against the skirting board. Trying the door it now opened properly. He bought hangers for it and over the following days he washed and ironed or dry-cleaned his clothes and placed them on the hangers in the wardrobe. He discovered black bin-liners full of his things at one end of the spare room: Ros must have sent over his stuff early in their separation and he had not bothered to go through any of it. When he opened one black bag a little cloud of moths flew out and in it lay a crumpled and utterly ruined Chittleborough & Morgan suit.

One evening, passing a corner store that sold little bunches of flowers, he bought one on impulse. On the way up to his flat he knocked at the door of Janet Obudjowe. After a short pause there was scrabbling at the door and it opened an inch or so on a chain. He could just see Janet's left eye.

'Yes?'

'It's William from upstairs.'

'Hello. What do you want?'

'I'd like to apologise for the nuisance I have been, up late at night and so on. I was on the wrong medication and was rather confused. I'm better now.'

'Oh. That's good.'

'Also, it was quite wrong of me speak that way to you and your, your … friends on the pavement that day. My girlfriend had dumped me and I was very upset, you see. I bought you these to make up for having been a bad neighbour to you.'

William could follow Janet's eye as it swivelled downwards to the flowers in his hand and then back to him. There was another pause, the door shut softly and then reopened fully. Janet stood there looking alternately at the flowers and at William.

'Oh,' she said. 'That's very kind of you.'

William proffered the flowers and smiled at her encouragingly. Finally she smiled cautiously and reached out for them.

'In our church we don't approve of girlfriends,' she said, holding the flowers in her hand and staring at him.

'Oh.'

'We believe in the sanctity of marriage.'

'Oh, so do I. Marriage. Yes.'

She frowned. 'Thank you,' she said, and closed the door.

He still had a lingering hope of traces of his therapy period. Perhaps he had deleted the therapy files, and had been using a mobile phone long since lost. He was used to misplacing things. After all his bed and wardrobe had been placed all wrong and he hadn't noticed in four years. You can't misplace a warehouse though, so he finally launched on a trip filled with dread to Old Street. Yes, there was an old warehouse there, yes it had been converted into a therapy centre, but no, there was no trace of 'Transcarnational Multiverse Therapy' or a Stefan Kolakowski. Neither did it look anything like how he imagined it. His exchanges with the receptionist were quite forlorn, and afterwards he felt very low again – the therapy centre must have featured in one of Veronica's case studies. It was horribly sobering, that last withdrawal of hope, which his mother had compounded in a phone call that he had finally decided to answer, hoping in fact that it would be Ros. After a little reassuring small-talk Belinda was careful to ask if it was okay for her to mention another doubt that had crossed her mind. William could not but agree, having made his apologies for having left so abruptly on his last visit. He was not angry with her any more.

'William, darling, it's funny how the details of your story have stuck in my mind. I am sure on the one hand that there is meaning in it, but on the other hand you need to see your therapy world and its characters as a delusion brought on by the wrong medicines. So here is another thought: did you know that the Belsfield Hotel really was a women's Air Force training school in the war? I looked it up.'

'Yes, Mother.'

'No doubt the hotel brochure mentioned it, and perhaps also mentioned the flying boat factory?'

'Quite possibly.'

'Well, you said that the Scottish superintendent at the Belsfield in your story was called Alexander Turnbull, do you remember?'

'Ah, yes,' said William warily. He did not really need any more painful reminders.

'And did you say that his nickname was "Ecky" for wearing spectacles?'

'Yes.'

'Well, said Belinda, 'I thought so. It rang bells when you said it but I couldn't think why. So I mentioned it to Pop who said that it was a character from The Thirty Nine Steps. He'd been reading it to you at bedtime when you were seven. He is still upset about it as far as I can see because we went to the first screening of Star Wars with you as a treat around that time – all the way to London – and when you got back you told him you wanted stories more like that, and not such old-fashioned stuff as the adventures of Richard Hanney. I think it was the last time he read you a bedtime story actually.'

'The Thirty Nine Steps?' asked William faintly.

'Oh it doesn't matter, darling. Just a boy's own sort of story of a heroic Englishman saving his nation from the Germans. Could be a coincidence of course.'

Poor Pop, William was thinking. And then: poor me. I have never read a bedtime story to Tommy. Not once.

'William?'

'Yes?'

'Are you alright?'

'Yes, Mother. But this is hard to deal with.'

'Sorry, William.'

There was a pause.

'William?'

'Yes?'

'Paul had an Airfix Sunderland when he was little, amongst all his model aeroplanes. I asked him, and apparently he remembers being annoyed with you because you knocked it off his desk, accidentally of course.'

'Really?'

'Apparently it fell on its nose and broke the forward gun turret.'

There was a long pause.

'Christ ...' murmured William finally.

Slowly, on his own, William began to come to terms with it. He had to accept that the entire therapy world had been the production of his fermenting brain seething under chemical imbalances wrought by the clash of medications. Scrambled synapses, as Parkes said. That was it. Each morning he woke up, scrabbled to remember the horrible nature of this revelation, lay there with it for a while, and then got up in progressively more resigned and accepting mood.

One small detail seemed to help him bid farewell to this world made up of imaginary characters like Eric, Ambrose, Peter and Deirdre from the past, and a more recent one made up of equally imaginary characters like Stefan, Felicity, Admiral D'murr Pilru and Anita. It was 'orangeberry and pine herbal tea sachets'. He was making coffee one morning, staring into the cupboard over the sink when it dawned on him. There was no such thing as 'orangeberry', was there? He looked it up on the internet, an exact search on 'orangeberry and pine'. Zero search results were produced in 0.29 seconds. Bursting into laughter, he felt a liberation. It was comical wasn't it? That he had never once suspected 'orangeberry and pine' as a herbal tea. Instead it was a mirage, just part of a huge delusion that the drug clash had constructed for him to justify having an affair.

Funny thing, he thought, the unconscious.

While clearing away the junk on his computers, he came across the Eliza II material. At first he winced at memories of talking out loud with Eliza, but then, out of curiosity, he logged onto the shared workspace on the college system. His password was still valid, so he could now track all the developments made by Spindler and Piatagorsky. He looked at these for a while and decided that they had missed something. Over the next few days he worked on the material, and then posted his conclusions to them – it made him feel much better, having some mathematical work to turn to, however prosaic. Otherwise he rose each morning, took Prozac, waited for the little lift it gave him, and just sort of existed. After a while he took the next very difficult decision: to go off Prozac as well. He was sure, he explained, to Parkes, that the voices were gone; indeed that the symptoms that led him to take Prozac had all disappeared.

Two days after posting his suggestions on the Eliza II workspace, he had a long email from Simon Spindler. It rather gushed how much William had moved the project forward in spotting some wrong assumptions that he and Piatigorsky had made about implementation. Might it be possible to see him?

William arranged a meeting with Spindler. He showered, shaved and dressed carefully, and went into Imperial for the first time in many months. He was in the early stages of Prozac withdrawal and felt a little fragile.

Spindler was clearly nervous when they met in William's tiny office. 'Professor Strange, I owe you an apology,' he stammered.

'Do call me William, and what on earth for?' said William kindly.

'I feel terribly embarrassed that I made a complaint about you ...'

'Nonsense, Simon. You did absolutely the right thing. You were not to know, as indeed none of us did, that I was on the wrong medication. It sort of messed up my head. I imagine it must have caused you great concern. But that's all over. You'll see, I am all sorted out now.'

Spindler was relieved at William's approachability and went on to further discuss the Eliza II project. Piatigorsky, it seemed, had not been much help, insisting that they include a 'consciousness' module in its specification and then rather ignoring the whole thing, so they agreed to finish the project together, William having now provided the path forward. At a later meeting Spindler brought up another request: might William be interested in attending the maths discussion group that he chaired? William readily agreed, and found himself the following week with a nervous group of PhD students. William rather liked them, indeed he found their questions interesting, and though he could answer them all easily he was a little charmed how they had devoured his publications to date and seemed in awe of him. At the second fortnightly meeting the group had greatly expanded, and William found himself effectively leading a small master-class through the advanced material he had been developing.

111111

William faced an Adriana-style situation with his estranged wife. Ros's lover was gone, just as Adriana's Francis was, but Maria's exit did not at all signal his advantage. Seeing Ros that day with Tommy had brought home to him what a fool he had been with Adriana: he could now see that it had been a drug-induced obsession. 'Don't assume a thing,' Ros had said, however, and in such a final tone, that he dare not even ring her. He decided to write, instead, and awkwardly composed a hand-written note full of contrition and stating his longing to return to the family. It was ignored. But he was given, quite at random, occasion for hope – this was when Ros turned up, instead of Claire, with Tommy on the grounds of the non-availability of the au pair. At least that is what Ros said, but William hoped and suspected that her purpose was to form a new assessment of her errant partner.

'Did you get my letter?' he asked in a most tentative manner, on the first of such occasions.

'Yes…' she admitted, but then tilted her head back and stared at him severely as if he had overstepped some mark. He looked away. On another of these rare occasions Tommy asked again: 'Mummy and Daddy talk now? Daddy come home?'

William looked at Ros who bit her lip. 'Daddy been ill,' she explained. 'Not well enough to come back.'

William blinked at this. Ros leant over to him and whispered furiously: 'Don't you *dare* put ideas in his head.' She leant back to survey him. 'You are a *mess*,' she added cruelly.

The worst was the Christmas leading to Tommy's sixth birthday. William hardly dared hope for any concessions here, and yet was still deeply disappointed when none were forthcoming. He declined an invitation from his mother: he really was not in a mood for jollity of any kind, he told her, and also turned down an invitation from the Chatterjees. William sat out the festive days on his own, developing some coding for Eliza II and allowing the last of the Prozac to work through his system. He felt terribly alone again, but knew he was not really ready to rejoin friends and family in the holiday spirit. The long withdrawal from the drugs and his hallucinations demanded this lonely existence, punctuated only by the weekly access to Tommy and the rare torment of Ros in the place of Claire. He had let his family down badly. What worse thing can a man do than have an affair just after his wife gives birth to their first child? Whatever the nature of his delusions, they were telling him one thing loud and clear: he was a man who let others down. That needed some quiet contemplation. No drugs. No false companionability. Still, to be away from Tommy for yet another Christmas was a bleak atonement. And Ros stopped coming.

Instead of festivities he made a resolution to go to the gym. He had put on weight during the years away from Ros, and felt that this was just one more thing that made him unattractive to her. He rang for an appointment and turned up at a nearby sports centre for an induction with a pretty young trainer. She breezily showed him round the gym with its various threatening-looking machines, its denizens mostly under headphones and grunting, none of which appealed to him at all. Back in the office she ran through various training options: 'We can tailor a programme for you to achieve a number of different goals,' she said. 'For example you might focus on weight loss, toning, or training for any number of different sports, or running or cycling. How do you see your training goals?'

He looked at her unsure. 'Ah, my training goals are, er, to, um … I want to get my wife back.' He said the last in a low voice.

'Oh,' said the trainer, a little put out. 'I see. Well, we'll put you on cardiovascular machines: cycle, cross-trainer, wave machine, rowing machine, treadmill …'

'I suffer from asthma,' William pointed out. 'I probably should have mentioned that to you before.'

'Oh. Well in that case we focus on resistive work on machines: quads, abs, lats, pecs and biceps. That usually gets a woman's interest. Oh, and you have to diet of course.'

'Ah, thanks.' Apart from the dreaded diet thing, William wasn't at all sure what that all meant, nor what the other machines were, but was much relieved not to be on the treadmill at least. That sounded truly awful.

Months later, and quite out of the blue, Ros rang him and suggested dinner. She wanted to talk with him – how about that Hungarian restaurant not far from the Chatterjees? William agreed like a shot: it was what he had been desperately hoping for, any positive sign. It was why he had been to the gym every day, despite the utter boredom of exercising in that sterile environment to the point of panic-inducing asthma attacks and permanently aching muscles. And he didn't care that he used to avoid the Hungarian restaurant like the plague after Harry had first taken him there as one of his ten favourite eateries in London. Or that it had given William much satisfaction when Harry had downgraded it from 'posh nosh' to 'average' after a mix-up by the management had left only pork goulash on the menu and no beef. Apparently Harry had stormed out, having berated the puzzled maître d' that it might remain a perfectly good place for an apostate Muslim or Jew to dine, but not for an apostate Hindu.

It was not much more than four months from giving up the Prozac, and the worst was behind him. Parkes had been supportive, and regularly checked with William that his original depression was not returning. He was certainly clear enough in the head to make a thorough effort to dress well for his meeting with Ros. If his appearance had put her off sharing Christmas with him, then for the sake of seeing Tommy he would go through the works: he still felt the sting of her remark. He bought a new shirt and jacket in Jermyn Street, had an expensive haircut and shave for the first time in years, and tracked down a bottle of the Burberry aftershave that Ros liked on him. Perhaps its 'base notes' of guaiac wood, oakmoss, and opoponax would do it for him. Whatever they were. He felt strange though. Damn it, he grinned to himself in the bathroom mirror, he was like a teenager on his first date. He looked at his naked torso: was there some trace of this thing called 'definition' in his quads, abs, pecs, lats, and biceps? He wasn't sure. As to his stomach, it looked more like a one-pack than a six-pack, despite eating mostly salad. He sighed. What he clung to was the simple but terse statement from Ros that she wanted to talk with him – and the fact that she had not placed boundaries on this meeting, as she had at Eel Brook Common, with 'don't assume a thing'.

Ros welcomed him at the restaurant with broad smiles, but they soon faded into nervousness. She talked too fast about inconsequential things. They became aware of the waiter, which halted her flow, so William asked her what she would like. She wanted the red fish soup starter and then the mixed grill with lecsó – the Hungarian equivalent to ratatouille – followed by something called 'angel wing' cookies. William, caught unprepared but determined not to fall into the trap of his former dependence on her, glanced at the menu and ordered at random sour-cherry soup starter, pork tenderloin roulade, and a sweet quark cheese filled chocolate bar with cream for desert – hang salads for today. Ros gave him a curious look but made no comment.

'William,' she said once the meal had been ordered and they had tasted the wine to their satisfaction. 'Your dear mother sent me a copy of that strange book, The Ordeal of Gilbert Pinfold. You see I wouldn't listen to her, even though I wanted to in some way, I was still so angry with you. With myself too. But out of curiosity I read it, dull as it was; never liked Waugh anyway. Imagine being called "Gilbert", let alone "Pinfold"!' But I realised that if it could have happened to Evelyn Waugh, why not you? But of course I didn't want to hear of any excuse for your behaviour.'

As an opening shot in a tentative game of reconciliation it was everything he dared hope for. She stared at him as he ate his soup, and then looked down. He was making a mental note that there was garlic in it at the same time as he was mentally testing what he had heard. Perhaps something of Eric's caution had lingered in him, so he did not venture a response. 'Oh, William,' she was saying, 'what a terrible period for you. I spoke with Belinda after Christmas, and she said that after you switched asthma medications you improved dramatically. Also I understand you went off Prozac as well? How the hell is that going? I gather it's pretty grim for a while.'

'Not so bad, actually,' said William, quite unsure of what he should share with her. 'It was worst in the beginning when I thought the delusions were returning. But the auditory illusions on withdrawal from Prozac were different, more like thinking aloud. I rode them out, and am now pretty much clear of them.'

They ate the soup. Little more was said until they started on the main course, each stealing glances at each other when they could, unsure of themselves, very much conscious of how much more there was to broach with each other.

Suddenly she leant over and felt his collar. 'That's a Charles Tyrwhitt, isn't it William?'

He nodded, munching on the roulade. It has a sauce *totally* steeped in garlic, he thought to himself. He was still also utterly thrown by her proximity, juxtaposing in his mind this Ros with the one who turned into the lift with Piatigorsky at the mere sight of him, back at Imperial.

She frowned. 'I don't recall buying you that one.'

'No,' he smiled. 'I bought it yesterday in Jermyn Street. Is it alright?'

'It's very nice,' she said decidedly. Suddenly there was a tear in her eye. She wiped it away, annoyed. Half-angrily she then added: 'It's fine with the trousers, but the jacket's not quite right.'

'Monkeys with typewriters,' William excused himself, grinning sheepishly.

Ros's face softened. 'The fact is you do look so much better William. I have to admit I did a double take on seeing you.' She looked away and added quietly: 'And that's the Burberry London you're wearing.'

She grimaced and gulped down some more white wine, then hesitated as if she wanted to say more, her face full of conflicting emotions. She stared at him as he was placing another portion of the roulade in his mouth with what could only be called *confidence*, toyed with her lecsó, and then went on: 'I was still so angry that I didn't want you or any of your family to see Tommy over Christmas. But on Boxing Day I felt awful. It was a stupid decision not to let you visit, and Tommy was terribly disappointed. But I have to confess that the real reason I have put this off so long is an awful thing I have to tell you.'

Ros heaved a huge sigh and looked down. She then finished her glass, which William quite expertly topped up for her, using the crisp white napkin to hold the bottle, all the while trying not to place too much hope on what he was hearing – she had actually contemplated inviting him to Britannia Road for Christmas? They ate more of their main course in silence – he was in no rush to hear more confessions from her. Whatever nonsense had happened between her and Maria, he could not escape the conviction that it was he who had injured her, not the other way round.

A waiter came up to them with a fancy half-bottle of wine, and proffered it to Ros.

'This is a special appellation from the Puszta,' he said in a thick accent. 'A new Hungarian wine. A rich ruby red. Would madam like to try a glass?'

Eric. Ruby red, mind.
You're the governor.

Ros looked to William for a decision and then frowned. 'William, there's a funny look on your face, are you all right?'

William realised that his face must have been a little set. He blinked, shook his head, and then broke into smiles, looking at his wife and thinking how he loved her slightly snub nose. 'I'm fine,' he grinned, 'but I occasionally get little flashbacks off the residual Prozac and Psyllicontin. One of my hallucinations was about a man who wanted to buy ruby-red silk knickers for his girlfriend.'

Ros burst out laughing. 'So it wasn't completely awful then,' she commented.

William turned to the waiter. 'We'd love to try it,' he said. 'Let us have the bottle.'

They were silent for a while as they moved from the white to the red.

'Very good,' nodded William at the bottle. 'And the meal. How's yours?'

'Oh, very good,' she said in a distracted way, giving him another curious glance. Her brow furrowed. 'William, I didn't mean to be flippant about your delusions. It must have been a terrible period.'

'Well, the thing about delusions,' William mused, 'is that one suspects them at one level but is completely taken in at another. You won't believe this, but one delusion was really helpful though: for a long time I fully believed that I had been Alan Turing in a previous life.'

'No,' said Ros.

'Yup,' he grinned, 'it really did help me plough on with the maths you know. It was the one anchor through the whole period, apart from seeing Tommy, that is.'

Ros looked away at this. William continued. 'But the other delusion was a terrible thing: it was the idea that Adriana and I had been lovers during the war, you know, in our former lives.' William looked down. 'I actually used it as some kind of justification to myself for our affair. I told myself I needed to get to the bottom of what had happened to our former selves, as though it would explain some mystery for me.'

'And did it?'

William looked up, unsure. 'Parkes told me that it would take some time, even once the drugs were gone, for the full effects to be flushed out. So I don't know. I do know that I was delusional. Raving. Paranoid. But I can't completely let go of the story that unfolded. It was oddly coherent, though clearly constructed from buried memories of quite absurd things like my brother's model aeroplane; from things I had read or seen in films – you know, like Brief Encounter which I had totally forgotten seeing – and God knows what other influences. Of course I also know that the brain produced the whole thing just to ease my conscience.'

William looked at her. He shrugged. 'Or you could just say,' he concluded, 'that I was completely off my head.'

Ros just smiled at him distractedly, and they ate on in silence. William was worried that what he had just told her must sound like excuses.

'William,' she said suddenly, after placing her knife and fork carefully down on the plate in the proper way to indicate that she had finished the dish. 'You know of course that Maria and I became lovers. Whether you slept with that student of yours before I slept with Maria or not is a moot point. It's probably best we don't try and work it out. But William ...'

Ros trailed off. On impulse William lent over and took her hand: it was the first physical contact for many years, and he had no idea how she would react. She gripped him tightly however and then relaxed. She withdrew her hand slowly, as if to steel herself, William feeling for the first time that there was some real hope in all this. The waiter cleared their plates from the main course. She paused, and then went on:

'William. Here is the thing. She was a *con artist*. I handed thousands of pounds over to her boyfriend – of course I didn't know that then – to arrange architectural and interior design drawings for our new home together. Also handed over other money through the years. It came to more than a hundred thousand pounds altogether. I am so ashamed and angry with myself, but the lawyers can't help. I have tried for a whole year now, but have given up hope of recovering anything. Our lawyer says that even if we did, the bad publicity would make a laughing stock of Pierce & Fine. I am so sorry. If I had faced the truth of that earlier we could have met like this months ago. And poor Tommy is the one who has really lost out.'

She looked at him, but was interrupted by the arrival of deserts.

'And William ...' she continued after both had tentatively sampled their new course. He had been thinking that 'quark' – whatever that was – could easily have garlic in it, knowing the Hungarians, but was relieved to find that it merely tasted cheesy and a little sour. He was also desperately trying not to assume anything regarding all the positive signals that Ros was sending out, the sensation in his hand after touching her still resonating in him. She continued: 'I don't even have the excuse of bad medicines. I fell for it. I suppose I must be bisexual to some degree, they say everyone is. Really, she just manipulated me, hated you from the start, and made it impossible for me to go into mediation or marriage guidance with you. She turned me and Tommy against you, I don't even know how she did it.'

William looked at her. He smiled and said: 'I have no excuse either. It was simply the worst mistake of my life. I deserved all you threw at me. I was married with a new-born baby and I had an affair. It was disgraceful behaviour.'

Ros shook her head. They both picked at their deserts.

'You don't understand William,' she continued. 'When we were first looking for au pairs and came across Maria I only took her on because she was so ... pretty.' She looked down. 'Even as we were discussing how suitable Maria would be as a nanny for Tommy, I was having ... thoughts.'

William was trying to work it out. Did he have more of an excuse for his behaviour than Ros? However much clarity had returned to his mind now, the exact sequence of the last five or so years was pretty muddled for him. He just shook his head. It was an irony, he supposed, that it was the wife who was attracted to the beautiful au pair, not the husband.

'William ...' said Ros cautiously, 'have you ever thought that, er, have you ever been even slightly attracted to, you know, other men?'

He looked at her, gauging her anxiety. 'I have to say that in the period away from you,' he answered, 'I had to question just about everything I knew about myself. So, yes, for a while I did wonder if I was also a bit AC/DC.'

The look on her face told him everything: he could not have hoped to have made a more understanding remark. He laughed. 'Though I did reach the conclusion that I would stick to DC for now,' he added.

She laughed too in acknowledgement of this. It was a laughter of agreement, but after a while she frowned a little. The rapid changes of her mood, alternately lighting up and then darkening her face through their difficult conversation, roused his protective feelings towards her, roused his love.

'AC/DC William?' she was saying. 'Where did you pick up that expression? It's so old-fashioned.'

William was a bit stumped at this but offered: 'Perhaps it was mixing with all those humanities types at Birkbeck?'

'Must be,' she said.

They talked for a while about trivialities, and laughed over the Darth Maul battlecruiser. Apparently that incident had opened the floodgates for Star Wars-themed products to fill Tommy's world. 'Boys will be boys,' concluded Ros gaily on the subject.

The waiter appeared at their table, and they ordered liqueur coffees: hers with Tia Maria and his with Grand Marnier. Again her eyebrows raised a fraction at his choice.

As the waiter disappeared with their order Ros leant over to him.

'Give me a kiss, William,' she whispered. His heart leapt: what could it mean exactly? In response he moved his chair closer to hers around the table, leant over, and kissed her on the cheek. She looked at him quietly as he withdrew, and so he leant forward again, their faces turned to each other, and kissed her this time on the lips. Was it the wine and the hot Grand Marnier? His heart was pounding, he really was like a teenager on a date. They sat like that for a while, simply finishing their coffees. He thought: this is my Ros of old, and: she is pleasing to the eye.

When it was time to leave she said: 'William?'

'Yes?'

'In your letter you said that all you wanted was to come home to us.' She paused and swallowed hard, her face poignant, uncertain, bewitching. 'William ... after all I have told you, do you still want that?'

He answered without hesitation: 'More than anything in the world.'

In the taxi on the journey home to 54 Britannia Road they kissed again, a real passionate kiss. They disengaged and a slow smile spread over Ros's face: she remembered something. 'You ordered a desert with quark in it! You always hated soft cheeses. You used to say that the universe only needed one cheese and that was Cheddar.'

William grinned. Suddenly Ros sat further back in the taxi seat so as to take him all in. He continued smiling at her as she looked him up and down.

'You've changed,' she decided.

'I hope so,' he said softly, his face turning a little sombre.

Later she whispered something to him: 'William darling, we made a mess of Tommy's early childhood didn't we?'

'I guess so. I'm going to do a million things to make up for it.'

'Would one of them be… would one of them … William, darling … what would you feel about a brother or sister for Tommy?'

'Fabulous.'

She held his hand tight.

A doubt occurred to him however. 'Do you remember how Patricia was always banging on about artificial insemination? Ah …, you wouldn't be thinking of that, ah, method would you Ros?'

'I'm *definitely* not thinking about that method …' she whispered and then grinned: 'I need a man, not a turkey baster.'

Their eyes met. He was silent for a brief moment. Then: 'Good.'

Ros was thinking. 'William darling,' she said slowly. 'Do you blame Patricia, at least a little bit, for what happened? She was very keen on Maria you know.'

'Not in the slightest.'

'We don't have to include her in our circle of friends if you don't want,' said Ros cautiously.

Again, thought William, she is the one offering all the olive-branches.

'But Ros, darling,' he returned, 'Patricia's boy is a good friend to Tommy isn't he?'

'Yes.'

'So, they are welcome aren't they?'

'Oh William, that's thoughtful of you.' She paused and then grinned. 'Even though Douglass has a double "s" in his name?'

'You know I can't spell darling. They'll stay our friends I hope.'

Claire was waiting for them. She confirmed a few details about the passing of Tommy's bedtime ritual, and left. As Ros had explained, the help was now strictly non-residential. William peered into his son's room to gaze on the sleeping boy, his left arm around Ros's waist. 'We'll do him a really special birthday next year,' she said.

'And Christmas this year,' added William. He looked at the shelf over the boy's bed and spotted several toy replicas of the Star Wars robots in different sizes and colours. He grinned, waved his right hand, and said to Ros in low voice: 'These *are* the droids you're looking for.'

She just smiled and shook her head.

Leaving the boy's room she kissed William long and hard, took his hand and led him to her room. It had been a very long return to their marital bed.

William's reunion with Ros and Tommy was the major milestone in the restoration of William to his former life. He had of course never ceased to be a radically innovative mathematician, and confirmation of that came in April of that year. His solid helpful work on Eliza II – leading to yet another discomfiting of poor Emil – had brought him back into May's favour, though of course his generally improved demeanour and appearance all helped. May summoned William to his office, a move that no longer alarmed him. It was not just good news, however, it was staggeringly good.

'William dear boy. The editor at ACM Computational Mathematics has taken the highly unusual step of contacting me directly. His editorial board has declared your paper an absolute breakthrough.'

William's eyebrows shot up. At last! He had been strung like a wire waiting for news of his submission.

'Gosh,' he murmured.

'Wait, William. There is more. Much more. The board were apparently so taken with your work that they immediately nominated you for the ACM Turing Prize. As you are the youngest mathematician ever to be nominated for it, they wanted to inform you at the same time as letting you know about acceptance for publication.'

'The Turing Prize? I can't believe it!'

William had shot to his feet and stood in front of May, who nodded.

'Okay William, okay. So far it is only a nomination. I know that normally it is a formality, but we must anyhow not say a word to anyone until the formal announcement.' May shook his head with glee. 'It'll put Imperial back at the top of the international league table,' he declared.

William sat down again shaking his head in wonder.

'William. You do understand that a carefully managed public presentation of this is essential, and an opportunity we must not miss out on.'

'Ah. Of course.'

'So you don't mind if we all keep quiet about this until after the opening of the Turing exhibition?'

'No of course not. That's fine, just fine. Can I tell Ros?'

'Ah, would you mind holding back, old boy? We had to let Pierce & Fine go I am afraid. Rum do, your wife and that au pair. Slightly took the shine of the company I have to say.'

William did not know what to make of this, but agreed. It would be a wonderful surprise for Ros whenever it came.

'What about Emil?' asked William.

'Ah now, that's a whole other matter. I'll let him know in due course, but today I want to show you something.'

May beckoned to the door and took William to the third floor holography department, where they were welcomed by a team of largely Indian engineers and software developers who were waiting with a demonstration.

'Pop these on,' said May, handing William a prototype head-up display. He then led William around a large empty room. 'Okay,' he shouted, 'switch the simulation on.'

William took a little while to focus properly, but then realised where he was: it was a simulation of the sixth-floor lobby. They walked in the direction of Piatigorsky's office, but it had all been changed.

'This is the new Sir Richard May wing, or rather étage,' May said. 'Or will be.'

'"Sir" Richard May?' enquired William politely.

'Ha ha. Another secret you must keep old boy. I had notification of it in the same week as your Turing Prize. Can't get better than that. Actually we needed a bit of luck here, things had gone a bit pear-shaped for a while. I don't mind telling you that I had a hell of a job keeping SharpSoft with us. You turned it round just in time actually. Yes. "Sir Richard May". The nomination wasn't a complete surprise of course.'

The purpose of the holographic display was to show William the plans for Piatigorsky's office and a completely new hospitality suite with stunning views over London.

'It was all Ros's idea, you know. I'm hoping to rehire Pierce & Fine as soon as we can, now all that business is over. Fine lady your wife. These things happen you know. But this is the, er, key point of this demonstration.' May took off his goggles, followed by William.

'William dear boy. I am going to have to suggest to Emil that he considers early retirement. I want you to take up the new Aleksander chair in computational mathematics. You will have Emil's old, or rather new, office, and in the meantime, as of next week, I have a spacious temporary office for you on the fifth floor. I am being blunt now: we want to keep you here at Imperial. You will have plenty of other offers. '

It was all too fast. William was still reeling with the news of the acceptance of his paper, the Turing Prize nomination, and the virtual tour of the new facilities which had made him slightly dizzy. It hadn't occurred to him that other top universities would be interested in hiring him now.

'You can take as many visiting professorships as you like, it goes without saying. But I very much hope our developments here will persuade you to stay.'

'Ah. Of course,' said William. He couldn't think of any reason why he would want to leave. 'Of course I'll stay.'

'Good chap, good chap,' beamed May.

'Oh,' said William, suddenly aware of his dramatically improved bargaining position. 'One favour.'

'Just name it.'

'I'd like the words "The Chinese Room" to be placed on the door to my new office, spelled out in Chinese characters. Would that be possible?'

'Ah …' May was puzzled for a moment. Then: 'Of course! It's the Searle thing isn't it? Like you used to have? Of course dear boy, of course.'

This was not long before William was due to be keynote speaker for the launch and private view of the Turing exhibition at the Science Museum. It was the culmination of his work with Adriana, and necessitated some email exchanges with her that he found rather difficult. He explained to Ros that there was no way of avoiding Adriana's presence at the event but he terribly wanted Ros and Tommy to be there, to which she readily agreed.

On the night he could see Ros stiffen at the introductions, even though she had been prepared for it; he found it no easier to be shaking hands with Adriana's husband, Rich Taylor. He couldn't help recalling that 'Rich' is the English equivalent of 'Ulrich' and winced at the memory.

Professor May took the podium to make introductions to an audience of Imperial, Birkbeck and Science Museum staff, along with journalists and sponsors. 'Ladies and Gentlemen,' he began, 'I am delighted to be here tonight to introduce the key staff on this extraordinary interdisciplinary project. I have to say that when we started none of us knew that the key mover at Birkbeck, Doctor Adriana Russett, would in fact become Doctor Adriana Taylor by the time we finished.' He bowed in her direction to polite applause. 'Neither could I have conceived the possibility that by the time the project would finish that I would be forced to address you as Sir Richard May. Actually I am not of course, I have merely been nominated.' There was more polite applause.

'But more to the point, I want to introduce you to Professor William Strange. He was the youngest ever appointment to a chair in computational mathematics at Imperial.'

There was noticeably more applause for this, led, it seemed, by William's new admirers, his group of PhD students.

'Professor Strange has attracted steadily increasing plaudits for his work on frame theory in Artificial Intelligence, taking it, as our Princeton colleagues have suggested, to an unexpected new height. But for most of you that will be gobbledygook. What we are here for today is to mark the opening of a new exhibition at the Science Museum, a collaboration between the Museum, Imperial and Birkbeck, led by Professor Strange and Doctor Taylor. This has been an exemplary project of an interdisciplinary nature, bringing together the sciences and humanities. This is precisely what C. P. Snow was asking for back in the 1960s, the education of our humanities graduates in the sciences of our day and the public implications of them.' He paused to look at William. 'I am now asking Professor Strange to introduce to us the work of the foundational hero of computational mathematics, the subject of the exhibition ... Alan Turing!'

There was enthusiastic applause. May sat down and a red-faced William took to the stage. Adriana's baby took this moment to start screaming, and the embarrassed mother left with the infant.

'Ah, hello, everyone,' said William, some notes in his hand, his blond hair flopping over his eyes, and with a number of conflicting emotions bringing him to a sweat, not least over having to speak in front of such an audience. He was out of practice with this sort of thing. 'Professor May, or rather Sir Professor May,' he corrected himself, 'oh, actually Professor Sir-in-waiting May, I suppose ...' May frowned at this to some laughter, '... is absolutely right that a great deal of unexpected events transpired over the course of this project.' Ros winced from the front row, holding Tommy's hand. The boy was paying rapt attention. 'Ah, sticking to the academic side of things for now,' he continued, 'I have to admit that I was a reluctant convert to the humanities. I have a terrible confession to make: that when I was first approached I likened Turing's work on computing to the Stone Age man's invention of the wheel. Or whenever it was.' There were gasps and groans in the audience and May looked rather worried at William's turn of presentation. 'I am arrogant enough mathematically to still believe that,' William said calmly. 'But that does not belittle Turing's contribution, which has changed humanity as much if not more than the wheel has. But this was not for me the point of the project. Rather, what I learned from it was to consider the whole life of a man, a person remote from me in history, but whose struggle to be who he really was remains a lesson to us all.' He leant forward a little to make his point.

'Turing was simply an extraordinary man, an extraordinary mind. A beautiful mind. He was gay, as you all know. But without entering empathetically into that period in British social history, something I could never have done prior to this interdisciplinary project, I would just have said, sure, so what? But, being forced to acquaint myself with a bygone era of Bakelite telephones, scratchy nylon stockings, aeroplanes made crudely like boats, and the horrors of war including death by drowning of thousands of merchant seamen, I was able to understood the meaning of the Enigma-breaking machines, all of which you will see in the exhibition. Turing saved hundreds of thousands of lives, if not the very freedom of our nation. But behind the "boy's own" ...' William gestured the quote marks, '... stories of intellectual and physical daring in that era lies another story: of institutional prejudice, of institutional ignorance, all bound up with the British class system. In this exhibition you will see artefacts and explanations that will make you take pride in Britain as a nation. You will also see things that will make you ashamed. I think in particular of a small capsule of human female hormones. It is a replica of the one that Turing was forced to take to "cure" him...,' William made more hand gestures, '... of his homosexuality, then a proclivity that was against the law. It was against the law for Alan Turing to be Alan Turing. We are now horrified by that, but we must recognise that, historically speaking – and I must admit to finding myself astonished to be "historically speaking" ...' William made quote marks again, '– the law only changed very recently in this country. In other lands around the world homosexuality remains a criminal offence.'

William paused for a moment.

'It may be an urban myth,' he continued, 'but think of the Apple logo: an apple with a bite taken out of it. Should that be "byte" with a "y"?'

There was laughter from the geeks in the audience.

'Or, more tragically,' he intoned, 'is it the bite that Alan Turing took from the apple he dipped in cyanide in the act of suicide forced on him by a world that rejected him? An Establishment that rejected him?'

There were murmurings and shaking of heads. William surveyed them sombrely, and then let his visage relax into a smile.

'Ladies and gentlemen,' he concluded. 'It was a privilege to work on this project. I was dragged kicking and screaming into the past, and I learned things to be amazed at and also to be ashamed of, as I have just said. I have learned that there is a bigger life than mathematics. With the opening of this exhibition we are of course honouring the mathematical genius of Alan Turing. We are also honouring his life. We are also, I hope, sobered that human progress is very slow, to be greatly cherished, and that our advances must be always defended against backsliding. I hope you all enjoy this wonderful exhibition. I give you Alan Turing!'

Infectious with enthusiasm, a William of old was emerging. Ros clapped vigorously with the rest of the audience and Tommy followed suit. He flung his arms around William's waist when he left the stage and would not let go.

These were William's last recollections in Emil's office overlooking the park. What Emil was thinking about only he knew. William withdrew his gaze from the park; Emil too snapped out of his reverie. They looked at each other. Emil offered the paper and ACM letter back to William who took them in his left hand. He proffered his right. Emil leant forward and grasped it vigorously.

'Villy, I heff to be honest. You betrayed everyzing I ever stood for. But I can't help liking you. Good luck here …,' Piatigorsky waved round the room, '…or razher in ze new office once zey have taken ze broom to my old vun. Good luck.'

'You too, old chap. Good luck with retirement,' William responded, continuing to shake the old man's hand. On his final release he turned, left the office, and made for the lift. As he descended in the enclosed space he was once again grateful for the absence of voices, of paranoid feelings and of the mush in his head that bad medication had brought him, and as he watched the floor indicator he smiled that the passing levels marked the recent ups and downs of his career. On exiting the lift he looked around at the atrium: it was properly constructed on the cuboid grid principle; it featured glass and stainless steel, and was blissfully free of plaster wreaths, cherubs, cornices and porticos. Walking out onto Exhibition Road into bright daylight his heart was lifted further by the sight of the modernised street layout. He was on his way down to Carluccio's where Ros would have coffee with him after a business meeting in the area. He looked at one of the Victoria and Albert Museum buildings on the left as he passed it – he actually didn't mind its ridiculous frescoed excesses any more. The modern lighting posts – curved and tapered metal with indentations for the lamps themselves – pleased him anew however. The modern was infiltrating the old, if not actually replacing it, and the new marked better ways of being.

At Carluccio's William and Ros settled into a table under the still baffling – for William – poster that ran through a list of Italian olive oils, declaring them a 'condiment' of great variety. It was odd to be in the café with Ros given that the iceberg of Adriana had sunk him at the very same spot: she and 'history' had intruded on him here.

'It was nice to see Tommy play with Sonia last night,' Ros commented.

'Yes, it was great. But it was funny that Veronica insisted on us watching that film, Eyes Wide Shut, after the kids went to bed,' said William, stirring his coffee.

'Oh, yes, the whole point was that the Tom Cruise and Nicole Kidman couple went through some kind of obsessive hell, but saw in the end that their marriage was worth more than all their fantasies about orgies and so on. Trust Veronica to dig something out like that, you know, as a comment on what we've been through.'

'Yup, I guess that was the point. I'm just relieved that she's moved on from A Beautiful Mind.'

Ros giggled. 'Actually I would have loved to have seen your flat when you were at your most manic. I bet it was just like the film in fact.'

William shook his head, smiling.

'But darling,' continued Ros, 'I didn't get why Harryjee loved the Kubrick film so much. What was the deal with the Hindu thing?'

'Oh, apparently the religious Hindus forced Kubrick to cut some passages in the orgy scene where they recite from one of their scriptures. Backwards, I think. Harryjee has spent years trying to track down an uncut version.'

'Funny too,' Ros said, 'how Veronica thought you had now become a convert to Eastern ideas. You sure put her straight on that though. What did you say? Something like: "meeting our obligations to the few people we do know in our own lifetime is hard enough without dragging in potentially millions of other people we don't know from other lifetimes we can't ever be sure of." And Harryjee trumped that by saying that this was exactly what the Buddha said, not that Buddhism was any less rubbish than Hinduism. That shut her up!'

William smiled. 'But Veronica gives as good as she gets,' he said. 'When I complimented her on the kedgeree she teased Harryjee, saying "you know what it is, don't you?" which he didn't get at all. "Don't you remember?" she asked him to his confusion and then she came out with: "it's a tip top, top notch, posh nosh, fish dish" in a perfect Indian accent, making fun of him.'

Ros grinned at the memory of it, and then became serious. She had bad news about their finances.

'William, listen. I feel absolutely terrible about this,' she confessed. 'But things look worse than I had thought. Even without Maria we were living something of a credit-fuelled lifestyle. William: I can't see any way round it after talks with the accountant. Any move to a bigger house is out of the question. And I think we'll have to give up the cruiser.'

'Really?' said William unconcerned.

'You don't mind darling?' she asked, looking relieved. 'It was me who got us into this mess.'

He shook his head and then grinned. He had a surprise for her. There was a pause.

'By the way, I'm picking Tommy up from school tomorrow after all,' Ros said, changing the subject. 'But Claire has a cold. Can you do it the following day if she is still unwell?'

'Sure,' he said. He smiled again. 'But today I have something to show you.'

He withdrew a letter from his briefcase and handed it to her: it was the one Piatigorsky had just read.

'"The Association for Computing Machinery",' she read out and looked up. 'Boy, you people really know how to make something sound exciting.'

'Read on,' he said, grinning.

He reflected again on the fresco high up on the V&A. Extraordinary that the architects should spend so much money on something so few people would bother to look up at. It was of course an expression of imperialism, he decided. He had learned a word that expressed the contemporary distaste for the whole ethos of it: hegemony. He laughed inwardly. Fancy him actually thinking a word like that! There was no doubt though: the fresco was from the hegemonic past and the past for him was nothing more than an illness. Yes, definitely an illness, and an illness he had now pretty much recovered from.

Ros looked up.

'The Turing Prize! And a quarter of a million dollars! I had no idea! How on earth did you keep all of this under wraps? Was it that paper you mentioned? William! You're an absolute genius!' She was shaking her head in disbelief, and then leant over to kiss him vigorously.

William smiled at her.

'Perhaps,' he said quietly, 'we can keep the boat after all.'

'That's wonderful!' she cried. 'Yes of course we can, now.'

He nodded.

Ros looked at him thoughtfully.

'Oh, William,' she said. 'I suppose it all worked out in the end.'

'Yes,' he agreed. 'Tip top.'